ST. MARTIN'S

MINOTAUR

MYSTERIES

SKELETON
KEY

Jane Haddam

St. Martin's Paperbacks

SKELETON KEY

Copyright © 2000 by Orcinia Papazoglou.
Excerpt from *True Believers* copyright © 2000 by Orcinia Papazoglou.

Cover photograph of house by © Bret Morgan/Esto.

Library of Congress Catalog Card Number: 99-054816

ISBN: 0-312-97865-0

Printed in the United States of America

St. Martin's Press hardcover edition / February 2000
St. Martin's Paperbacks edition / March 2001

St. Martin's Paperbacks are published by St. Martin's Press, 175 Fifth Avenue, New York, NY 10010.

10 9 8 7 6 5 4 3 2 1

To Bill DeAndrea,
July 1, 1952–October 9, 1996,
who gave me everything important in my life,
including Gregor Demarkian

Acknowledgments

In this book, I have given the town of Washington, Connecticut, a police department and a police station it doesn't have. What it does have is two wonderful resident troopers who have been of great help to me when my car has broken down, my tires have exploded, and I've gotten lost on all those back roads with no road signs on them. Omitting them from this book was a judgment call on my part, and I don't want them to think 1 don't appreciate their work because I haven't put them here.

When this book started, the character of Grace Feinman and the matter of her harpsichord took up much more room and was of much more importance. Grace and her instruments have moved on to another book, but I would like to thank the invaluable help I have received for all things related to early music from Peter Redstone of Peter Redstone Harpsichords in Claremont, Virginia; Claire Hammett of Harpsichord Services of London (U.K.); and especially Igor Kipnis, harpsichordist, teacher, lecturer, and tireless advocate for the harpsichord and all it can do.

SKELETON KEY

PROLOGUE

I

Kayla Anson didn't know when she first realized she was being followed, but by the time she reached the Litchfield Road, the signs were unmistakable. It was seven o'clock on the evening of Friday, October 27, and the roads were awful. Three days of drizzle had been followed by three nights of below-freezing temperatures. There was patch ice everywhere, black and slick. The sky was cloudless and infinite. The moon was full. Lined up on the side of the road here and there, now that she was beyond the last little clump of houses, were harbingers of Halloween in the country: clothes stuffed with straw to look like corpses, skeletons made of plastic, jack-o'-lanterns with no candles in them, so that their faces looked like visions, etched in black. It all made her wish she had never come out tonight, on her own, even though she knew there couldn't be anything really wrong. Kayla Anson was nineteen and she got followed a lot. People recognized her car. People recognized her, too, from the picture that had appeared in *Town and Country* and been reprinted in the *Waterbury Republican*. Next week there would be a picture in the *Torrington Register-Citizen* and it would start all over again. "Debutante of the Year," the captions always read, and "the beautiful legacy of a graceful tradition." It made Kayla want to scream. She wouldn't have been a debutante at all if she had been able to go away to college this year. She would have been safely settled at Stanford if it hadn't been for Annabel. And Annabel—

Kayla slowed a little to get a look at whoever it was who was coming up behind her. For a moment there, she had started to be afraid. Once she saw the vehicle, she relaxed. It was one of those farm things with the big wheels. Kayla had never known the name of them. This one was relatively fast, although most of them were much slower than ordinary cars. Some of them crawled along the black-top at only a couple of miles an hour, so that traffic got backed up behind them so far it took half an hour to straighten it out after they pulled over to the side of the road. There were dairy farms all over this tiny northwest corner of the state, although a lot of them were moving out. You saw stories about it every other day in the local papers. The weather was bad and the soil was rotten and the taxes were much too high. People got tired of holding on.

This particular farm vehicle was very, very fast. It had come up behind her now and was staying a single car length behind. Kayla squinted into the rearview mirror and tried to get a look at the driver. All she saw were very bright headlights and the dark shape of something vaguely human. The headlights were so bright, she had to switch the mirror into night position just to go on driving. The vehicle had that grumbly roar of something with a muffler that wasn't working properly. Kayla wished she knew what to call it. It was so much easier not to be afraid of things when they had names.

The problem with all the publicity she'd been getting about being a debutante was that it was also publicity about other things, and the other things could be dangerous. Kayla Anson, only surviving child of multibillionaire venture capitalist Robert Mark Anson and his only heir. Kayla Anson, poor little rich girl, rich girl with everything, rich girl without direction, rich, rich, rich. Once, when Kayla was seven and her father was still alive, she had been almost kidnapped on the sidewalk in front of the Brearley School in Manhattan. She had just come out of the building with her books in a book bag when the long black car pulled up to the curb. She had just turned down the street in the direction of the bus stop when the man got out and came running through the crowd of children toward her. She hadn't been afraid then, either. She hadn't even been aware of what was happening. Her best friend at the time, Linda Markman, had pulled her out of the way. The man who was chasing her had gone careening out of control and fallen on his side. After that, everyone seemed to be jumping on him. Kayla had felt only this: that the whole thing was stupid, and that it should be happening to anyone on earth except her.

The farm vehicle was now only half a car length behind her. Kayla could finally see some things for sure. It wasn't an ordinary farm vehicle, in spite of the big wheels, because it was made by Jeep. It seemed to be a bright metallic blue. Kayla punched the buttons on her car radio and got Big D 103 FM out of Hartford. The Rolling Stones were singing "Under My Thumb," but that was beginning to fade. What was coming up next was the Beach Boys doing "Fun, Fun, Fun." Right up ahead of her on her left was the Victory Independent Baptist Church. The sign out front said: HELL IS TRUTH, SEEN TOO LATE.

"Crap," Kayla said out loud. She pressed her foot down on the gas and felt the car underneath her speed up. It was a good car, and it could be fast: a BMW two-door with a German engine, imported, literally. Her lawyers had had it shipped over from Frankfurt in May. She streaked on up the hill in the direction of Litchfield and thought about her mother, who had been so very opposed to the whole idea of Kayla's buying a car.

"You could always get someone to drive you," Margaret Anson had said, in that pinched-face, salt-of-New-England way of hers. "A car like that would only be calling attention to yourself."

Some men marry for love, and some men marry for position. In Kayla's father's case, it had definitely been for position. Margaret was the last living descendant of two signers of the Declaration of Independence and a delegate to the Constitutional Convention, as well. She had roots in Boston and Connecticut and Philadelphia and social connections everywhere. Kayla had always thought that if her father had lived long enough, he would have divorced and married again, this time for sex. God only knew there was never much to do with sex around Margaret Bell Anson.

Kayla looked in the rearview mirror again, but the vehicle was still there. In fact, it was closer than ever. She
was really beyond it now, on that long stretch past White
Flowers Farms with nothing in the way of buildings on it
at all. Even the Halloween decorations were missing. No
one had thought to come out here to scatter straw corpses
on the grass. No one had thought to use this empty place
to play a practical joke. No one was walking by the side
of the road, hoping for a ride. Kayla felt a thin line of sweat
make its way across her neck and swiped at it. She tried
looking in the side mirror and got only the vehicle's headlights. She thought of the way her mother was always trying
to get her to carry a cell phone and how she always refused,
because she hated cell phones, and because they seemed
like such a rich-snot thing to have.

The Beach Boys had become the Supremes, singing
"You Can't Hurry Love." Kayla pressed down even harder
on the accelerator. She heard the vehicle come up even
closer behind her, its unmuffled engine making a sound like
spitting nails. This was beginning to feel crazy. If he
wanted to pass her, he should pass her. The road was
empty. There was nothing holding him back. She tried to
pull over a little to the right-hand side of the road, without
actually stopping. It didn't work. He came closer still, and
then he bumped her from behind.

Kayla's little BMW did a shudder and a jerk. It was
incredible that she'd never realized how dark it got out
here. Every once in a while there were streetlights, but they
seemed to do more harm than good. Mostly there were trees
and grass and bits of rock littering the edges of the blacktop. Kayla was sure it couldn't be all that far to Litchfield
from where she was. In Litchfield, there would be lights
and people and restaurants that stayed open into the night,
so that she would be able to get to a phone.

The vehicle came up behind her and bumped her again.
This time the bump was hard and deliberate. The force of
it made Kayla's back wheels sway as if she had hit an ice

patch. She tried to put her foot on the gas again, but when she did the car seemed to go out of control. The vehicle stayed right behind her anyway. Then suddenly it swerved out to her left and came up on her side. Kayla thought it was going to pass. Whoever it was would turn out to be just some local yokel, all pissed off because the rich girl hadn't been going fast enough on the Litchfield Road. When he got in front of her, she would get his license plate number and be sure to remember it. Tomorrow or the next day she would go into the Department of Motor Vehicles and have his ass.

The vehicle drifted closer and closer to her on her left. It bumped against her sideways and made the BMW rock madly. Kayla thought she was going to turn over. The vehicle got its nose a little ahead of hers and began to edge into her lane—except that he didn't have enough room to go there. Kayla couldn't just slow down and let him in. She couldn't go sideways in either direction. To her right there was a ditch. To her left there was still the vehicle, flanking her, boxing her in.

Kayla pumped the horn.

The vehicle got closer.

Kayla pumper her horn again, long and loud.

Up ahead there was a side road, on her right. She had never noticed it before. There was no sign on the road and no lights to light it. It looked like one of those town access things where the paving only went a few feet from the main blacktop and then stopped. Kayla put the flat of her hand on her horn and held it there, letting out a long, wailing shriek. There had to be someone around to hear this. There had to be. This wasn't the middle of nowhere. This was Connecticut.

"Crap," Kayla said again, but this time it was a whisper. She was so frightened, she could barely breathe. The vehicle was coming closer and closer on her left. It hit her broadside again and again. Its wheels were bigger and thicker than ordinary wheels. It didn't even rock when it hit. The BMW did dances all over the road.

"Son of a bitch," Kayla said, and then, because there was nothing else she could do unless she wanted to die right there, she pulled off to her right, onto the dark side road.

As soon as she had done it, she knew she had made a mistake. It was what he had wanted her to do. He was coming right up behind her. The BMW was not suited for this kind of road. The ruts were too deep and the weeds were too high. She was jouncing and shaking over the unpaved surface. She had lost all semblance of control over the wheel. She tried to remember what it was she had gone to Waterbury for, but all that came to mind was the Barnes & Noble near the new Brass Mill Center Mall, and she hadn't even gone inside it. She wasn't thinking straight. She wasn't thinking. Everything inside her seemed to have frozen up.

Kayla put her foot on the accelerator to give it one more try, but she was stuck in a rut. Her wheels wouldn't move. She even thought she heard the sound of a puncture.

Then the vehicle came up behind her, fast, and smashed into her back end. She was thrown forward in a rush. Her seat belt locked into place. Her horn went off, and only seconds later did she realize she was pressing it.

"Now what?" Kayla asked the air—and then she turned around and tried to see who was coming for her, in the dark.

2

Margaret Bell Anson had always believed that life had rules, and one of the most important of those rules had to do with the duty a person owed her friends. Cordelia Day Hannaford had been a good friend of Margaret's until the day she died. They had gone to boarding school together and come out together in Philadelphia, too, because Margaret had been doing a national season. It wasn't Cordelia's fault that she had married That Man and been shut away from everybody in Bryn Mawr for decades. It wasn't Cordelia's fault that so many of her children had grown up to be psychopaths, either—although, Margaret admitted to herself, you had to wonder about that one. There were two children in jail, from what Margaret had heard, and another one who was some kind of failed academic. The two in jail had both been part of really enormous scandals. It went around and around, in spite of the fact that Cordelia's husband had been far better off in the family department than Margaret's. One of the rules Margaret had been brought up with was the one that said Blood Will Out, and it bothered her no end when something made it seem as if it weren't true.

At the moment, it was after nine o'clock at night and Margaret wanted to be in bed. What she was doing instead was sitting in her own living room, dressed in a good shirt-waist and a pair of heels, making small talk with Cordelia's third-oldest daughter. That was the other thing about Cordelia that Margaret had never been able to get used to. She bred like a nineteenth-century matriarch or a welfare queen. She had baby after baby, seven of them in all, so that it wasn't strange that some of them had turned out badly. Margaret had had exactly one child, Kayla, and she had never wanted to have another. The idea of being weighed down by pregnancy and bloodied by delivery sickened her. She was sure it sickened all decent women everywhere, and that they only put up with it for the survival of the species.

The young woman sitting across from her in the yellow wing chair was perhaps not so young, and she had a bad cough, the kind of thing Margaret herself would have had a doctor look after. The age was questionable. Margaret's best guess would have been around forty. On the other hand, she was truly one of the most astonishingly beautiful women Margaret had ever seen, with the sort of face that existed nowhere else on earth and worked perfectly. It gave her authority in spite of the fact that she was actually rather short, which Margaret always thought made people look ridiculous. Margaret was five-foot-nine herself. There were people who said that when Kayla finished growing, she would be something over six feet.

Unless, of course, Kayla had already finished growing. Margaret couldn't remember when that stopped. She couldn't remember exactly how old Kayla was, either, although she could make a good guess at eighteen or nineteen, because that was when girls came out. This was the year that Kayla was coming out. Margaret didn't think Bennis Day Hannaford had ever come out, but she might have, in a small way, and Margaret might have missed it. There was something un-debutantelike about Bennis. Margaret couldn't put her finger on what.

There were little demitasse cups on the coffee table between them, and a silver serving set just for demitasse that Margaret had gotten as a gift for her wedding. All of Margaret's really good pieces had come to her as wedding gifts or been inherited from her mother. Her husband's taste had run to the obviously expensive, and—as he had told her, time and time again—he was the one with the money.

Margaret crossed her legs carefully at the knee—when she was growing up, ladies crossed their legs only at the ankles, but now it was considered much more sophisticated to do it this way, even in the Northwest Hills—and folded her hands in her lap.

"So," she said. "Abigail van Dern sent you. But you could have come on your own, you know. Because of your mother."

Bennis Hannaford was wearing a pair of canvas jeans and a cotton rollneck sweater, as if she were about to model for the cover of the J. Crew catalogue. She had her legs crossed like a man's, and she was leaning forward to get at the demitasse. She turned her head sideways and coughed twice into her hand.

"I think my mother was part of Abigail's thinking," Bennis said. "Although, of course, I had no idea if the two of you had been in touch. And mother has been dead now for several years."

"Yes. Yes, I heard about that. It's terrible when someone

we love has an illness like that. Incurable. And debilitating."

"Yes. Right. At any rate, Abigail was feeling a little diffident about it, you see, because it had to do with your husband's family instead of yours. I'm not entirely sure what kind of difference that was supposed to make—"

"I am."

"—but she kept stressing that I was to tell you that she didn't mean any offense of any kind, and that it was just because Julia Anson's paintings are having a vogue at the moment. I feel as if I've been left out of the loop here a little, if you know what I mean. I think it's wonderful if Julia Anson's paintings are having a vogue."

"Oh," Margaret said. "So do I. So do I. Abigail really has nothing to worry about."

"Anyway, Abigail just wants to know if you'll lend the ones you've got, so that she can hang a show in Philadelphia. The museum would be very grateful, you know, and it would be for a good cause. It would bring people in to look. Because of the publicity value, if you know what I mean."

"Mm," Margaret said. She picked up her own demitasse cup and put it down again. She really did not like this young woman, with her straight gray eyes and too-straight spine. She didn't like her at all. It was just too bad that she couldn't do anything about it, instead of just sitting here being polite.

"You know," Margaret said, "I think what Abigail is worried about is Viveca Bell. Have you ever heard of Viveca Bell?"

"No."

"She was a painter, too. In Paris. In the late twenties and early thirties. She was my great aunt. Of course, she wasn't like Julia Anson. She didn't know those people."

"Those people?"

"Yes, you know. Hemingway and those people. Gertrude Stein. Picasso. Viveca was really quite a great lady in her time, and she didn't see the point of walking away from everything she had ever known just to call herself an artist. It's really a twentieth-century idea, don't you think, this business about the artist as an outsider. It came in with existentialism."

"I think existentialism came later, after the war."

"Did it? Well, Viveca was a lot like Edith Wharton, if you know who that is. Edith went to Paris to be a writer, you know, but she was true to her class. She lived among her own people. She was a friend of Henry James's."

"I think it's all fashion anyway," Bennis said. "Who gets hung and who gets reviewed and all the rest of it. There's a tremendous vogue now for all the women who were working in Paris at the time that Julia Anson was. For all the women in that group of people."

"For all the lesbians, you mean."

"Were they lesbians?"

Bennis Hannaford seemed to swallow hard. No, Margaret thought, I do not like this woman. I do not like anything about her. Margaret had a sudden vision of something terrible happening here—of Bennis choking until she died and lying in a heap on the floor, of Bennis struck down by an aneurism or a stroke and rendered unreal, but the vision passed.

"They were all lesbians," Margaret said, "all the women in that group, and I'm not just saying it the way some people do, to make them illegitimate. But it was an organized thing, the lesbianism of that time. It included Stein and Toklas, of course, and Sylvia Beach and Adrienne Monnier. And it included Julia Anson."

"Did she have a regular lover?" Bennis asked. "I've never heard of one."

"She was part of Natalie Barney's set. Natalie had a house with a garden in the back where she used to hold pagan rituals of some sort. Goddess worship. It's odd to think that all kinds of perfectly respectable young women want to worship the Goddess now."

"I don't think it's anything very serious."

Margaret put her demitasse cup down and smoothed the

skirt of her dress. "Quite frankly, if it were up to me, I would turn down this request. I know Abigail means well, but I do think she's encouraging a cultural vogue that could turn out to be very dangerous. It doesn't do any of us any good when women run off and chuck their responsibilities, all for the sake of becoming artists. In spite of the fashions, Miss Hannaford, I don't really think any woman has ever been an artist. At least not a great artist, like Michelangelo or Raphael."

"Well," Bennis Hannaford said, "of course, you're entitled to your opinion. But Abigail will be very disappointed."

"Abigail will not be disappointed," Margaret said. "The decision is not, as it happens, up to me. It's up to my daughter. Have you met my daughter?"

"Once or twice. I saw her picture in *Town and Country*."

"Quite. I was debutante of the year when I came out, too. Not that it's an official designation. Did you—?"

"At the Assemblies."

"Oh, yes, of course. I should have known. Your mother was presented at the Assemblies. Kayla is of a different mind about almost everything from me. I think she's only coming out because she had to postpone college for a year and she has nothing else to do. Kayla is very interested in Abigail's project, and of course Kayla is the one who owns Julia Anson's paintings. Kayla is the one who owns everything, including this house. The papers aren't exaggerating when they say she was Robert's only heir."

"I thought that sort of thing could be set aside," Bennis said. "If you went to court about it and worked it out with a judge."

"I'm of a generation that does not resort to courtrooms except from necessity, and there is no necessity. I'm not destitute. I'm merely very angry. Does that surprise you?"

"No," Bennis said.

"Good." Margaret stood up. "Kayla's gone to Waterbury to buy a few things. She's put you in the front guest room that looks over the porte cochere. I've always thought it was very noisy there, but Kayla likes the view."

"I'm sure it will be fine."

"Kayla can show you the paintings tomorrow, if you want to see them. Or she can give Abigail a call and arrange a meeting in Philadelphia. She has some papers, too, diaries and address books that belonged to Julia Anson. I'm sure it will all come in for good use when Abigail gets hold of it. From what I've seen, however, the diaries are rather explicit."

"I don't think Abigail wants to do anything explicit."

"There will be a publisher out there who does. Did I tell you that one of the reasons that Kayla is so excited about this project is that she thinks she can talk someone into letting her write a book? Kayla is very ambitious. And very bright, I might add. She's much more like her father than she ever has been like me."

"Oh," Bennis said.

"I'm going to go to bed now. I'm very tired."

"Oh," Bennis said again.

Margaret waited. A woman of her own generation would have made a protest, or looked angry, or given some indication that this sort of behavior was highly irregular. Bennis Hannaford did none of these things. She simply sat where she was, holding a demitasse cup and looking polite.

Margaret inclined her head, turned away, and went out of the living room into the hall. She paused at the bottom of the stairs to see if she could hear Bennis getting up to move around, but it didn't happen. She went up the stairs slowly, making sure to let them creak. This house was over two hundred years old at its core, and over a hundred at least in both its extensions. It was the oldest and most historically important house in all of Litchfield County. Margaret had picked it out when she was pregnant with Kayla, at a time when Robert was disposed to give her anything she asked for. Later, he made no secret of the fact that he hated the place without reservation. The rooms were small. The floors creaked. The walls bulged in odd places, even after thousands of dollars had been spent to make them straight.

Actually, Margaret thought, as she came to the top of the stairs and paused again—there were still no sounds coming from the living room—there was still no indication that Bennis Hannaford had gotten off her chair and started to snoop. Actually, the real problem was that Robert had hated her without reservation, as she had come to hate him. They had had year after year of each other, and year after year of angry sex, and the point of it all had never been anything but Kayla. If it hadn't been for Kayla, they would have been divorced and gotten it over with. If it hadn't been for Kayla, they would have seen nothing of each other at all.

Margaret had a very distinct memory of sitting up in bed next to Robert sleeping, right here in the master bedroom of this house. She sat there and stared down at his neck, wondering what it would be like to get her hands around the bones there. She imagined the bones breaking, fragile and small, like bird bones in a stone vise. Then she blinked, and the face on the body beside her changed. It was Kayla's face, wide awake, laughing at her so hard that tears streamed out of the corners of her eyes. Then the face changed to Robert's again, the features thickened with age and wrong experience. Margaret got up and went into the master bathroom and closed the door.

Now she went into the bedroom and closed *that* door. Bennis Hannaford wasn't moving around down there, poking into all the private things. She wasn't even taking out a cigarette and lighting up, although Margaret had it on good authority that Bennis smoked, like some half-witted factory worker with no self-discipline at all. There were times when you went right to the edge of the universe and looked over the side. You found out that there was nothing there but darkness and fear, so deep and so wide and so pure that you couldn't even move in it.

Down in the living room, Bennis Hannaford coughed, long and hard and chokingly.

Margaret locked the bedroom door and went to sit down on her bed—and that was when it struck her, for the first time, that she should not have let Bennis Hannaford come here.

3

Annabel Crawford had bought a lot of fake IDs in her life, but this one—with its State of Ohio logo and bright-colored picture—was the best one yet. It was so good that the bartender of the Lucky Eight barely looked at it before setting her up with a St. Pauli Girl Light, and that in spite of the fact that Annabel knew she looked nowhere near twenty-one. She barely looked eighteen. It was a kind of curse that had happened to her and to no one else in her family. She was very short and very fine-boned and very small. She was also very flat-chested. All of the slightness taken together made her look like a child, and year after year, in one boarding school after another, Annabel's teachers had called her out and rechecked her records just to make sure she was old enough to be there. It was Annabel Crawford's boast that she had been expelled from more boarding schools than anybody else in the history of American private education, and she may have been right.

At the moment, all she was being right about was the beer, and the attention of a boy named Tommy Haggerty, who had just graduated from Choate. Unlike Annabel—who had so few high school credits she couldn't qualify for Quinipiac Junior College—Tommy was just back for the weekend from Princeton, and until Annabel had brought up the story of her last expulsion, Princeton was all he had wanted to talk about. Annabel was beginning to think she had made a mistake in picking him out from all the other boys at the club this afternoon. He was giving every indication of wanting to get as drunk as possible as quickly as he could, and that always ended up being boring as hell for Annabel. What Annabel liked to do was have a couple of beers and a couple of joints and then drive out to Bantam Lake to neck. If you knew what to look for, you could find a place out there that was totally hidden in the trees. Annabel had lost her virginity at Bantam Lake on the day after she turned sixteen, and she had never looked back. It seemed incredible to her that anybody would ever do anything else when they were out with a boy.

The Lucky Eight was a roadhouse, freestanding and made of wood out on Route 209. The lake was only half a mile away, driving toward Washington Depot. Tommy had brought them out here in his brand-new bright red Corvette, which was what his father had given him to congratulate him on getting into Princeton. All the kids Annabel knew had gotten their cars as congratulatory presents on getting into the Ivy League.

Annabel poured beer into her glass, very carefully. She was trying to make it last. She was trying to will Tommy into making his last, too, but she wasn't getting anywhere. His glass and his bottle sat in front of him, empty, for the third time already that night.

"So," he said. "First there was a horse—"

"No, no." Annabel waved her glass in the air. "It was Kayla, you see. You can't just do anything with Kayla. She gets suspicious."

"I think that's natural." Tommy sounded drunk. "I mean, a girl in her position. All that money. I bet she has to be suspicious."

"Maybe. But I didn't mean she was suspicious of people. I meant she was suspicious of me."

"For good reason, I bet."

"Well, I've known her all my life, for God's sake. It's not as if I have anything to hide. I knew her for years and years before Daddy bought our house out here."

"In New York," Tommy said helpfully. "At Brearley."

Annabel took a long sucking swallow of beer. This was really hopeless. Tommy was already beyond the point where he was going to be of any use to her, and then what was she going to do? He'd end up passing out in the bathroom and she would have to drive him home, in spite of the fact that she didn't have a legitimate license from any state. She rubbed the side of her face with the flat of her hand and tried to think. Tommy was snaking his hand up under the skirt of her metallic green minidress, but he seemed to have lost his sense of direction, or his focus, or something.

"So," he said finally, having lost the thread of whatever it was that had started his caressing her leg. "You were going to elope."

"No," Annabel said patiently. "I only said I was going to elope. Because I had to. Because the guy I wanted to neck with was a Christian."

"Oh."

"People think of Virginia as this very sophisticated place where senators live, but it isn't really. It's full of rednecks. And this guy belonged to one of those churches where, you know, they speak in tongues. And sex is evil unless you're married. Do you think sex is evil?"

"I think it must be weird. Being someone like Kayla Anson. Being, you know, set apart like that."

"Set apart?"

"Well, you know," Tommy said. "That's what happens. We had a guy at Choate who was a Rockefeller. I mean, you know, that wasn't his name, because it was his mother who was the Rockefeller, but everybody knew who he was, and so he was—well—set apart."

"I've always thought of Kayla as a perfectly ordinary person. With money."

"Maybe. But she gets to go back and finish the year come January, and you don't."

Annabel's St. Pauli Girl Light was finished. She'd taken nearly an hour to drink it, but now there it was. The bartender caught her eye and she nodded, slightly. Then the bartender looked at Tommy and shook his head.

"The thing about people like Kayla Anson," Tommy said—and he was slurring his words, too, close to losing it; it had to be all that stuff that he'd had out at the club—

"is that you can't help hating them. No matter what kind of person they are. If they're shits, you hate them for being able to get away with it. And if they're not, you hate them for being perfect. Do you see what I mean?"

"No," Annabel said.

"I bet you do see what I mean. I bet you do. And every time Kayla Anson complains about anything, I bet you just about erupt, you hate it so much. Because people like that don't have any right to complain."

"I don't think you ought to drink any more of that," Annabel said. "I think you're going to end up passing out."

Tommy smiled politely. Then he put his head down on the bar and closed his eyes. He wasn't going to pass out. He was just going to go to sleep. The bartender put her new St. Pauli Girl Light down and waited. Annabel opened her purse and got out a five-dollar bill.

"You're going to have to do something about him," the bartender said.

"I know," Annabel replied.

"It's college boys," the bartender said. "You see it all the time. They don't know the difference between getting high and getting stewed. Most of them don't know the difference between getting high and getting sick. At least he isn't sick."

"No," Annabel said. "He isn't sick."

The bartender made change. Annabel put the change down on the bar next to her glass.

"You're going to have to do something about him eventually," the bartender said, again, and then he moved away down the bar.

Annabel poured beer into her glass and swung her legs. It wasn't true that she hated Kayla Anson—at least, it wasn't true exactly. It was just that it sometimes seemed as if she'd gotten the wrong end of some cosmic bargain. Kayla didn't even care about acting out and having fun. Rules didn't faze her. She never felt suffocated by the things everybody expected of her. Even that last night at school, when she was helping Annabel down the sheet rope from their dorm window and onto that idiotic old horse, she had only been in it out of general good nature. She was helping Annabel. It didn't even occur to her that she could come into town herself and find a boy of her own.

No, Annabel told herself again. It really isn't true that I hate Kayla. I've known her forever. And if there are times I sometimes wish I could wipe her face out of existence, that's only natural. Because she is who she is. And it's frustrating.

Annabel got down off her barstool and moved as close to Tommy as she could. With his head down on the bar like that, he was in the best possible position. All she had to do was run her hand over the back of his pants—it made him smile, in spite of the condition he was in—and there was his wallet, right where she would have expected it to be. She got it out and put it into her purse, careful not to appear self-conscious. She was a woman with a drunk on her hands. Nobody was going to be surprised at anything she did. She moved her hands around to the front of Tommy's trousers and went looking for the keys. That was harder, because he was lying sideways across the place where the pocket she needed had its opening. When she finally got in there, she could feel his penis against the side of her hand. It was limp as a worm. She got the keys and got out.

"You're going to have to take him home," the bartender said. "You don't want him driving you anywhere, the condition he's in."

"He couldn't drive me anywhere," Annabel said. "All he'd do is fall asleep behind the wheel."

"You're going to have to drive him home," the bartender said again.

Annabel waved the keys in her hand. "Before I drive him anywhere, I'm going to go to the bathroom. Then maybe I can find somebody to help me get him to the car."

"Maybe," the bartender said.

Annabel walked away from the bar to the back of the room, where the rest rooms sat on a small corridor near the kitchen. The Lucky Eight had a whole menu full of food it said it served, but Annabel had never seen anyone eat anything there except big plates of nacho chips with melted cheese and salsa. No one she saw tonight was eating even that. The small round tables were mostly full of couples drinking beer. Every once in a while, somebody had a shot glass or a cocktail. Off to the side, the band was setting up for the night. It would start at 10:00 P.M. and play country music until well after 2:00, or as late as it could until the state police decided to shut it down.

Annabel went into the small corridor where the rest rooms were and looked into the kitchen. The cook was smoking a cigarette and watching a game on a small television set up near the microwave. Annabel thought it must be a rerun of some kind. She kept on going and went through the back door into the parking lot.

The bright red Corvette was not difficult to find. It was especially easy because Tommy had parked it across two spaces, diagonally, to make sure nobody scraped his sides. When people did that, other people sometimes took their keys and scraped for real, but this time the car had been left alone. Annabel found the key for the door and got inside it. The alarm whooped once and stopped when she pushed the safety button. She slammed the door closed and went for the glove compartment.

It wasn't true that she hated Kayla Anson, any more than it was true that she hated any of them, all those people she had gone to school with and grown up with, all those people who seemed to be able to get away with anything while she was left making it up as she went along. It was just that she was a little—angry—with Kayla now, because this last expulsion had been completely unnecessary. They could have lied their way out of it. It was Kayla who had insisted on coming clean and telling the truth.

Annabel took the road maps and the owner's manual out of the glove compartment. Under all that there were two little Baggies, one full to bursting and the other with just a little in the bottom of it. The one that was full to bursting had marijuana in it. The other one had a fine white powder. Annabel supposed it was cocaine. She couldn't be sure. These days, some of the boys had heroin. It was the latest thing in drug chic on all the best campuses in the Ivy League.

Annabel shoved everything back into the glove compartment and got the compartment shut. Then she hooked her seat belt into place and put the key in the ignition. The Corvette started up without any problem at all. She maneuvered it out of its parking space—not easy, with a diagonal position like that to start with and the rest of the lot chock full—and headed out on 209.

What she really wanted to do, right now, was find a pay phone and turn the Lucky Eight and everybody in it over to the police. She would have done it, except that she knew that if she did she would only shut the Lucky Eight down and make all the other roadhouses in the Northwest Hills scared to death of serving underaged drinkers. Tommy would not get arrested. He wouldn't even get turned over to a drug and alcohol program.

What she was going to do instead was drive home to her own driveway and park the car and get out, with the drugs safely hidden away in her purse. Then she was going to call Tommy's parents and tell them, more or less, what had happened and where he was. That wouldn't get him in trouble, either, but at least she'd have the dope.

She got to the junction of 209 and 109 and turned right, toward Washington Depot. The road was dark and deserted and quiet. The moon overhead would have been full and bright, except that it was covered by clouds.

It wasn't true that she hated Kayla Anson, Annabel told herself again. It was only true that she sometimes wished her dead.

4

Faye Dallmer believed in the Goddess. She thought she might always have believed in the Goddess, even when she was small and going to Methodist Sunday school—but she knew for sure that her belief had been strong at least since 1978, which was when she had moved to the Northwest Hills. Before she had come up here for the first time, with the man who was then her husband, Faye hadn't realized that there were places like this left anywhere in New England. Well, maybe there were, up in Maine, say, or in northern Vermont or New Hampshire, places that were too far away and too isolated to do her any good. The Northwest Hills were the best she could have hoped for, under the circumstances. They were prime antiquing country for every overpaid corporate manager in New York, and they were home to a lot of wealthy people with pretensions about wanting to save the earth. Fay made handmade quilts and elaborately crocheted afghans, among other things, and she had a good eye for her potential customers. They almost always came from the city, and they almost never knew anything important about anything.

Faye had decided to go out tonight because the moon was full, even if she couldn't see her fullness. She had closed up the small shop she had had built right next to the edge of the Litchfield Road and made sure that all the doors were locked. This close to Halloween, she couldn't be too careful. Then she had gone back to the house and picked up Zara Anne, who was sitting in the kitchen as usual, trying to read a book. Zara Anne was the latest in a long line of Faye's lovers, each picked for her supposed commitment to Preserving the History of the Crafts, and each stupider and more leaden than the last. Zara Anne was thin, as well, as skeletal as some of the white trash women Faye sometimes saw buying beer at the gas station at Four Corners—except that Faye would never call anybody "white trash." People were not trash, not even if they were men, and calling these people white would have been superfluous. One of the truly shocking things about this part of Connecticut was that it was practically *all* white, and mostly Anglo-Saxon white on top of it. Maybe the ethnic people didn't feel comfortable here, or maybe they were just too smart to get stuck in the snows that hit so regularly during the winter. The first snow of this year was very close. Faye had been feeling it coming on all day. If the bad weather started this early, there would be hell to pay by Christmas, which was when most of the towns would run out of money to plow the roads. Then they would plow the roads anyway, and there would have to be town meetings to impose surcharges that would make up the difference. It was as if nobody thought of planning ahead.

When Faye came into the house, Zara Anne was watching some news program on channel 8. That meant it had to be eleven o'clock, which seemed to be damned near impossible. Faye took the white gauze scarf off her head and put it down on the little table in the hall. Her earrings tinkled like wind chimes, mostly because they were like wind chimes, tiers of metal that knocked against each other. All of Faye's jewelry was big and bright and loud. It contrasted well with the skirts and sweaters she wore, which were always in blacks and navy blues, to disguise the fact that she was getting a little thick around the middle, now that she had reached the menopause. She wasn't getting really fat, though, only *just a little* thick around the waist. She couldn't help feeling proud of herself for that. Sometimes she wanted to take Zara Anne by the neck and wring the life out of her. At least it would be some kind of change, when Zara Anne was usually as placid and immobile as a rock sealed into a vacuum chamber.

"I thought we'd go out and cast stones," Faye said, as she came through the hall into the living room.

Zara Anne was sprawled out on the couch with her legs twisted into something vaguely yoga-ish, covered in a batik cotton something whose colors all looked vaguely wrong. Faye had no idea what Zara Anne called the things she wore—dresses, maybe, or saris, or wraps—but she'd always thought there ought to be something special to say about them, as if they were an art form of their own. Fay had no idea where Zara Anne got them, either, since Zara Anne didn't drive and never wanted to shop.

"I thought . . ." Faye started again.

Zara Anne moved her entire body sideways, as if she could no longer move just her neck. "Somebody took the Jeep again," she said. "I heard them."

"Excuse me?" Faye said.

"Somebody took the Jeep again." Zara Anne hauled herself forward, so that she was almost sitting up. Why couldn't she move the way normal people moved? Why did she always look like a robot? "They came in the garage. It was hours ago. When the other news was on. I heard them."

"And you didn't come and get me?" "The other news" would mean the six o'clock, or maybe even the five-thirty.

"You were working. And besides. You'd already said. It's because it's Halloween. And they always bring it back."

This made sense, although it didn't seem to. In the weeks around Halloween, Faye's Jeep did get stolen, on and off, by kids who liked to trawl it up and down the blacktops. That was because it was a regular Jeep with a regular Jeep engine, but fitted out with extra large farm vehicle wheels, so that Faye could drive it around her back lot whenever she needed to. She'd had it customized that way at Z & J's in Danbury, to use for gardening. She had an ordinary car—a little Escort with a hatchback—that she used for actually driving on the roads.

Now she went to the door that led to the garage and opened it. The space where the Jeep usually sat was empty. The Escort was where it always was. She closed the door again and went back down the hall to the living room. Zara Anne was still watching television. Zara Anne still hadn't moved enough to be occupying any really new space.

I brought this woman here, Faye reminded herself. I met her at the naturopath conference and brought her here, all the way from Hartford. I can't just kick her out the door and expect her to fend for herself.

"Zara Anne," Faye said. "Do you remember at all, when it was this happened? How long ago exactly?"

"It was after six. Ann Nyberg was on the news. And

Diane Smith had already been. But I didn't worry about it. Because you said—"

"Well, yes. I know what I said. But it's after eleven."

"I heard it go by later," Zara Anne said. "I recognized the noise. And I went out on the porch and looked at it."

"You looked at it going by."

"She was going by, too. You know. That girl. The one with the millions of dollars who lives in Washington Depot and is on the news all the time."

"Kayla Anson."

"I don't think people should have millions of dollars like that, when so many other people have nothing. I don't think it's fair. Do you believe in Marxism?"

The last thing Faye wanted was to get into a discussion of Marxism with Zara Anne. Then she tried to remember Zara Anne's last name and couldn't, which made her feel incredibly stupid. Maybe she was getting too old for this. Years ago, she had left her husband because the sex had been so awful. She had wanted nothing more in her life but lover after lover, male and female, orgasm after orgasm. She'd even written a philosophy about it, and the philosophy had been published as a book by a small press in New Jersey. The small press was dedicated to feminist and environmental issues, with (of course) a definite political slant. The same press had published four of Faye's other books. Then one of the books had made it onto one of the national bestseller lists, and Faye had switched her allegiance to Simon and Schuster. Her reasons were entirely practical. Under all the outsized jewelry and flowing, not-quite-over-being-a-hippie clothes, Faye Dallmer was a supremely practical woman. Simon and Schuster paid advances in six figures. That was all she needed to know.

Faye went back to the door to the garage one more time. The Jeep was still gone. The Escort was still there. At this point, it didn't matter so much if the Jeep had been stolen by kids or professional car thieves. If it had been stolen by thieves, she ought to call the police on principle. If it had been stolen by kids, she had to worry that they'd had an accident in it. The Jeep didn't go missing for hours at a time like this. The kids always brought it back and parked it where it belonged before she'd even had a chance to worry about it.

Faye went back to Zara Anne. The phone was on a small table between the couch and the biggest armchair. Faye sat down on the armchair and began punching numbers into the pad.

"I'm going to call the town police," she said. "We should have done this hours ago. There may have been an accident."

"You told me not to worry," Zara Anne said stubbornly.

The phone rang and rang in Faye's ear. Then it was picked up and Faye recognized the voice of Rita Venotti, who seemed to have been on the night shift at the police department before forever.

"Oh, Rita," Faye said. And then she explained, in detail, so that Rita wouldn't say what Zara Anne had, that it had happened before, that there was nothing to worry about.

"I could send somebody out," Rita said. "I could send Danny Hazelton. Would that be all right?"

"That would be fine," Faye said.

"We don't have any accidents over the radio," Rita said. "I don't think you have to worry about that. We monitor the state police all the time."

"Maybe it was professional thieves, then," Faye said. "Although it hardly seems possible."

"I know, I know," Rita said. "It hardly does seem possible. It used to be you never had to worry about any of that out here."

Faye put the phone down. Zara Anne was wielding the remote, punching channels as if her life depended on them. Sometimes, late at night, she settled on the Trinity Broadcasting Network and watched the PTL club as if it were a documentary. Now she had found a rerun of an ancient *Hawaii Five-O* episode. Jack Lord was looking just as tense and phony as he ever had.

"Zara Anne," Faye said carefully. "I've been meaning

to talk to you about some things. I've been meaning to talk to you about us."

"You've been meaning to throw me out," Zara Anne said. "I could see it coming."

"I don't think it's a question of throwing you out," Faye said. "I think it's more of the order of, well——"

"Sometimes I really do believe in God," Zara Anne said. "I believe in a God of the devil. If you get what I mean."

"No. No, I don't."

"I bet nobody ever threw that girl out. The rich one. I bet she gets to stay anywhere she wants for as long as she wants. I bet all she has to do to get a lover is say she wants one, and there it is."

"It?"

Zara Anne swivelled her head around. Her face was mottled with red. The skin of her face was slack and loose and creased, like polyester that has been left to wrinkle at the bottom of a laundry basket. Faye didn't think she could have been this unattractive when she first came here. In fact, Faye was sure she couldn't have been. If Zara Anne had been this unattractive, Faye would never have brought her home.

"If you think you're going to get rid of me just by saying so," Zara Anne said, "you're going to have to think again. I'm not a piece of cardboard. I'm not here just so that you can push me around."

"I don't want to push you around," Faye said, automatically, but the thought came to her that this possibly wasn't true. It would be a great deal of help if she *could* push Zara Anne around, at least to the extent of getting her to move a little. Sweep the floor. Remember to pick up her clothes instead of leaving them where they fell as she took them off, even if they fell in the middle of the upstairs hall, because she took them off on the way to the shower.

Zara Anne had drifted off again, her mind on the television set or the air or wherever. "You can't push me around," she said again, but her heart wasn't in it.

Faye looked at the set and saw Ann Nyberg on News

Channel Eight, tapping papers together on the anchor desk. The graphic behind her said CHILD ABUSE, but there was no way beyond that to tell what the story was about.

Faye left Zara Anne to it and went through the living room to the little back hall. She went down the back hall to the kitchen, where the dinner dishes were still piled in the sink and three dirty coffee mugs were standing out on the counter. She began to put things away automatically, at the same time she was filling the kettle and putting it on to boil.

It was time she rethought her life, all of her life, from beginning to end. Lesbian or not, New Age or not, she was behaving just like a man with the way she chose her lovers. Maybe she was behaving worse than a man, because no man would have chosen Zara Anne out of the dozens of women wandering around the Hartford Civic Center that afternoon. No man would put up with Zara Anne's wild clothes, or her Depression-era Okie thinness, or her stupidity.

The kettle whistled and Faye took it off the stove. She started to put a Red Zinger tea bag into her favorite mug and then opted out. Red Rose would be better. She could use all the caffeine she could get.

She left the tea to steep on the counter and went out the back door to stand on the little porch there. Through the small back windows, she could see the lights she had left shining in the garage, and the hulk of her Escort. She could see the empty space where the Jeep had been, too. Obviously, Zara Anne wasn't the only thing in her life that was out of control.

If there was one thing Faye Dallmer couldn't stand, it was being out of control. She had been that way once, when she was very young. She didn't intend to be that way for any length of time again. Not even by accident.

5

It was fifteen minutes after eleven, and Sally Martindale was having a hard time keeping her stomach under control. It had been bad enough when she was still out on Interstate 84, with wide empty roads and good road lights and nothing to be afraid of except the existential kinds of things that had plagued her, endlessly, ever since Frank had moved back to New York. Losing Frank and getting fired all at once—it was exactly the kind of double whammy Sally had always been suspicious of when it happened to other people. Surely there must have been something they'd done. Surely it couldn't be plain old innocent bad luck. Now that it had happened to her, she hadn't the first idea of what to do. Tonight she had simply driven out to Ledyard, where the Mashentucket Pequots had their gambling casino, and used her last two hundred dollars to give the slots a shot. She had kept back fifteen dollars for a full tank of gas, which was a good thing. The slots had been absolutely dead for her all night, the way the rest of her luck had been dead for her for almost two years. It was amazing how luck always seemed to travel in packs. It was even more amazing just how long a string of bad luck could go on, without even taking a break for air.

Right now, she was driving under the dark cover of the trees on Swamp Tree Road, heading for the main lodge of the Swamp Tree Country Club. She thought she ought to know this road by heart by now, since she drove it every morning of her life. Doing the books for the Swamp Tree was the only job she had been able to get after she had been fired from Deloitte, Touche in New York. At the time she had been offered it, she had been glad to get in, in spite of the fact that it was part-time and didn't come with benefits. It was only that she realized what an impossible position she was in: still a member of the club, still cheerfully intending to bring her daughter out at the Swamp Tree's

Midnight Cotillion, and so short of cash that she was afraid to go to the doctor when she got a little sick. She hadn't been to a dentist for over eighteen months.

Sally looked across at her daughter, Mallory, sitting in the other bucket seat, her hands folded in her lap, her mouth set. Mallory had always been heavy, but since Frank left she had literally ballooned. The dress she was wearing now had to be at least a size twenty-four. It wasn't only the size, either. Mallory had changed in every way it was possible to change. Frank was willing to pay for her college tuition, but Mallory wasn't willing to take it—in spite of the fact that she'd fantasized forever about going to Smith, and had even gotten accepted. These days Mallory was in a nursing program at the University of Connecticut branch campus in Waterbury. She drove into class every morning just before Sally went to work, except on weekends. On weekends Mallory went to the club and sat at the big circular tables in the main dining room with all the other girls, acting as if nothing had happened. It was all wrong, Sally thought, all wrong, everything that had happened to them. Things like this were supposed to happen to other people, who deserved them.

The road dipped and swayed. Up ahead, Sally suddenly saw the lights she had been looking for, winking like fairy auras in the blackness. She relaxed a little, but only as much as she thought she could afford.

"Well," she said, "we're practically there. I thought I'd gotten lost for a moment."

"You took the right road," Mallory said. "I saw you do it."

"I know I did. It didn't look familiar. Maybe I'm not used to being out here so late."

"I can't believe you've done this before," Mallory said. "I can't believe it. What are you going to do if they catch you at it? What am I going to do if they put you in jail?"

"We've got to eat," Sally said. "We can't go on keeping the thermostat at sixty-eight all through the winter. We can't live on the cranberries I grow in the backyard."

"We could sell the house and move someplace smaller."

"It would take forever to sell the house."

"If we moved someplace small enough, you could take the extra money from the house and use that to help us live on. We could quit the club. We could give up on my being a debutante. Lots of people live on less money than you're making now. I've met them."

"I don't want to live on less money than I'm making now," Sally said.

Mallory turned her head away, so that she was looking out the window on her side, into the dark. "It's like a disease you have," she said. "It's like you think there's some kind of cosmic meaning to all this stuff. It doesn't have anything to do with life."

"You don't know the first thing about life," Sally said, feeling suddenly furious—but she had to tone it down. The lights were right ahead of her now. She could see the two low stone pillars that marked the entrance to the club. She could see the gravel drive winding up the hill right to the lodge itself.

"Here we are," she said, making the car turn slowly. She didn't want to end up in a ditch with all this ice on the road. "When we get there you can go into the dining room and see who's around that you know."

"I don't want to see who's around that I know. I don't like the people I know. Not at this place."

"Even your father understands the need for contacts, Mallory. These are the best contacts you're ever going to have, unless you come to your senses and let your father put you into college next fall."

"Contacts for what?"

"Contacts," Sally said stubbornly. "You really have no idea how the world works. No idea. I wish I could get you to see what you're trying to get me to give up on and throw away."

"I wish you could see what I see."

"You're romanticizing poverty. That's all you're doing.

It's very common in adolescents who've never had to fend for themselves."

"You're romanticizing money."

They had reached the wide gravel parking lot. This was a weekend night in the country. The lot was more than half-full. Sally put the car into a space at the back, being careful not to hit either of the two Volvos that surrounded her. Her own car was a Volvo, too, because it had been bought before Frank left them. If she'd had to buy a car of her own these days, she wouldn't have been able to afford anything expensive, because she wouldn't have been able to get the credit.

She pulled the key out of the ignition and dropped it into her purse. "I don't know what you're going to do if you don't go into the main dining room," she said. "You'd look much too conspicuous if you came with me. And you can't hide out in the ladies' room for an hour."

"Maybe I can just go into the library and read."

"On Friday night?"

"Some people do read on Friday night, Mother. Some people work, too. Some people even just stay home and don't see anybody."

"This is the club on Friday night. You'll look ridiculous. Sometimes I think you want to look ridiculous."

"Maybe I just want to look like myself. Or maybe I just don't want to look like a debutante."

"Stay in the car for all I care," Sally said, popping her door open and letting the wind rush in. "Stay out here and freeze. If I don't do what I came here to do, we're not going to eat next week."

She climbed out onto the gravel and slammed the car door shut behind her. It was freezing out here, not only late October but early frost. She had left her coat in the backseat of the car. She didn't want to get it. Mallory was fumbling around in there, getting ready to come out. Sally didn't want to talk to her again.

Sally wrapped her arms around her chest and started across the lot, wobbling so violently on her high heels that

she thought she was going to break an ankle. When she got
to the lodge's front door, she turned back and saw Mallory
lumbering toward her, not wearing any kind of coat, either.
Maybe with all that fat on her she doesn't get cold, Sally
thought—and then she was ashamed of herself, because
that seemed spiteful.

She turned away and let herself into the lodge. There
was no one at all in the front lobby although Sally could
see a few couples in the dining room beyond, and one or
two of the girls in Mallory's group. The girls were not the
ones Sally most wanted Mallory to know—but then they
wouldn't be, since girls like that almost always had other
things to do on weekend nights besides hang around at the
club. That was true even if they were heavy and unattractive, like Mallory was. Money covered a multitude of sins.
It was one of those things Mallory just didn't understand.

Sally bypassed the main rooms and went down to the
back where the administrative offices were. Her own office
was the second-biggest one on the corridor, after the club
manager's. SALLY MARTINDALE, FINANCIAL OFFICER the
sign on her door read. Sally made a face at it. Of all the
things she found it hard to take, this was what she found
the hardest: that there was a sign on her door that announced, unequivocally, just how far she had come down
in the world.

She went into her office and turned on the lights. She
punched at the keyboard of her computer and waited for it
to boot up. Then she sat down in the little chair and
punched at her keyboard some more, until she brought up
the file she had to have to do what she wanted to do. It
was only then that her fear came back to her, and it came
back in a wave. Mallory thought she did this without a
qualm, but it wasn't true. Sometimes she lay awake in the
night, imagining all the worst things happening to her, getting caught, going to jail, watching Mallory move to New
York to live with Frank. Except, of course, that Frank
wouldn't take Mallory. The last thing Frank wanted was a
fat, sullen, unattractive daughter hanging around the apart-

ment, letting all his perky little girlfriends know exactly how old he was.

Sally scrolled up the page, looking for the names she liked the best. It was not a good idea to take money out of the same accounts two weeks in a row, even small sums of money, like one or two hundred dollars, which was all Sally ever took. She didn't want to turn into a real-life embezzler. She just wanted enough to get by, to keep the phone and the gas on, to make sure she didn't have too many calls from the people she had her credit cards with, wondering where their money was going to come from this month. In the past six months, Sally had been threatened with law suits twice, both by out-of-town banks where she had Visa cards. When she and Frank had been together and she had been working for Deloitte, it had seemed like the most natural thing in the world to run up huge balances and pay them off only sporadically. It had seemed like the most natural thing in the world to drop a thousand dollars in a single afternoon at the West Farms Mall, just because she was bored.

The problem was, not every member of the club kept significant amounts of money in their club account. Sally couldn't always alter the list of people she was taking fifty dollars from here and twenty-five dollars from there. She kept coming back to the same names over and over and over again, and that was dangerous.

Actually, if she was honest about it, she kept coming back to the same name over and over again—name singular, not plural. She looked down at the screen and bit her lip.

"Anson, Kayla," it said, the letters pulsing a little on their dark blue background. Kayla's club account had over fifteen hundred dollars in it. It was the largest of any account kept at the club. Even other very rich women, like Penny Harrison or Dee Marie Colt, rarely kept more than a couple of hundred on account at any one time.

Sally punched at her keyboard again. Kayla Anson's fifteen hundred dollars became thirteen hundred dollars. Sally punched at her keyboard again and Kayla's name disappeared. All Sally had to do now was wait for the morning, when she picked up the club's weekend cash at the bank. She could take the two hundred dollars off the top right in the car. All anybody would know if they checked was that Kayla Anson had spent two hundred dollars at the club on Friday, October 27, and that the spending had been done on food and liquor. The club was not supposed to serve liquor to minors, but it had been doing it for decades, and it wasn't going to stop now.

Sally exited the program and put her screen saver up. Then she stood and got her purse from the floor. Kayla Anson wasn't in the club tonight. Her little BMW was not in the parking lot. As far as Sally knew, Kayla hadn't been in the club all day. When Sally had first started doing this, she had been much more careful about making sure that the dates of her withdrawals matched the dates on which the account holders were really here. After a few months, it had been impossible to keep that up. It was incredible how fast money went, and how much there was to spend it on. It was incredible how completely broke a person could get and not be dead.

Sally turned off the lights and went back into the hall. Nobody was around. The club manager went home on weekend evenings, in spite of the fact that they were often the busiest nights of the week. The very busiest night of the week was Thursday. That was the night the maids traditionally had off, and nobody wanted to stay home and cook.

Sally went into the main lobby again and then through to the dining room. Mallory was sitting alone at a table near the kitchen door, reading a ragged copy of *Field and Stream*. At a table in the center of the room, three girls from Mallory's coming-out class—including one Vanderbilt connection and a girl whose mother was related to Jacqueline Onassis on the Bouvier side—were huddled over gin and tonics, giggling.

If Sally Martindale could have done anything at all right

that minute, she would have strangled her daughter and thrown the body in the duck pond beyond the terrace. Maybe the ducks would be able to get through to Mallory where she could not. Maybe the ducks would come up with a reason why Sally should go on living.

6

It was almost 11:30 by the time Peter Greer got home, and he was tense as hell about it until he came through his garage and into the main room of his Adirondack-style house. That was when he heard the giggling coming from his sunroom, where the hot tub was—giggling that meant that Deirdre had waited for him after all, and gotten herself fairly drunk on champagne in the process. That was almost too perfect to believe: a drunk and naked Deirdre, in a good mood. Peter had been jumpy all night. It was impossible not to think of all the things that could go wrong if he didn't keep an eye on his life every single moment. He had so many balls in the air right now, he wasn't even juggling anymore. He was just flailing, pinwheeling his arms and living on hope. One of these days it was all going to come crashing down on his head, and then what was he going to do with himself?

He went past the massive stone fireplace with its framed poster on the mantel: the cover of the first Goldenrod catalogue he had ever produced. He dropped his scarf and his down vest on a black leather love seat and kept moving toward the sunroom. Almost everything he owned had appeared in one Goldenrod catalogue or another over the years. When he really liked something, he tried to get a franchise to sell it. Goldenrod was all about his personal taste. No, that wasn't it. It was all about his personal *identity*. Either that, or the kind of identity other people thought he had. Everybody was looking for an image these day. Everybody wanted to see themselves living out their lives on a big screen. Peter had no idea what people had done in other eras, when there hadn't been so much media around, or so many opportunities to appear in public. He had always thought anonymity was a little like death, or maybe something worse. If a tree falls in the forest and nobody hears it, did it really make a sound? If a person lives a life that nobody else notices, was he ever really alive? The trick was to call as much attention to yourself as possible. That way you could be sure you wouldn't just disappear.

Peter ducked his head into the sunroom. Deirdre was lying in the hot water, letting her body float to the surface every once in a while and then forcing it back down. She really was naked. When Kayla came here—and Peter brought her here often; it was the most sensible thing he could do—she always wore a bathing suit.

"You look like you're in a good mood," Peter said. "I take it there haven't been any interruptions."

"Your Kayla called," Deirdre said. "It's on tape."

"What did she say?"

"I didn't pay much attention. And it was hours ago. It was before seven o'clock."

"She was supposed to go into Waterbury and do some shopping. Whatever she said didn't get your nose out of joint, for once."

"I was hoping she'd show up. I was hoping she'd find me in the hot tub."

"And?"

Deirdre's eyes narrowed. They were small eyes to begin with. They turned into slits. It reminded Peter of how dangerous she was. He needed to be reminded. He found it far too easy to think of Deirdre as a kind of classic bimbo, all oversized breasts and no brain, instead of as the mercenary little whore she really was. Mercenary little whores could be something worse than dangerous. They could be fatal.

Peter backed out of the sunroom and took the stairs up to the loft where he slept. He saw the light blinking on his message machine and pushed the buttons he needed to play the message back.

"Hello, Peter, this is Kayla," Kayla's voice said. "I'd ask you where you've gone, but I wouldn't get an answer. It's six-fifteen. I'm on my way back any minute now. Maybe I'll stop by and see if you've wandered in. One way or the other, I'll talk to you later."

Peter turned the machine off. Kayla must have decided not to wander in. Either that, or she had come to the door and knocked, and Deirdre hadn't let her in. Peter thought Deirdre would have said something about that, if it had happened. Kayla Anson drove Deirdre crazy.

Peter dropped his shirt and trousers on the floor. He stepped out of his boxer shorts and admired himself in the mirror. He was very careful about working out, and it had paid off. His stomach was flatter than it had been when he was a jock at Brown. Even women like Deirdre were attracted to him, and women like Deirdre weren't attracted to anything, except money.

Peter went downstairs again. One wall of his living room was nothing but windows, but it didn't matter, because the windows looked out on a thickly treed wood that went on for miles. He went back into the sunroom and found that Deirdre had managed to get herself a brand-new bottle of champagne. It was the kind she liked best, that he bought only for her: cheap, pink, and very sweet. He got a glass from the bar and poured himself two full shots of un-blended scotch. It looked as clear as water, but it tasted better.

"So," he said, getting into the water next to Deirdre's impossible blondeness. Everything about Deirdre was impossible. It was what he liked best about her. In spite of the fact that her accent was a nasal mid-Connecticut whine, she reminded him of the low-rent town he had grown up in, where women tried as hard as they could to "beautify" themselves, even when they were only running out to the corner store.

Peter anchored himself to the bench—he hated floating in the hot tub—and took a long sip of scotch. "You're in a remarkably good mood for a night when Kayla called.

What did you do, catch her trying to get in the front door and throw her out?'

"No," Deirdre said. "I couldn't throw her out if I wanted to. She has a key."

"You have a key," Peter said.

"Maybe half of Litchfield County has a key. The female half."

Peter didn't answer. Deirdre slugged back pink champagne.

"I was just thinking," she said. "About you. And about me. And about Kayla-rich-as-shit-Anson."

"And?"

"And I was thinking I wouldn't complain about her so much if I was going to do something about her. Only I couldn't think of what to do about her. You don't see her because you like the way she is in bed."

"Maybe I do."

Deirdre made a face. "She's got money, that's what it is, lots and lots of money and there isn't anybody on earth who can compete with that. All those old movies about how men don't want to marry an heiress because she'll end up taking their balls away is just so much crap. Men don't care what happens to their balls at all."

"I don't think that's entirely accurate. Besides, I don't see what it is you think you're—"

Deirdre's champagne glass was empty. The bottle was on the tub collar next to her elbow. She got it and filled up again, squinting at the glass as the liquid went into it, as if she were measuring something and the measurement had to be precise. Her blonde hair was so close to white, it looked like light. Her eyelashes were at least half an inch thick, plumped out by mink strips.

"Somebody else called while you were out," she said. "Except this time I picked up."

"While the message was still running on the machine? How did you know who it was?"

"I didn't."

"That was stupid, Deirdre."

"Maybe. Maybe not. Do you want to know who it was?"

"I take it it wasn't Kayla."

"It might have been. It might have been anybody."

"Whatever that's supposed to mean."

"It's supposed to *mean*," Deirdre said, "that there wasn't any voice after I answered the phone. There was breathing. There wasn't any voice. But I don't think it was Kayla Anson's breathing."

He should have brought the bottle of scotch to the tub with him, instead of leaving it on the bar. Now, if he wanted to fill his glass, he would have to get up and walk across the sunroom to do it. He would have to walk out there in the open, as naked as the day he was born.

"Well," he said, very carefully, "that could have been anything. That could have been a telephone solicitation."

"Funny time of night for a telephone solicitation."

Peter's glass was empty. It was so empty, it looked as if it had never been used. He stood up carefully and began to climb out of the tub.

He could not possibly know who that call was from. It didn't make any sense. There was no such thing as telepathy. It could have been a phone call from Santa Claus at the North Pole as easily as it could have been a phone call from anybody else.

"So," he said, "you mean this person just called up and breathed in your ear."

"For a long time."

"Maybe it was a random obscene caller. Dial the first number that comes into your head. Get a woman. Hit the jackpot."

"It wasn't that kind of breathing."

"That must have been bizarre. I'm surprised you didn't hang up on him."

"I thought it was a woman I'd be hanging up on. It was a woman's breathing. If you know the kind of thing I mean."

Peter knew nothing at all about the kind of thing she meant. He got to the bar and started pouring scotch. He would have ditched his drink glass for a tumbler, but he thought it would be too obvious. He hoped Deirdre would think he was sweating because of the water in the hot tub. He hoped he wasn't breathing too hard.

"It doesn't matter who it was," he said finally. "If it was anybody important, he'll call back."

"You're really a snot, do you know that?" Deirdre said. "You pick your friends out of the *Social Register*. You care more about your image than you do about your bank account."

"If that were true, you wouldn't be here."

"Oh," Deirdre said, "I think I'd still be here. Even men who are listed in the *Social Register* go slumming."

"I've never called seeing you 'slumming.' And you know it."

"You've never called it anything else, either. Are you going to marry Kayla Anson?"

"I doubt if she'd have me."

"But you would marry her, if she'd have you? Because of all that money?"

"Kayla is a wonderful girl. But she's a girl. She's very young."

"Jesus Christ," Deirdre said.

Peter turned around with his drink in his hand. His penis was waving in the air. He felt so exposed, he wanted to duck, except that there was no place to duck into, and nothing to hide behind. Deirdre put her glass down on the tub collar and hauled herself up. She was exposed, too, but she didn't seem to mind it.

"You know," she said finally, "you really shouldn't treat me like an asshole, because I'm not an asshole. Do you get my meaning?"

"I never treat you like an asshole."

"You never treat me like anything else. But if you really think I'm going to let you get away with pushing me around the way you push around your debutantes, you're going to be very surprised. Have I made myself clear?"

"I never push you around."

"Jesus Christ," Deirdre said again.

She walked around the tub collar until she got to the towel rack. She got a towel and wrapped herself up in it, tucking the edge between her breasts to make it stay. Deirdre was the only person Peter had ever known who could do that and walk around without the towel coming lose and falling off. She was the only woman he had ever known whose breasts pointed at the ceiling like missiles at a launch pad. He supposed she'd had them done.

"I'm going to get dressed and get out of here," she said. "You're beginning to piss me off. But try to remember a few things, will you please?"

"Like what?"

"Like the fact that you have caller ID."

"I don't get it."

"I'm going home," Deirdre said again.

On any other night, Peter would have gone to her and tried to make her change her mind. He would at least have grabbed her arm and tried to do something physical. Now he just watched her walk away, her hips moving like waves under the pink terrycloth of the towel. She reminded him of Marilyn Monroe in some old movie.

When she was out of the room, Peter got a towel for himself and brought his scotch out into the main room. He could hear Deirdre in the loft, getting herself dressed, but he didn't go up to see her. He sat down on the love seat instead and closed his eyes.

He felt as if he were a single wagon, detached from a wagon train, and the Indians were attacking.

7

The call came in at 11:37, and Eve Wachinsky almost didn't hear it. She had an uneasy feeling that she might have failed to hear a number of calls tonight. With Darla upstairs, sick as a dog, and nothing going on down here but a movie on HBO with the sound turned down too low to hear, the world could have come to an end without her noticing. Darla Barden was the woman whose house this was, and who owned the answering service that was run from this broad front room. The front room had once been a porch off the living room and had then been enclosed. Now it was an alcove off the living room, and the living room had no furniture in it. Eve rubbed at the side of her face and looked at the machine blinking in front of her. This room was full of machines: computers, telephones, fax machines, devices to contact beepers, radios turned to the police band. The movie on HBO was *Wag the Dog*, which was what everybody had been watching since August, when President Clinton had bombed the Sudan. Eve Wachinsky was not sure where the Sudan was—in Africa, she thought, but she wasn't sure which part—but it bothered her to no end that her last name was so much like the last name of That Woman.

Now she rubbed the side of her face and stared at the blinking light on the machine in front of her. The light told her which account the call was related to, so that she knew whether to say "Good evening, Southbury Diagnostics" or "Good evening, Holden Tool and Die" when she picked up. Right now, it felt to her as if everything on her body itched. She'd been sitting in the same place so long, it seemed as if every part of her body had gone to sleep. She wanted to cry, too, that was the thing, as if she had nothing to do with her life anymore except break down.

She put the headset on, punched into the machine, and said, "Waterville Physicians Services. Can I help you?"

"Oh," Rita Venotti said. "Eve, I'm sorry. I couldn't remember the number I'm supposed to use, and I knew you'd be doing this one, so—"

"It's all right," Eve said. It was, too. She hated taking calls for doctors more than she hated anything. The patients were all crazy, and too many of them got abusive. "Bitch," the women called her, when she would not give them their doctor's home telephone numbers, or put them through to some doctor who was not on call. "Scum cunt" one of the men had said to her once, and she didn't even remember why. The patients had terrible symptoms and waited for hours before calling in. They got addicted to their pain-killers and then wanted more and more of them, from different doctors, called into different pharmacies. Eve rubbed the side of her face again, as if there was something there she needed to rub off.

"Eve?" Rita said.

"I'm sorry," Eve said. "I'm a little tired tonight, I guess."

"Could I talk to Darla?"

"She's upstairs asleep. She's got some kind of food poisoning, I think. Anyway, she was throwing up nonstop when I got here. And then she passed out."

"Oh, dear. Well, I don't suppose it matters. In fact, I know it doesn't matter. I don't know what's wrong with me tonight. I need the road crew sent out to Four Corners. There's a telephone pole down on Capernaum Road. You know that road?"

"No."

"One of those dirt things that's really a mess, but the thing is, it goes out to that little cemetery and a few other places, so people actually want to use it. And according to the guy who called me, the pole is leaning practically sideways."

"I'd better call SNET, as well."

"No, don't do that. Let the town people do it when they get out. It's so frustrating, really. I mean, Capernaum Road in the middle of the night. You'd think it could wait until morning. But I know what they'd say around here if I let it wait."

"I don't think it's good to let it wait with the telephone wire being interfered with," Eve said. "Aren't there other things up there on those poles, electrical stuff, that kind of thing?"

"I don't know. I don't understand any of it. I just know that when the poles come down everything stops and they close off the road for half a day. You'd think they could have thought of a better way after all this time."

"Mmm," Eve said.

"Well, it doesn't matter. Just get the road crew out to Capernaum Road and tell them to go from there. That will take care of it. I hope you're feeling good these days."

"I'm fine," Eve said.

"Everything's a mess over at my house. It always is. Did you know that my Michael got into Harvard University?"

"No," Eve said.

"He got a scholarship, too. And he's going to have to take loans. But we worked it out. We thought it was really important, if he could get into a good school like that, he should go. And now Lisa is saying she wants to go someplace good herself. Wellesley, that's what she's thinking of. I don't know how we're going to afford it."

"Mmm," Eve said again.

"It's going to be a kick anyway," Rita said. "Both my children in the Ivy League. Or whatever it is they call those girls' schools. I must say I never expected, when they were born, that they would both turn out to be so smart."

"If I don't call the town, you're never going to get a road crew out to Four Corners."

"What? Oh, yes. You're right. Of course you're right. I'll hang right up. It just gets so lonely around here at night, with nobody to talk to. I wouldn't work nights at all except that it pays so much more money."

"The road crew—"

"Yes, yes," Rita said. "I'll be quiet now. I've got to find out what Danny Hazelton is doing. I sent him out to Faye Dallmer's to find out what happened to her Jeep, and it's been simply forever. More than half an hour, at least. What do you think he could be doing out there for half an hour?"

"Maybe this time somebody really stole it."

"I don't think that's likely. Well, whatever. I'll talk to you later. Tell Darla I hope she's feeling better."

"I will," Eve said.

The headset sent up a buzzing dial tone in her ears. Eve took it off and put it down on her keyboard. It was too dark outside. She had come to hate fall and winter in New England. Everything was always black. She turned sideways and began to punch the message—*Tree down, road crew to Four Corners Capernaum Road*—into the machine that sent messages to beepers.

The thing was, it had suddenly occurred to her that she was getting old. Not old old. She wasn't ready for Social Security, or a candidate for a nursing home. She was, in fact, exactly forty-nine years old. In two months, she would be fifty. The number kept stopping her dead, every time she thought of it.

Fifty was what her mother was, the year Eve had graduated from high school—graduated in the very same class with Rita Venotti and at least a dozen other people who were still in town. Rita had a husband and two children and a house out at Mount Fair Farm. John Candless, who had been president of their class senior year, had a wife and four children and a dermatology practice in Waterbury. Even Jenna Borman, the class slut, had surprised them all by entering a convent and becoming a teacher. Now she was Sister Jenna Marie Borman, and principal of Holy Name School in Waterbury.

I should have more to show for my life than this, Eve kept thinking—and by "more" she really meant anything at all. She kept trying to remember what she had been doing for the last thirty years or so, what she had been thinking, that she could get to the age she was now and almost literally not exist. She'd had boyfriends, but none of them had ever asked her to marry them. None of them had really been all that good in the way of catches, either, but that was something else. She had had jobs, but they had mostly been jobs like this one. She had worked for a long time as a cashier in a supermarket, and then for a little longer as a nurse's aide in a convalescent home. She had worked at Sears, too, selling perfume. It had probably been the best job she ever had—it had at least come with health insurance—but she had left it eventually, she wasn't sure why. She hadn't even had what she could call a lot of fun. Now

she rented a three-room apartment in a cut up old house in
Watertown, and came to this job here, and played the lot-
tery, but not too much. She couldn't play the lottery much.
She didn't have enough money.

Her machine began to beep again. Eve clamped the
headset on her head and picked up.

"Road Maintenance Department. Can I help you?"

"There's a telephone pole down on Capernaum Road?
Are you kidding me?"

"Ask Rita. It's Rita who would be kidding you."

"Jesus. In the middle of the night like this. What would
bring a telephone pole down in the middle of the night like
this?"

"Wind, maybe."

"There isn't enough wind to blow over a matchstick.
You'd need a major hurricane."

"So maybe it's been down for a long time and somebody
just noticed it now."

"Not likely. Half the world uses that damned road as a
shortcut. You sure Rita didn't say anything about an accident, about some *car* knocking over a telephone pole on
Capernaum Road?"

"Nope."

"Jesus."

"Craig?" Eve said. "Do you ever think that you've had
enough of it? Your life, I mean. Do you ever think that you
really have to change everything around right now?"

"I think that if I ever win the lottery I'm going to retire
to Florida. Are you drunk or something?"

"No. No, just a little tired. I'm sorry."

"You can tell Rita we'll be out there in about twenty
minutes."

"She says the report says that the pole may be leaning
into a set of power lines. You may need SNET as well as
CL and P."

"Right. Shit. Just what I need when it's right before Halloween."

"Sorry."

"Do you realize you apologize for everything?" Craig said. "You apologize for stuff you didn't even do."

"Sorry," Eve said again—but there was nobody to hear her. The dial tone was buzzing in her ears again. She took the headset off again and pushed her chair away from the computer.

It wasn't stupid, or drunk, to ask the kind of questions she was asking now. Eve was sure of it. Everybody had to ask those questions. The lucky ones asked while they were still in high school, when they had a world of time to do something about their dissatisfaction.

She got up and went into the living room. There was a fireplace there with a big mirror over the mantel, but nothing else except boxes of files and manuals, pushed up against the wall on the north side of the room. Eve went to the mirror and looked at herself. The image she got back was murky and inconclusive. She went out the front door that stood at one end of the living room and out onto the front stoop. With the door open, she would be able to hear the machine if it beeped.

What was it that people did that put realness in their lives? That was what she didn't understand. How did people end up with families, or jobs they had for twenty years, or nice little niches in groups like the Friends of the Library or the Town Benevolent League? How did they start? To Eve, life was like a dust storm, pulled this way and that, with no particular direction.

There has to be something else besides this, she told herself—and then she realized that she was freezing. She was standing on the stoop in her light cotton shirt and polyester-made-to-look-like-cotton vest, and the air around her had that unyielding hardness that meant a major frost.

She turned around and went back into the house and closed the door behind her.

I'm forty-nine years old, she told herself, and I have to do something about it.

8

Because it was the Friday before Halloween, the noises out back had been awful all day, and even more awful once it got to be dark. Martin Chandling found himself having to go out back to take a look at least once every half hour. He wouldn't have bothered, except that a couple of years ago they had had real trouble. That was when Jackey Hargrove had gone in with two of his friends and tipped over half a dozen gravestones and then tried to dig up a grave. It only went to prove that Jackey was just as stupid as everybody thought he was, because the grave he had tried to dig up had a cremated man in it, and if he had managed to get down to the box, all he would have found was a marble urn with a pile of ashes in it. Still, Martin thought, you had to be careful. There had been a couple of incidents in other parts of the state in recent years. Down in Danbury, there had been a real mess, complete with desecrations. All Martin needed now was to have one of his two-hundred-year-old skeletons pulled out of the ground and dragged into Washington Depot. All he needed now was to have something come along and make him lose this job, which he had had as far back as he could remember, maybe as far back as time. Other people might have found it disturbing, living in a little house right next to the cemetery grounds, but Martin rather liked it. It was quiet, and cool, too, even in the summer, because of all the shade trees. He thought he would have felt differently about one of those new cemeteries, run by a corporation, with professional landscaping and paved roads between the graves. This cemetery went all the way back to 1697. One whole section of it, up in the back near the rotting wood building that had once been a church, was given over to the members of a single family. That was why this was called the Fairchild Family Cemetery, even though there were other people besides Fairchilds in it. Martin often wondered what it had been like for them, when they were still almost the only family here.

Actually, Martin could remember a lot of his life before coming to the Fairchild Family Cemetery. He couldn't have forgotten it if he'd wanted to, because his brother Henry lived at the cemetery with him, and always had. Sometimes it seemed to Martin as if he and Henry had done everything together all his fifty-six years. They had even gotten married together, once, back in 1962, but it hadn't lasted long for either of them.

"I could understand it if you were twins," Martin's wife had told him when she left. "I still wouldn't like it, but at least I would understand it. But you aren't even close. There's three years between the two of you and your sister Esther besides. I don't understand what it is you think you're doing."

It was Henry who was the older. He would be fifty-nine in November. Martin's wife had been a schoolteacher, and Martin had always thought that that was the real problem there. It was a mistake to get involved with an educated woman. They always wanted to be someplace they weren't, and they ran a man's life ragged in the process. Martin's wife had taken a job in Westport—"where I'll be halfway close to civilization," as she put it—and then married a professor at NYU. Martin thought about her sometimes, during all those crazy riots in the late 1960s. He hadn't been able to decide whether she would like them or hate them. She had liked flowers growing in flower boxes in the spring, and instrumental music with a high twangy sound to it she bought in record albums put out by some outfit in Germany. She liked Christmas at her mother's, too, which Martin had never been able to stand.

He was standing on his own back porch, trying to listen to any sounds that might be coming from the cemetery. All he heard was his brother Henry, tramping along on the frosted grass and swearing, not quite under his breath. Other than that, the world might as well have been empty. There weren't even any cars going by on 109.

"Henry?"

"It's that Dallmer woman," Henry said. "She's probably dead in a ditch up there. Her car's sure as hell about as dead as it can get."

Martin switched on his flashlight and waved it into the dark. He caught Henry, looking furious.

"Her car's where?" he asked. "In the cemetery?"

"Of course it's in the cemetery," Henry said.

"But how can it be in the cemetery? There aren't any roads in the cemetery. Nobody's supposed to drive in there."

Henry reached the porch and came up the steps. "It's the Jeep with the wheels, the one she has done up like a damned tank. It went right over the meadow and in where the Gordons are buried."

"But . . ." Martin said.

Henry went past him, into the house. Martin heard him pick up the phone and punch the pad. He hated Touch-Tone phones, all those weird beepings they made. If he'd had the money, he would have gone to one of those antique stores and got himself a rotary model. The rotary models always reminded him of his own mother.

Henry came back onto the porch. He looked angrier than he had when he went in.

"I talked to Rita," he said. "She says the Dallmer woman called the thing in stolen, almost an hour ago. Kids, she says. There were kids in it."

"How does she know?"

"I've got to go back up and look around. I can't leave some asshole teenager lying in a hole up there with a broken neck and then all the TV stations saying what a bastard I am when he dies. Did I ever tell you all teenagers are assholes?"

"Yes," Martin said.

Henry walked down the porch steps and into the dark. "If it was that Dallmer woman, I could have left her where she was to rot, and nobody would give a damn. If it's some kid, everybody will say they care even if they don't. Ass-holes."

Martin shined the flashlight at Henry's back. He didn't want to be left here on the porch alone. It was close enough to midnight for him to be getting the heebie-jeebies. He didn't like the idea of a fresh body out there, never looked over by a funeral parlor. Martin liked his dead men to be really dead, sucked dry of blood, immobile.

"Henry?" he said.

Henry stopped walking. Martin's flashlight caught the red and black of his checked flannel shirt.

"Come on if you're going to come," he said. "Don't just stand there getting cold."

"All right," Martin said.

He came carefully down the porch steps and onto the bed of leaves that made up their backyard every fall. They were going to have to get around to raking it pretty soon. If they didn't, the snows would come and dump on top of it all. Then, when the spring thaw came, the yard would be nothing but slime.

"Hurry up," Henry said.

Martin drew up behind him and trained the flashlight on the ground just ahead of them. It didn't help much.

"I'm beginning to see the point of that priest used to be over at St. John's," Henry said. "Halloween is the devil in disguise. Halloween ought to be abolished. Maybe they should just get Jackey and his friends and put them in jail every October first, and not let them out again until Thanks-giving."

It wasn't Jackey anymore, Martin thought. Jackey worked at a gas station in Middlebury. It was Jackey's brother Skeet, who was just as bad and just as stupid. They were rounding up the hill now, though, and Martin could see the Jeep. It was lying all the way over on its side, with its oversized wheels mostly in the air.

"That wasn't an accident," Martin said, waving the flash-light. "Look at it."

"I am looking at it," Henry said. "What is it if it isn't an accident?"

Martin went up to the Jeep. "There's no ditch here. There's just an incline."

"So?"

"So what would you have to do, to tip a Jeep over like this, with no incline and those wheels? You'd have to push it."

"Push it."

"Yeah. You'd get it up on that little ridge there and wait till it was leaning, and then you'd push it."

"Christ on a crutch," Henry said. "What for? And if it was leaning, it could have fallen over."

"It wouldn't have been leaning enough."

"Jesus."

"And if it had fallen, there would still be people in it. They would be all caught up in their seat belts. We'd be able to talk to them."

"I think they got out of their seat belts and out of the Jeep and took off. I think they didn't want to get into any more trouble than they had to get into. That's what I think."

"Maybe Miss Dallmer did it herself," Martin said. "Maybe she drove out here and tipped the Jeep over, and then went back to her house to call the police."

Henry made a snort and stomped off. He was looking through the weeds for footprints or other signs of someone running—although there couldn't be much in the way of footprints out here. Martin walked around and around the Jeep, shining his flashlight at it. It looked the way it always looked when Faye Dallmer drove it in and parked it next to the house where Martin and Henry lived. One of the things Faye Dallmer liked to do was to take rubbings of gravestones. It had always seemed like something worse than a stupid idea to Martin. Maybe it really meant something, all those herbs and crystals she used. Maybe she was worshiping the dead.

Henry came back around the other side of the car. "We'd better go back to the house," he said. "We don't want the cops showing up and nobody being there. They'd mark us down for being drunk and forget all about us."

"Uh huh," Martin said.

Henry was moving very quickly. Martin looked up at the moon for a minute—it was coming out of the clouds now, looking full and bright—and followed. Henry's wife had been a nurse. When she left him, she told him that he had been more dangerous to her health than any of the infectious patients she cared for, even the one who had cholera. Martin had never been able to understand it, since Henry had never been a very physical man.

"Christ on a crutch," Henry said, coming to a full stop.

Martin came to a stop just behind him, and then moved around to his side so that he could see what Henry could see. He still had the flashlight on, but he didn't need it. The moon was full out now. The backyard was as lit up as it would have been on a fairly cloudy day. Martin aimed the flashlight at the back porch anyway, because it seemed to be the thing he was supposed to do.

"Christ on a crutch," Henry said again.

Martin felt himself backing up, automatically. He didn't remember deciding to move.

"Henry?" he said.

"When I get hold of Jackey screwing Hargrove, I'm going to kill him," Henry said.

"Skeet," Martin said, just as automatically as he had moved backward. The muscles in his arms and legs were twitching. He was clamping his jaw so hard, it hurt.

Lying across the porch steps in front of him was a skeleton, and there was no way of mistaking it for anything but the real thing. It wasn't strung together in a whole the way fake skeletons and medical school models were. It was just lose bones, pushed here and there along the steps, barely held together at all. And the bones were dirty, not polished white. They looked wet and cold and gray, as if they were oozing slime.

"Christ on a screaming, frigging crutch," Henry said.

And then Martin started to laugh, because he couldn't

help himself. They had been out here all these years, with never any trouble to speak of for either of them, and now this, now this.

Martin started to laugh, and once he started he couldn't stop. He laughed so hard that he sat down on the ground, doing nothing to break his fall. He felt his tailbone hit a rock and the pain shoot up his spine. It seemed to him to be happening to somebody else in some other universe. Then his stomach began to heave and he swallowed against it. He was laughing so hard he couldn't inhale worth a damn.

"This is funny," Henry said, looking about ready to kill him. "You think this is funny?"

Martin got an arm up and a finger pointing in the skeleton's direction. The skull was hollow and blank. He could see how people could have something like that polished to use as an ornament on a desk.

"It isn't ours," he said, when he could make himself talk. "That thing. It isn't ours. It doesn't come from here."

"What the hell are you talking about?"

"It's much too young," Martin said.

And that was the truth. Every single grave in the Fairchild Family Cemetery was at least a hundred and fifty years old. The bones were brittle and thin and dry. They weren't—they weren't—

When the first of the bile came up in his throat, he wasn't ready for it. It slammed into the top of his esophagus like a fist. He threw himself sideways and let it all come up. He wanted to keep it off himself. He didn't exactly make it. His throat felt so raw and torn he thought he must be throwing up ground glass.

He was still throwing up, fifteen minutes later, when the cops drove into the driveway at their front door and Henry went around to let them in.

9

Margaret Anson had gone to bed, but she hadn't gone to sleep. Bennis Hannaford knew that, because she could heard pacing in the room down the hall, punctuated periodically by the sound of drawers slamming, or maybe furniture being moved. Bennis tried to tell herself that this was simple maternal concern—Kayla was still out; it was the Friday before Halloween and half past midnight—but she didn't believe it, and she didn't think anyone else would, either. Her own family was screwed up enough so that she didn't expect much of anything from anybody else's, but Margaret had struck her as an unusually cold and ruthless woman. Bennis tried to remember what Kayla had been like, on the one or two occasions when they had met. The occasions had been too brief to allow her to form an opinion. Maybe Kayla would turn out to be just like her mother. Maybe it was the money that did that to people, although Bennis had grown up with money, and around people with money, and most of them hadn't been infected with Margaret's pinching contempt. Maybe it was just that she should not have made this trip, for Abigail or anybody else. Bennis had a lot to do at home lately. She had people she cared about and responsibilities of a sort. It had been stupid to give in to her restlessness. It had probably been stupid to get restless in the first place. Sometimes Bennis thought she was the worst mess of anybody she knew. She couldn't make up her mind about anything. She was practically forty, and she still didn't know what she wanted to be when she grew up. Even Gregor got exasperated with her now and then. He was probably exasperated with her right his minute, sitting back on Cavanaugh Street by himself, wondering what it was she thought she was doing.

And then, of course, there was this cough she had. And had and had.

What she was supposed to be doing was trying to go to

sleep, which was why she had come upstairs to her assigned bedroom, a low-ceilinged, cramped little space under one of the west ell gables. She had even gotten out of her clothes and put on her nightgown and a robe. It was Gregor's robe, and much too large for her, but she liked the way it smelled. It had a warm aura, like French toast with butter and cinnamon on it. It was hard to say what it meant, that that was the kind of thing that reminded her of Gregor. She had taken her books out of her suitcase and laid them on the bed, too. One of them was a mystery novel by P. D. James called *Original Sin*. The other was a book about Paris in the 1920s that had a lot about Julia Anson in it. Julia Anson the painter. Julia Anson the collector. Julia Anson the lesbian—and famous for it, too, long before it had been fashionable to be famous for any such thing.

It was impossible to concentrate on P. D. James when the wind was rattling against the house the way it was. Bennis wanted to call Gregor, but she didn't want to wake him up, or be accused by Margaret of using the house phones for long-distance calls. Margaret Anson seemed like just the sort of woman who would make that kind of accusation, without bothering to find out first if Bennis used a calling card. This room was so small, there was no point to pacing in it. She just kept bumping up against the green-and-gold wallpapered walls. Julia Anson had lived the last fifty years of her life in two small rooms off the rue Jacob. Her parents hadn't had any money then, and people didn't pay serious money for paintings by women. Abigail had Julia's diary from that period, and it was all about half-starving in the midst of some of the most wonderful food on earth. Bennis couldn't imagine being in Paris and not being able to afford to eat.

Bennis went to her gabled window and looked out. She'd thought she'd heard a car coming up the drive, but there was nothing out there but trees. She went back to the narrow bed and sat down on it. She wanted a cigarette, but she wasn't allowed to smoke in the house. It was time to quit smoking, it really was, but somehow she didn't want to do it right this second.

She got up off the bed and went back to the window. She left the window and went back to the bed. She was feeling frustrated and she was beginning to feel angry. She got her cigarettes out of the side pocket of her tote bag and stuck them in the pocket of her robe.

Out in the hallway, the lights were all turned off, except that there was a stream coming from under the door of Margaret Anson's bedroom. Bennis stopped there and listened, but Margaret seemed to be doing no more than she herself had been doing only a few moments before: pacing, and getting no joy out of it. Bennis went on down the hall and came to the stairs that led to the front entry. She went down those and ended up in a long, high-ceilinged hall. This part of the house had been built later than the part where she had her bedroom. Very early New Englanders always seemed to need wombs more than they needed rooms.

Bennis went out the front door and looked around. There was nothing to see, and it was very cold. She should have put something on her legs and feet, but she hadn't thought of it, because she never wore anything on her legs and feet when she was padding around her apartment in her nightgown. She came back inside and closed the door behind her. Then she headed through the living room and the rooms beyond. If this had been somebody else's house, she would have gone into the kitchen and made herself a cup of tea, but she wasn't going to take anything here unless she had Margaret Anson's permission for it.

She got to the kitchen and walked straight through it, into the pantry. She looked at the open shelves of canned corn and flour sacks and rose hip preserved in glass jars. One wall was free of shelves and had pegs on it instead. Hanging from each of the pegs but one were jackets that looked as if they belonged to a man. Underneath them were shoes that looked as if they belonged to a man, too. Robert Anson's shoes.

Bennis went out the other side of the pantry and onto the back porch. There was a security light here, turned on and pointing to the yard. Bennis could see the raked gravel of the driveway's turnaround and the outline of the long four-car garage. The garage had been a barn once. The shape was unmistakable. The last bay of it was standing open.

Bennis got her cigarettes out and lit one up. She took a deep lungful of smoke and let it out slowly, as if she were smoking marijuana instead of tobacco. Then she started to cough again, but she held it in. She could do that sometimes. It was really cold out here—freezing, in fact. The least she should do was to put on a pair of Robert's shoes, so that her toes didn't freeze to the wooden floor of the porch. She didn't want to do that any more than she wanted to get herself a cup of tea in the kitchen, though, because Margaret was always hovering in the background, looking for something discreditable to report.

Bennis went down into the drive. The gravel hurt her feet. She moved to the grass and shivered. There was enough frost on the grass to make it stiff. She had to be out of her mind, wandering around like this. She walked over to the barn and looked at the side of it. Its paint was peeling and its wood was gray and dry. It wasn't really being taken care of. She wasn't taking care of herself, either. She seemed to be willing herself into a bout with pneumonia.

Bennis's cigarette was out. She knelt down and ground the butt against the grass, making the frost melt. Then she put the cold butt into her pocket and got another cigarette out. The problem wasn't that she went on smoking, but that she went on chain smoking. She had to keep reminding herself that there was nothing romantic about dying young.

She walked around the side of the barn, back onto the gravel drive. She walked past the three closed bays and stopped at the open one. All the bays were full of cars. There were too many of them for the people who lived in the house. Bennis supposed that at least one of them had been Robert's own, like the boots and the jackets in the pantry. Probate was supposed to take care of all that, but maybe it hadn't been a very thorough probate. Maybe Robert Anson had had so many things that it was easy to forget about a car parked in a garage at a house in the country.

The car in the bay in front of her was a Mercedes four-door sedan, painted a murky brown. It looked like it belonged to Margaret Anson. The car in the bay farthest from where she was standing was a Jaguar. She could tell that just by the shape of it. It was the one she thought was most likely to belong to the dead man. Margaret would say that that was just one more proof that Robert Anson had been flashy and superficial, and the flashy part was probably true enough.

The car in the next bay was a little BMW and, by some trick of the moonlight that was streaming in through the open bay and the barn's few small windows, it looked as if there were a person there, sitting bolt upright in the front passenger seat. Bennis stared and stared at the shape, willing it to go away. It was spooky in a way she didn't like to think about. Her cigarette felt hot and hostile in her hand. It kept burning down to the skin on her fingers. Bennis took a long drag and rocked from foot to foot. The barn floor had been paved over with cement. Her feet weren't being hurt by the small rocks of the drive anymore. It was still cold.

The best thing to do about fear is to face it. Bennis had made that rule for herself years ago, when she had first escaped from her father's house. If you are afraid to face your fear, you simply fold. Bennis wasn't sure what folding would mean in this case. She wasn't even sure if it would matter. She dragged on the last of her cigarette—she always forgot how much faster they smoked down outside than in—and ground it out against the cement.

It was going to turn out to be a jacket left lying across the back of the seat, or a large tote bag stuffed with junk that someone had forgotten to take inside. Bennis wrapped her arms around her body and walked up to the side of the car. This close, she could see even less than she had from the open bay, because it was darker. She put her face to the glass of the passenger side window and got nothing at all. A shape. A hulk. A ragged piece of darkness. Nothing.

"Ass," Bennis said, meaning herself. She was an ass sometimes, too. She blew things out of all proportion. Gregor always said that she cared more for her imagination than she did for practical reality. She made her living on her imagination. Gregor also said other things, though— such as that she always tried to find the most expensive price for anything she wanted to buy—that weren't strictly true. They had been together for so long now, in one way or the other, that they exaggerated the things that seemed to them unique in the other person. It was a way of marking territory and soothing the nervousness that came with any serious human connection. A relationship could always fail. A love affair could always fall apart. A friendship could always disintegrate.

"I am killing time here," Bennis said, as loudly as she could, just to hear the sound of her own voice. If she had brought Gregor with her, she could go back into the house and get him to help her with this. Of course, if she had brought Gregor with her, she wouldn't have come out here to begin with. She would probably have had a better bedroom, too. She didn't believe her bedroom had been Kayla's idea. Margaret Anson struck her as the kind of woman who always gave the best she had to men, and then resented them for it.

Bennis got her arms unwrapped from around her body and her hand on the car door's handle. She held her breath and counted to ten and jerked the car door open. When she heard something start to slide out, she thought she had been right about a tote bag. It made the kind of sound cloth bags make when they are full of clothes. Then she felt something brush against her legs and looked down.

Eyes, Bennis thought a second later. Those are eyes I see, staring straight up at me. This must be some kind of ventriloquist's dummy.

But Bennis knew enough about ventriloquist's dummies to know they didn't have eyes like that, eyes that stared straight up, eyes with whites that were threaded through with tiny red veins. This was a body she had lying against her legs. It was a body that had been dead for at least some time. It was stiffish and awkward, as if it were just beginning to freeze with rigor.

Bennis backed away from the car, moving very slowly. She backed away until she hit the Mercedes in the open bay. By then the body was off her legs and wholly on the barn's cement floor. It lay on its back with its legs splayed and its clothing spattered with blood. Hit on the back of the head, Bennis thought. And then she started to half-run, half-walk to the house.

Outside, the full moon was floating in a sea of black, free of even the trace of clouds. The house looked backlit and deserted, so dark it might as well have been haunted. How long would the body have had to be out there, in the cold like that, before it got into the condition it was in? How long had it been tonight since someone had bludgeoned Kayla Anson to death?

The first thing Bennis Hannaford wanted to do was to call Gregor Demarkian and tell him what had happened. The next thing she wanted to do was to pack her things and move right out of this house.

Somewhere in there—maybe when this latest coughing fit was over—she would have to find the time to call the state police.

PART ONE

One

I

For Gregor Demarkian, the most frightening thing was not that he couldn't sleep when Bennis was not at home, but that it mattered so much to him that Bennis shouldn't know he couldn't sleep when she was not at home. Like everything else about his relationship with Bennis Hannaford, this was a thought so convoluted that he almost couldn't express it in words. He got it tangled up. He started talking nonsense, even in his own mind. Then he would get out of bed and go down the short hall to his living room. He would make himself coffee strong enough so that he wouldn't even have to think about trying to sleep for hours. He would stand in front of the broad window in his living room and look down on Cavanaugh Street. This morning, like all mornings, was a dark and silent one. There might be crises in other parts of Philadelphia, crimes and accidents, parties that raged so loudly they broke windows in houses across the street, but in this place there was only sleep, punctuated by streetlamps.

He had a digital clock on the table next to his bed, one of the kind with numbers that glowed red. When he woke up, it said 2:37:09. He turned over onto his back and stared up into the dark. When he had first bought this apartment—when he was still newly retired from the FBI, and newly a widower—there had been times when he had thought he could hear his dead wife's voice in the hallway, or her movements in the kitchen. That was true even though she had never been in these rooms. She had never even been on Cavanaugh Street when these rooms were in existence. Her memory of this neighborhood had been like his, then: a marginal ethnic enclave, marked by decaying buildings and elderly people who just didn't have the resources to move. He still thought of the street that way sometimes, the way it had been on the day he and Elizabeth had come to Philadelphia to bury his mother. Sometimes he thought of it even further back, when he was growing up, when it was full of tenements and ambition. This was something he had never been able to work out. How much of a person's childhood stayed with him forever? How much could he just walk away from, as if it had never been? Sometimes, sitting with Bennis in a restaurant or listening to her complain about work or parking tickets, it seemed to Gregor that the gulf between them was unbridgeable. Bennis, after all, had been born in a mansion on the Philadelphia Main Line.

When the clock said 2:45:00, Gregor sat up and got one of his robes. When Bennis was here, she always took one. It felt wrong, somehow, to actually be able to lay hands on his favorite and use it, for himself. He went down the hall and through the living room into the kitchen. He opened his refrigerator and took out a big plate of stuffed grape leaves. Lida Arkmanian had brought them over to him, as she did even when Bennis was here. Bennis couldn't cook. Gregor and Lida had gone to school together right here on Cavanaugh Street, in the days when children got new shoes only for Easter and getting them was an event.

"Stuffed *grape* leaves," Lida had told him, when they first began having coffee together, that Christmas after Gregor had moved back to Philadelphia. "Not stuffed *vine* leaves. For goodness sake, Krekor, you sound like a yuppie."

Stuffed grape leaves didn't have to be heated up. Coffee did, but that meant only putting the kettle on the stove and getting out the Folgers crystals. Gregor took a large white mug and a small white plate out of the cabinet and put them on the kitchen table. He took stuffed grape leaves out of the bowl and put them on the plate. He made a mountain of grape leaves, high enough to be unsteady. He wished somebody was awake, somewhere on the street, or that Bennis was staying in an ordinary hotel where he could call her at any hour of the night. Instead, Bennis was staying in some rich woman's spare bedroom, and even Father Tibor Kasparian would be passed out on his couch with a book on his chest.

Was it even possible, to find someone to love when you were nearly sixty? And what was it supposed to mean? With Elizabeth, he had had all the usual things. They had started out together young. They had built a life, and would have built a family, if they had ever been able to have children. That kind of marriage was made of little things—a tiny apartment made the scene of many small sacrifices, endured to save the money for the down payment on a house; a period of trial and error over cookbooks; the choice of lights and decorations for a Christmas tree. Gregor understood that kind of marriage. He understood what it was for and why he had gone into it. He even understood, finally, that it had not all been ruined because Elizabeth had died badly. It was terrible what cancer did to people, and not just to the people who had it.

The problem with this—situation—with Bennis was that he didn't have a name for it. It wasn't a marriage. They weren't married, and Gregor wasn't even sure that Bennis would marry him if he asked. They had other things together, things Gregor had never had with anyone else— they had gone off alone together, to Spain, for an entire month, just a little while ago, and the memories of it could still make Gregor turn bright red—but he was sure you couldn't base a life on that kind of thing. It wore off eventually, or the woman got tired, or you did. Besides, he and Bennis had been together for years before they had been together like *that*. Bennis had bought her apartment, on the floor just below this one, just to be near to where he lived. They had to have something going with each other, something deeper and more complicated, maybe even something simply more mundane, than—

—sex.

The water was boiling. Gregor took the kettle off the stove. He dumped a heaping teaspoon of Folgers crystals into the bottom of his mug. Then, thinking better of it, he added another. He took the water off the stove and poured it over the instant coffee. He watched the water turn a darker brown than he should have allowed himself to make it.

Maybe this was the problem, the thing he hadn't been able to get past. Maybe it was the *sex* that was bothering him. Because the more he thought about it, the more he realized that sex had been filling his life, taking it over, ever since they had gone to Spain. It wasn't that they spent all their time actually having sex. If it had been that, it would have been over very quickly. Gregor wasn't twenty anymore, and he had no intention of getting addicted to Viagra. It was that he seemed to spend all his time thinking about sex, or about things related to sex. Before Spain, when he had called up an image of Bennis in his mind, it had been Bennis in her working uniform: jeans, knee socks, turtleneck, cotton crew-neck sweater. Now, when he called up such an image, he saw her in the gray silk nightgown she had bought especially to be with him in Spain, or in one of his shirts, buttoned only halfway up, and asleep next to him in bed.

"Sex gets in the way of friendship," he said aloud, trying it out. He felt instantaneously foolish. That was the kind of thing boys said to girls in high school, or girls said to boys—the kind of thing that, before you knew any better, you thought was kinder than coming right out and telling someone you found her unattractive.

Gregor considered putting milk in his coffee and rejected it. He didn't want to cut the strength of the caffeine. The caffeine was the point. He picked the mug up in one hand and the plate of stuffed grape leaves in the other and went into the living room. He put the mug and the plate down on the coffee table and went over to the window.

Cavanaugh Street, these days, was not a marginal place. The tenements were gone. The brownstone row houses had been converted into single-family townhouses or, like this one, refurbished into three or four floor-through cooperative apartments. The cramped little rooms Gregor remembered from his childhood had been knocked together. His own apartment had a living room large enough to play table tennis in and a big fireplace with a grey marble surround and a mantel made of polished walnut. Across the street, one floor down, Lida Arkmanian's townhouse had a living room that took up two-thirds of the entire second floor. The last third had been made into a dining room.

Things change, that was what he had to remember. Things change, and not all the changes are for the worse. Elizabeth had died, yes, but Cavanaugh Street had gotten rich. Bennis had given up her restlessness to settle with him. The local school district had given up on corporal punishment and rote learning to dedicate itself to critical thinking. Richard Nixon had resigned.

Gregor thought he might be losing his mind.

Instead of sitting down on the couch, he picked up his coffee and grape leaves and took them into the bedroom. He put them down on the table in the corner and sat at the chair there to boot up the computer. The computer had been a gift from Bennis, as had a year's subscription to America Online. Gregor still hadn't been able to get the hang of the Internet. It still seemed to him like a waste of time.

Gregor waited for the desktop icons to settle on the screen—there was cat wallpaper, engineered for him by Donna Moradanyan Donahue, who hadn't been able to stand the gray ugliness of the default background that had been built into the machine—then clicked the mouse in all the right places and brought up the Free Cell board. He had never in his life heard of Free Cell before he got this computer, and now he seemed to be addicted to it.

The real problem with the—situation—with Bennis, Gregor decided, as he moved cards around the board, was that they'd both spent so long deciding to create it that they didn't know what to do with it now that they had it. If they were honest with each other, they would have to say that they had both wanted to be lovers from the moment they first saw each other, in Bennis's father's Main Line house. Even though Gregor had not been over the death of his wife. Even though Bennis had been living with a man in Boston. They had wanted to be lovers and resisted their desire, and now all they really knew how to do was to go on resisting each other.

This was beginning to sound like a college bull session going on inside his head—except that Gregor had never been part of a college bull session. He had graduated from the University of Pennsylvania, but he had been a commuter student, living right here in a tenement on Cavanaugh Street, taking the bus across town.

If I'm going to go on thinking like this, Gregor told himself, I'd better start drinking. At least then I could blame it on the alcohol.

Then he bent toward the screen and concentrated on the cards, red queen to black king, three of hearts to the stack pile at the top.

He was still bent over the screen an hour later, when the phone rang.

2

It wasn't until he heard the sound of her voice, going rapid-fire through all the details, that Gregor realized that he really had been worried about it—worried, on some level, that Bennis was just going to disappear. Now he knew he should be concerned about this mess she had gotten herself in, about the body she had found in the car, about the way she had had to, or felt she had to, pack up and move in the middle of the night. Instead, all he could feel was calm, and a certain light happiness at the sound of her voice. Even the cough didn't bother him, although it had in the weeks before she left for Connecticut. That cough had been going on much too long. It seemed to have become harsher and more insistent in the less than a day she had been gone.

"So," Bennis was saying. "That's where we are. I'm at the Mayflower Inn. Which is beautiful, really, but it's about two hundred and fifty years old."

"You like old."

"Not after Margaret Anson's house, I don't. God, that woman is unbelievable. And I'm not going to be able to get rid of her for weeks now. Not until this is over. If this is ever over. I keep reminding myself that the police fail to solve crimes all the time. Are you going to come out here and help?"

"I'll come out and help you." Gregor stood up and pushed himself away from the computer table. He couldn't concentrate on the cards anymore, and he'd been losing so badly it was embarrassing anyway. Bennis sometimes said he had a learning disability that applied only to games of solitaire. He didn't tell her how miserably he lost at poker. Now he sat down on the bed and switched the phone from one ear to the other.

"I can't just go rushing in and disrupting a police investigation," he said. "It's not my investigation."

"Well, it can be if you want. The thing is, they've got this police department, it's maybe got two people in it. And then they've got the state police."

"I think it's the local police departments that investigate murders, Bennis. Not the state police."

"Well, actually, that's not exactly clear. You see, the thing is, there's more than one town involved. There's Washington Depot, but then there's also Watertown, and maybe Morris."

"Are these towns all close together?"

"Yes. Exactly. They all bump into each other. And about the first thing that happened, after we called the police, is that the call was picked up by the state police, because one of the towns has something called a resident trooper—"

"Resident trooper?"

"Right. That's where, if a town is too small to be able to afford its own police force, the state pays to have a state trooper live in town and do the police stuff. And there isn't usually a lot of it, because these are really small places and nothing much happens in them."

"All right."

"Anyway, one of these towns has a resident trooper, and he picked up the police call and checked on it, because it turned out that he'd seen the car."

"The car?" Gregor was beginning to feel a little dizzy.

"Kayla Anson's car," Bennis told him. "It's this little BMW. And according to this guy—the resident trooper—it went through the center of Morris about ten minutes after eight this evening, doing maybe ninety, ninety-five miles an hour on this road that's narrow and all hills and twists and turns and—"

"Are you sure this woman didn't die in an automobile accident?"

"Yes, Gregor, of course I'm sure. The point is, the resident trooper isn't a resident trooper for the town of Morris, because Morris has its own police department. He works in—Cornwall Bridge, I think. I'm not sure. He just happened to be in Morris at the time. And he saw the car. And he was in his cruiser, but he couldn't really chase it because he didn't have jurisdiction, and also I don't think he wanted to. I mean, that kind of behavior on the roads out here is suicidal."

"This is the car she died in," Gregor said.

"Well, it's the car I found her dead in, Gregor. I don't think there's any way we can know right now if she actually—"

"Okay. Yes. Now—"

"Oh, well. So what the resident trooper did was call ahead to Washington Depot and warn them about what she was doing. Anyway, when the police call came about her being dead there was one of those technical descriptions of the car going back and forth, you know, and so the resident trooper picked up the message and got in contact, and then some guy on the Watertown police department—no, wait, that's not right, some woman—"

"I don't think it matters."

"Whatever. Anyway, the thing is, the Watertown police had this stolen car case, and they were looking into it, and one of the things they had some witness saying was that they saw this stolen car, this Jeep, and it seemed to be following the BMW."

"Wait. The BMW is the one you found the body in. The one that was doing ninety miles an hour."

"Right. And this was about seven o'clock or so. So the Watertown police got into it. And now they're saying that they might just bring in the state police and let them handle it, because when you have a bunch of towns like this it can be hard to sort out jurisdiction, because you don't know what happened where. Do you see what I mean?"

"Sort of. It still doesn't mean I can go barging in there throwing around advice nobody has asked me for, Bennis. Much as I'd like to. Because you're involved."

"Oh, I know. But that's the thing. I talked to the resident trooper. And he knew who you were. And he thought—"

"*He* thought?"

"Well, okay. I brought it up. But they've spent money on psychics in this state, Gregor, at least you'd actually do some good. And they all know who you are. Even the town cops do. And they want you to help. It's not as if you'd gone and retired or anything."

Gregor lay back on the bed and put his feet up. It was true. He hadn't retired. He just hadn't taken much work lately. He wasn't quite sure why that was. There had been times in his life when he had been thoroughly sick of work. He had spent twenty years in the Federal Bureau of Investigation, the last ten of them as head of the behavioral sciences unit, the section dedicated to the tracking of serial killers. That had gotten old so fast it had left him breathless. There had been times, with one more string of child murders lying on his desk, or the arrival of a new set of photographs meant to show what had been found in yet another series of unmarked graves, when he would gladly have chucked it all and become an accountant. There had been other times, like when he had first started consulting for police departments after he'd moved to Philadelphia, when he'd been enormously gratified to be able to do the work he could do. Lately he'd just been—distracted.

"Gregor?

"I'm here," he said. "Are you sure you're all right, where you are? At this hotel?"

"It's a Revolutionary War–era inn. And it's beautiful. And I'm fine. Except that I miss you."

"I miss you, too."

"So come on out. At least keep me company. You can talk to the state police when you get here. And you don't have to consult if you don't want to."

"Are you going to have to be there for any length of time?"

"I don't know," Bennis said.

"All right," Gregor said. "Do you mind if I tell you that this sounds like a script for a Woody Allen movie?'

"No, Gregor, I don't mind. You should have been in the middle of it. I think there must be all kinds of people around here who do nothing but monitor the police band. You wouldn't believe the commotion. And Margaret Anson. I mean. Oh, hell. Margaret *Anson*."

Gregor turned over on his side. "So," he said. "Have you worked it out? Can I get there from here? Washington Depot sounds like a train station."

"It used to be. It isn't anymore. And I have worked it out. Do you mind?"

"Not at all. You've always been—meticulous about that sort of thing."

"Thanks a lot."

"It wasn't an insult. Besides, I like you to act like yourself. How complicated is this going to be?"

"Not so much complicated as long, Gregor. You take the Amtrak to New York. You take the shuttle to Grand Central. You take the New Haven line to Bridgeport. You take the bud car to Waterbury. I'll pick you up in Waterbury. Tomorrow."

"All right."

"There's just one thing. There's only one train to Waterbury a day. So—"

"*One* train?"

"You've got to be at Grand Central by nine-thirty in the morning. That will get you here around twelve. You got that?"

"Bennis—"

"I'll talk to you tomorrow," Bennis said.

"I love you," Gregor started to say, but Bennis was already gone. The phone was humming in his ear.

He got up and put the receiver down, so that he would no longer be cut off from the world.

3

Twenty minutes later—suddenly tired, but still not able to sleep—Gregor went to his closet and got out his most casual pants. They were khakis, not jeans, because no matter how many times he tried jeans he felt silly in them, and he suspected he looked silly, as well. Some things did *not* change, and one of those things was that he was a very formal man. He found a shirt and put that on, too, a white one with a button-down collar. He found a sweater he'd left lying over the back of a chair. He put his loafers on without bothering with socks. This was as rakish as he got. It was also the best he could do at four o'clock in the morning.

Four o'clock.

In the apartment upstairs, Donna and Russ and Tommy were sleeping out one of their last nights before they moved to a townhouse down the street. In the apartment on the ground floor, old George Tekemanian was curled up in a bed that his grandson had bought him, a bed that did everything but sing the theme song from *The Sound of Music*. Down the street, the Ararat restaurant was closed, and wouldn't open for another three hours.

Gregor let himself out into the hall and closed the door behind him. Then he pulled at the knob to make sure it was locked. He walked down one flight of steps and stopped in front of Bennis's door. He checked to make sure that that was locked, too, although he'd done it half a dozen times in the last day. It hadn't been locked right after she left, of course, because Bennis never bothered to lock doors. But Gregor had been ready for that.

He made his way down the rest of the stairs and through the foyer onto the stoop. The air was cold and bright under the streetlamps. The street looked naked. In any other year, Donna would have decorated by now. She would have wrapped their brownstone in black and orange crepe paper and put out jack-o'-lanterns and plastic goblins and cardboard witches riding on real broomsticks that went right across the roof. This year, Gregor supposed, she had just too much to do.

Some things change that *are* for the worse.

Gregor went down the street to Holy Trinity Church. He went around the back on the little cobblestone path and let himself through the low wrought-iron gate into the courtyard. He noticed that the vines that wound around the pillars next to Tibor's front door were out of control again. Tibor never remembered to call the yard service that was supposed to take care of things like that.

Gregor knocked, got no answer, and used his key. He fumbled with the door for a good three minutes before he realized that the door hadn't been locked in the first place, and that he was only locking himself out. He got the mess turned around the right way and stepped into Tibor's foyer. Stacks of paperback books rose from the floor on both sides, leaning dangerously toward the center, ending well above his head. He took one down at random and found he was holding a copy of *Men Are from Mars, Women Are from Venus*. He put it back.

"Tibor?" he called out.

There was no answer. He made his way through yet more stacks of books and into the living room. Tibor was, as usual, laid out on the couch, fully clothed, with books all over him. Gregor didn't think the man ever actually slept in his bed.

"Tibor," Gregor said again. It wasn't a question this time. It was a command.

Tibor squirmed slightly on the couch. Gregor went over to him and took the books off his chest. He had Betty Friedan's *The Feminine Mystique,* in hardcover; Aristotle's *Nicomachian Ethics,* in ancient Greek; and a paperback copy of John Grisham's *The Street.* Gregor was very careful not to lose Tibor's place in any of them. He left them open on the floor.

"Tibor," Gregor said, louder this time.

Tibor stirred on the couch, turned on his side. Squinted his eyes open.

"Krekor?"

"I need to talk to you," Gregor said.

Tibor turned side to side, and then seemed to make up his mind. He let his legs swing off the side of the couch and brought himself slowly, more or less, upright.

"I fell asleep on the couch again," he said. "Did I sleep through my alarm clock again? Is it time for breakfast?"

"It's four o'clock in the morning."

"Four."

"I needed to talk to you about something."

"You should not let Bennis go away on her own, even overnight," Tibor said. "When you do that, nobody can sleep."

"Tibor—"

"I know, I know," Tibor said. "You need somebody to help you understand love."

Gregor turned away and went looking for a chair. He had to take two piles of paperbacks off an ottoman to find a place to sit down. Maybe he was getting obsessive about this. Maybe he needed to do something—stabilizing—with his life.

Or something.

He sat down on the ottoman and stretched his feet out, trying to think of some way to begin.

Two

I

One of the good things about insomnia is that it always ends in a crash. Gregor Demarkian found that out on the long trip from Philadelphia to Waterbury. It could have been a much shorter trip, if he had known how to drive. According to Donna Moradanyan Donahue, who had given him a ride to his first train, it took only a couple of hours to get from Philadelphia to that part of Connecticut if you had something in the way of a Volvo and a decent set of maps from the AAA. Gregor had been too tired to listen to her, about this or anything else, and Donna had been too wound up to be perfectly clear. Her honey blonde hair had bopped restlessly in the breeze that came through the open car windows. Her very young, still unlined face had been set in frowns and furrows.

"The thing is," she said, getting off the subject of Gregor's inability to drive for the fifth time in thirty seconds, "I wouldn't mind if I thought he actually wanted a relationship with Tommy. I mean, he's Tommy's father. Tommy should know his father. Do you see what I mean?"

"Yes," Gregor said. This was still in Philadelphia, at the very beginning of the day, so he was more than a little wound up himself. He couldn't have fallen asleep if he'd wanted to, then, but even the air around him looked too bright. Philadelphia looked dirty and vibrant, which is how he thought of it when he was being kind.

"And the thing is," Donna said, "that of course I've talked this over with Russ, and for the first time, I'm just about ready to kill him. I mean, he thinks like a lawyer. Have you ever realized that?"

"He is a lawyer."

"Well, yes. I know. But this isn't his work we're talking about. This is his life. My life. Tommy's life. Don't you think it would be a good thing if Russ adopted Tommy?"

"Yes," Gregor said.

Donna Moradanyan and Russ Donahue had married only a few months ago—back in June, in fact, when Gregor had been distracted, too. Donna had a small son from a previous *liaison,* as Lida Arkmanian called it, with a man named Peter Desarian. Actually, Peter wasn't really a man. He was no older than Donna, who was barely twenty-one herself, and he was, in Gregor's opinion, one of the great examples of arrested development. Some boys grew up to be men. Peter Desarian had grown up to evolve a strategy for avoiding responsibility. Whenever he got into more trouble than he could handle, he moved back into his mother's house.

"Anyway," Donna said, "the thing is, according to Russ, if Peter wants to fight the adoption he can stop it. Because the law wants to keep families together. I mean, does this make any sense to you? Peter and I were never a family. We were never even a couple except when he wanted to, um, I mean—"

"I think I get the point," Gregor said.

"Well, it embarrasses me. I mean, no woman wants to admit that she lost her virginity to a jerk."

"No woman has to worry that she's alone in that circumstance."

"I guess not. But you see what I mean. First he wanted me to have an abortion. Then when I wouldn't have one, he refused to have anything at all to do with Tommy for years. Bennis went to the hospital with me when I was in labor. Lida Arkmanian bought him his christening gown. Father Tibor and old George Tekemanian taught him his first words. I mean, where was Peter Stupid Desarian?"

"He came back for your wedding," Gregor said drily.

"Don't remind me. Okay. I had cold feet or something. I don't know. Something. But the fact is, he's back again now, and I'm just not going to put up with it. Tommy's very happy with Russ for a father. He really is. He's got somebody to play board games with on Sunday afternoons. He's got somebody who understands the Cartoon Network.

I mean, Father Tibor's a really wonderful man and all, but his idea of a bedtime story for Tommy was passages from the *Odyssey*."

"I think you've got to go around here or you're not going to have anywhere to park."

Donna leaned over the steering wheel and made a pretense of paying attention. Traffic was almost nonexistent— it was quarter to six in the morning, and the yuppies were still at home in bed. If there were still yuppies. Gregor thought he might be out of date. He also thought that he had reached that point in lack of sleep when his condition was on the verge of dangerous.

"So," he said.

Donna had made the turn. They were gliding down a short block whose tall buildings all seemed to be made out of beige stone. Donna adjusted her rearview mirror.

"So," Donna said, "I've thought it all out, and I've decided that you've got to do something about it."

"Excuse me?"

"You've got to do something about it," Donna insisted. "I mean, it obviously can't be allowed to go on the way it's going. Peter's a spoiler. He'll wreck everything if he can manage it. And you *know* that. So you have to do something about it."

There was a parking space just ahead of them. In fact, there were several. Donna didn't even have to parallel park. She glided up along the curb and positioned the car's nose right in front of a parking meter.

"Gregor," she said.

Donna and Bennis were very good friends. Sometimes Gregor found that hard to understand. Now he thought it made perfect sense, because in at least this way they were exactly alike. He turned around and looked at his big black suitcase in the backseat of the car.

"Donna," he said carefully.

"I know what you're going to say," Donna said. "So don't bother. You got him away from me at the wedding."

"That was different."

"Exactly. That wasn't anywhere near as important. This is vital. Tommy doesn't need Peter Desarian hanging around his life. He really doesn't. Nobody needs Peter Desarian hanging around his life."

"Peter is still Tommy's natural father."

Donna got out of the car and opened the back door. She got his suitcase out and put it down in the street. The street cleaners had done a good job this morning. There were no stray papers or cigarette butts in the gutters that Gregor could see.

He got out of the car himself.

"I can't just do something," he said reasonably. "Peter *is* Tommy's natural father. And that matters. It's even going to matter to Tommy one of these days."

"I'll cross that bridge when I come to it."

"But the thing is—"

"Don't you want Russ to adopt Tommy? You've said all along that it would be a good thing. It *would* be a good thing. And you know it. And you can do something about it if you think it over long enough."

"Like what?"

"Like find a way for us to prove abuse or neglect," Donna said triumphantly. "Russ explained it to me. If there's cause to believe that Peter abused or neglected Tommy, then we can get his rights terminated and Russ can go ahead with the adoption. And Lord only knows, Peter has neglected Tommy. He's barely set eyes on him the whole time he's been alive."

"I don't think that's the kind of neglect that qualifies—"

Donna turned around, so quickly that Gregor was startled into stepping back. Her blue eyes were large and dark in her white face. Her body was very still. Gregor suddenly realized that he had never seen her really angry before, white hot angry, angry to the bone. He'd seen her blow up at Russ. He'd seen her exasperated and annoyed. He had never seen her like this.

Donna's going to be very beautiful when she gets older, Gregor thought, with the half of his mind that was operating on automatic pilot. You could see the change that would come in her face. It was there right under the surface. The anger made it plain.

"Listen to me," she said slowly. "I have no intention, no intention at all, of letting Peter Desarian mess this up. Which means we're going to have to find a way to fend him off, and find a way soon, because Russ was meaning to file those adoption papers next month. And he's going to. So start thinking, Gregor. We have to do something."

Then she bent over, picked up Gregor's suitcase in one hand, and headed out across the street for the train station. In the faint gray of the early morning not-quite-light, she looked like a Valkyrie.

Other men found docile women who made breakfast for them and cleaned house without complaint. Other men found pliant women who wanted only to please, or directionless women who wanted only a man to guide them, or even simply polite women who believed it was only fair to let a man have his own way at least every once in a while.

Gregor Demarkian found Valkyries.

There was a moral in there somewhere, but Gregor was too tired to think of what it was.

2

The ride up to Connecticut was more than just long. It was interminable. From Philadelphia to New York was not too bad. It was fast, at least, although it did seem as if Amtrak stopped at every small town in the hinterlands. The shuttle from Pennsylvania Station to Grand Central wasn't too bad, either, although it was definitely strange. Gregor always forgot just how odd New York really was, especially underground. Today there were three transvestites in the shuttle with him, obviously coming off an unbroken night of something. One of them had his wig off and lying in his lap, so that it looked as if his legs were erupting into curly blonde hair. Gregor didn't mind the transvestites at all. He did mind the two young men huddled in the seats at the front of the car, clearly wasted on drugs and close to being sick. This was how he understood that he was not a modern man. It was inconceivable to him that anybody would want to do this with his life—and yet they were everywhere, these people, cowering in doorways, curled up in abandoned buildings. It was even more inconceivable to him that anyone could fail to realize that this was the kind of thing that happened to you if you insisted on taking drugs, and yet children—even intelligent children—started taking drugs every day.

In the world in which Gregor Demarkian grew up, even alcohol was confined to parties, and those came only two or three times a year. He couldn't imagine anything more shameful on the Cavanaugh Street of his childhood than for a man to be known as someone who drank. Women never had more than two or three glasses of wine a year. Nobody had ever heard of drugs—or if they had, it was mostly rumors, passed on from people who had been to other places, like the army, where farm boys from Texas and mechanics from New Mexico sometimes brought little bags of marijuana to sell to anybody who would pay.

Gregor got off the shuttle at Grand Central and made his way upstairs. He found the next train to Bridgeport on the New Haven line and headed for track 19 on the main concourse. He had only fifteen minutes before the train left. That meant that the train would be parked in its appointed slot and open to take on passengers. That was a good thing, because there didn't seem to be anyplace to sit in Grand Central anymore. Everything looked boarded up, or worse. The concourse itself was full of litter. The boards that hid what had once been the seating areas were covered with graffiti. You had to ask yourself how quick these kids were, with their spray cans. Grand Central was policed continually, from what Gregor could see. Patrolmen paced the corridors from one end to the other without stopping. When did anyone have time to spray three big red initials and a number on a barrier, without getting caught?

When Gregor was growing up on Cavanaugh Street, even almost-grown children, boys of seventeen, girls as old as twenty, went to church every week with their parents, walking in straight and unyielding lines down the block to the high steps of Holy Trinity Church. The old priest from Armenia who had been at the church in those days would stand out in front of the big doors and wait for them all to come in. He was a filthy old man, and nasty in his habits in more ways than one, but they all stopped in front of him and greeted him. They took his hand and wished him well. That was God's representative on earth, that old man. You could feel the power of omniscience behind him.

When it got close to time for the liturgy to start—the old liturgy, the one that seemed to take hours and probably had—the priest would turn his back to them and go inside. He would disappear behind the iconostasis to dress. The children would sit in the long wooden pews with their hands held together in their laps and wait, unprotesting, until it was time to pray. They all had special clothes for church. The girls had white dresses and white socks. The boys had miniature little suits with ties they borrowed from their fathers and tucked inside their shirts. The old ladies wore black lace kerchiefs on their heads and black lace gloves.

The church itself was a cavernous space, filled with icons, and many of the icons were bloody. A saint pierced in the breast by a long sword. Another tied to a stake with his back whipped into shreds of skin and bright red wounds. They were all reminded, over and over again, that the martyrs had died horrible deaths for the faith, that it wasn't so much to ask them to sit still and be quiet for a couple of hours every week.

And then, of course, when it was over, there was always a little reception in the basement of the church. The ladies put out thick black coffee and little pastries on a table covered with a plain white cloth. The fast before Communion was so long that everybody was starving. They took little round plates and passed from one kind of pastry to another, trying to decide. Nobody ever took more than one. That might have meant that somebody got nothing. Gregor remembered Lida Arkmanian and Hannah Krekorian, standing side by side, in an agony of indecision—until two of the old ladies came up and took the last of the *banirov kadayif*, and the indecision was over. There was nothing but *loukoumia* left.

Did I really think that was a suffocating life? Gregor asked himself, as he tried to get comfortable on the hard plastic seats. It seemed he had. It was to escape the suffocation that he left Philadelphia the first time, for the army—and then, when the army was over and he had come home, left it a second time for the Harvard Business School. Those were the days when all special agents of the FBI were required to have a degree in accounting and a degree in law, and he had been sure he would never be able to stomach the full course in a law school.

It was a suffocating life, but it had edges. Maybe that was the thing. The lives some people led these days seemed to have no edges at all, so that drifting into a heroin stupor looked no different to them than going to night school for their GED, or even making love. Equal opportunity indirection, Gregor thought, and then he thought that it made no sense. He had no idea what he was trying to get at.

Outside on the platform, a man who was probably homeless was bending over to pick three quarters up off the dirty floor. There were always coins on the platforms, because people lost them while they tried to get things out of their pockets and walk at the same time. The man was wearing clothes so ragged that the bottom of his pants looked like a fringe. His hair was matted to his skull.

Gregor twisted on the seat again, and prepared to sit up awake and miserable all the way to Bridgeport.

3

The first time Gregor Demarkian fell asleep, they were just outside Stamford. He would have gone right on past Bridgeport, and maybe all the way to New Haven, except that the young woman in the seat next to him woke him up.

"Didn't you say you were getting off here?" she asked him. "This is Bridgeport. Didn't you say you had to make a connection?"

She was really very, very young. Gregor thought she was a student. She was reading Peter Kreeft's gloss on St. Thomas Aquinas, *A Summa of the Summa*. Maybe she was just religious, or the kind of person who enjoyed philosophy as a hobby. She had very wide eyes and pretty glasses. Gregor said that he did, indeed, need to get off at Bridgeport, and thanked her for waking him up.

"That's okay," she said. "I fall asleep on this train all the time. But New Haven is the last stop, you see, so I don't have to worry."

The train station in Bridgeport was very clean and very small. Considering the kinds of things Gregor had heard about Bridgeport—that it was drug and gang central, that it was decaying into an unbroken slum, that it was so violent even its own police refused to live there—he was very favorably impressed. He got himself a copy of *The New York Times* from one of those vending machines and a cup of coffee from the little diner in a corner and checked the time for the train to Waterbury. He had just about fifteen minutes. He sat down in a molded plastic chair and wished that his coffee was stronger. There wouldn't be anything about the death of Kayla Anson in the *Times*, of course. The body had probably been discovered after the paper had been printed. There would be something in the paper tomorrow, however, and probably in every other paper in the country. Gregor wondered if Bennis had considered the implications of that.

Gregor still had half a cup of coffee when his train was called. He went back out onto the platform to find that it was the wrong platform. He had to take the long tunnel to the other side of the tracks.

There were two other men and a woman heading for the same train. They all went racing through together, although they were all middle-aged. Going up those two flights of stairs at the end wasn't easy for any of them. When they came out on the platform they found not a train, but a single train car, oddly built, so that it could go in either direction. Gregor went inside and found a seat next to a window in the back of the car, near one of the exit doors.

"They used to have runs up to Waterbury four or five times a day," the woman who had come over with the rest of them said to him. "But I suppose this is better than nothing. Do you know that Governor Rowland wanted to eliminated this service entirely?"

"No," Gregor said.

"Then there wouldn't be any public transportation out of the Northwest Hills at all. It's the way they think of us out in Hartford, and down on the Gold Coast. As if we were all a lot of movie stars with our own limousines. Susan St. James. Meryl Streep. As if nobody else lived up in the Hills at all. Although you'd think Governor Rowland would know better."

"Excuse me?"

"Governor Rowland is from Middlebury. That's right on the border of Litchfield County. You'd think he'd know better."

"Oh," Gregor said.

The woman was that sort of not-quite-thin, not-quite-fat that women in their late forties and fifties often got if they had had a couple of children and no dedication to serious exercise. She was standing in the aisle near Gregor's seat, as if she were waiting for the train to start before she let herself sit down. Gregor sipped his coffee and stared at her politely. He wanted to read his paper and think about Bennis, in jeans or otherwise.

The woman shifted from foot to foot. She adjusted the strap of her black leather bag on her shoulder.

"You're that detective, aren't you?" she asked him suddenly. "The one that was in *People* magazine. Gregory Demarkian."

"Gregor," Gregor said. It was automatic.

"Gregor. I'm sorry. But I remember that story. Or rather I remember you. You have a very unusual face."

"Ummm," Gregor said.

"And of course you'll be coming up to look into what happened to Kayla Anson. That's the only thing that makes any sense here, for you to be on this train. I wouldn't be on it myself except that I was going to take a few days in the city and I didn't want to bring my car. And now, of course, I simply can't. Of course, of course, of course. I keep repeating myself. I'm glad I ran into you."

"It's very kind of you to say so."

"I'm going to sit down now. This car is nothing to stand up in when it gets moving."

Gregor watched her walk away, down the aisle, and take a seat in the middle of the car. Was it surprising that she knew that something had happened to Kayla Anson? Probably not. These were small towns up there. Everybody in them probably knew by now that something had happened to Kayla Anson, and if Gregor had been able to get to a television set he was sure he would find that CNN knew it, as well.

The train jolted and moved a few feet forward. Gregor looked down at the front page of the *Times*. There was a story about the still-evolving investigation of that mess the United States had gotten itself into in the Sudan. There was another about the upcoming elections and whether being known as a Friend of Bill would help candidates or hurt them in the coming races. Gregor finished off the rest of his coffee in a gulp and put his head back on the seat and closed his eyes. The bud car was moving, but not very fast. It felt to Gregor as if he were being rocked to sleep in a cradle.

Then, what seemed like moments later, he felt himself being shaken hard. Someone was holding him by both shoulders and slamming him against the back of his seat. He opened his eyes in a squint and saw what looked like Bennis standing over him, although he was sure that had to be an illusion. Bennis was waiting for him in the train station in Waterbury. She was supposed to be bringing her car.

"Gregor," Bennis said.

"It's going to be an unbelievable mess," Gregor told her.

Bennis shook him hard, again. Her thick black hair was coming lose from its pins. Wisps of it were floating around her face.

"Wake up, Gregor, for God's sake. What's wrong with you? This car is going to take off again any minute."

Gregor sat forward and hunched over his knees. He felt sick to his stomach, but at least he no longer thought he was hallucinating. He felt sick enough to pass out. He had to do something about the not sleeping.

"Are you all right?" Bennis asked him.

He stood up and looked around the car. There were three people in it, but not the same three people who had been with him on the ride out from Bridgeport. These had to be people hoping to take the train *into* New York.

He made his way out into the aisle and looked around.

"Sorry," he told Bennis. "I fell asleep."

"I could see that. You looked white as a sheet. You scared me to death. Come on out and get into the car."

"Right," Gregor said.

He followed Bennis through the narrow door and out onto the platform. The train station in front of him was made of red stone and boarded up. The small city beyond it looked empty and down on its luck. All the buildings were both old and dirty, except for the big clock tower that rose almost exactly over his head.

"That's the *Waterbury Republican,*" Bennis told him, as she threw his big suitcase into the space behind the backs of the seats in her little orange Mercedes. "It's the local paper, more or less. Except that all the elite types get the *Litchfield County Times*. Are you sure you're all right?"

"I'm fine." Gregor settled himself into his seat. "I need some rest. Have you seen anything of the news this morning?"

"I've seen all of it."

"What's it like?"

"It's a circus. What did you expect it would be like?"

Gregor sighed. Bennis pulled the car out on a dilapidated city street that was so full of potholes, Gregor had a momentary fear for the tires.

"It's that I didn't think about it at all, and I should have," he told her. "Because the media climate matters."

Three

I

Eve Wachinsky had a ritual for deciding when she could go to the doctor. First, she had to be sick enough so that she was sure she had no other choice. It didn't make any sense to spend all that money just to be told that she didn't need any medicine, that she would have been better off if she'd stayed at home and stayed in bed. Second, she had to call the doctor and find out exactly what it would cost—although that was not, really, entirely possible. Her doctor charged sixty-nine dollars for a standard office visit, and eighty-nine dollars for something longer. Eve always counted on the eighty-nine dollars. There were always tests, or blood work, or something else that needed to go to the lab, and that she would be required to pay for right up front. This was the bottom line with not having insurance. People who had it sailed in and out without ever being questioned. Even if their insurance ended up refusing to cover whatever it was they'd had done, even if they ran up a bill for thousands of dollars they ended up having to pay for themselves, nobody in the doctor's office thought twice about it. People who did not have insurance had to have money, right away, or they would just be told to go home. Or Eve thought they would. She had never dared go into the doctor's office without at least thinking she had enough to pay her bill. On the one occasion when she had figured wrong and had been able to pay only part of it, she had had to listen to Moira Rackhorn lecture her on taking advantage of the doctor.

Actually, Eve thought, turning over in bed and wishing the chills would stop, it wasn't true that every patient without insurance had to have money right up front. There were people, like that writer who lived in town, who just seemed to call up depths of sympathy in doctors and dentists and nurse practitioners. Eve had read an interview with the writer in the *Waterbury Republican*—about how this woman had lost her insurance when she lost her husband, young, to cancer; about how good and helpful and kind all the medical professionals had been, a year later, when she fell in her driveway and sustained a multiple fracture of her right leg. Eve could see the difference, even in the grainy black-and-white photograph—although she couldn't have said exactly what it was made up of. It was a kind of a puzzle she had spent her whole life trying to solve, without success. For some reason, she could just tell that the writer was someone who had gone to a good college, had grown up in a family that owned a decent house, had learned to expect that she would be treated well. She could tell this even though the writer was wearing jeans and a sweatshirt and sitting cross-legged on the floor of what looked like a wide front porch.

Eve turned over in bed and tried to breathe. Her chest hurt. Her head hurt, too. When she tried to move her head from side to side, there was so much pain in her neck she almost cried out. She had no idea how much money she had in the bank, or how she was going to find out. When she tried to move, everything inside her seemed to explode.

If worse came to worse, she could go to the emergency room at St. Mary's Hospital in Waterbury. St. Mary's was the one that took anybody in. Their waiting room was always full of Spanish boys who had cut each other and pregnant women with four other children in tow. There were policemen stationed there, at the doors, all the time. It had always made Eve wonder. Did the doctors and nurses feel they were under attack? Did the people come in from off the street and try to steal things?

Eve's apartment was just one big room, at the front of a house just off Hemenway Place, in Watertown. From that window she could see the tiny mall called Depot Square and one side of the old Hemenway School. The house was an old clapboard one with a barn out back that had been converted into a garage. Her car was in the garage with four others, the ones that belonged to the other people in the house. She had to get out of her bed and out of her apartment and out to her car, and then she had to drive it.

She did manage to get out of bed. She mostly fell onto the cold linoleum floor, but she got out. She looked at the faded black-and-pink-and-silver pattern of swans and thought that she should have done something about it long ago, bought a rug or had the floor pulled up at her own expense. The pattern was so ugly. She grabbed the side of the bed and pulled herself up. She could stand if she held onto things. She was holding onto the wall.

She had gone to the Hemenway School herself, when she was small. She had walked up the hill from the little house where her family had had their own apartment and watched the big yellow school buses come in from the subdivisions in the north part of town. In those days she had wanted nothing as much as she wanted a split level, with two bathrooms, and a room that wasn't the living room to put the television in.

She looked around and saw that she had made it to the door. She was still wearing her nightgown. She was still shivering. She was sure she had forgotten something, but she couldn't remember what. She had to get to her car, that was the thing. It didn't matter if she was in her nightgown. Nobody would see her until she got to the hospital, and at the hospital nobody would care.

She went out into the hall and looked around. She could hear music coming from the apartment across the way. Classical music, that was what it was called. Except that it sounded funny, even for classical music, tinny, maybe, or very high-pitched. Eve's head hurt so badly that she thought it was going to pop open.

The door had clicked shut and locked behind her before she realized what it was she'd forgotten—and then it was too late, of course. She didn't know what she was going to do.

Her keys. She didn't have her keys. She was in her nightgown, and her keys were in her pocketbook on the table with this morning's breakfast dishes. She had sat down to eat just after she got in from work, but she had already been feeling awful. She'd been feeling worse than awful. She never threw food away. She couldn't stand the idea of wasting it. This food she'd left sitting in its dishes, as if fairies would come to eat it in the night.

If her keys were still on the table, she wouldn't be able to drive her car. She wouldn't even be able to get back into the apartment. The door locked automatically when it closed. She felt the tears well up behind her eyes. It wasn't true that everything was her fault. It really wasn't. Some things just happened.

She was only half aware of slipping to the floor, of sitting there hunched with her back against the wall. The chills were so bad now that she was shuddering more than shaking. She felt like one of those old cars you see on the highway sometimes, rattling so much that you think they're just going to fly apart.

If she couldn't get to the car, she couldn't get to the hospital. If she couldn't get to the hospital, what would happen to her? Maybe she would die here, in this hallway, and the next person to come through would find her body on the carpet, curled into a ball like a sleeping cat.

She took a deep breath. She wished with everything she had that her neck didn't hurt so much. She counted to ten and got lost in the middle somewhere.

Then she felt a heaviness on her shoulder, and turned to find a young woman standing beside her, dressed in jeans and the whitest sneakers that had ever existed on the planet. They were so white, they hurt Eve's eyes.

"Excuse me?" the young woman said. "You're Ms. Wachinsky, aren't you? You live right over there? Are you all right?"

Eve tried to look up and started crying, instead. She saw that the door to the apartment across the hall was open. The music had stopped. This must be her neighbor, the one she had never seen, the one who had moved in just last month. She buried her head in her arms and rocked.

A hand came down on her head, then on her forehead.

"Jesus Christ," the young woman said. "You're burning up. Do you need to go to a doctor?"

Eve kept her head very still. Her neck hurt so much she never wanted to move it again. "Hospital," she said. "Going to hospital."

"You want to go to the hospital. Good plan. I can do that. Do you want me to take you to the hospital?"

"Hospital," Eve said again. "St.—"

"St. Mary's. Right. Okay. Look, let me go get you a sweatshirt or something to wear—I've got some that are as big as coats. Then I'll go get the car. Then we'll take you to the hospital. Will that be all right?"

Of course it would be all right, Eve thought. This was ridiculous. This woman was ridiculous. She was dying, of course she had to go to the hospital. She wondered what had happened to the music. She wondered what was going on.

The young woman disappeared and came back with a big red sweatshirt. Eve let her force it over her head and only cried out once, when her neck was moved too far.

"Damn," she heard the woman say, "you've got meningitis. I'll bet anything."

Eve tried to remember what meningitis was and couldn't. Something terrible. Something people died of. She tried to remember if it was catching, and couldn't get hold of that information, either.

"Listen," she tried to say.

The young woman was pushing her out their mutual front door. The car was right there. Eve had no idea when the young woman had had a chance to go get it. The whole world seemed cold and hot at once. The sun was much too bright. Her eyes hurt. She felt herself being folded into a bucket seat and began to shudder again.

The door next to her closed. On the other side of the car, the driver's side door opened, and the young woman climbed in behind the wheel. Then that door closed, too—

God, but the noise was loud; it was explosive—and the engine started up.

"I'm Grace Feinmann, by the way," the young woman said.

That was when a voice from the radio started talking about how Kayla Anson had been murdered, only the night before, and something in Eve's head began to struggle mightily to put the information in context. BMW. Jeep. The Litchfield Road.

The cold gave way to heat. Eve was suddenly burning up, so hot that there was no way she could move, no way she could shudder, no way she could do much of anything except sweat and sweat until big rivers of water ran down the front of her chest.

But the car was out on the road now, moving, and that made her feel a little better.

2

Annabel Crawford knew that the death of Kayla Anson had done her at least some good—although she didn't like to think about it like that. She didn't like to think about Kayla dying at all. It had been so odd to get up this morning and see it all over the news like that. It had been odd, in fact, just to see the television on at ten o'clock. Annabel's mother always said she hated television, the way women like her were supposed to hate it. The set was kept in a cramped little "sitting room" at the back of the house, off the kitchen, and only turned on in the early evenings, when Jennifer Crawford had nothing else to do. Annabel's father wasn't home enough for decisions like that to matter. Annabel thought she should have known, as soon as she came downstairs looking for coffee, that something was terribly wrong. Her mother only kept the television on like that for major league airplane disasters.

"I've been trying to get through to Margaret all day," Jennifer said, when Annabel came down and began moving around the kitchen. "The phone's on the answering machine—I don't suppose I blame her. There must be reporters crawling all over that place by now. And it's only going to get worse."

Annabel found grapefruit in the refrigerator. She got one out and cut it in half. She hated the taste of grapefruit, but that was the point. If you hated the taste of something, you didn't eat too much of it. She put the half a grapefruit in a little bowl, and found a spoon, and sat down at the table. The red Corvette was parked right outside the kitchen window, in that part of the drive that came up to the back porch. Annabel was surprised that she hadn't thought to put it away in the garage.

"There's something I've got to talk to you about," Annabel started.

Jennifer was still on a roll. She was a fine-boned woman with too much hair and clothes that had come straight out of the Talbot's store in Southbury. She looked like any one of a hundred Litchfield County ladies.

"Strangled," she was saying, pacing back and forth from the kitchen to the little sitting room and back again. "That's what they said on the news. Strangled. And hit on the head, too, or something. I don't know. The news is very confusing. But I don't think there's a safe place left anywhere in the world."

"She was strangled in her house?" Annabel asked.

"She was strangled in her car. Or strangled and then put in her car. Really, Annabel, it's impossible to sort it all out. There are all these news reports, but I don't think anybody really knows anything. And there were pictures . . . of them bringing the body out. You know. The bag. And all I could think of was that Kayla Anson was in that bag."

Annabel felt suddenly very ill. Kayla in a body bag. Body bags in general. She pushed her grapefruit away from her.

"Mother, listen to me," she said. "I sort of stole this car."

"What?" Jennifer said.

"Well, I didn't really steal it. I just—I was out with this

guy. Tommy Haggerty. You know. He goes to Princeton. His parents belong to the club."

"It's going to be really awful if it turns out it wasn't some thug from the neighborhood. So to speak. If it turns out it was one of Kayla's boyfriends."

"Kayla only had one boyfriend. He wouldn't strangle her. The thing is, Tommy and I went out to the Lucky Eight last night, and he was drinking, and—"

"You can just imagine what Margaret is going through. Especially given the fact that Margaret is Margaret, if you know what I mean. A more tightly wound, unforgiving woman I've never met. Margaret hates publicity."

"He got too drunk to drive," Annabel said, plowing on gamely. "So I took his keys and left him in the bar and drove his car back here. And now it's in our driveway. That one. The Corvette."

"Well, dear. I think that's only sensible. You wouldn't have wanted the boy to drive you home if he was drunk."

"Right," Annabel said.

On any other day, Jennifer would have caught onto it immediately—if the boy was drunk, the chances were that Annabel had been drinking. Her father would catch onto it, if her father heard about it. He didn't seem to be around.

"Did Daddy go into the city?" Annabel asked.

"What? Oh, yes. He had some kind of conference or something. They say they're going to get that famous detective out here to help. You know the one. The Hungarian."

"Hungarian?"

"Gregory something."

"Oh," Annabel said. "Gregor Demarkian. He's not Hungarian. He's from Philadelphia."

"When I was growing up, you never heard about people with names like that. If they got famous, they changed them. Now, I don't know what to think, half the time. I wish they'd be more clear about what happened. They keep saying she was found in her own car in her own garage, as if she'd committed suicide with carbon monoxide. Or somebody had killed her that way. Do you think that could be it?"

"I think I've got to get the car back to Tommy," Annabel said.

Jennifer blinked. She wandered back into the little sitting room again. Annabel heard her sigh. "Now they've got Diane Smith at the scene," she called out, "except it isn't exactly at the scene because the driveway's blocked off. It's just out in front of Margaret's house. Oh, Margaret must be having a *fit*."

"Right," Annabel said.

Her pocketbook was just where she had left it the night before, on the kitchen counter next to the refrigerator. She picked it up and made sure she still had Tommy's keys tucked into the open pocket on the side. She would drive the car over to Tommy's house and ask him to drive her home—if he was in any shape to do any such thing. If he wasn't, she would explain the whole thing to Tommy's mother and have Tommy's mother drive her home. Annabel didn't think she had to worry about Tommy's father. None of the fathers she knew was ever home, not even on the weekends. If they didn't work themselves to death, they wouldn't have enough money to buy their children Corvettes.

"I'm leaving," Annabel called out.

"Drive carefully," Jennifer called back.

Annabel went out and got into the Corvette and started it up. The radio was on. A woman announcer was giving a little capsule report on "the murder in Washington Depot." She said something about "tragedy" and something about "the only child of entrepreneurial pioneer Robert Anson." Annabel turned her off.

Now that she was out here, on her own, without her mother nattering to her, Annabel suddenly realized that this was all for real. Kayla was really dead. It had happened and it would not un-happen. The whole thing seemed worse than impossible. People didn't just die. They didn't get murdered in the Northwest Hills, either, where nothing much ever happened in the way of violence except wild turkeys chasing small cats. In all the years and years Annabel and her family had been coming to Litchfield County, there had only been one murder, not counting this one. A few years ago, a boy had gone into the convenience store in Four Corners and shot his ex-girlfriend and then himself. They were both in high school and she had wanted to be free to date other people.

If it had happened in Waterbury, that would be a different thing, Annabel thought—but that wasn't really true, of course. It wouldn't have mattered where it happened. It wasn't where it happened that was bothering her.

If it was really real, she thought to herself—and then it struck her. This was it. This was what was bothering her.

She didn't know what was really real. She had no idea what she was talking about when she said something was really real. She had no idea what "real" meant.

It seemed to her that she had lived her whole life in a fog.

3

It was well after noon before Peter Greer decided that he had to go to sleep—to bed, to sleep, to the medicine cabinet in the bathroom off the loft, where he kept a small bottle of contraband prescription sleeping pills. The first news of the murder had come across in a bulletin on WTNH. The next thing he knew, it seemed to be all over everywhere, on CNN, on the major networks. It made sense, of course, because she had been who she'd been, because she'd had so much money. It was the money that really made all the difference.

Years ago, when he had been growing up in Litchfield County, Peter Greer had made decisions for himself, decisions he had known, even then, that he would never change. Unlike Kayla Anson and her friends, Peter had not been part of the country-club and private-school segment of

Litchfield County. His parents had had a small Cape Cod house in Morris, and he had gone to Morris Elementary School and to the regional high school, just like everybody else. He couldn't even remember when he had first realized that there was a difference, or that the difference would matter in the long run in ways nobody ever admitted to themselves out loud. He did remember walking down South Street in Litchfield and looking at the big houses there, the white ones set back from the road with their tall columns and curving front drives. He did remember sitting on the Litchfield Green and listening to them talk, the ones they called the pink-and-greens, who went to Rumsey Hall and then got sent away to prep school. Their voices were so different from the ones he was used to, it was almost as if they were speaking anther language.

There were people who said that Peter Greer was an opportunist, and a social climber, but it wasn't exactly true. It was true that he had always intended to live in *that* Litchfield County instead of in the one that he was used to. He thought anybody on earth would want to make that change, once they understood what it was about. It was even true that he intended to make as much money as possible, without having to be tethered to a desk like the Wall Street bankers who kept houses out here for the summer. In his better moments, he imagined himself becoming his generation's version of Steve Fossett, a multimillionaire adventurer, taking up mountain climbing or around-the-world sailing as a hobby in his old age.

What he really wanted, when he thought about it, was a kind of rest—the end to his own dissatisfaction, the end to this feeling he had had all his life that he wasn't getting enough, wasn't doing enough, wasn't respected enough to be able to relax and let it all go. It was as if he were strapped to the front of an express train and being pushed ever onward, ever faster. He had worked for years to be valedictorian of his high school class, and when he had achieved it he felt only that it would have been better if his grade point average had been five points higher than it was, if it had been perfect. He had worked those same years to make sure he got a scholarship big enough so that he could go to Amherst without piling up debts he would never be able to pay. Then, when he got to Amherst, he thought only that he should have tried for Harvard. It went on and on, on and on, and there didn't seem to be any way he could stop it.

For a while there, he had thought Kayla Anson was going to stop it for him. He had thought she was going to be his resting place. He honestly couldn't imagine how much higher he could go, than being married to her and having for himself what being married to her would mean. Even if it didn't last forever. Even if she couldn't love him always. None of those women could ever love for always. They weren't built for it.

Right now, he could hear Deirdre in his shower. She had slept through the night and the morning. She didn't give a damn about the news or even about the way Kayla Anson had died. She seemed to think it had nothing to do with her.

Peter wondered if he would feel differently if he and Kayla had been closer than they were, if what they had had together hadn't already begun to wind down, if she hadn't been on her way out his door. On her way, but not completely gone yet. On her way, but waiting for the right time to make a scene. All women felt they had to make scenes, to justify the end of a relationship. Even Deirdre was going to feel the need to make a scene, and she was going to be good at it.

Once, when he and Kayla were first going out together, she had taken him to a hunt breakfast up in Salisbury. They hadn't actually gone on the hunt—Kayla didn't approve of hunting, but she didn't disapprove of the people who approve of it—and they had walked together along the wide halls of one of those mock-Tudor houses everybody had been building in the twenties. In that one moment, Peter Greer had been perfectly and unquestionably at peace. He had suddenly been able to see himself in just the place where he belonged. It was so far in the past, he could never reach it, but it was there. It wasn't just a figment of his imagination.

Now he would never reach even an approximation of that place. He was sure of it. She would not be coming back to him.

And although it was true enough that she would not have come back to him even if she had lived—that she was more than on her way out the door the last time he talked to her; she was all the way out and just running back to clear up a few loose ends—it somehow made an enormous difference that she was dead.

That did not, however, mean that he was sorry she was dead.

The news reports all said strangled, and he could see her strangled. He could see the hands around her throat and the arms pressing her neck down, down, so far down that it would break. He could see her eyes bulging in their sockets and the skin of her face going red.

His anger was so broad and so deep, it welled out of him like lava.

Four

I

The newspapers were lying in a stack at the foot of the bed when Gregor Demarkian woke up—lying there in the way, so that every time he turned he brushed them with his feet. He felt fuzzy, the way he often did when he was off-schedule. He liked to keep regular hours. He couldn't remember when he had last slept in this off-and-on way. Maybe it was when he had still been on kidnapping detail, sitting with a partner in an unmarked car at the side of some road somewhere, drinking bad coffee and waiting for hours for something to happen. Mostly, nothing ever did. In those days, all new agents with the Bureau started either on kidnapping detail or on tax patrol. It was either boredom in a car or boredom in a back office somewhere, trying to decide if one mobster or another might be illegally deducting hit men fees from his income taxes. Although why such a deduction would be illegal, Gregor thought now, wasn't that easy to explain. He could make a decent case in tax court that hit men were a legitimate business expense, at least if the businessman in question was a member of the Gambino family.

In those days, too, there was the ethnic thing. There were no black agents, and Gregor was one of the very few who could not claim to be at least partly Anglo-Saxon. Hoover had been strange that way, as he had been in many ways. It wasn't quite that he had been an unrelieved bigot. He didn't hate all people who were not "true Americans," as he put it. He just picked and chose. The Bureau had a good sprinkling of Greeks, but no Italians. It had Armenians, but no Portuguese. People of color, as they would be called now, were simply out of the question—but if Hoover had been required to hire one, he would have taken an African American over a Chinese or Japanese. He was, however, passionately committed to Irish Catholics. He always said he thought they made the best Americans. It made no sense, because Hoover himself made no sense. Even in Gregor's earliest days at the Bureau, the consensus had been that the old man was not really mentally well—and that was when the agents were being polite. A dangerous paranoid jerk, was what Gregor had thought, the third or fourth time he met the man. By now he knew perfectly well that he'd been right.

He swung his legs over the side of the bed and looked around. This was Bennis's bedroom in the Mayflower Inn. She also had a sitting room. The bed was a big antique-looking sleigh, piled high with blankets and quilts and pillows. Bennis must have asked for extra. Gregor pulled the papers to him and looked at their front pages: the *Waterbury Republican*, the *Torrington Register-Citizen*, the *Litchfield County Times*. The *Litchfield County Times* was set up to look exactly like *The New York Times,* so much so that Gregor had thought it was *The New York Times* until he'd brought it closer and could read the masthead. The other two papers were standard small-town sheets. They used the cheapest possible ink. Their headlines were much too large. None of them had anything at all about Kayla Anson's murder.

Gregor got off the bed and went to his suitcase. His favorite robe was still there, folded. Bennis not only hadn't taken it, she hadn't even gone looking for it. Gregor put it on over his pajamas and tightened the belt on his waist. He thought of how surprised Bennis had been when she saw he wore pajamas and then put it out of his mind. In his day, nice men didn't go to bed in the nude, or just their underwear. He was far too old to change now.

He folded the newspapers and put them under his arm. He opened the bedroom door and looked out into the sitting room. Bennis was sitting at a small writing table next to a window, working away busily on a laptop that was plugged into the wall. The window was open, letting in air that was downright cold. Bennis's hair was pinned up and coming undone. Great black clouds seemed to surround her head, like some kind of alternative halo. Gregor suddenly felt wonderful, watching her sitting there. This was the way he wanted to think of her, the way he wanted to remember her, not the way he had been remembering her the last day while she'd been gone.

He shifted the newspapers from one arm to the other and cleared his throat. Bennis turned away from the keyboard and looked at him.

"You're up. It's after five o'clock. I thought you were going to sleep through dinner."

"I couldn't have. I'm too hungry. What are you doing?"

"E-mail. I've got an address just for fan mail. It's on my interview at Amazon-dot-com. You want to see some of this stuff?"

"No." Gregor dropped the newspapers on a coffee table near the small couch. Bennis wrote fantasy novels, full of knights and ladies and trolls and jousts. Her fan mail tended to consist of long missives from middle-aged women who used the word *forsooth* at least once every paragraph.

Bennis was still pecking away at her fan mail. "So," she said. "I'm glad you're here. We're supposed to have dinner later with the resident trooper up in Caldwell. That's where he's from. Not Cornwall Bridge."

"I was thinking about J. Edgar Hoover," Gregor said. He sat down on the little couch, in front of the papers. There was a television across the room and a remote on the coffee table. He picked up the remote and turned the set on.

"Start with channel eight," Bennis said. "That's WTNH. It's the one I like best. Thinking about Hoover always puts you in a bad mood."

"My mood is fine. I was thinking about the Bureau, maybe. About who Hoover hired and who he didn't hire. About racial and ethnic discrimination, we'd call it today."

"Ethnic?"

"In my class at Quantico, I was the only Armenian. There was one Greek. Everybody else was at least white.

And WASP or Irish Catholic. It was a strange situation."

"Did it bother you? Did you feel—I don't know. Disrespected?"

"Not really. I was just thinking that it explained some of the things some of those people did later. Charley Constantinus going to jail for trying to cover up for Nixon. Mike Seranian going into the State Department and becoming such a bloodthirsty hawk he embarrassed Lyndon Johnson. Hyper-Americans, if you know what I mean. Going that extra mile just to prove that their loyalty was absolute."

"And you didn't do that?"

"I think it's because I knew the type. Hoover's type. I knew what was wrong with him. Although I don't think I could have explained it at the time. We had a priest at Holy Trinity when I was growing up who was very much the same as Hoover was. I've come to think of it as a syndrome."

"You've got to stop reading Tibor's copies of *Psychology Today*."

Gregor pumped up the sound on the television. A blonde woman—"Ann," everybody kept calling her—was reporting a story on child abuse in a town called Manchester. She had a serious look on her face, but it was a pixie-ish face. He could imagine her laughing.

Bennis stopped doing e-mail and shut down her machine. Then she came across the room to sit in the small armchair next to the couch.

"So," she said. "Is that what we're doing today? Thinking about J. Edgar Hoover? Have you thought about Kayla Anson at all?"

"I haven't had much to think about. Except that I've been wondering about people—about how many people seem to need to fight other people off. How many of them need to be isolated. Not that they're forced to be, but that they want to be."

Bennis got out a cigarette. There was an ashtray on the little writing table next to the laptop. Gregor hadn't noticed it before, although he had noticed the smell of smoke in the room. It hadn't registered as smoke, because it was the smell he'd come to recognize as part-of-Bennis, along with the lavender sachet that she put in all her underwear drawers. Now Bennis lit up and then went back across the room to get the ashtray. She dumped the small pile of butts into the wastebasket next to the table and brought it back almost clean. Gregor could see traces of ash in the bottom of it.

"I wish you'd stop doing that," he said.

"You were telling me about people being isolated."

Bennis was coughing. It was a sort of underground cough, held back, not full-throated, but it was there. Gregor pumped the volume on the television even higher.

"I was just thinking what I was telling you I was thinking. About how so many people seem to want to chase off anybody who might be close to them. Anybody who even tries to get close to them. I keep trying to come to some sort of understanding about why people kill each other. Not people on the street—not killings in the middle of a robbery, or drive-by shootings, or that kind of thing. I don't even mean serial killers. Do you remember Ginny Marsh?"

"Ginny Marsh who killed her baby."

"That's right. And all the others, really. The people who do it deliberately. Who do it out of some sense of connection, out of wanting to get rid of that sense of connection. I suppose I'm not making much sense of anything, myself."

Bennis blew smoke into the air. "Did you know they'd set the date for execution?" she asked abruptly. "They sent me an invitation for it, in the mail. The twenty-fourth of November. Less than a month away."

Gregor watched the smoke of Bennis's cigarette curl into the air. He had forgotten this part, of course. He always forgot this part. His relationship to murder was professional. He always had a certain amount of detachment when he approached it. Bennis's relationship to murder could never be truly detached at all.

"Her lawyers will make another appeal," he said carefully—but Bennis's head was already shaking, and his voice hadn't carried much conviction. It had, after all, been almost ten years.

"They're finished with the appeals. I got a letter from her lawyers, too."

"And?"

"She's still refusing to speak to us. To any of us. She's still—herself. My brother Teddy sent her a little crate full of holiday jellies last Christmas. She sent it back without opening the package. I keep wondering if she'll change her mind when it gets closer to the day."

"You don't have to go see it. You don't have to go see her, if you don't want to."

"I know." Bennis had smoked her cigarette to the filter. She stubbed it out and reached for another one. "I don't even know what I want. Except that I don't want her to be dead. That just seems wrong to me. Even though I know she's—what she is. That's she's not safe. That she would do it again. To me, if she had the chance."

"She almost did."

"Do you get like this? With the people you work on, the people who get arrested in the cases that you do? Do you ever just not want them to die?"

"I don't want anyone to die," Gregor said. "I don't believe in capital punishment."

"Oh, I know. But that's not what I mean. I'm being as idiotic about this as you were being about Hoover. Maybe it's a sign that we're both getting old."

"I'm a lot older than you are. When is this dinner with the resident trooper?"

"Eight-thirty. We could go downstairs and get some appetizers, if you want. Bar food, really, but it's not bad. Hot nibbles. That kind of thing."

"Hot nibbles would be fine. I don't suppose they have a television in the bar."

"I don't know."

Gregor leaned forward and squinted at the television set. It was a large one, really, but the focus seemed to be off. The woman named Ann had been replaced by another one, named Diane. She was a blonde, too, but she had bigger teeth.

"All right," Gregor said abruptly. "Let me get dressed."

2

Later, standing in front of the mirror in the small bathroom and trying to make sure his tie was straight, it occurred to Gregor that he was not really suited for this—relationship— he was having with Bennis. In his day, people hadn't had relationships. They had had marriages, or friendships, or love affairs, and those were very stylized things, where everybody's roles were clearly defined. Women emoted and men stayed stoic in the face of it, that was the thing. Women had feelings and men took care of them when they got that way. Gregor knew what to do in a situation like that. It was what he had done for Elizabeth, all the long months of her painful dying. He did not know what to do now, for Bennis, who was getting dressed in the living room and smoking nonstop in the process. She expected something else from him besides stoic support. He knew that. He just didn't know what. The Commonwealth of Pennsylvania was about to execute Bennis Hannaford's sis- ter—for a murder Gregor himself had solved and that Ben- nis herself had been some help in solving. Gregor was shocked to realize that he didn't even know what method Pennsylvania used in executions. Gas chamber, electric chair, lethal injection: It would make a difference.

Christ, Gregor thought. Of course it would make a dif- ference. He shoved the knot of his tie all the way up to his Adam's apple. It made him feel strangled, and he didn't even care. He wished he knew what he felt for Bennis *re- ally*. He wished he could sort out and put a name to all the things that had him so confused. When he wasn't paying attention to them, there seemed to be millions, all swirling around in his head and chest and groin. When he turned his attention to them, they reduced themselves to one—this desperation, this feeling beyond desperation, to be wherever she was, in her sight, in her hearing, every day and all the time, without ceasing. If this was love, then he had never loved Elizabeth. He had never felt this way about anybody else in his life.

He gave up on the tie and stepped out of the bathroom. Bennis was pacing through the tiny living room, still smoking. She had on one of those plain black dresses that her closet seemed to be full of, even though they looked mostly alike. This one had short sleeves and a little jacket that went with it. The jacket was lying over the back of the couch. Bennis was coughing. Sometimes she had to stop dead in the middle of the carpet and bend over double to let it happen.

"You ought to get somebody to check out that cough," Gregor told her.

Bennis stopped coughing and stood up. "I'm fine. I'm a little hyper. You ready to go?"

"Absolutely. Do you ever feel like you were born out of time and out of place?"

"Are we going to do philosophy again?"

"No," Gregor said.

He got his coat from where he had left it lying on a chair when he first got to this room. He draped it over his shoulder. As he passed the couch he looked down at the little black jacket and saw the Chanel label inside the collar. Bennis would never consent to wear a real coat over a Chanel jacket/dress. It would spoil the line.

"Ready," Gregor said.

Bennis got her bag—more Chanel. Gregor recognized the double-C bit on the handle. What was going on here? Bennis never dressed up like this, unless she was going to be interviewed on television. She hated shopping for clothes, and hated even more spending money on them, even though she didn't really have to worry about what she spent. Here it was again: one more thing to make him feel confused; one more thing to make him feel off-balance; one more thing to convince him that he was somehow getting it wrong.

He opened the door that went from the living room to the hall. He waited for Bennis to go through and then walked out behind her.

Just a few minutes ago, he had been thinking about people who craved isolation, who hated connection. He had been thinking that that was true of everybody, to some extent. Now he thought he was thinking nonsense. It was not true about him. He had no need for isolation at all. He hated the very thought of it. If he remembered himself as he had been between the time Elizabeth had died and the time he had first met Bennis Hannaford, it was only because he now knew that he had been dead.

Then he remembered the title of a book he had seen once in an airport a couple of years ago, a paperback book in a rack with a dozen other books. All the other books in the rack had had something to do with diets. This one had been called *New Hope for the Dead*.

He started to laugh out loud. Then he realized that Bennis was looking at him oddly, as if he had lost it, which maybe he had.

He bit his lip and made himself stop.

3

Half a minute later, they were in the lobby in front of the check-in desk, standing on thick rugs that were patterned with gigantic roses. The lights were all amber-tinted and soft. The people going back and forth all looked like they had children at good prep schools, which they probably did. What other reason could there be to come to Washington Depot, Connecticut, at the very end of October, except to go to Parents' Day at the kind of school that charged more in tuition than most people paid for their cars, brand new?

Bennis stopped at the desk to hand in her key and ask them to take any messages. Gregor noted idly that she looked a little too fashionable for the people in this lobby, who tended to the kind of good wool and cashmere classic cuts that used to be sold at Peck and Peck. Even so, she looked good. He took a lot of pleasure watching her cross the room. She said hello to one or two people, as if she half knew them, maybe because she had run across them a couple of times in the halls. In some ways, Gregor realized, Bennis ran very much to type. You could tell just by looking at her that she had come from money, and never really fallen off the perch.

"Ready?" she said to him, as she came up beside him and laid a hand on his arm.

"Ready," he told her.

Then he let himself be guided down a small hall toward a sign that said TAP ROOM. Tap room was a much better name for it than bar would have been. He understood that immediately. Places like the Mayflower Inn did not have bars.

They were just sitting down at a sturdy wooden table for two near one of the windows that looked out onto the inn's front drive when the woman walked up to them, and for a moment Gregor couldn't remember who she was. Her familiarity was overwhelming, but that was as far as he got. She was middle-aged and a little heavy, but definitely not obese. Her clothes were determinedly but unobtrusively provincial.

"Excuse me," she said.

Gregor's head went up. The voice he remembered. He had always been better with voices than with faces.

"The woman on the train," he said.

"Excuse me?" Bennis said.

The woman was nodding. "That's right, Mr. Demarkian. We met on the train. Or on the bud car, really. Coming up to Waterbury from Bridgeport."

Bennis got her cigarettes out. The woman frowned at them, but she didn't protest. Gregor was sure that she wouldn't, no matter how much she wanted to.

"I'm Iris Brayne," the woman said. "You wouldn't recognize the name. I work for the *Torrington Register-Citizen*. In about half an hour, I'm going to file a story about you."

"Ah," Bennis said. She blew a thick stream of smoke in the air—directly at Iris Brayne, Gregor was certain, although he wouldn't have accused her of it out loud.

Iris Brayne waved smoke away from her face and grimaced. "I thought I'd give you a chance to comment," she said. "You're here. You're with the woman who discovered Kayla Anson's body. You might want to say something the general public would understand."

"Why should I say anything?" Gregor asked her reasonably. "I don't even know what's going on. I just got here. Miss Hannaford and I have barely had a chance to talk."

"You've been here for hours. I know that. We came up together on the train."

"I've been asleep. I was asleep on the train, if you were paying any attention."

"She was the one who told me where to find you," Bennis said drily.

"There, then," Gregor said. "Why don't you just let us talk, and then after I know something I might have something to tell you."

"You consult with police departments," Iris Brayne said. "I want to know which one you're consulting with now."

"I'm not consulting with, or for, any police department."

"Your own—lady friend—found the body. Did you know Kayla Anson well?"

"I never met Kayla Anson in my life," Gregor said.

"Did your lady friend know Kayla Anson well?"

There was something about this woman that was all wrong, mean-spirited and pinched. The lines in her face were too deep. She wouldn't look at Bennis Hannaford, even when she wanted Bennis to answer a question she obviously felt she needed to ask. Gregor looked down at her hands clutched together on the table and saw that the nails were bitten ragged.

"I think it's about time you went someplace and left us

alone," he said, as pleasantly as he could. Then he stood up, as if he were about to help her—guide her—in getting where she was supposed to go.

By now, Bennis had finished her cigarette and started another one. This was defensive smoking, the kind of thing she did when she was trying to ward off some evil, like someone she thought might be stalking her on a city street. Iris Brayne had begun to rub her hands together fretfully. Her shoulder bag—the same one she had had on the train— was slipping down along her arm. Every once in a while she pushed at it, as if it were in her way.

"Everybody's going to know one way or the other," Iris Brayne said. "It's going to be in the morning's paper. Even if you don't make a statement. It's going to be in the paper with a picture from the Associated Press."

"That way," Gregor said, pointing toward the door.

Iris Brayne looked at him long and hard, and then quickly at Bennis and quickly away. Gregor knew it would be a mistake to put a hand on her, even just on her elbow, to move her away. He had had run-ins with small-town reporters before. He had had run-ins with big-town reporters, too. If this woman had not been a reporter, he would have been worried that she was on the verge of becoming irrational.

Of course, the only way he knew she was a reporter was because she said she was. She might very well be lying.

Gregor was just making up his mind to do something— or to go to the bartender and ask him to do something— when Iris Brayne stepped away from him. The movement was abrupt and deliberate. She moved not a single millimeter more than she'd wanted to.

"It'll be in the paper tomorrow," she said. "All about you and your lady friend and Kayla Anson. I bet it'll be picked up by the wire services, too."

She hitched the strap of her bag back up on her shoulder and turned away.

She walked out of the tap room at a small-stepped, hitching half-run, as if she'd suddenly realized that she was going to be late for her deadline.

There were millions of them like this, at small-town newspapers all across the country. Gregor had met them and understood them, just as he had met and understood their better halves, the reporters who liked being where they were. They didn't bother him, except that they did. Connection and isolation. He couldn't make it any clearer than that.

"So," Bennis said. "What was that all about?"

"That," Gregor told her, "is a harbinger of things to come. I'm going to be panned unmercifully in the *Torrington Register-Citizen*."

Five

I

Later, Sally Martindale would think about this weekend as a movable apocalypse. She would go over and over the particulars in her mind, the way people do when they are the victims of a preventable disaster. Because this disaster was certainly preventable. It would never have happened at all if Frank hadn't left her. It would never have occurred to her at all to take money out of Kayla Anson's account—or anybody else's—if she hadn't been left to rattle around on her own in this big, ancient house, if she hadn't already been forced to sell all the furniture she could get away with just to go on getting by. As far as Sally could tell, it was *all* Frank's fault, all of it, even her getting fired from Deloitte. It was true that she had been late more often than not in that last year before they had let her go. It was true that she had been distracted. It was even true that she had known all along what the competition was like, and that there would only be one or two of them asked to stay on to be partners. Nothing mattered except for the fact that Frank was leaving her. She couldn't think about anything else. She didn't even see why she should have been expected to.

The particulars that were going through her mind that weekend, though, were about different things. They were about the obvious. She had been careless these last few months—sloppy, really, tense and in a hurry all the time. There was that. There was also the fact that the murder had happened on a Friday, so that she hadn't even heard about it until Sunday morning. If it had happened on an ordinary weekday, she would have caught it on the radio news on her way in to work. Then it would have been easy to fix what she had done, at least well enough to get away with it just a little bit longer. She would only have had to move a few things around and transfer a few dollars out of other people's accounts. She would have been careful to pick the right kind of people with the right kind of accounts, the kind she should have been using all along, except that it had seemed so much simpler to use Kayla Anson's. What she really needed was young mothers with young children— healthy but not reckless, distracted by baby-sitting and classes in Mozart for Toddlers.

The right kind of accounts, she had thought compulsively as she switched the television back and forth from CBS to NBC to ABC to CNN. The story was everywhere. It was just beginning to heat up. She had missed the beginning of it, because she had been so tense that she had just slept through most of Saturday, and then she had driven out to Ledyard again and given it one more try. All she had gotten for her trouble was one hundred dollars poorer. She hadn't dared to risk any more.

Now she pulled into the parking lot at the side of the club and looked at the long, low mock-Tudor building. She was finding it very difficult to breathe. Her chest hurt. Her muscles seemed to be knotted tight, so that when she tried to move, everything on her body resisted. This building had been put up in the twenties, when the first of the serious New York money began to move north—serious *old* money, that was the ticket. Down on the Gold Coast it was all stockbroker fortunes and people who'd made a million overnight. They liked everything shiny and new and very up-to-date. Sally liked things like that, too. She'd just learned never to say so when she was with people up here, who all seemed to think that a cramped little house where the plumbing was falling apart was more impressive than any other kind, as long as it had been built in 1676.

If I ever win the lottery, I'm going to run away to New York, Sally told herself. Then she bit her lip and put her head down on the steering wheel. She had lottery tickets, of course. She had them every day. She had to have them. It was the only thing in her life that gave her hope. She wished she knew what people did for money, how they got it, how they handled it. She wished she knew where money came from. All her life, even when she was working, it had seemed to her that it had just fallen out of the sky.

Mallory had been sitting at the kitchen table when Sally first heard the news of Kayla Anson's murder, and Sally had felt Mallory watching her every move.

"I don't understand what your problem is," Mallory had said. "You barely knew her. I barely knew her. She wasn't one of my *contacts*, Mother."

Sally had considered telling Mallory all about it, about which account she had taken the money from and about what would happen to that account now that the account holder was dead, but she was stopped by the cold flatness in Mallory's eyes, the thing that was very near hate. Was it true that her daughter hated her? It seemed to be, although Sally knew she ought to be careful about this, because Mallory was still an adolescent. Adolescents went through phases where they thought their parents were beneath contempt. Even so, Sally didn't want to tell Mallory anything, not now and maybe not ever. She didn't want Mallory to see her any more clearly than she already did. Besides, the feeling was somewhat mutual. Mallory might hate her, but she hated Mallory, or at least spent some of the time wishing her dead. Sally only wished that her own mother had been for her what she was being for Mallory—her own mother, who thought the height of success was to be able to buy a sofa and love seat combination at Sears.

"I'm going into my office," was all she said, gathering up her pocketbook and keys. She thought for a moment that she ought to change into something more professional, and then decided against it. Nobody dressed up to spend Sunday at the club, no matter what they were doing there. She didn't want to be conspicuous, or conspicuously odd.

"You never go into the club on Sundays," Mallory said, "except when I've got something on, and then all you do is *police* me."

Sally kept her head against the steering wheel and began to count. She couldn't go inside when she was this obvi-

ously upset. They would pick it up right away. She tried
to call up Kayla Anson's face and found only Kayla's
cousin Annabel instead—and this in spite of the fact that
she had just seen Kayla's picture on the news. She had the
radio on and turned to a classical music station. In a couple
of minutes, the station would break for the hourly news and
she would have to hear the whole story again. She made
herself take a deep breath, and then another, and another.
She counted to one hundred and then started from one hundred and counted backward. She heard a car pulling into
the lot somewhere behind her. She couldn't sit here like
this forever.

The car belonged to Marian Ridenour—one of those
young mothers with young children. Sally sat up and
watched them all pile out of the Volvo station wagon, two
young girls and a tiny boy. The girls were dressed in cham-
bray jumpers with very white turtlenecks under them. Sally
took her keys out of the ignition and opened her own car's
door. The cold poured in on her and made her shiver. Marian Ridenour's husband worked for Goldman, Sachs. Sally
couldn't remember what he did, only that he got paid a lot
of money—and that Marian was his second wife.

She waited for Marian and the children to be out of
hailing range, and then started into the club herself. She
took the front entrance, even though it was more likely to
get her seen, because there was something about going
around to the side that smacked to her of sneaking. The
last thing she needed was to have somebody see her here
and conclude that she was hiding in some way. If she had
any chance at all, it was to do what she had to do before
anybody else even thought about the account that Kayla
Anson, like all the other members, kept at this club.

She got down to her office without seeing anybody. She
sat at her computer and booted up. The club seemed very,
very busy, full of people. It was a Sunday afternoon in
October and people didn't have anything else to do.

She got to her desktop screen and then from there to the
accounts. She typed in Kayla Anson's name and waited. A

second later, a window popped up, making a sound like a cymbal being struck, that said FILE NOT FOUND.

"Shit," Sally said, under her breath. Then she felt instantly guilty. You didn't use words like *shit* at this club. Even the men didn't use them.

She tried Anson, Kayla. She got another window: FILE NOT FOUND. Then she tried the account number. She knew that number by heart. The cymbal went off and the window went up: FILE NOT FOUND. Just to check, just to make sure, Sally typed in "Marian Ridenour." The account document flashed into the window, accessible and complete.

There was a small rivulet of sweat going down the back of her neck. Sally could feel it. Any minute now, it would soak into the silk of her pale blue blouse. Somebody had deleted Kayla Anson's account file, or moved it, or put it off limits. She had absolutely no idea what she was supposed to do now.

"Did we mess up your program?" a voice asked from the doorway. "I told them to be careful, but you know what those people are like. And they were in an incredible hurry."

Sally looked up and saw Ruth Grandmere standing in the doorway. Ruth was the club's weekend manager, a salt-and-peppered-hair woman with a sensible figure and a penchant for dresses in floral prints. Unlike Sally, she had never been a member of the club—and never even wanted to be.

"What *what* people are like?" Sally asked her. "Do you mean someone's been in here playing with my machines?"

"The Anson people. Kayla Anson's trust lawyers. Tons of them. Well, I suppose it was only three. But still. Can you imagine getting three eight-hundred-dollar-an-hour white shoe Wall Street lawyers out to the Northwest Hills of Connecticut the first thing Saturday morning just to get the records on an account that had, what, in it—maybe a thousand dollars?"

"I don't know," Sally said. Her throat felt raw and bloody, as if she'd swallowed glass.

Ruth had come all the way into the office. Now she sat down on a corner of Sally's desk.

"If you ask me, it's Margaret. I don't mean Margaret made them come out. I mean they don't trust Margaret. Not as far as they can throw her. And I can't say I blame them. Lord, but that woman is god-awful. And I don't think she ever cared about Kayla at all, except for the money. That girl lost everything she had when her father died."

"Yes," Sally said.

"Anyway," Ruth said, "they wanted the account records, so I gave them to them—I hope you don't mind. You weren't here and I couldn't get you at home. Not that there's anything wrong with that. It's your weekend. But they were in a hurry. And I called Mortimer and he said to make every accommodation."

Mortimer was the club's regular manager.

"No," Sally said. "I don't mind."

What was she supposed to say?

Ruth hopped down off the desk. "I didn't think you would. And you'll get the account documents back— you've still got them, really, they've just been moved and protected with a password or something, I don't remember how it works. They just want to dot all the i's and cross all the t's, if you see what I mean. Did you really come in to work today?"

"What? Oh, no. No. I came to have some coffee and get out of the house. I just thought I'd check on some things while I was here."

"Well, good. Good. I keep telling Mortimer that we ought to put you on full-time. We need you on full-time. But you know how Mortimer is. Now I've got to go and make sure that the golf caddies aren't ready to kill Stephen Holdenbrook again—why that man has to be so awful to the caddies, I don't know. It's a terrible thing, isn't it, about Kayla Anson?"

"What? Oh, yes. Yes, it is."

"There's nothing else on tap for conversation around this place today. If you want to get away from the news, you'd better go to Hawaii. I can't imagine what it would be like, to be dead at an age like that."

"Yes," Sally said again.

Ruth retreated into the hall. Sally looked at the screen of her computer. There wasn't anything she could do about this mess, not here, not now. Maybe there was nothing she could do about this mess ever. She wrapped her arms around her chest and held herself tight.

She needed to get up and close the office door. She needed to lock it tight.

She didn't want anybody to see her in here, bent over her keyboard, breaking down.

2

Faye Dallmer had thirteen earthenware pots of mint to put out on the boards in the roadside stand this morning. She normally hired somebody to do that kind of thing for her, but today she needed to do it herself. She needed to be out of the house. She needed to be away from Zara Anne. Most importantly, she needed to be doing something physical. Ever since she had heard about the death of Kayla Anson, she had been agitated, and she wasn't even sure why.

It isn't as if it has anything to do with you, she kept telling herself, as she set mint pots into even, orderly rows. You didn't even know Kayla Anson. You were out back mucking around in the dirt when whatever it was that happened, happened. You didn't even have the Jeep.

It was the Jeep that was nagging at her, although that made no more sense than anything else. She had the Jeep back, after all. It was sitting right next to her little Escort in the garage. It was just more than a little banged up, that was all. There was bark all over it, as if somebody had smashed it into a tree, except that it wasn't that smashed. She wondered who had taken it, back on Friday night. When kids took it, they always brought it back. They put it in the garage or left it parked in the driveway. Maybe this time, after they hit the tree or whatever it was, they had been too ashamed to return it.

"It was chasing that girl's car," Zara Anne had said, that night, to the policemen who showed up at the door.

Faye had been able to tell that the policemen had not been taking Zara Anne seriously. Local people rarely did take her seriously. She was a hard young woman to take. By the time the policemen got there, she had put on all her jewelry, necklaces and bangles and earrings that dangled and shone. She sounded like a jewelry store walking whenever she moved. She had put on more eye makeup, too, including thick black liner that she had painted into wings at the sides of her eyes. Faye wondered why she had never noticed it before, this need of Zara Anne's to be as ridiculous as possible.

"It was right up on the back of that car," Zara Anne told them, "practically climbing up the bumper. Tailgating, that's what it's called. And it didn't have to be. There wasn't anybody else out there. It could have passed anytime."

"I didn't make it up," Zara Anne had told Faye herself, the next morning. "I really did see it happen. I don't understand why you won't believe me."

It wasn't that Faye didn't believe her. Not exactly. It was more complicated than that. Part of it was that Faye was used to Zara Anne's exaggerations. Five hits out of twenty on an ESP test became an "incredible proof" of extrasensory perception. The failure of a checkout girl to make eye contact at the supermarket became "irrefutable evidence" of her Christian fundamentalism and hatred of Wicca.

"They all want to go back to burning witches at the stake," Zara Anne would say, as they got back into the car after a long day of grocery shopping.

Faye had given up pointing out that nobody had ever burned a witch in the American colonies. Witches here were hanged, not burned. The hangings took place in Hartford.

Part of it was that there was something wrong with this—this vision of the Jeep chasing the BMW, tailing it, out there on the Litchfield Road. Faye made sure her rows of mint were straight and then went to the back of the stand to see what she still had in boxes on the ground. She took a box full of organically grown beets with their greens still on and lugged it to the front. She had on two thick cotton sweaters over her turtleneck, but she was still cold. If the weather went on like this, she didn't know if she would be able to keep the stand open until November. She thought of Towne Corn out in Morris, where they kept the stand open almost forever. The people there wore heavy corduroy jackets lined with fleece and thick suede gloves.

I couldn't do it like that, Faye said to herself, outside. Then she stopped working for a moment to watch a car pass on the road. On Sunday mornings like this, the road was nearly empty. They wouldn't start to see any serious traffic until people started coming out of church.

"I think I could tell what he was thinking," Zara Anne had said stubbornly, the next morning, when the news was everywhere that Kayla Anson was dead. "I didn't know she was dead last night. I wasn't trying to get in on the publicity. I didn't know there was any publicity to get in on."

"I wasn't saying you were trying to get in on it last night," Faye said. "I know we didn't know anything last night. I said I thought you were trying to get in on it now."

"By talking to you."

"By working this whole story up in your head. And it is a story. Because you know they're going to be back."

"Why should they be back?"

They had been standing in the kitchen by then. Zara Anne had been all pouty and furious and rumpled. She was always rumpled when she got up in the morning. It was as if she had a disorganized soul.

"Kayla Anson's been murdered," Faye told her. "In her car. The one you said the Jeep was chasing. Not just happened to be behind. Chasing."

"Somebody stole the Jeep and then they killed her," Zara

Anne said. "You're just jealous I knew it before you. Wiccans always have to be careful about their powers. Other people get jealous."

"I'm not getting *jealous* of your *powers*," Faye said.

"I could feel it the whole time they were driving by," Zara Anne said. "I've got the sight that way. I could feel the badness coming right out of that Jeep. That's why I didn't go and tell you about it. That's why I just waited until you came home. I didn't want you chasing that Jeep with all the badness in it."

"You're going to bring a million reporters out here, do you understand that?" Faye asked her. "You're going to bring Geraldo Rivera and Ricki Lake and I don't know who else. You're going to turn this place into a circus."

"It will be good for the movement. It will be good for people to see that we aren't just making it up."

"You're going to get a reporter from the *Weekly World News* to camp on our doorstep. They'll find aliens landing in my pumpkin patch. It will be nuts."

"You're only jealous because it's me instead of you. That's all this is. You think you have a right to be the big important one all the time."

"Fine. Wonderful. Then we'll let it all be you. When they start inundating this place, and clogging up the parking lot so that nobody can get to the stand, you can just move out and take a room at the Super 8 in Waterbury. You can clog up their parking lot and talk to reporters there."

"You're just jealous because it's me instead of you," Zara Anne said again.

The beets were all put out on the stand. She had a box of zucchini the size of jousting lances at the back that needed to be put out, too. Had she ever really made love to Zara Anne? Had she really done all those physical things, and allowed them to be done to her, that should only be done between two people who were very much in love?

And never mind the fact that Faye Dallmer hadn't been in love with anybody since her marriage went bad, or maybe even before.

Zara Anne was up at the house, wrapped in a quilt, watching television.

Faye just wondered what it was she really knew.

3

In the next day or two, they would release the body from the morgue and bring it to the Hitchcock Funeral Home in Watertown. That was where Margaret Anson had arranged to have the funeral, in spite of the fact that Kayla's lawyers were very much against it. Kayla's lawyers wanted the funeral to be in New York. In this one thing, Margaret had had the moral authority to resist. They couldn't very well tell a mother where and how to bury her own daughter, even if they thought the mother had never liked the daughter at all. In fact, Margaret knew, they knew that. They had all been thoroughly briefed by Robert, before he died. They all considered her the prime bitch of the Western world. It didn't matter, in this case. They didn't want to see themselves on the pages of *People* magazine, charged with persecuting the grieving mother.

Funerals and bank accounts—that was what this was going to come down to. That, and the reporters already camped outside her door, sitting there stretched along Sunny Vale road like a dismembered centipede. It was all over the place already, as she knew it would be, but she was ready for them. She had locks for the windows as well as the doors, and shades she could pull down tight. Right now the whole house was closed off. The gate at the bottom of the drive was locked. She could sit here in the big keeping room off the kitchen with her glass of sherry and not be bothered by them at all.

What kept coming back to her, what she couldn't get rid of, was the day of Kayla's delivery, at Lenox Hill Hospital in New York. By then, the hospitals had given up using twilight sleep. They were committed to using nothing at all.

"We want a drug-free delivery," her doctor had told her confidently. "It's what's best for the baby."

It was always what was best for the baby. The whole long stretch of that pregnancy, it had been as if Margaret herself had ceased to exist. No pain was supposed to be too great, no inconvenience too shattering, if what resulted was what was best for the baby. Margaret thought she had hated that baby from the third month of its gestation. She had hated the morning sickness and the bloating. She had hated not being allowed to take Contac when she had a cold or allergy medications when the pollen got high. She would have had an abortion if she could have done it without Robert knowing about it—but that would have been impossible, because Robert knew about everything. She would have gone ahead and taken the Contac and the antiallergy pills, except that she was afraid of the birth defects. She was afraid of what it would do to her life, to her self, if the baby she was carrying was born with too much damage. By that time she had hated Robert, too, of course. She had come to see him for what he was. She had come to understand that he would never mean anything more to her than money.

In Margaret Anson's perfect world, money and merit would go together. The people who really understood opera and art and history would be in charge of everybody else, and recognition would come for taste instead of for overwhelming effort. The truth was, Margaret didn't really have it all worked out, what she would like the world to be instead of what it was now. She only knew that she hated almost everything about what it was now, and what it had forced her to become. She was with the feminists on at least one thing, although she thought of most feminists as lower-class and overly fond of talking about their genitals. Marriage and prostitution were one and the same thing. You sold your body for money. You handed it over for sex and procreation. Robert hadn't been much interested in sex, in the end. He had wanted another child, to try for a son, but he could have gotten that much by presenting her with a loaded turkey baster.

When Kayla was small, she had raced around their big apartment in the city, falling from things, jumping on things. Nannies had despaired of her. Maids had tried to stay out of her way. Margaret had seen from the beginning that she was Robert's daughter and not hers. She had been born with all the vitality and all the crudeness of her father's less-than-admirable social class.

I will not have her here, Margaret thought now. It was the only thought she could hold in her head. Even this one glass of sherry was making her wobbly. These last two nights of not getting enough sleep had made her something worse.

The body could stay at the funeral home; that's what it could do. The body could stay there until it went to rot. Margaret had no intention of ever seeing it again. If there was a hell, she hoped that Kayla was in it. She hoped that the flames licked up from the molten lava on the ground and burned great blisters in that stupid girl's feet. At least she would no longer have to open *Town and Country* to see her daughter's face.

Life was not fair, that was what the problem was. Life had not been fair to her, to Margaret Anson.

And if life wasn't fair, somebody had to pay for it.

Six

I

All murder is random. That was what Gregor Demarkian's most formidable instructor at Quantico had said, when Gregor was young enough to think that murder was rare, except in war. Maybe the truth was that in those days murder *was* rare. It was the year before John F. Kennedy would be assassinated in Dallas. Television was full of happy families. Television news was careful to report only on those people who could be considered "significant." If the denizens of the local trailer park got liquored up and slaughtered each other at will, nobody in the nicer subdivisions on the other side of town would ever hear about it. If children were beaten to death by their mother's boyfriends, if they were left to starve and die by their mothers themselves— well, it all happened *over there,* in that part of town, and there was nothing more you could expect from those people. It didn't make any difference to *you.* Gregor remembered sitting at a small desk with a little writing-desk extension on one side, trying to take notes in a spiral notebook. He was not only young enough to still think that murder was rare, but young enough to still be uncomfortable with his size. He sometimes thought he was still growing taller, in his sleep, and that every morning when he woke the world around him was a little smaller. He imagined himself as Alice, growing larger. Any minute now, he would grow too big for his own apartment. His arms and legs would push through the windows and leave him trapped.

All murder is random. At the time, he had thought the man was insane. Murder was deliberate. That's why people were executed for it. He couldn't remember how many years it had taken him to understand what had been meant, or how thoroughly he had to agree with it.

Now he let Bennis pull her car up in front of the tiny white clapboard house on Caldwell green, and felt again how foolish it was not to be able to drive. He was an urban animal, but all those years in the Bureau should have egged him into it at one point or another. Lord only knows, he had spent enough of his career as an agent in cars. The problem was that somebody else had always had a car. Now he felt oddly silly—the Important Consultant, being chauffeured around like a ten-year-old with a Little League game.

Bennis put the car into park and leaned toward the windshield to take in the green and what surrounded it. Gregor was fascinated with it all himself. It was so—New England. So exactly what it was supposed to be. The not-quite-rectangular patch of brown grass at the center. The churches on each of the four sides: Congregationalist, Methodist, Presbyterian, Episcopal. The Congregationalist and Methodist churches were white. The Presbyterian and Episcopal were made of flat gray stone. The whole collection looked forbidding and completely empty.

"You'd never know that the Methodists are discussing holding blessings for same-sex marriages," Bennis said.

Gregor got his coat out of the little well behind the two front seats.

"I'll see you for dinner at the inn. I think we're going around and looking at lab work. At any rate, I don't think we're staying here. You ought to try to stay out of trouble."

"You ought to get a driver's license. Although I don't think you'd really be safe. Are you sure you don't want me to come in with you? Just to make certain that somebody's here?"

"Somebody's here." The tiny white house with the sign in front of it that said RESIDENT TROOPER had a driveway. Gregor pointed down the flat cut of it to the garage at the back, in front of which a state police car was parked in full view of whoever wanted to look. "The rest of them will be here in a few moments, I'm sure. Unless they're already here and parked somewhere out of sight. To make sure we don't all get caught doing this."

"You make it sound like you're about to rob a bank."

"We've been very lucky to avoid all the media nonsense that's going on out there," Gregor said. "They haven't caught up to you at the inn. They haven't caught up to me. It isn't going to last forever. You might try being careful with yourself this afternoon."

"I'm going to the mall. There's a new one in Waterbury. Gregor, do you know the JonBenet Ramsey case?"

"Yes."

"Do you know who did it?"

"Yes."

"And you're not going to tell me who it is? Why not?"

"For the same reason that the Denver police aren't making an arrest. They know who did it, too. They just can't prove it. Cases like that aren't really all that difficult, Bennis. They're sort of standard operating procedure. Every police detective anywhere who deals with homicide on a regular basis has half a dozen like it in a drawer somewhere, all of them officially unsolved. You have to be careful with them. More careful with them than you are with the others."

"Why?"

"Because juries want to bring back convictions in child murder cases. They don't like findings of not guilty when a child is dead. Even if the defendant doesn't look to be guilty. Even if they don't think the defendant is guilty. They want to convict somebody. What's got you started on JonBenet Ramsey?"

"I don't know," Bennis said. "I was wondering about this, I guess. About Kayla Anson. I was wondering if you knew who had killed Kayla Anson."

"I've only just got here, Bennis. I don't even know who the suspects are."

"Her mother."

"Who, as far as I know at the moment, was sitting with you at the time that the murder occurred, making conversation about lesbian painters in Paris in the twenties. Why are you in such a hurry to convict Kayla Anson's mother?"

"I've met her. Never mind. Are they all going to be there today, all the police officers from all the towns?"

"I don't know. But you're not going to be."

Gregor opened the car door and climbed out. There was a jack-o'-lantern on the tiny clapboard house's front stoop. It was the only sign of Halloween on Caldwell green. He leaned back into the car and gave Bennis a chaste peck on the lips. It was the best he could do. Contorted into that particular physical position, it was all he could do to get his lips properly puckered.

"Go to the mall," he said. "I'll talk to you later. Nothing is going to go on for the rest of today but procedure. You'd be bored if you were here."

"I know." She gave him a peck on the cheek to go with the one he had given her on the lips. "Take care of yourself."

"My biggest problem is going to be finding myself some decent food."

Gregor stepped back out of the car. He slammed the door shut after himself. Bennis rolled down her window and stuck her head out.

"I'll talk to you later," she said.

Then she drew her head back into the car and rolled the window up again. A moment later, the car was moving away from the curb and out onto the narrow country road. What did it say about this place that even its main roads were narrow?

Gregor put his coat over his shoulders and went up to the resident trooper's front door.

2

The resident trooper's name was Stacey Spratz, and he was very young. Gregor had noticed that the night before, when they had met for the first time under Bennis's watchful eye.

It hadn't been much of a meeting. Gregor had been too tired, and strung too tight, to be much help, or even to make much sense. All he and Stacey had been able to accomplish was to make it clear that, yes, Gregor would not mind looking into this particular case if the law enforcement agencies involved wanted him to—and no, Gregor did not charge fees for his work, although he did appreciate it if the people he helped out gave a donation to Foodshare or Mother Teresa's Missionaries of Charity. This business about not paying him always held people up. They had contingency funds in their budgets for this kind of thing. Why wouldn't he want to get paid? Gregor always found himself going into a long, convoluted explanation of something that should have been very simple. To be legitimately paid, he needed a private detective's license. He had no intention of getting a private detective's license.

That stopped them, too. Why wouldn't he want to get a private detective's license?

He went up to Stacey Spratz's front door, found the bell, and rang. You did not go from being a special agent of the Federal Bureau of Investigation—from being the founder and head of the FBI's behavioral sciences unit—to being a private detective. It was like starting out as Picasso and then going to work painting Mickey Mouse on clock faces.

Stacey Spratz opened the door and looked out. His face was tense. When he saw Gregor, he relaxed.

"Oh, it's you. I keep expecting to be invaded. They *have* been invaded, out in Washington Depot. Cam Borderman called and told me they've set up a press room right there on the premises. It was either that or have reporters crawling all over the building at all hours of the day and night. And they still find the idiots all over the place."

Stacey was headed toward the back of the house down a long narrow hall that went through the middle. The place was just as cramped as Gregor had expected it to be, with the added discomfort of having very low ceilings. Old, Gregor thought automatically. Probably as old as the churches. He had to duck to go through doorways.

Stacey Spratz did not have to duck. He was very short, for a man, and on top of that he was used to the house. He led Gregor into the kitchen and then motioned him to sit down at a round kitchen table. The table was covered with papers and file folders and Post-it notes stuck all over everything.

"Let me get you a cup of coffee," Stacey said. "Then I'll tell you where we're at. I talked to my captain this morning. You're officially on as a consultant as of this morning at eight o'clock. We had to get five people out of bed to authorize it, but nobody wants a mess on this one. Washington and Watertown are formally giving up jurisdiction to the state police—we don't know where she was killed yet anyway. It could even have been Morris. Morris will give up jurisdiction, too. I think we've got everything settled that has to be settled."

"I think so, too."

"The thing is," Stacey put a mug of coffee in front of Gregor, in spite of the fact that Gregor hadn't actually said he wanted any. "I mean. Well . . . I tried to head them off. But they want to have a press conference. A big press conference. With the governor."

Gregor thought this over. "Isn't the governor in Hartford?"

"Yeah, but he's from Middlebury. That's right next to Watertown. Anyway, he'll come out here. That's not the thing. The thing is, this is going to be one hell of a press conference. We've got people out here from the networks. From CNN. I don't know if you mind that kind of thing or not, but it scares the hell out of me."

"It's probably inevitable," Gregor pointed out. He tried the coffee. It was as bad as Father Tibor's. It might be worse. He put the mug down.

Stacey Spratz rubbed his hand across the side of his face. In spite of the youngness of it, Gregor could see where the lines would be, when they came. Stacey had the sort of pale skin light blonds often do in their teens and twenties. It went quickly to hell as they aged. Gregor's guess was that Stacey Spratz was not very bright. His virtues ran to loyalty and honesty and the desperate need to do good in a world he found inherently confusing. It was not a personality type Gregor would have chosen if he were doing the hiring for his own police force. Maybe it was just what was needed in the way of a resident trooper.

"Mr. Demarkian?" Stacey said.

"Sorry," Gregor said. "I was thinking about what you do. About what it consists of, being a resident trooper."

"Mostly it consists of getting Mark Wethersfield off the road when he's been drinking. And checking out break-ins. Which always turn out not to be break-ins. Not a lot goes on out here, Mr. Demarkian. We did have a murder out in Morris, back in ninety-one or ninety-two. At Four Corners. At the gas station there. This kid went in and shot his girlfriend and then he shot himself. Ex-girlfriend. She wanted to break up. They were both seventeen."

"We get that kind of thing in Philadelphia, too."

"I know. And they get it in Waterbury, too. The point is that we don't get much else. And we're all very—conscious, I guess the word is—we all know that we're in way over our heads. That this thing is beyond us. If you know what I mean."

"I know the feeling of being in over my head," Gregor said.

"I'm supposed to lay all this out for you and then take you out to Washington Depot for the press conference. If that's okay with you."

"That's fine with me."

This seemed to be not quite fine with Stacey Spratz. He was hesitating, as if he were expecting Gregor to do something else, want something else, make some objection. When that didn't happen, Stacey got up and got himself a second cup of coffee. Gregor didn't understand how he'd managed to drink the first.

"All right then," he said, coming back to the table and sitting down facing Gregor on the other side. "This is what we have, then."

3

This was the part about a case that Gregor liked best—the part where you could put the pieces on the table and make order out of chaos. Gregor was a very orderly man. That had as much to do with his success as a detective as any trained intellect he could be said to have, or any talent, either. Life was never completely orderly. There were always loose ends. Still, a crime had a narrative, if it was any kind of crime at all. The kind of crimes that were really something else—the violence of too much dope or too much liquor—didn't interest him at all.

Stacey Spratz was not an orderly man. He couldn't even be said to be reasonably neat. Before he could get started telling Gregor what had gone on the night Kayla Anson was murdered, he had to hunt through the papers on the kitchen table three times to find his notes.

Gregor abandoned his coffee, stood up, and began to put the papers on the table in neat stacks, sorted by type. He did it as much to give himself something to do as to be any great help to Stacey Spratz. He had no idea if this case would be furthered or hindered by having a stack he thought of as "Watertown police reports" separate from the one he thought of as "Washington police reports."

"Okay," Stacey said. "The thing is, earlier that evening, around four-thirty or five, Kayla Anson went into Waterbury. She went out to the Brass Mill Center, which is the new mall. It's actually in the town of Waterbury, right in the middle of it, right off Main Street. Not out in the country the way malls usually are. You see what I mean?"

"Yes," Gregor said. He just didn't see why it was important.

"Anyway, she went out there and did some shopping. She stopped at Waldenbooks. We talked to the manager. The manager knew her. Actually, most people did. She got around town a lot the past few months. Did I tell you she'd been expelled from her boarding school?"

"No."

"Well, she had. Christmas last year. Actually, I think what it was was that she was asked to stop out for a year. She was supposed to go back this January. She and her friend Annabel Crawford got thrown out together. From the Madeira School, out in Virginia."

"What for?" The Madeira School was the one Jean Harris had been headmistress of, before she drove up to Westchester and murdered Dr. Herman Tarnower.

"This Annabel Crawford was going to elope. Or said she was. With some local kid. And they'd been friends forever, so Kayla Anson helped her out by getting her horse out of the stables and parking it where Annabel could ride off on it. Do you know that some of these girls bring their own horses to boarding school with them?"

"I'd heard of it."

"Well, they got caught. Actually, if you ask me, I think Annabel was pulling some kind of stunt and got Kayla Anson involved in it. We all know Annabel out here. She's got more fake IDs than an Iranian terrorist. And she's something of a rip. I don't think she'd marry some local boy with no money and no prospects. He couldn't keep her in shoes."

"But they both got expelled."

"Annabel got *expelled* expelled—don't ever darken our door again. Kayla got held out for a year. Annabel had it coming. It wasn't the first time she'd pulled something. She was suspended for a term the year before, but I don't remember what that was about. Anyway, they came out here, because their families have houses here. Annabel's actually live in Washington Depot practically full-time. And Kayla's mother has that big yellow thing out on Sunny Vale Road. So they've been around almost full-time for nearly a year now."

"And they made friends?"

"Out at the country club their parents belong to, yeah, I

think so. The Swamp Tree Country Club. Out on Swamp Tree Road. They've all got names like that up here."

"Did they have jobs?"

"Not that I know of."

"Were they doing anything in particular? Volunteer work? Writing memoirs?"

"This fall they were coming out. Being debutantes. There was a big write-up about it in the *Litchfield County Times*. I don't understand much about that, but it seems to mean they had to go to a lot of parties. And give a lot of parties. I'm from out by Manchester. We don't do a lot of that kind of thing out there."

They did do a lot of that kind of thing in Philadelphia, but Gregor's understanding of it was hazy at best. He supposed that if he needed to understand it better than he did, he could always ask Bennis. Bennis had been a debutante.

"So," he said, "on the night of the murder—"

"Oh. Well. She went to Waterbury. She went to Waldenbooks. She stopped at the salad place at the food court and got herself some kind of veggie sandwich in a pita to go. The girl there remembered her, and we found the wrapping paper in the car when we found her. She bought a bunch of stuff at Sears. They didn't remember her there, but the bags were in the car. A pair of running shoes, good ones, Nikes. Three packages of white athletic socks. Three pairs of sweatpants and a sweatshirt. Plain solid gray. Nothing fancy."

"Was that like her? To buy clothes at Sears?"

"Well, it wasn't clothes exactly. If you see what I mean."

"Yes." Gregor did see what Stacey meant. "What happened next?"

"Well, that was it, really. She headed back to Washington Depot, except that she didn't take Route Eight, which she could have. She came back the regular roads through Watertown. Route Sixty-three, that would be, to One-oh-nine. A lot of people do that. They don't like the highway. Or they don't like it in the dark."

"All right. She was seen on the trip home?"

"She was seen on Route Sixty-three by a woman named Zara Anne Moss. You'll get to meet Zara Anne Moss. She's not exactly a reliable witness. She's not—you ever know anybody who claimed to be a witch?"

"You mean this woman says she saw Kayla Anson in tea leaves?"

"No, no. With ordinary eyesight, going by on Route Sixty-three sometime during the six o'clock news. Which fits, time wise. The thing is, Zara Anne Moss lives with Faye Dallmer—"

"I know Faye Dallmer," Gregor said. "She's the one—the organic everything woman. Who writes the books. And does the advice thing on the *Today* show."

"Right. She lives out here. Has a place on Sixty-three with a vegetable stand and sells quilts. That's how she started, actually. The other stuff came later. Anyway, she's, um, she's uh—"

"Gay."

"Right. And Zara Anne is her latest live-in. There have been a lot of them. They've all been a little flaky, but this one is way flaky. Anyway, Faye Dallmer has this refitted Jeep she uses to do truck farming stuff, and it looks like a monster but it goes fast, so kids like to steal it and drive it around. It happens all the time. And Friday, it looked like it had happened again. And Faye was out back somewhere doing some work, and Zara Anne noticed that the Jeep was gone, so she went out on the porch and looked around, and saw it coming, bad-assing down Sixty-three, going really fast. And following Kayla Anson's BMW."

"Following it?"

"Well, here's what we're not sure of. Zara Anne says following, but it might just have been behind there accidentally. There's no way to tell. She might actually have seen them half an hour apart. Anything."

"What happened to the Jeep?"

"Well, that's an odd thing. What usually happens is that the kids just bring it back. Faye doesn't even bother to call anybody anymore. But Friday it was a long time, hours, really, so about eleven Faye called the police in Watertown and they sent somebody out."

"And?"

"And they finally found it up in the Fairchild Family Cemetery in Morris. Turned over on its side way up on the hill. It's one of those really old cemeteries. Goes back before the Revolutionary War. They've always got trouble up there. Besides the Jeep that night there was a skeleton up there, sitting right on Martin and Henry's front porch, turned out it came from the anatomy exhibit at the Litchfield County Museum. But in case you're wondering, there was nothing in the Jeep that had anything to do with Kayla Anson, as far as we could tell. Although it was smashed up a lot, like it had been run into something."

"Kayla Anson's car?"

"More like a tree. But we're going to check that, too."

"What did happen to Kayla Anson's car?"

"That's a good question," Stacey Spratz said. "I saw it, like I told you, going through Morris like a bat out of hell around eight-ten and I let it go. And that's it. That's all anybody saw of it until your friend Bennis found it in the Anson garage and Kayla Anson in it."

"Was Kayla Anson in it when you saw it in Morris?"

"I've got no idea. I didn't get any kind of look at all at whoever was driving, and I didn't see if there was a passenger, either."

"So Kayla Anson could have been driving. Or she could have been being driven. Or she could have been dead in the car. Can you remember, where was she sitting in the car when her body was found?"

"Front passenger seat."

"Passenger seat."

"I know what you're thinking," Stacey said. "I've been thinking the same thing myself. She could have been alive when the car went by me in Morris. If I'd chased it instead of let it go, she could be alive. I've been over and over it. But I just can't figure out what else I could have done. The car was going at least ninety. It might have been a hundred.

I'm surprised everybody in the thing didn't end up dead on the road somewhere."

"But you called ahead to the Washington police."

"Yes, I did."

"And what did they do?"

"There wasn't much they could do. They sent a car out to the Morris line, but if the BMW was going like that, it would have been long gone by the time they got there."

"Is it far, from the town line to Kayla Anson's house?"

"It's practically a straight shot on One-oh-nine. Maybe five miles. Then a left turn and maybe fifty feet. And that's the Anson drive."

"I'm surprised nobody else heard the car. You'd think somebody would. Going at that speed. Or that Bennis or Margaret Anson would have heard it."

"Well," Stacey said, "I don't think your friend Bennis could have heard it. Not if it got to the house at twenty after eight or half past. She didn't get there herself until quarter to. If then. She had dinner at the McDonald's off Exit Eight on I-Eighty-four at ten minutes after eight. That's what she said she did, and we checked. Three people there recognized her. From stories about you. In *People* magazine."

"Ah," Gregor said.

He and Stacey both looked down at the dining room table, now covered with neat stacks of paper, not a thing out of place.

"Well," Stacey said, "I guess I'd better get you to this press conference. If I don't, they'll probably send somebody out to pick you up."

Seven

I

What Bennis Hannaford really wanted to do was to drive out to Margaret Anson's house and get a look at the garage—now, in the daylight, when she would be able to see what she was doing. Something had been bothering her about the garage ever since she had found Kayla Anson's body in it, but the more she thought about it, the less she was able to see what it was. She went over and over it in her mind. The big barnlike place. The car. The cement floor. The light from the one small window. When she came to the light, she always stopped and thought of it again, because there seemed to be something there that was important. Then she decided that it was lost to her. Maybe she was just obsessing on the scene because it had been such an awful scene, something she would rather have had no part in at all. Remembering what the light had looked like, falling over the tops of the cars, was so much easier than remembering what Kayla Anson's face had looked like in that same light.

In the end, she did drive out to Sunny Vale Road. It was actually on the way from Caldwell to Waterbury, except that she had to turn off 109 for a few feet to reach the front of the house. As it turned out, she didn't even do that. The trip was ridiculous on the face of it. She wouldn't have been able to get a look at the garage unless Margaret Anson had opened the gate and let her in. That was as likely to happen as Tinker Bell was likely to get a religious vocation. Once she had got to the road, though, Bennis could see that she wouldn't even be able to go to the front door and ask. Sunny Vale Road was packed with cars and minivans and people.

Media, Bennis said to herself, slowing down as she went up the hill. She recognized one or two of the people pacing back and forth on the narrow blacktop. She felt her lungs begin to convulse again and let herself cough. There was nobody here to lecture her about smoking. This time the cough went on and on, giving way suddenly to dry heaves. When it died down, Bennis found herself shaking.

When this was over, she was going to have to go someplace and get it checked out. That was what she was going to have to do.

She slowed the car literally to a crawl. It was a good thing there was nobody behind her on the road. It was a good thing she didn't want to go down Sunny Vale, too. She could see the CNN van, open at the back, with people jumping in and out of it. She could see a blonde woman she was sure was one of the anchorwomen for WVIT, without a coat and walking in little circles to ward off the cold. Why were local anchorwomen always blonde?

Bennis put her foot on the gas; 109 was hilly and long. When she got to the center of Morris, she slowed, because the Morris cops often had a car out by the traffic light, on alert for people who might be speeding. All of this part of Connecticut looked to her, suddenly, shabby and small, pinched, at war with modernity.

At the blinking red light at Four Corners, Bennis turned right onto the Litchfield Road. This was the way Kayla Anson had come the night she died, except that she was going in the other direction. Bennis tried to imagine it all in the dark. Halloween was now only two days away. The little red fabric store had a banner outside with a pumpkin on it. One of the houses that sat very close to the edge of the road had a jack-o'-lantern and a straw man arranged on the steps of its stoop. It was a gray day—the kind of day, later in the year, when Bennis would have expected snow.

She rode the Litchfield Road to its intersection with Route 6, when it became Main Street in Watertown. She watched people standing in little groups in front of the big white Methodist church and then, a little ways down, other people making their way to their cars in the massive parking lot that belonged to the Roman Catholics at St. John the Evangelist. St. John the Evangelist was made of brick, as were most of the buildings on Main Street. Some of the stores had Halloween cut-out pumpkins in their plate glass windows. Toto Mundi, one of them was called. It looked filled with the sort of all-cotton, peasant-inspired "natural" wear that had been popular when Bennis was in college, with the same people who had tried to learn to play the dulcimer and listened to Sally Rodgers on Wheatland Records.

People who wear Birkenstocks, Bennis thought idly. The red brick of central Main Street gave way to a sort of strip-mall-like area where one chain store seemed to follow another—Brooks Drugs to Dunkin' Donuts to Burger King to Carvel. The road veered off and became Straits Turnpike. A short stretch of green and residential housing gave way to yet another strip-mall-like area, this one full of car dealerships and offering K-mart and McDonald's.

"Watertown in the gateway," Abigail had warned her, when she'd packed her off to try to "talk sense" to Margaret Anson. "It's half Litchfield County and half not. You'll see."

Bennis saw the signs for I-84 and headed for those.

There was something else that had been nagging her, of course, as well as the problem with the garage. Gregor was here, and she was glad he was here, but his coming had not given her the peace she had expected it to. Maybe he had been too tired, what with all the hauling up and down the countryside she had put him through on almost no notice. Maybe whatever was wrong was entirely her fault. That was more than possible. She didn't think she had ever in her life been able to maintain a relationship for more than a year. Usually, once she had sex with a man, the connection lasted barely a few months. She didn't think she could be that stupid about Gregor—about somebody she had known for so long, and had cared about so much—but the possibility was there. The possibility was always there. Sometimes, when she tried to stay with men after she knew she should leave them, she started to hate them.

It was age that was doing it to her, she thought, age that kept getting in the way, making her options unclear. She was over forty years old. She couldn't shake the conviction that she should be settled by now, that she should have done something with her life besides produce a whole raft of best-selling sword-and-sorcery fantasy novels. Women her age had husbands and children and houses and volunteer work as well as careers. They had families and commitments. She never seemed to do anything but bounce from one thing to another, on the emotional level. Even her commitment to Cavanaugh Street was tentative, and alienated in conception. She had her apartment and her routines, but she was always aware of being the only non-Armenian American on the block, the odd woman out, the curiosity. It said something about her, she thought, that she was only really comfortable when she was absolutely sure she didn't fit. It said something even less flattering that she was so protective of her isolation—that she sometimes felt, in dreams, as if she would rather die than give it up.

She had gotten on I-84 without realizing she was doing it. She saw the signs looming up for Exit 23 and headed toward them. She had directions from the woman at the desk at the inn, and so far there seemed to be nothing wrong with them. The highway was broad and well-kept, but it was also stark and inhuman. The Waterbury that flanked its sides was run-down and dispirited. Bennis was aware of feeling much better than she had.

She went down the long ramp that led to what seemed like three or four little mini-exits, then off onto a short country road with signs clearly posted saying: MALL. She followed the arrows and saw that she couldn't have missed it. God, but she hated malls. She hated them almost as much as she hated reruns of *Gilligan's Island*, which at the moment were Father Tibor Kasparian's favorite method of relaxation. Still, she couldn't think of anywhere else to go.

She entered the mall at the far end, near Sears, because it seemed to her easier to get in that way. She parked in the half-empty little section of lot and got out and made sure that all her doors were locked. She was doing things by rote, moving because she had to move. She couldn't just stand still. Past the mall she could see the middle of Waterbury, right there, with its storefront windows boarded up and the boards spray painted with uninspired graffiti. People came here on foot. She could see three of them walking down the hill in her direction, women dressed in spandex, with too much hair.

She was almost to the little-found entryway when it struck her—what it had been about the garage, what was wrong with the light.

It was coming from the wrong direction, that was what was wrong with it. Or some of it was. The light on the tops of the cars was coming from the little window on the wall, but the light that had struck Kayla Anson's face, that had made it possible to see that Kayla Anson was dead, that had had to come from somewhere else.

Behind. And lower. Maybe. Somewhere.

Bennis shoved her hands into the pockets of her jacket and tried to think.

2

There had been a man out from the Litchfield County Museum all Saturday afternoon, but Martin Chandling had had hopes that Sunday would be better. Who worked on Sundays, after all, especially out here? People went to church, that's what they did on Sundays, and then after church they went to the Farm Shop or Denny's to get something to eat. Catholics ate a lot when they went out, because they'd had to fast all morning in order to take Communion. Protestants ate less, but still enough to make them fat. People got fatter and fatter every day. Martin had seen them. It was pitiful, what went walking around in the middle of town these days, and dressed in stuff so tight you could see their nipples right through the fabric. In Martin's opinion, no woman had a right to dress like that unless she looked like

Gwyneth Paltrow. In Henry's opinion, it was a good thing if he got a chance to see nipples.

They were sitting together at the breakfast table, eating toast and coffee and arguing about the paper, when the car drove up. The paper was full of stories about the elections. There was even a picture of Monica Lewinsky on page six, next to a story about the "moral backlash" the *Waterbury Republican* thought was going to happen to Democrats running for Congress. Martin thought the *Waterbury Republican* was very aptly named. They hadn't endorsed a Democrat at that paper since Franklin Delano Roosevelt, and maybe they hadn't endorsed him. Or maybe they had. Martin didn't really pay much attention to the paper. He was just tired of stories about Monica Lewinsky.

The car parked right on the grass at the side of the house, as if there weren't a perfectly good dirt drive to put a car on. Henry looked up over the top of his section of the paper and said, "Christ on a crutch. It's what's-his-name. Back again."

"Jake Sturmer," Martin said. He was the one who had written the name down on their calendar yesterday afternoon, so that they would have a record of who had been here and why. "Different car, though."

The car yesterday had been a little red Toyota, with the words *Litchfield County Museum* stenciled in white on the doors. This car today was a much larger Volvo, and it gave Martin a great deal of satisfaction to see it. He had thought from the first time he saw Jake Sturmer that the man was the kind who ought to own a Volvo.

Henry had put the paper down on the table and was standing up. "What can he possibly want? We went all over it with him yesterday."

"Well," Martin said reasonably, "we did have his skeleton. I mean, it was in our possession."

"It still didn't have anything to do with us."

"Maybe he didn't get all the parts of it and he wants to look for something that's missing."

Henry was out of the kitchen. Martin could hear his heavy boots, clunking down the hall. He finished his own coffee and stood up himself. The last thing he wanted to do today was to talk to Jake Sturmer about the skeleton, or about anything else. Halloween was only two days away, for God's sake. If they didn't get some work done and the place protected, all hell was going to break loose on the night. It didn't matter that they didn't usually have much trouble. They'd been in all the papers now, what with the skeleton, and with that girl dying at the same time, and not all that far from here—Martin could just see how it was going to be. There were going to be a couple of dozen teenagers out here on Tuesday, and half of them were going to want to get laid on the graves.

The other half were going to be girls.

Martin got up and headed outside himself. Henry was standing on the porch, talking to Jake Sturmer over the rail. A wind was blowing through their chimes, making the world sound full of metal.

"So," Martin said, coming out.

"I was just telling your brother here that there are a few little details we have to clear up," Jake Sturmer said, "just a few little things that are bothering me. I was hoping the two of you wouldn't mind."

Jake Sturmer was a small man, short and wiry. His hair was cut very close to his head, and his small mustache was neatly trimmed. Today he was wearing jeans and a flannel shirt and a black cotton sweater. Yesterday he had been wearing jeans and a flannel shirt and a blue cotton sweater. It was like a uniform, the I-moved-out-here-from-New-York-City uniform. Or one of them. This was really the I-moved-out-here-from-New-York-City-with-a-big-fat-stock-portfolio uniform. There was another one—consisting of heavy leather sandals, batik print peasant blouses, and wool ponchos made in Guatemala—for the people who had moved out here from New York City to go back to the land.

"It's two days before Halloween," Martin pointed out. "We're not ready."

"Ready?" Jake Sturmer looked confused.

"For the invasion," Henry said. "Christ on a crutch. What more can you possibly want to know? We came back from finding that damned car overturned in our own grave-yard and there was your skeleton. If you ask me, it's all connected. Whoever took the car took the skeleton."

"Well, yes, Mr. Chandling. I think that's what the police are thinking of—"

"So there's nothing we can tell you about it," Martin said. "That's what we're trying to say here. We don't know anything about it. We didn't hear anything we didn't go investigate. We went over all this stuff—"

"Yes," Jake said. "I know. But the thing is, I just real-ized."

"Realized what?" Henry asked him.

Jake Sturmer was energized. "It was while I was in the shower this morning that I realized. I drove to get to your place, you see, so it wasn't clear at first, because of the way the roads go. You have to go around. But if you didn't have to use the roads, then we'd be right up there." He pointed into space behind the house.

"What would be right up there?" Martin asked.

"The museum," Jake said. "It's right up there. Right through that stand of trees. It's maybe a thousand yards from here. You could have walked it. I could have. Any-body could have. So you see, it makes more sense than we thought it did. For the skeleton to have ended up here."

"Okay," Martin said.

"It's an invitation to Lyme disease, that's what it is," Henry said. "It's crazy. Those trees are thick."

"It's not much farther, if you go around the side of them," Jake Sturmer said. "Then there's a little field. You could even have driven the Jeep. It has those big wheels. It's supposed to go over terrain. That's the point."

"I don't see what we're getting at here," Martin said.

Jake Sturmer hesitated, as if he didn't either—which he

might not, Martin thought, because he was so obviously the sort of man who needed to do things. Some people should never retire from their jobs. It made them anxious and over-wrought.

"Well," Jake said finally, "I was just going to ask. If you'd mind. If I walked it myself. First through the woods and then across the field."

"Why?" Henry asked.

"I don't know. To see if I could find anything. To see if—I don't know."

"Asshole," Henry said.

"I don't see how it would do any harm to let him walk around in the trees," Martin said.

"I didn't say it would do any harm," Henry said.

"I'm just going to go up there and check it out," Jake said. "I won't bother you at all. I promise you. I just want to—look around."

"Go right ahead," Martin said.

"Asshole," Henry said again.

Henry turned around and stomped back through the front door, slamming it behind him. The sharp noise made Jake Sturmer jump.

"Well," he said, looking Martin up and down. "I guess I'll just go on up. If you don't mind."

"Don't mind at all," Martin said.

"Right," Jake said.

He smiled weakly and then took over, looking back over his shoulder every few steps to see if Martin was still watching him. Martin seemed to be, but he wasn't. He was looking up into the stand of trees that started maybe thirty yards from the house and covered the rise of the hill at that end of the property. At lot of things out here were close together, but you didn't realize they were. The roads were odd, and there were so many trees. He couldn't believe that anyone would come down through that stand in pitch dark-ness carrying a human skeleton, even one that had been cleaned and polished to make an exhibit in a museum.

"Martin?" Henry called from inside the house.

Martin turned away from the sight of Jake Sturmer plodding through the thick underbrush at the start of the trees and went back into the house.

3

Out at the Swamp Tree Country Club, Annabel Crawford was sitting at a large round table near the bar, sipping neatly from what was supposed to be a Virgin Mary. A Virgin Mary was what the bartender had served her. She'd bloodied it up on her own with a couple of little airline bottles of vodka. On the other side of the room, at another table, Tommy Haggerty was sitting with a big groups of boys, ignoring her. He was still furious at her for taking the car and leaving him stranded at the Lucky Eight. By now, Annabel had come to the decision that everything that had happened had been his fault, and that she didn't want to see him again anyway, never mind sleep with him. She could do much better if all she was looking for was somebody to sleep with. She could do much better just by standing up in the middle of this room and announcing that she wanted to get laid.

The bloodied Virgin Mary tasted raw. Annabel wished that everybody wasn't so wrapped up in the press conference that was supposed to happen any minute now, that people could talk about anything—*anything*—that wasn't the murder of Kayla Anson. She also wished that she were someplace else besides this table, anchored unmercifully to the low droning voice of Mallory Martindale. Annabel Crawford had never had any use for Mallory Martindale. Fat girls made her furious. They were only taking their neuroses out on themselves.

". . . so you see," Mallory was saying, "I've decided not to come out, and I've got that magnificent dress, the Carolina dress, that you were saying you liked so much. And of course she doesn't do copies. So you couldn't have it.

But since I'm not coming out, I'm not going to need it. If you see what I mean."

"Why aren't you coming out?" Annabel asked. "That doesn't make any sense."

"I never wanted to come out," Mallory said. "It was my mother's idea. I'm going to nursing school. I just finally made her see reason."

"I can't imagine not coming out," Annabel said. "You won't get invited to any of the parties."

Mallory Martindale was drinking a vanilla Coke. It looked thick and syrupy, even in the glass.

"I thought you might like to buy the dress," she said. "The Carolina dress. You'd have to take it in. But you said you liked it. And it's never been worn. And I'd charge a lot less for it than Carolina would if you got if from her."

"I don't really think you've got your mother's permission to do this," Annabel said. "I think you're trying to put something over on her and then when she finds out all hell is going to break loose. And I'm in enough trouble already."

"All right. I'll ask Bronwyn Kidd. She liked it, too."

Bronwyn Kidd was one of the Goody Girls, as Annabel thought of them. She had gone through four perfect years at Choate-Rosemary Hall and was now at Vassar, where she was intending to major in something esoteric and intellectual, like philosophy. Annabel's mother was always pointing to Bronwyn Kidd and her two best friends whenever Annabel said that it really, really hadn't been her fault that all the trouble had started.

"So," Mallory Martindale said.

"Wait a minute." Annabel got up and brought her glass back to the bar. The bartender made her another Virgin Mary and handed it over. Annabel came back to the table and took two more airline bottles of vodka out of her bag.

"Excuse me," she said. "Right now, I have every intention of getting thoroughly drunk."

"Is there a reason for that?"

"Yes," Annabel said. "Because I want to."

"They know you're doing it, you know. Or at least, the bartender does. What are you going to do if he throws you out?"

"He won't throw me out. He just won't let me drive home. Which is beside the point anyway, since I don't have a car. My mother will have to drive me home."

"Won't she be upset? At the drinking?"

"No more upset than she ever has been before. We were talking about the dress."

Mallory Martindale looked down into her vanilla Coke and then looked up again. "Do you have any more of— whatever that is? What you're drinking?"

"Vodka?"

"Whatever. Could I have some to put in my Coke?"

"I think it's rum you usually put in Coke."

"Do you have any rum?"

"No," Annabel said.

Mallory shrugged. "I'd take fifteen hundred dollars for the dress. It cost my father nearly six thousand. And it wouldn't be hard to get it taken in. It's not the kind of thing that needs to be precisely fitted anyway. I thought vodka tasted good in everything. I thought vodka didn't have a taste."

Annabel reached into her bag, got out another bottle of vodka, and handed it over. She was not drunk, but she thought she could get that way, if she worked at it. Now she thought she would like to see Mallory Martindale drunk.

"You're different," she said accusingly.

Mallory Martindale dumped vodka in her drink and smiled.

Eight

I

The press conference was due to be held at the Washington Police Department—Washington Depot, it turned out, was the unofficial name given to a part of the town, not the whole town itself. There were other sections of town with names. Stacey Spratz drove Gregor through at least one of them, called New Preston. He also drove Gregor past some of the most spectacular houses Gregor had ever seen, even more impressive than the big ones in the best parts of the Main Line suburbs. Large brown-and-beige Tudors and white clapboards sat high on hills so steep Gregor had no idea how anybody managed to mow the lawns. Blank-faced brick Federals with half a dozen additions sprawled across three hundred feet of frontage, looking more like institutions than private residences, but private nonetheless. No more than a third of the roads they passed had road signs.

"People steal them," Stacey Spratz said when Gregor asked. "The theory is, if you don't know where you are, you don't belong here. And if you don't belong here, you've probably got it in mind to steal something, so we're not going to make it any easier for you. Although I don't know why they think somebody's going to come out here and steal something. Nobody like that even knows this stuff is here."

This seemed true enough. It seemed unlikely that some ghetto gang from Hartford or New Haven would come all the way out here to rob a ten-thousand-square-foot house, when they could take the bus into one of the nearer suburbs and rip off something there. Still, Gregor found the effect unsettling. The Main Line was a rather straightforward place. Rich people lived there, in sight of one another, and nobody who entered the precincts of Bryn Mawr or Radnor expected anything different. Out here the impression was given, possibly deliberately, that the area was nothing more than a country way station, an old New England outpost that had more in common with small towns in Vermont than pricey suburbs on the Gold Coast. In some ways, the impression was very much wrong.

The Washington Police Department was in a small brick building on a side street in the middle of what Gregor was coming to think of as a moderate-sized town. Before he'd seen Morris, and Caldwell, he would have called Washington "small." Stacey Spratz pulled up to the curb outside the parking lot. He had to, because the parking lot was full.

"Here we are," he said.

He and Gregor both looked at the cars and minivans crowding the small space in front of the police station's doors. A small podium had been set up on the steps, with a wooden lectern backed by half a dozen chairs. The lectern had a microphone on it, with cables running down and off to the side. A lot of the people in the minivans had microphones, too, big boom ones. Cables for camera feeds were everywhere, but Gregor saw few nationally recognizable faces. Cokie Roberts and Sam Donaldson were probably still enmeshed in presidential scandals. Dan Rather had never had a taste for this kind of thing.

"I was hoping we'd get somebody famous," Stacey Spratz said, "but none of the really big reporters came. You figure it's the elections?"

"Probably," Gregor said.

Stacey got out of the car. "There's some guys in there want to talk to you. Mark Cashman. He's on the PD here. Tom Royce. He's with the ME's office. You know we got a central state medical examiner's office?"

"No."

"Yeah, well, we have. Dozens of small towns like this. Each of them gets a murder maybe once every twenty years. I think if we go around back we can avoid all the cameras until the press conference starts. And it won't start until the governor gets here."

"How are you sure he's not already here?"

"No limousines."

This made sense. Gregor let Stacey Spratz lead him up the street past the parking lot and then around the back on the lawn. There was a door back there, but no path going to it. It made Gregor wonder if the door had been put there only to cover contingencies, like fires or raids. Who would raid the police station in Washington, Connecticut?

Stacey climbed the two little steps in front of the door and knocked. After a certain amount of fuss, it was opened to them. Gregor wondered irritably why they didn't just establish a ritual—*Halt! Who goes there?*—and be done with it.

The door opened onto a back hall, all white walls and shiny fixtures. There was a stainless steel water fountain along one wall. There were also too many people here for a Sunday afternoon, and way too many people in suits.

"Security for the governor," Stacey said, waving at the men as they passed.

Gregor let himself be led into a small room with a large table in it—a small conference room, maybe, or a place to eat lunch. The two men sitting at the table rose when he entered. One of them was as young as Stacey Spratz, but far less raw. The other was middle-aged and in a bad mood.

"Mark Cashman," Stacey Spratz said, pointing to the young one. He turned to the other and said, "Tom Royce. This is Gregor Demarkian. Our consultant."

"Glad to meet you." Mark Cashman held out his hand.

Gregor took it. Mark released him and sat down again. Tom Royce didn't offer a hand, and didn't look like he wanted to sit down. Instead, he gestured at the pile of papers in the middle of the table and shrugged.

"Did anybody tell Mr. Demarkian that we don't actually have anything yet? Anything conclusive, that is? Is there a *point* to this charade beyond getting our esteemed governor's face in the papers right before the election?"

"I'll tell you what the *point* is," Mark Cashman said. "The *point* is that I don't want to be left out to hang on this by myself, that's what the *point* is. I don't have the firepower and I don't have the authority."

"Any police detective has the authority," Tom Royce said.

"You weren't here yesterday afternoon when those lawyers descended. Jesus God. It was like something out of a John Grisham novel. It was worse."

"What lawyers?" Gregor asked, in as neutral a tone as he could manage.

Mark Cashman got out of his chair again. "Her lawyers. Kayla Anson's. From some big firm in New York. They handle her money."

"And they were out here?" Gregor asked.

"You bet."

"Why?"

"They closed her accounts at the banks and those places," Mark Cashman said. "They just came in and shut it all down. The ones at the local banks, I mean. She had this checking account at Webster."

"They could do that on a Saturday?"

"Well, they did it. That's the thing, isn't it? They did all kinds of things, on a Saturday, that maybe you and I couldn't do. And they don't talk worth a damn."

Gregor considered this. "Did they say they were interested in anything else? Besides closing her accounts? Besides the money?"

"They asked to be kept informed on the progress of the investigation." Mark Cashman's voice was dry. "I thought the whole time that they'd do better just bribing the hell out of somebody to feed them the news, and maybe they did. They were certainly well-heeled enough to manage that kind of thing."

Gregor sat down at the table. The papers in the middle of it, unlike the ones on Stacey's table in Caldwell, were actually in use. Gregor saw several black-and-white photographs of what he was sure was the body of Kayla Anson, spilling out of her car. He pulled one of them toward him and looked at it. She had been alive when she had been strangled. If she hadn't been, her eyes would not have protruded in that characteristic way.

"Those don't amount to much," Tom Royce said. "We'll have better ones coming in a day or two. Those were—just to be going on with."

"Tom wanted to have a little show-and-tell with the governor," Mark Cashman said.

"Well, you'd think he'd take an interest, wouldn't you? Even him. This is going to be an enormous case. As big as JonBenet Ramsey. You'd think he'd at least pay attention."

"He'll talk to Dr. Lee when Dr. Lee gets back," Mark Cashman said. Then he turned to Gregor and explained, "That's Dr. Henry Lee. The state medical examiner. Big wheel. Testified in the O. J. trial. He's on vacation in Colorado. He's flying back tonight."

Gregor had heard of Dr. Henry Lee. Now he put the photograph of Kayla Anson back on the table and said, "She was alive when she was strangled."

Tom Royce shook his head. "That's my guess, too, but it's still a guess until we're finished running all the tests. And until Dr. Lee has had a chance to check over the work. This one isn't going out of the office without his personal say-so."

"But you were the one who actually examined the body?" Gregor asked.

"Yesterday morning, yeah. I did an autopsy and set up the lab work."

"And?"

Tom Royce sighed. "And it looks to me like she was strangled and strangulation was how she died. The cord was still around her neck, by the way."

"What kind of cord?"

"A white nylon shoelace. New. The kind you use for athletic shoes."

"She had a whole package of them in one of the bags from Sears," Mark Cashman said. "You know she'd been to Sears?"

"Mr. Spratz told me."

"Stacey," Stacey said automatically.

"The problem with the shoelaces is that they're every-where," Mark Cashman said. "We ran across a half dozen of them in Margaret Anson's kitchen the night of the mur-der. They were sitting in a kitchen drawer right next to the mudroom. You couldn't go anywhere in the rich part of Litchfield County without finding them by the dozens. At the Swamp Tree Country Club. At Rumsey Hall and Taft. Everybody's athletic these days."

"Rich people have always been athletic," Tom Royce said.

"What about the strength required to get the job done?" Gregor asked. "Was she a strong young woman? Would she have struggled?'

Tom Royce shifted uncomfortably from foot to foot. "Here's where we get into territory I don't like. I really couldn't tell you that unless I'd talked to Dr. Lee. There are things—"

"What things?"

"Well, for one thing, how much strength was required would depend on whether or not she was conscious when she was strangled. She could have been alive and not been conscious."

"Do you have reason to believe she wasn't conscious?"

"Sort of. Maybe. But it's all speculation. Completely speculation. I don't have any proof of it at all."

"Would you like to tell me proof of what?" Gregor asked.

Tom Royce started to pace. From the way Mark Cash-man was staring at Tom, Gregor knew that this was the first of this Tom had mentioned to anybody. Holding back the information wasn't going to do him any good, at least with the Washington Police Department. Tom's pacing was jerky and uneven. He kept taking his hands out of his pock-ets and putting them back in again.

"Okay," Tom said. "This isn't even speculation. This is a guess. A pure and simple guess. I think she was hit on the back of the head."

"Why?" Gregor asked him.

"If you mean what makes me think so, it's because she had a bruise. On her forehead. Her left temple just above the eye."

"And that makes you think she was hit on the back of the head?'

"And fell forward into the steering wheel and got a bruise. Yes. That's it exactly."

"But there was no mark on the back of the head?'

"No obvious mark, no. But there are ways to do that. You can knock somebody out cold without causing any visible damage. And that's a good place to go for, because it's effective but it's covered with hair. Especially in women. Lots of hair. So if you do some damage, it's not necessarily going to be seen."

"But what about the autopsy? Didn't that reveal any evidence of concussion?'

"I don't know. What I have is inconclusive as hell."

"I see."

Tom Royce sat down abruptly. "If Henry responds the way you're doing, I'm dead in the water. But nothing else makes much sense. She was a young woman in good health and good shape. She played a lot of tennis. She worked out. There should have been—I don't know. More signs of a struggle. Something. She should have kicked out or hit at things—"

"Maybe she did," Mark Cashman said. "Maybe she wasn't killed in the car. I've said before—"

"She was killed in the car," Tom Royce said. "*I've* said before. She was killed sitting in the passenger seat of that car. If she hadn't been, there would have been other kinds of bruising that came from getting her in there, and there wasn't anything like that at all. Not a thing."

"Not a thing," Gregor repeated.

He was just about to ask them all the most obvious question—what was Kayla Anson doing in the *passenger* seat of a car she'd been driving when she left Waterbury?—when the door to the little conference room swung open and a harried middle-aged woman came bursting in.

"The governor's here," she announced dramatically, "and he's got about half the state with him, and I don't know what to do next. You guys had better come on out and take care of him before something goes wrong and I get blamed for it."

"When Ella Grasso was governor of this state," Tom Royce said, "she could get to a press conference with fewer people than Elvis's entourage in attendance."

"Tom is a Democrat," Stacey Spratz said. "Let's go."

2

Gregor Demarkian had never seen the governor of the State of Connecticut in person before. The only time he had ever seen him in action on television was after the 1997 mass shootings at Connecticut Lottery headquarters in Newington, when a disgruntled employee just returned from medical leave had shown up for work armed to the teeth and then walked around the facility blasting away at one lottery corporation executive after another. Gregor could remember, in the aftermath of that case, thinking that for once the killer had got it right. He had gone after the people in power instead of the people he worked with, although that was going to be cold comfort to the families of the people who had died. All Gregor remembered about the governor was a round fair face at a press conference—that, and a very good suit.

"The governor doesn't really travel with an entourage the size of Elvis's," Stacey Spratz said unnecessarily. "From what I hear, he's actually pretty easy to work with. You should hear some of the stories going around about some of the others."

Gregor had a few stories of his own about various government officeholders, including two speakers of the House and a president, left over from his days at the Federal Bureau of Investigation. He let himself be led down the narrow corridor to the front of the building. The governor was standing with a small clutch of people near the station's front counter, enveloped in a very good winter coat. This governor seemed to like good clothes. Bennis Hannaford would have approved.

"Governor?" Stacey Spratz said, "I'm Stacey Spratz, of the state police. I'm the resident trooper in Caldwell? And this is Gregor Demarkian."

The governor's face did not look blank, even for an instant. Either he'd been very well briefed for this meeting, or he liked reading true crime stories in *The New York Times Sunday Magazine*. He put his hand out and grabbed Gregor's.

"Mr. Demarkian," he said. "You have no idea how grateful I am that you agreed to come. We're all grateful. This is a terrible situation. The murder of any young person is a terrible situation, but the ramifications here—"

"Governor?" It was one of the men in the plain black suits.

The governor dropped Gregor's hand and turned away. "Are we ready?"

"You'd better be ready," somebody else said. "They're ready to eat raw meat out there. And they're cold."

"Does everybody know what it is we're doing?" the governor asked.

A young woman raced up to Gregor and brushed his hair out of his eyes. She had a clipboard and her hair held back in the kind of hairband Hillary Clinton had favored before the professional handlers had gotten to her.

"The governor's going to make a short statement," she told Gregor, "and then he's going to introduce you and you're supposed to make a short statement. Just that you're glad to be here and that you'll help in any way possible. That kind of thing. You don't actually have to say anything. Would you like to have something written out for you?"

"No," Gregor said.

"It wouldn't be any trouble. In fact, I've already got something. I took the liberty—"

"No," Gregor said again.

"It will be all right," the governor said. "Mr. Demarkian has handled press conferences before. I've seen him."

"If they try to ask you any questions, don't answer," the young woman said. "Or don't be too specific. Are you sure you're going to be all right?"

"Let's go," the governor said.

Somebody opened the police station's front doors. Gregor wondered what a person would do if he actually needed police protection at this moment. Nobody who didn't know about the back door would even be able to get into the station. Was the dispatcher sending out cars when people called in? He hadn't seen a dispatcher.

The governor stepped outside first, followed by two men Gregor assumed to be either aides or security personnel. The young woman in the hairband pushed him out immediately afterward, followed by Stacey Spratz and Mark Cashman. Tom Royce stayed behind. As soon as the group of men filed out onto the station steps, the people in the minivans came to life. Men with cameras on their shoulders moved in close. Gregor saw that, between the time he and Stacey Spratz had left the car on the side of the road and now, somebody had put up extra folding chairs.

"Sit here," the young woman in the hairband told Gregor. Then she nodded at the governor and retreated.

At a federal press conference, there would have been more of a sense of ceremony. Here, although there was a press officer to make introductions and serve as a sort of informal director of the proceedings, he seemed to be mostly making it up as he went along. He stood at the lectern, leaning toward the microphone, until the people in the parking lot started to settle down. Then he said, "Ladies and gentlemen, the governor will speak first, followed by a short statement from Gregor Demarkian. When Mr. Demarkian is finished talking, the governor will take questions."

"Will Mr. Demarkian take questions?" somebody asked.

"Yes," the press officer said.

"What about somebody from the medical examiner's office? What about somebody from the police?" somebody
else asked.

"The medical examiner's office has no statement to
make at this time," the press officer said, "and will not have
such a statement until Dr. Lee returns from Colorado and
can review the evidence. The Washington Police Department also has no statement to make at this time."

"What about the state police?" a third person asked. "I
thought this was being handled by the state police."

The press officer ignored the question, and the statement,
and everything else that was going on in the parking lot.
He leaned into the microphone and said, "Ladies and gentlemen, the governor."

The governor stepped up to the lectern, and Gregor let
his mind drift. The press officer should have said "the governor of the State of Connecticut" instead of just "the governor." It would have sounded better. This press conference
should have been held inside someplace, at the town hall
or in a movie theater. That way it would have been warmer
and less chaotic. They should have announced a time limit
for questions. It would have helped keep things from getting out of hand.

The governor stepped back. He did not sit down. The
press officer went back to the lectern and announced, "Mr.
Gregor Demarkian."

Gregor went up to the lectern. He never took the canned
statements he was offered before press conferences, but
sometimes he thought he should. He never really knew
what to say in situations like this.

"I have been asked," he said, "by the governor's office
and by the Connecticut State Police, to provide consultation
and aid in the investigation into the murder of Kayla Anson,
and I have agreed to do so most willingly. I will be serving
in an advisory capacity only. I hope that my experience,
both in the Federal Bureau of Investigation and more recently as a consultant to police departments faced with dif-

ficult homicide investigations, will prove valuable for all
the parties concerned in this case."

Gregor stepped away from the lectern and sat down. He
thought he'd sounded more bureaucratic than most bureau-
crats. At the very worst, he'd sounded like a pompous ass.
He wondered if Bennis was back at the inn, watching this.

The press officer had stepped up to the lectern again.
"We'll bring the governor back and you can start your
questions. If you could try to raise your hands instead of
calling out, I'd much appreciate it. I—"

There was a sound from behind him, and he turned. So
did the governor and Gregor and everybody else on the
station steps. The people in the parking lot did not have to
turn. The front doors of the station were opening.

"Excuse me," a woman said—it took Gregor a moment
to recognize her as the one who had come to the conference
room to tell them that the governor had arrived. She looked
out at the sea of faces in the lot and nearly retreated. Her
confusion was as plain as the bold red print on her dress.
"Excuse me," she said again.

The young woman with the hairband rushed up to her.
"We're having a press conference here," she hissed. "If you
need to leave the building, go out to the back. You can't—"

"But I don't need to leave the building. I don't. I need
to talk to Mark. I have to talk to Mark. He's the only one
here who can do anything about it."

"Whatever it is, it can wait," the girl in the hairband said
firmly, pushing the older woman forcefully back into the
building. "Right now, we're having a press conference, and
anything short of bloody murder—"

"But that's just *it*," the older woman said, pushing back
hard enough so that the younger woman stumbled. "It is
bloody murder, it is. It's another bloody murder and nobody else is on duty right now but Mark and he's the one
I have to talk to. He's the one I have to talk to right now."

Suddenly, she seemed to realize that they were all frozen—the people on the steps, the people in the parking lot.
They were as still as statues and they were all staring at

her. She pushed her way out farther onto the steps, clear of the young woman with the hairband. Once she was out there on her own like that, her posture improved. She threw her shoulders back and stood up straight. She seemed to gain two inches in height.

"It's happened again," she said, in a stentorian voice that needed no help from a microphone. "There's another body lying dead in Margaret Anson's garage."

PART TWO

PART TWO

One

I

The first thing Gregor Demarkian noticed about Margaret Anson's house was that it was enormous, a parody of a big old house, with long one-story wings stretching out from a boxlike central two-story core. It looked more like an institution than a private house, except that the low white-picket fence that ran along the road in front of it was so studiedly domestic. The flowerpots in the windows near the front door were studiedly domestic, too, but they looked out of place. It was late fall and cold. The flowers were dead.

The second thing Gregor Demarkian noticed about Margaret Anson's house was that it was almost aggressively ugly. For one thing, it was painted a garish yellow color with black shutters. The color would have done well on the walls of the kind of nursery school that has become over-anxious about its pupils' self-esteem. For another, the proportions were all wrong. The central core was clearly early eighteenth century. The additions were clearly later. The collection didn't match. Gregor looked up the long gravel drive to the long garage at the back. That had once been a barn, and it still looked like one. It was as out of place here as a pig would have been, penned up in a mudhole on the front lawn.

"CNN was faster than we were," Mark Cashman said, turning the police cruiser into Margaret Anson's drive.

The drive was being guarded by two state policemen. The whole house was being guarded by state policemen. Calling in reinforcements was the first thing Mark Cashman and Stacey Spratz had done after that woman had made her dramatic announcement at the press conference.

"The word *zoo* doesn't even begin to describe what we're going to have," Mark had said as he hit the phones to make sure that there would be something like a crime scene left by the time they got to the house.

Gregor could see it was a good thing that he had done what he did, too, because the road in front of the big yellow house was clogged with reporters and camera crews, and they were being anything but cooperative. As Gregor watched, a woman in high spiked heels walked up to one of the state troopers and began stabbing him in the chest with her forefinger, over and over again.

"The public has the *right to know*," Gregor could hear her saying.

"Crap," Stacey Spratz said.

The troopers let the cruiser through. Mark pulled it up in front of the barn and got out to look around. Gregor got out, too. It was almost as crowded back here as it was down on the road, but everybody up here was a law enforcement officer of one kind or another. Even the men who weren't in uniform were law enforcement officers. Gregor knew the type. The bay doors that had been cut into the side of the barn were standing open. Gregor saw a succession of cars inside, all expensive. The barn was full of people, working with concentration—that meant that whoever it was must have died in the barn. But who? Margaret Anson herself? It suddenly struck Gregor as odd that nobody had yet said anything about who or what had died—male or female, old or young.

Gregor went up to one of the bays and looked inside. The body was lying out on the floor, presumably untouched. From where he stood, he couldn't quite make out its relevant features, but he was sure it wasn't going to turn out to be Margaret Anson. What he could see was a bright, garishly printed fabric—batik, the style was called, he was pretty sure. Margaret Anson didn't sound to him like the sort of woman who would wear batik.

Mark Cashman came up behind him, followed by Stacey Spratz. "All right," Mark said. "I've got a handle on it. It's a woman, name of Zara Anne Moss. She—"

"She was the one who saw the Jeep following the BMW

on the night of the murder," Gregor said. "I remember the name. It's an odd name."

"It may turn out to be fake by the time we're done," Stacey said. "I talked to her once. She was a little—"

"Nuts," Mark finished.

"Nuts," Stacey agreed.

"Does anybody know what she was doing out here?" Gregor asked them.

"I haven't got the faintest idea," Mark said. "I haven't talked to anybody yet."

"Who found the body?"

"Margaret Anson did." Mark nodded toward the house. "She's the one who called the police department, anyway. That much, I have been able to figure out."

"Interesting," Gregor said.

There was a sound in the driveway and they saw Tom Royce and his people come in in an unmarked car. Tom looked harried. Gregor could imagine what the guards at the bottom of the drive had put him through, just to make sure he was a legitimate player. Royce got out from behind the wheel and opened the door in the back so that he could get his bag from the backseat. The rest of his people seemed to grow equipment like centipedes grow arms. None of them were wearing coats. Gregor thought they must all be freezing.

"Can we talk to Margaret Anson?" Gregor asked. "Is she still here? In the house?"

"I'll check," Stacey said.

He walked over to one of the uniformed state policemen standing near one of the house's many back doors, spoke for a few moments, and then nodded. He came back to Mark and Gregor.

"She's in the house. She's not against making a report. She's already talked to her attorney."

"Already?" Mark asked.

"I guess you pay these guys eight hundred dollars an hour, they've got to do what you want them to do when you need them."

Gregor went back over to the barn and looked inside again. Two of the bays were empty. One of them had probably held the BMW that Kayla Anson's body had been found in. That had been impounded as evidence, Gregor knew. He wondered if the other bay was usually left empty for guests or if there was something else that belonged there, in the shop for repairs now or out in the hands of a housekeeper or a driver. The house looked big enough to require a staff, but Gregor had no idea if Margaret Anson kept one. He looked at the closer side wall to the garage and saw that there was a narrow window there. There was no counterpart to it on the far side wall, but down at that end, on the back wall, was an ordinary egress door. Gregor backed out away from the garage.

"We're okay to go inside," Mark Cashman said. "I'd like to do that if you don't mind."

Gregor didn't mind. Stacey Spratz seemed to be in a hurry to see Margaret Anson, too. Gregor was interested in seeing her himself—if only to find out if he agreed with Bennis about her awfulness.

2

The inside of Margaret Anson's house was a model of fidelity to historical period. All the furniture in the back hall through which Gregor, Mark, and Stacey passed on their way to the living room was antique, and good antique at that. Unfortunately, the house itself was antique. If it had been a couple of years older, the ceilings would have been higher and the dimensions of the rooms more forgiving. Instead, in spite of its enormous size, the house felt cramped. Gregor felt downright claustrophobic. He was six feet, three inches tall. These rooms had not been made for him.

They passed into the front hall, and that was a little better. The stairwell gave the illusion of expansive height, at least for a few moments. There were glass doors that opened onto the living room. Gregor knew enough about architecture to know that they must have been added some time in the twentieth century. Women in Revolutionary War America did not want doors of any kind to their main reception rooms. He stopped to look at a pen-and-ink drawing in a small frame on the wall next to the front door. It was yellow with age under its glass, and it showed the devil prodding sinners into the flames of hell.

"Charming," Gregor said.

Mark and Stacey ignored him. They were already through the glass doors into the living room. Margaret Anson was sitting on a long low couch upholstered in something murkily floral. Everything about this house was murky. It was as if Margaret Anson worshiped the darkness.

Margaret Anson herself was unexceptional—a woman in late middle age, with all the usual lines on her face and a body that was thin and wiry in the way bodies get after a lifetime of riding horses. There were probably two dozen women in Litchfield County who looked exactly like her.

Stacey and Mark were standing in the middle of the room, not quite sure what to do next. Margaret Anson wasn't helping them. Gregor stepped to the front of the group.

"Mrs. Anson?" he said. "My name is Gregor Demarkian. I believe we have a mutual acquaintance."

"I have been informed by my attorney," Margaret Anson said, "that I do not have to answer any questions I do not want to answer, and I do not have to talk to any person not directly associated with the police department investigating this case. I do think that means I don't have to talk to you, Mr. Demarkian."

"The police department investigating this case is the Connecticut State Police," Stacey Spratz said. "Mr. Demarkian is our consultant. He *is* directly associated with us."

"You mean you've hired Mr. Demarkian as a consultant in your investigation of this young woman in my garage?"

"We've hired Mr. Demarkian as a consultant in the investigation of the murder of your daughter, Mrs. Anson," Stacey said.

Margaret Anson smiled thinly. "You are not here, at the moment, on the matter of the murder of my daughter. You are here on the unrelated matter of the murder of this young woman. Whoever she was."

"Her name was Zara Anne Moss," Mark Cashman said.

"Was it? Well, it has nothing to do with me. And as far as you know, it has nothing to do with Kayla. Once you've taken Mr. Demarkian on in the matter of the death of this young woman, I would of course be more than happy to talk to him."

Stacey and Mark looked at each other, momentarily brought up short.

Gregor cleared his throat. "I can't really believe," he said, "that you think the two things are unconnected. Do you often find the dead bodies of young women in your garage?"

"I don't often find much of anything in my garage, Mr. Demarkian. But it is a detached garage, well to the back of this house, and this house is very large. Anything at all could be going on out there without my knowing a thing about it."

"I'm sure it could," Gregor said. "But doesn't the timing seem strange to you?"

"I have no idea what you mean."

"Well, the reporters have been out here, in front of the house, most of the day, haven't they? I saw a picture of this house on the news last night, and there were vans and reporters parked all over the road, making it nearly impassable."

"So?"

"So," Gregor said, "you can see the garage bays from the road. I don't think anyone could have brought that young woman's body in here—or that young woman herself, alive and well—without the reporters on the road noticing. Unless there's a way into the garage to the back?"

"There's a door in the back, yes." Margaret Anson said. "I still don't see what you're getting at."

"Could you tell me if the garage bays were open earlier today, Mrs. Anson?"

"I have no idea. I haven't been out. I haven't even been interested in going out. I had to see Kayla's lawyers, but they came here."

"In full view of the television cameras parked outside."

"Of course."

"But then for a while the television cameras left the scene," Gregor said. "They took off for the Washington Police Department, to cover the press conference. I saw many of the same people there that I'm now seeing here."

"We did have a few moments of calm, yes," Margaret said. "I don't know if they all went, though. I didn't check."

"But you went outside."

"Did I?"

"You must have," Gregor said. "You found the body in the garage. To find the body in the garage, you had to have gone to the garage. Unless you're claiming clairvoyance. It doesn't seem your style."

Margaret Anson looked down at her hands, folded calmly in her lap. If she was going to notice the fact that she was talking to him even though she had declared that she wouldn't, she would notice it now. She didn't. Instead she seemed to be studying the pattern of her good wool dress. Gregor realized that Margaret Anson looked dressed for church, at least, if not for a full day of professional obligations in the city. Either she had changed into formal clothes in anticipation of the arrival of the police, or she lived an unbelievably formal life.

"I grow herbs," she said now. "On a window shelf—a whole series of window shelves—in the kitchen. I like to put up vegetables in the fall."

Gregor waited. The nails on Margaret Anson's hands were short and blunt but very well cared for, professionally manicured hands. She did not put those hands in dirt.

"I went out to the garage," she said, "to get a couple of small clay pots. It's what I grow the herbs in. And I walked through the bay and there she was."

"The bay was open?"

"One of them was."

"Was it the one where she was lying?"

"What? Oh, no. It was the one in front of Robert's car. The Jaguar. Robert always had very flashy taste in cars. I once threatened to divorce him if he insisted on buying a Rolls-Royce."

"And this young woman was lying there, in one of the empty bays, on the ground?"

"Yes, she was. Except that I didn't know it was a person at first. It was dark in the garage. It looked like a pile of garbage. So I went over to check it out. And there she was."

"Dead."

"I assumed she was dead."

"You didn't get down on the floor to check?"

"I could see her eyes. They were—coming out of her head. Is that the way to put it? I knew she was dead."

"What did you do then?"

"I came back to the house and called the police department."

"You didn't touch the body in any way?"

"No," Margaret Anson said. "Not at all. Not even with a single finger. I didn't even want to look at it."

"What about the reporters? Were there any in the road?"

"I didn't notice."

"What did you do after you called the police?"

"I came in here and made myself a cup of tea," Margaret Anson said. "And then I drank it. And then I waited. And the next thing I knew, everything turned into a circus again. And here you are."

"Do you really think that this murder and the murder of your daughter are unconnected?"

Margaret Anson stood up. "I think you've had enough questions," she said. "I think I've talked entirely too much.

I think it's about time you left this house. You can come back when I have my attorney present."

"We'll need you to come down and make a formal statement," Stacey Spratz said quickly.

Margaret Anson waved him off. "I'll come down and make a formal statement when I have my attorney present. That should be tomorrow. I don't have to make one today in any case, and I don't have to come with you anywhere unless you're arresting me on some charge. Are you arresting me on some charge?"

"No," Mark Cashman said.

"Good." Margaret Anson nodded to each of them in turn. "Then I think, gentlemen, that it's about time that the three of you left my house."

3

Back out in the driveway, Gregor could see that the road was once again so clogged with reporters that it was unpassable. While they had been talking to Margaret Anson, the work in the garage had been proceeding quickly, but the body was still lying on the concrete floor. Gregor went inside and stood over it, trying not to get in the way of Tom Royce and the uniformed officers doing routine evidence gathering. Margaret Anson had been telling the truth about at least one thing. Zara Anne Moss's eyes were indeed protruding from her head, one of the common symptoms of death by strangulation. Gregor could see others. There was a deep welt in the part of her throat that Gregor could see. On cursory examination, there didn't seem to be anything about this welt that was inconsistent with the idea that it had been made by a nylon athletic shoelace. The mouth was hanging open.

Gregor backed away from the body and looked around. There was no sign of clay pottery in the garage, but he hadn't expected there to be. There was a shed-roofed box built into the side of the house near the back door. Gardening things would be kept in there. He went to the back of the garage and looked at the rear door. It was an undistinguished wooden door, and it was unlocked. He opened it and looked outside. There was more lawn and a few trees, nothing special. There was no sign of anyone having gone back and forth through it anytime recently. He shut it again and went back across the garage and through the bays to the drive.

"So?" Stacey Spratz said, when he walked up.

"So," Gregor said, "she's lying about why she went out to the garage. She's never grown herbs in her life, she doesn't even garden, and the pots for that kind of thing aren't kept in the garage in the first place. The interesting question is why she bothered to tell that particular lie."

"But if she's lying, can't we do something about it?" Stacey asked.

"What?" Gregor asked him. "She wasn't under oath. She wasn't even making an official statement. By the time she gets down to making that statement, she'll probably have figured out what was wrong with what she said and changed it. And you're not dealing with some street kid here. You're dealing with a very rich woman who has lots of legal help. If there are discrepancies between the story she just gave and her eventual statement, she'll just say— perfectly plausibly—that she was too upset to know what she was talking about when she first talked to us."

"I don't believe that woman is ever too upset to know what she's talking about," Mark Cashman said.

"I agree," Gregor said. "But the problem remains, at the moment, why she told this particular lie. There's always the possibility that she killed Zara Anne Moss herself."

"But you don't think so," Stacey said.

"No, I don't. Take a look at those hands, the next time you see her. How do you strangle somebody—how do you strangle a vigorous young woman—and have hands that look like that when you're done?"

"If she didn't kill her, why is she lying?" Mark Cashman asked.

"Oh," Gregor said, "people lie all the time. They lie to hide what they think is discreditable in themselves, so that you won't know that they knock wood or cross their fingers or refuse to walk under ladders. Or because they've maxed out their credit cards and are ashamed of it. Or because they spend their spare time imagining themselves being interviewed by Ed Bradley on *60 Minutes* and they're just too embarrassed to tell you about it. No, what I want to know is, why this particular lie? Why pots and herb gardens?"

"I'd say she was lying to protect somebody," Mark Cashman said, "but I can't see that woman protecting anybody but herself. You should have seen her Friday night, when we found the body of Kayla Anson. I mean, it was her daughter, for God's sake."

"She's a cold woman," Stacey agreed.

"Cold doesn't mean murderous," Gregor said. "Do they have anything in the way of preliminary findings around here? Did they find one of those shoelaces, like the one they found on Kayla Anson?"

"Just a minute," Mark Cashman said.

He disappeared momentarily, and came back with Tom Royce. Tom looked dispirited and cold. He also looked angry.

"It had to be set up," he said. "Don't you agree? It had to be set up for the time of the press conference. It was done on purpose."

"Murder is usually done on purpose," Stacey Spratz said. "That's what makes it murder."

"A white shoelace," Gregor Demarkian said.

Tom Royce sighed. "It was lying half under the body. We found it when we turned her over. I don't know how it got there. It had to have been taken off. It wouldn't have just fallen off. If it was the murder weapon."

"Why not?" Stacey Spratz asked.

"Because it would have gotten embedded in the skin," Gregor answered. "What about signs of struggle? You said that with Kayla Anson—"

"In this case, there's no way to tell, assuming she was actually murdered in that garage. Which I think is a very good assumption, this time. Kayla Anson could have been murdered anywhere and then her body could have been driven home. This one, though, with all those reporters outside—"

"There would have been a very small window of opportunity when she could have been brought here, or come here, without being noticed," Gregor said. "Has anybody checked with the press to find out if somebody did see her?"

"I'll get somebody on it," Stacey Spratz said.

"How about what she got here on," Gregor said. "Or in. She lived—where? You've mentioned her before, but I didn't quite get the geography."

"On the Litchfield Road," Mark Cashman said. "In Watertown."

"And that's how far from here?" Gregor asked.

"About ten, fifteen miles," Stacey Spratz said.

Gregor stared at the two of them in astonishment. "Ten or fifteen miles? But how did she get here? There isn't a car in the place that doesn't belong to the Ansons that I can see. Did she hitchhike? Did somebody give her a ride? How did she get all the way out here?"

Two

I

On the day that Peter Greer was formally admitted to the Swamp Tree Country Club, he came into the clubhouse bar at exactly six o'clock and had a double Glenfidditch whiskey, neat. That was two years and four months ago, and now, sitting alone in a booth in the bar's far corner, he could remember it in perfect detail. That was the day my life changed, he had sometimes told himself. The thought did not embarrass him, even though he knew it would sound overdramatic to anyone who might hear it. It *was* the day his life changed, the day he had passed through an invisible barrier that separated *that* part of Litchfield County from *this* one. It had been the day he had started thinking of himself as something other than a poor boy making good. Later that week he had gone down to South Street in Litchfield and walked it from one end to the other. He had a fantasy of living in the big white-columned house there, the one that almost looked like the White House transplanted—except that it was better. Now he thought it might be just as well if he didn't think of the White House, because it also made him think of bimbo eruptions, which he was somewhat prone to himself. He had five messages from Deirdre on his machine back at the house. He knew that if he were to go back there now, he would find her in his hot tub, floating naked in the swirling water and ready to cut his throat.

"You really can't discard me like waste paper," she had told him the night before. "What is it that you think you're dealing with?"

"The police are going to want to talk to you just as much as they want to talk to me," Margaret Anson had said, also the night before.

Margaret had called. She never came to his house, and

Peter never expected her to come. Deirdre had been on his living room couch, having one of her patented tirades.

"You've got a woman there with you," Margaret had said. "How very sweet."

"I have a friend here who's a little upset. As you should be able to hear."

"I hear more than you think I do. But you were Kayla's lover, Peter. They're going to want to talk to you. They're going to be very interested in anything you have to say."

"I'm very easy to find, Margaret."

"So am I," Margaret said. "That may be my trouble."

The television in the bar was full of the story of the death of Zara Anne Moss. The graphic behind Ann Nyberg's head showed a folk Victorian farmhouse with the words *Death House* stenciled over it. Margaret's house was nothing like a folk Victorian, Peter thought irrelevantly. Then the screen went to a large picture of Zara Anne Moss's head, except that she looked far younger than she was supposed to be. Peter supposed it was a high school graduation photograph. It had that kind of posed quality to it.

A waiter went by, and Peter snagged him. He pointed to his glass and the waiter nodded. This was one of the good things about the club. They kept tabs on what you were eating or drinking. You never had to give elaborate orders or worry that what you ordered would be translated by the staff into something you didn't want.

Peter finished the rest of the whiskey in his glass in a single gulp. There wasn't much of it, less than a quarter of what he'd started with, but it went down as a shock nonetheless. He watched the waiter come back to him with another glass on a tray and sat still and polite while it was delivered to him. Then he signed the check he was presented with. Everything at the club was on account. You could sign for anything, and the charges were simply piled on and on, until the end of the month, when the bill came. Peter had heard rumors that there were members who let their bills go from month to month, who ran up thousands of dollars in charges and never seemed to get around to paying it, but he had never felt secure enough to let a bill slip for even a single month. With his luck, he would be called into the bursar's office and given a lecture the very first thing. You probably had to have a name like Ridenour to get away with something like that. Peter wondered if he'd feel differently about it, if he had serious money, like Bill Gates. Somehow, he thought he wouldn't.

When the waiter had gone, Peter picked up his drink and made his way to the bar. The stools there were mostly empty, but Sally Martindale was sitting at one end, nursing what looked like an elaborate ladies' drink. Pousse-café. Piña colada. Café frappé. Peter couldn't remember what they were all called. They were just silly drinks, with too much fluff and not enough alcohol in them.

Ordinarily, Peter would not have made an effort to talk to Sally Martindale. Since Sally's divorce, she had had too much of the smell of failure about her, too much of an air of desperation. You could see it in what was happening to her body. She had always been thin. Now she was emaciated, and it was the wrong kind of emaciated. Her body looked hard and undernourished. Her arms and legs seemed to be made of interlocking strings. Her face was a mess. A few years ago, she had had a network of fine lines at the sides of her eyes. Now the skin there was a holocaust of folds and gashes, as if someone had come along and cut it with a razor, and it had only inadequately healed.

Peter put his whiskey down on the bar next to Sally's stool and took a stool himself. He needed to talk to someone, and there was no one else to talk to. There was certainly no one who was safe. He had been revved up and in high gear all afternoon. There wasn't anywhere to put his energy.

At the other end of the bar, the television news had turned to something less combative than the death of Kayla Anson. Peter thought it was a consumer report on baby car seats.

"Well," Peter said.

Sally slid her eyes sideways to look at him, rather than turning right around. She sucked at her drink, which seemed to be all foam.

"Hello," she said.

"Do you think Margaret Anson has gone on some kind of killing spree?" Peter asked. "Maybe she's offing debutantes in her garage."

Sally Martindale twisted on her stool. "I didn't know this girl was a debutante. I thought she was some kind of hippie."

"I was being metaphorical. I think she was the right age."

"Mallory's decided she doesn't want to be a debutante. She wants to sell her dress to Annabel Crawford."

"I think a fair number of girls don't want to be debutantes these days. I don't think there's anything unusual in that."

"There's nothing unusual about it. It's just a disaster, that's all. She can't see that yet, but she will. And then I don't know what she's going to do."

"Maybe she just doesn't want to live a social life."

"Oh, they all think they don't want that when they're seventeen. They all think they're too pure and noble, and they just want to be authentic, and all the rest of it. It's all rot. You know it's all rot. They change their minds as soon as they grow up, and then if you haven't forced them, they're doomed."

Peter looked back at the television. There was an announcement on, highlighting a coming retrospective on the Monica Lewinsky affair. *All Monica All the Time*, Kayla had called it, when she'd gotten fed up with the way the story seemed to jam even her favorite radio stations. He had a sudden vision of her, the last time he had seen her alive: her hair blowing a little in the wind, her wide eyes so perfectly blue. Then he thought that that might be a trick of his memory. That might not have been the last time he saw her alive.

"Well," he said, looking down into his drink.

Sally finished hers. "I know how desperately important it all is, so of course I do a lot of work to make sure it comes out right. That only makes sense. Wouldn't you agree that that only makes sense?"

"Sure."

"Sometimes you have to do what you have to do to get what you want. You have to understand that. I know you understand it."

"Anybody would understand it."

"No, not anybody would," Sally said. "Those people, the ones who belong here, the ones who got into the club because their grandparents belonged and their mothers came out here, they wouldn't understand it. Annabel Crawford. Kayla Anson. Everybody says you were sleeping with Kayla Anson."

"Do they?"

"Mallory even says it's true."

"It was true. For a time."

"It wouldn't have lasted," Sally said. "She wouldn't have stayed with you. Those kind never do. When it comes time to marry they always find one of their own."

"Nobody was talking about marriage."

"I'll bet you were thinking about it," Sally said. She caught the eye of the bartender and signaled him. "I don't think Mallory is ever going to marry. She's never going to marry one of *them*. Too fat. Too stupid. Too sullen. Way too sullen. She takes a Nobel Prize in sullenness."

"What an ugly thing to say about your own daughter."

The bartender had arrived with another frothing drink. Sally signed for it and took a long pull on it. Then she hopped off her bar stool and brushed out the wrinkles in her skirt.

"I'm not saying anything everybody else isn't saying. I hear it all, sitting in that goddamned bursar's room. And it suddenly hit me today, that I've gone through it all, I've done everything I could and more than I should have and it's not going to matter. It's not going to matter at all. It's all going to be for nothing."

"Right," Peter said.

"Like you and Kayla Anson," Sally said.

She picked up her drink and started off with it, swaying a little as she went. It was the first time Peter realized that she was drunk.

No, Peter thought, he really did not like Sally Martindale. She was a dangerous woman, at the moment. She had lost her nerve.

Peter did not think it was possible for him ever to lose his own.

2

Her name was Zara Anne Moss, and she had graduated from Nonnewaug High School in Woodbury in the class of 1992. Faye Dallmer kept repeating that information to herself, over and over again, as if it had some kind of special significance. She wasn't too sure what that might be. They had given her a lot of information about Zara Anne, these policemen who had come to sit in her living room this early evening. They had told her things she had never expected to know. Zara Anne was much younger than she had thought she was, for instance. Zara Anne had been part of a local dramatic group for two years and taken the lead in a production of *The Glass Menagerie*. Zara Anne had spent a year at Trinity College in Hartford and been required to leave when her grade point average dipped consistently below a D.

There were so many policemen in the living room, Faye didn't know what to do about them all. There were policemen from Washington, where Zara Anne's body had been found. There were policemen from Watertown, where Faye's house was. There were state policemen. Faye concentrated on the one civilian, the big man she now knew to be Gregor Demarkian.

"This is only preliminary information," he was saying. "The things that have popped up automatically once the news of her death became generally known. We'll know much more about her in the next few days."

"I didn't know very much about her at all," Faye said. Then she blushed and looked away. She had never been so ashamed of having to say anything in her life. She rubbed her hands together in her lap. "We met at a natural foods fair. At the Hartford Civic Center. I was giving a speech, you see, and I showed up a little early to look around, and we ran into each other."

"She was interested in natural foods." It was a statement, not a question.

Faye sighed. "I don't know what she was interested in, really. In being—a certain kind of person, I think. In having a certain kind of life. And she was very devoted to Wicca."

"What's Wicca?" one of the policemen said.

"Oh, well," Faye said. "Witchcraft, I suppose you'd call it. It's the name of what's supposed to be an ancient religion, to which the witches in the Middle Ages and later were supposed to belong. I've never credited the analysis much myself. I don't mean that I don't think there was a religion called Wicca. There was. We can document that. I mean I don't think that the witches they burned in the witch-hunts were practicing Wicca. I think they were ordinary Christian women who got caught in the wrong place at the wrong time. If you see the difference. I'm not making any sense, am I? I'm going on and on."

"You're doing fine," Gregor Demarkian said.

She was swimming in Jell-O, that's what she was doing. She had been doing it since the moment she had turned on the news and heard Zara Anne's name coming across on a bulletin, coming across with no warning at all. It shouldn't have happened like that. Somebody had messed up. They should have sent a message to her privately one way or the other before they released Zara Anne's name to the press.

"Anyway," Faye said. "Zara Anne liked to think she was a witch. She liked to believe she had powers. And so, you know, on the night the Jeep was stolen—Friday night, the night before last. It's so odd. On the night the Jeep was stolen she decided she could feel the thoughts of the person she saw driving it. That's what she told the police. Or at least that's what I think she told them. That she saw the Jeep following Kayla Anson's BMW and that she could just tell, I guess, that there was malevolence, that something awful was going to happen."

"Do you think she got a look at whoever was driving the car?"

"I don't know. If she did, it must not have been somebody she knew, because she would have said, I think. I think she would have liked being able to give definite information, to point a finger. To get on the news, I guess. And how could she have seen? It was a dark night. We have streetlights out there. The glare would have kept her from seeing anybody through the windows of a car."

"Probably true," Gregor Demarkian said.

"I think she wanted to set herself up as a psychic," Faye said. "Except that she wouldn't have called herself that. And I told her at the time that it was dangerous, to say the things she was saying, when there was somebody out there who had already murdered one person. But she said them anyway. And not just to me."

"Do you mean to the police?" Gregor Demarkian asked.

"I mean to all sorts of people. To a reporter who came here, for one thing. It was on the news on Saturday, I remember, and some woman reporter asked Margaret Anson what she thought of it, the things that Zara Anne was saying. Margaret Anson didn't give an answer, of course. They were trying to catch her as she left the house. They were just sort of following her in her driveway. And she ignored them. But it was right there on the news. Zara Anne liked that. She liked it very much."

"And today?" Gregor Demarkian asked. "Did she do anything special today?"

"I don't know," Faye said. "I've been out at the stand most of the day. It's a busy day once the churches let out. People stop by and get vegetables for Sunday dinner. And then, later, I had to go out myself. I had to pick some things up at the Portuguese food store in Waterbury."

"What time was this?" It was one of the policemen again.

"I left here around one-thirty. I was gone until just after four. I would have stayed out longer, there were still things I needed to do, but I got into my car and there it was on the radio. About Zara Anne. It was just right there on the radio."

"Yes," Gregor Demarkian said gently.

"Somebody should have warned me," Faye said. "I know that with the press in the kind of insane snit it's in now, it's hard to do the right thing, but somebody should have warned me. I shouldn't have had to hear it on the news like that, out of the blue."

"Her parents are going to be saying the same thing," one of the policemen said.

Gregor Demarkian moved closer to where Faye was sitting and bent toward her. "Listen," he said, "this is important. Did you give Zara Anne a ride out to Margaret Anson's house?"

"No, of course not."

"Did you know she was intending to go to Margaret Anson's house? *Was* she intending to go to Margaret Anson's house?"

"I don't think so. She didn't mention it to me. And I think she would have. She wasn't good at keeping secrets, especially of information she thought might make her seem important."

"Would she have hitchhiked out to Margaret Anson's house?"

Faye sat up a little straighter. "I don't think so. She wasn't an energetic person, if you know what I mean. She tended toward lethargy. Hitchhiking is a lot of work, especially on back roads on Sunday afternoon. And there's one other thing."

"What?"

"I'm not sure she actually knew where the Anson house is. I know she'd seen pictures of it, but I don't think she'd ever been out there. And it wasn't in a direction she would be likely to go. To Waterbury to the mall, you know, or even here in Watertown to Kmart or one of those places, but not farther up into the hills. Unless there was a meeting or a conference or something of the sort, and then we would have gone together."

"And you didn't."

"No."

"All right," Gregor said. "One more thing. What about friends. What kind of friends did she have, who did she see, other than yourself?"

Faye blushed. "No one," she said. "The whole time she was here, she never saw anyone at all except me."

"Really? But that's—she was local, wasn't she? Woodbury is somewhere close to here?"

"Oh, yes, it's very close. But I was just as surprised as you seem to be. I thought she must have been from out of state, or at least way off on the eastern corner, because she never saw anybody. Or called anybody. Or wrote to anybody. Not anybody at all. And now it turns out she had parents in Woodbury. I can't believe it."

"Did you know if she'd had problems with her parents? If there was some reason for an estrangement?"

"Well, there must have been, mustn't there?" Faye said. "You don't just stop talking to your parents completely unless something has come up. But she never mentioned anything to me. She never even mentioned her parents. She never mentioned school, or friends—and yet she was always talking about herself. How she felt about things. What she meant to do. I don't know what to make of it."

"I think it's nuts," one of the policemen said. Faye noticed that it was the state policeman this time, the one with the very blond hair.

"I think it's nuts, too," she said. "But it's the truth. I don't know what else to tell you."

Gregor Demarkian nodded a little and stepped away. "Well, we'll just have to talk to her parents, then. And any acquaintances from high school we can find. But you must realize how important it is, determining just how she got out to Margaret Anson's house."

"Oh, yes."

"And why," Gregor Demarkian said.

"I think I'd stopped thinking about why when it came to Zara Anne," Faye said. "I think I'd just come to accept that Zara Anne did what she did."

Gregor Demarkian nodded a little—and then, suddenly, the whole lot of them were in motion. Faye stood up herself, realizing with something like franticness that they were all headed out her front door. They were going to leave her alone. And what was she going to do when she was alone?

She trailed behind them through the front hall and stood in the doorway as they filed out. She watched them get into their cars one after the other. Gregor Demarkian got into the state police car. He was not driving. Faye pulled at her hair and felt a raft of pins come lose.

It was worse than swimming through Jell-O. It was like being drugged. She had no idea what she was going to do now that she was on her own. She only knew that she did not want to be on her own, here in this house, by herself. She wished she had thought to ask them how Zara Anne had died. She envisioned Zara Anne's face, mottled and bug-eyed from strangulation, which was what was supposed to have happened to Kayla Anson. Then she bent double and wrapped her arms around her body. She thought she was going to be sick.

She had never wanted Zara Anne to die. That was the truth. She had only wanted to be on her own again for a while, to have some quiet, to be able to think. Now she had all those things, and she hated them.

3

Back at the Mayflower Inn, Bennis Hannaford was stretched out on the bed, feeling awful. The television was on. She had heard much of the press conference, and she had gone on watching after everybody had taken off for Margaret Anson's house. Breaking news, they called it— an excuse for hyperactivity. She knew nothing at all about this young woman, Zara Anne Moss. She wondered just what it was Gregor was doing. She wished she could stop coughing. That was the thing. She couldn't stop coughing.

Actually, she *did* stop coughing, on and off. She stopped and felt the muscles in her arms and chest relax—and then, as soon as they did, the coughing would start again. It had gotten to the point where she was afraid to sit up. Any movement at all seemed to trigger another set of spasms. She didn't even move to answer the phone when it rang. She was afraid to turn over, or that, if she did answer it, she would start coughing and not be able to stop. She willed herself to lay still until the ringing stopped. Then she closed her eyes and tried very hard not to yawn, even though she needed to. Yawning was the most treacherous thing of all.

She was just beginning to drift off to sleep when the phone started ringing again. She sat up to answer it without even thinking about it. She got the receiver off the hook and said, "Bennis Hannaford speaking" before the cough started in again.

"Bennis?" Donna Moradanyan asked.

"Donna," Bennis tried to say, but it didn't work. The coughing hit her like a wave, and in no time at all it was much worse than just coughing. It was something like convulsions.

She stood up and bent over at the waist.

"Bennis?" Donna said again.

Bennis felt something come up her throat, something thin and raw. She convulsed one more time and spat it out, and then the coughing stopped.

Then she looked at the floor, and saw what she had left there.

It was a thick clot of blood.

Three

I

Bennis Hannaford was asleep in bed when Gregor got back to the inn that night, carrying an armful of notes that made him feel as if he were back in college and had lost his briefcase. She was awake when he got up the next morning, running the water in the shower and muttering behind the bathroom door. Gregor got up, discovered that the bathrobe he'd brought was gone—this was nice, it meant that Bennis was behaving according to type—and took up his notes of the day before. It felt to him as if he had seen a million people in just a few hours. It might even have been true. Kayla Anson. Zara Anne Moss. The two deaths were almost undoubtedly connected. Gregor just didn't understand why investigating them required riding around in cars for the better part of the day.

Bennis was done in the bathroom. Gregor waited politely for her to come out and then went in himself. She did not look well. Her eyes were pouchy. Her skin was much too white. Gregor took a shower and brushed his teeth and looked at himself in the bathroom mirror. His eyes were pouchy. His skin was much too white. Maybe there was nothing wrong with Bennis except that she was a forty-year-old woman and he was seeing her the first thing in the morning. Maybe the other mornings when he had seen her first thing, and she had not been like this, had been the real exceptions.

He went back out into the main room and found Bennis sitting at a small round table, eating breakfast. The table was set for two, and the wheeled cart beside it had urns for both coffee and tea. She must have called room service.

"Good morning," Gregor said.

Bennis waved at him with her cigarette. "Donna Moradanyan called. Last night. She said it was important, but you can't call her back today. She's out until just around dinnertime."

"Did she say what it was about?"

"Something about Peter. She didn't go into a lot of detail."

"She didn't go into detail with you?"

"I was throwing up at the time. I think I've got a touch of . . . food poisoning. Or something."

"I thought you looked ill," Gregor said. "Do you want to see a doctor?"

"I don't see what for. I'm not throwing up anymore. I don't feel as if I'm about to die. I'll be all right."

"Maybe you should just stay in and take it easy."

"Mmmm," Bennis said.

Gregor sat down at the chair that was waiting for him and got himself coffee. It was decent coffee, properly perked, as he would have expected it to be. There were Danish pastries and doughnuts on the tray, too, and he took one of those. Bennis, he saw, was having her usual fruit and cheese, but she had barely touched it.

"I'm going to have to do quite a lot of running around today," he said. "I've got Stacey Spratz picking me up about quarter to nine. I think we're going to interview the boyfriend."

"Boyfriend?"

"Kayla Anson had a boyfriend."

"Oh." Bennis stirred out of her lethargy. "I've heard about him. From Abigail, my friend who sent me down here. Margaret was supposed to be livid."

"Why?"

"Because he's self-made, or something. Abigail said he was really quite respectable. You couldn't tell he hadn't been to Taft and Yale. But apparently he has no real background, the way Margaret would define the term, and he's in business for himself, by which I suppose she'd mean that he doesn't have enough money. I mean, her own husband was in business for himself."

"I'm not too sure if you describe the founder of a global conglomerate as 'in business for himself.' "

"Well, maybe not. But you see what I mean. And I don't really see why it would have mattered anyway, unless he was a beach bum or a ski instructor, and Abigail says he definitely isn't that. He owns Goldenrod. The catalogue company."

"Am I supposed to know what that is?"

"You've seen enough of their catalogues," Bennis said. "They sell natural fiber clothes for the country. Sort of like an East Coast Sundance. I buy a lot of my flannel shirts from them."

"And they're successful?"

Bennis shrugged. "I suppose you can never tell without a financial report, but I'd guess that unless the man's an absolute ass of a businessman they must be. Their stuff is everywhere. They're the most status-ridden label on any college campus. I don't think they're outsold by anybody except J. Crew and L. L. Bean."

"Sounds good."

"One would hope. But that's just like Margaret Anson, you see. I suppose you've met her by now. You must have seen what she's like."

"She's an unattractive woman."

"Unattractive nothing," Bennis said. "She's a rattle-snake. I don't think I've been so upset by anybody in my entire life. Do you think she's some kind of serial killer, luring young women into her garage and then—"

"I doubt it," Gregor said. "In fact, one of the few things I'm sure of is that Margaret Anson did not physically strangle either one of those two women."

"Is there a way to strangle somebody that's not physical?"

"I meant strangle with her own hands. Rather than induce somebody else to strangle. Pay somebody else to strangle. That kind of thing."

"Oh," Bennis said. "Well, that's a possibility. Do you

think there's something about mothers that makes them hate their own daughters?"

"What?"

"I don't mean all mothers," Bennis said. "I mean, obviously, I got along wonderfully with mine. I mean some mothers. And the hate is so deep that it's like acid. Deeper than hate could ever be otherwise."

"I think in a case like that, the hate is usually mutual."

"Well, Margaret Anson hated her daughter. I can tell you that absolutely. I don't know if Kayla Anson hated her mother. I only met her superficially once or twice."

"You only met Margaret Anson once."

"It was enough."

Gregor stood up. "I'd better get dressed and ready to go. Stacey Spratz seems to think that we're going to tour most of the state today. And maybe we are. I think I need to get him to make me a map. I never know where I am."

"I'm going to stay in and drink tea and read P. D. James."

Bennis was already almost reading P. D. James. She had picked the book up from the floor and laid it in her lap. Now she was rubbing the tips of her fingers against the cover. Gregor hesitated. The way she was this morning made him uneasy. She was so—worn out.

"Well," he said, "if you're sure you'll be all right here alone."

"Of course I'll be all right here alone. And you couldn't take me with you. You know that. I'll be fine."

"Of course you will."

"Of course I will." Bennis looked up. "Go get dressed, Gregor. You're hovering over me like a storm cloud."

It was Bennis's hair that looked like storm clouds. Gregor had always thought so.

He left her sitting at the little table and went back into the bathroom to get dressed.

2

Gregor was already sitting in the lobby when Stacey Spratz showed up. It took no time at all for Gregor to realize that Stacey was full of news, since Stacey tended to announce it, out loud, to everybody assembled near the inn's front desk.

"I got you all those things you asked for," he called out, in a voice that could have carried across a football field. "The police report sheets from Watertown, Morris, and Washington for Friday night. What a zoo that was, Friday night."

The people in the lobby all looked excessively well-heeled. The women wore good wool slacks with creases in them instead of jeans. The men wore sport coats. They turned first to look at Stacey Spratz, and then to look at Gregor. Gregor sighed.

"I take it you left them out in the car," he said, in as quiet a voice as he could manage.

"They're right on your seat," Stacey said. "But I'm impressed, you know. You were right. All kinds of stuff went on that night, and all in the right areas as far as we know. Well, not out near Margaret Anson's place, but where the Jeep and the BMW were seen together. You wouldn't believe what I found—"

"Let's go out to the car," Gregor said.

The woman behind the reception desk was glaring at them. They were mucking up her atmosphere.

Stacey trailed Gregor happily across the lobby and out the front door, talking all the way. Gregor stopped on the inn's front steps and looked around. Fall was here for real. The air was cold. The trees were nearly bare, and the leaves that lay on the ground were yellow and red. Stacey's state police cruiser was one of only six cars in the small lot.

"You want to hear this list of things we've got?"

"Absolutely," Gregor said.

He had reached the cruiser. The doors weren't locked. Gregor was beginning to wonder if he was one of the last people on earth who locked his doors. He opened up and climbed into the passenger seat, waiting for Stacey to come around and get behind the wheel.

"So," he said, when Stacey was settled in. "Tell me."

"I've got copies in the back," Stacey said, "but I'll give you a rundown. First, Watertown. The Jeep was stolen. And Zara Anne Moss saw it pass."

"We knew that."

"Right. But then it gets more interesting. Then we get to Morris."

"And?"

Stacey started the engine. "And Martin and Henry Chandling. Two old guys who do caretaking work at this historic cemetery. The Fairchild Family Cemetery. It's protected, or something, as a landmark. Established up here in sixteen eighty-six. Closed pretty much before the Civil War—lack of space, and lack of Fairchilds. It sits up there on its hill, you know, and the gravestones are all a hundred years old at least, and people come to take stone rubbings. You know about that, people bring tracing paper and pencils or charcoal and they rub against the stones and get the words and stuff on the paper?"

"I've heard of it, yes."

"Well, I don't get it, but it's really big with a certain kind of woman from New York. Anyway, that's what they do. That's where the Jeep was found."

"In the cemetery."

"Right. Tipped over on its side and a real mess. We can look at that, too. But that isn't all. This is the part I thought you'd be interested to hear. Thing is, they heard this noise and they went out to investigate it and it was the Jeep. But then when they got back to their little house, they had another surprise. They had a skeleton. Not one of their own skeletons. A strange skeleton."

Gregor considered this. "Strange in what way? Do you mean fake?"

"If you mean fake plastic, or that kind of thing, no. I talked to the Morris PD. This was a real enough skeleton, only it came from an exhibit up at the Litchfield County Museum. That's this little place some foundation has set up that does educational exhibits for schoolkids to take field trips to. You know the kind of thing."

"And they were doing anatomy?"

"They were doing bones. They've got all kinds of skeletons—a beaver, I think I heard, and an ostrich. I don't know where they got that one. And I don't know what the exhibit was supposed to be in aid of, either, so don't ask me. But somebody took their human skeleton and put it on Martin and Henry Chandling's front porch."

Gregor drummed his fingers against the top of his knees. He hated details like this. They almost always meant trouble, even if—like this one—there was a good chance that they had nothing to do with the case in hand. It was Halloween, after all. The skeleton could have been put on that porch by anybody at all, just as a trick or treat prank.

"Did they have to move this skeleton a long way to get it to this porch?" he asked.

"Just down the hill to the back," Stacey told him. "Guy I talked to out in Morris was fit to bust. Seems like the guy who runs this museum, Jake something, anyway, he's some kind of obsessive. He spent yesterday afternoon going back and forth from the museum to the house where Martin and Henry live, over and over and over again, and measuring everything—"

"Why?"

"Nobody knows. But he did it, and he wrote the measurements down in a notebook, and then he showed up at the Morris Police Department and tried to get them to listen to his theories about how the skeleton was carried and what the thief must have been wearing and whatever all else. And then Martin and Henry called in, and they were fit to bust, too, because this guy had been bugging them. It really was a mess."

"It probably doesn't mean anything."

"I'm with you. Kids out to have a good time and the museum was handy to the porch. There are always kids going out to that cemetery and trying to drive Martin and Henry nuts. They're a little eccentric."

"I wish I had a map of the area, though," Gregor said. "Something with the roads on it but not much else, and the relative distances, and the incidents marked out. Maybe we could make something like that if we wanted to take the time."

Stacey was surprised. "Sure we could. But I never expected you to want such a thing. It sounds like something out of Agatha Christie."

Sometimes far too much of Gregor's life sounded like something out of Agatha Christie. He looked out the windshield at the country they were passing through. It was odd the way you could tell the affluence of a town by the shade of green on its lawns. Rich towns had deep, jewel-like greens, even in the winter. This was definitely a rich town.

They passed a few small houses, built very close to the edge of the road. They passed a few more that were much larger and set well back. There didn't seem to be a single person anywhere.

"Does he live out here, Peter Greer?" Gregor asked. "Is that where we're going?"

"Oh, no," Stacey said. "I forgot to tell you. We're going out to the Swamp Tree Country Club. There's a manager there, a Mr. Mortimer. Thomas Mortimer. Anyway, he said it was urgent, about where Kayla Anson was on Friday night. He was all worked up. So I told him we'd be right out."

"But we know where Kayla Anson was on Friday night," Gregor pointed out.

"He seems to think we don't," Stacey said. "And I thought it wouldn't hurt us to check it out. Don't you agree with that, Mr. Demarkian? Should I have asked you first?"

The last thing Gregor could do was insist that Stacey Spratz check in with him before he made a single move. Going out to this country club would not hurt either one of them, if it gave them information about the life of Kayla Anson.

Gregor didn't think he had ever investigated a murder before where he had so little sense of the deceased. He knew more about what Zara Anne Moss was like than what Kayla Anson was like—and really, considering the time he had spent thinking about Kayla Anson, it should have been the other way around.

3

The Swamp Tree Country Club was at the end of a long and winding drive, and totally hidden from the road. Approaching it made Gregor think of the opening scene in Daphne du Maurier's *Rebecca,* and especially of the Alfred Hitchcock version. The vegetation at the side of the drive was something worse than overgrown. A lot of it seemed to be made up of bushes with brambles on them.

They made a turn and then another turn, and the vegetation ceased abruptly, replaced by a broad lawn in perfect order. The clubhouse was long and low and substantial-looking. Behind it, a golf course meandered up a gentle hill. At least one foursome was playing, making their way from the fifth to the sixth hole.

Stacey parked the car as close to the front door as possible and got out. Gregor got out, too.

"We're supposed to go right in and tell the man at the door that we need to see Thomas Mortimer," Stacey said. "I guess he's some kind of bouncer. To keep the nonmembers out."

Gregor didn't think that a lot of nonmembers showed up here, demanding to be let in. He didn't think a lot of nonmembers even knew that this was here. He followed Stacey toward the front door. Halloween might as well not have been happening at all, as far as the Swamp Tree Country Club was concerned. There wasn't so much as a jack-o'-lantern on the front porch.

The man just inside the front door was not a bouncer. He was far too old, and far too dignified, and dressed in a white tie and tails. Stacey explained what they had come for and the man retreated for a moment into a little wooden booth at the side of the wall. Then he came out again and asked them to take a seat while they waited.

They might as well not have bothered. It took no time at all for Thomas Mortimer to come out to get them, bustling with officiousness like a minor bureaucrat at the head of an even more minor department. Gregor knew the type all too well, and hated it. This was a man who would interrupt his subordinates at every opportunity. If you wanted to question those subordinates, you would have to get them out of the room.

"Mr. Demarkian," he said, holding out his hand to Gregor and ignoring Stacey Spratz completely. "It's such an honor and relief to have you here. Truly. I've read about every one of your cases. And this must be Officer—"

"Spratz," Stacey said.

"How good of you to come." Thomas Mortimer was staring over the top of Stacey's head. Then he turned back to Gregor.

"Come this way now, come this way," he said, leading them off down a hall to the side. "You'll see what the problem is immediately. We would have seen it ourselves except that the lawyers had the records all day Saturday and most of Sunday. They only got them back to us at nine o'clock last night."

"Lawyers?"

"Kayla Anson's lawyers. They came on Saturday morning and took the records of Kayla Anson's account here. If I'd been on duty I never would have allowed it. The account is really our responsibility. But Mrs. Grandmere was here instead, and she was quite at a loss for what to do, so she let them into the system. The computer system. We've been fully modernized here for at least the last three years."

"Ah," Gregor said.

Thomas Mortimer stopped before a heavy wooden door.

It had a brass plate on it that said OFFICE OF THE MANAGER. He opened it and shooed them inside, to a big room with its own fireplace and what was almost a wall of windows looking out on the golf course. Gregor stepped inside and saw that there were two women there, a dark one sitting calmly in a big wing chair and a blonde who was pacing back and forth in front of the bookcases at the far end of the room. Gregor didn't think he had ever seen anybody so tense in all his life.

"Well," Thomas Mortimer said. "This is Mrs. Grandmere." He nodded toward the dark-haired woman. "And this is Mrs. Martindale." He nodded toward the blonde.

"Ms.," the blonde woman said, but it was automatic. Gregor didn't think she even realized that she had spoken.

"Well," Thomas Mortimer said. "To explain. Mrs. Grandmere—"

"Yes," Mrs. Grandmere said. "Well. I would never have noticed it myself. It's not the kind of thing you do notice. But the lawyers saw it right away. Could you tell me what time Kayla Anson died?"

"I don't think we could tell you that," Stacey Spratz said. "I don't think we know exactly yet. We don't have the full medical examiner's report."

"But it was earlier on in the evening. Before, say, eleven o'clock?"

"She was found just around twelve," Gregor said, "and she'd been dead then for some time. I don't know if it's impossible that she was alive at eleven o'clock."

"How about at eleven twenty-two?" Mrs. Grandmere said. "Could she have been alive and here at eleven twenty-two?"

"She wasn't here at eleven twenty-two," Ms. Martindale said suddenly. "I would have seen her. I brought Mallory in for a drink at about eleven."

"I keep telling Sally that Kayla may have been here but out of sight," Mrs. Grandmere said. "This is a large place. And very—convoluted, so to speak."

"Well," Gregor said, "for what it's worth, I don't think

she could have been here, alive and well, at eleven twenty-two. Not unless I've got my geography all mixed up again—and even then, it would be pushing it. How far are you from Margaret Anson's house?"

"About six miles by the roads," Thomas Mortimer said. "Less than a ten-minute drive."

"I still don't think it would have been possible," Gregor said.

Mrs. Grandmere shifted in the wing chair. "I don't think it's possible, either, and neither did the lawyers. That's why they asked me about it. Because it really is right there, plain as day, as soon as you know to look for it."

"What is?"

It was Sally Martindale who spoke up. "A withdrawal from her account. From Kayla Anson's account. She kept a cash account here at the club."

"A large withdrawal?" Gregor asked.

"Two hundred dollars," Sally said.

"Was that a large amount of money for her to take out? Did she usually take out less?" Gregor asked.

Sally Martindale shrugged. "I could look it up for you. It sounds like a normal amount. People take that sort of money all the time, and more, really, when they play golf or they've got a bet in a football pool."

"I don't think the problem is the amount of money," Mrs. Grandmere said. "It's who took the money. It couldn't have been Kayla Anson. She wasn't here at the time. She might not even have been alive."

"It might have been her killer," Thomas Mortimer said. "That's what I was thinking. Somebody might have murdered her to get access to her accounts, and then—"

"If they did, they'd have to be a member of the club," Sally Martindale said. "We don't have cash machines here. Anybody can't get in the front door. You have to find a club officer to get to your account for you."

"And that club officer would be—?" Gregor asked.

"It could be any of us in a pinch," Mrs. Grandmere said. "That's not a problem. It's just that none of us seems to have been the club officer involved in this case. I have talked to the night manager, and you can, too, but the fact is that he says he gave nobody at all any money on Friday evening, never mind somebody as prominent and easy to remember as Kayla Anson."

"Nobody asked me for any money, either," Sally Martindale said. "And I was right there in the open. In the bar. It's not like I was hiding out."

Gregor considered the possibilities. "Are you sure of the time when the money was taken out?" he asked. "Could there be a mistake in the records?"

"It's done by the computer," Sally Martindale said. "I suppose if you knew how to override the program, you could change the time. I wouldn't want to do it."

"Could anybody at all have had access to the computers?"

"In the middle of the night like that, it might have been possible," Mrs. Grandmere said, "but it would have been risky. We don't keep the rooms locked. This is a private club. But people are in and out of these offices all the time. And even on a weekend night, if the night manager had seen a light he wasn't expecting coming from under Sally Martindale's door—well. He would have looked."

"I think we ought to keep the doors locked," Sally Martindale said. "It isn't the way it was when I was growing up. People aren't the same. Kids aren't the same."

"I'm not going to turn my club into an armed camp," Thomas Mortimer said. "The members would never stand for it."

"The members won't stand for having their accounts stolen from," Mrs. Grandmere said sharply. "I mean, Thomas, really. That's what we're talking about here. Somebody stole two hundred dollars from Kayla Anson's club account on the night she was murdered."

Sally Martindale put her face in her hands.

Gregor stood looking at the three of them. He was half-sure that they must have thought of what he was thinking of now, but he could never tell. Some people were almost criminally naive. He looked from one to the other of them and then at Stacey Spratz, who for all his loud-voiced bumbling had picked up on the thread immediately.

"Do you have access to the rest of Kayla Anson's records?" he asked them.

"We've got copies," Mrs. Grandmere said.

"And you have records on all the other accounts for all the other members of the club?"

"Yes, of course we do," Mrs. Grandmere said. "What *are* you getting at, Mr. Demarkian?"

It was Sally Martindale who said it. It burst out of her like an explosive cough. "He's saying we should check it all," she said, seeming near tears. "Every last account. Because two hundred dollars from Kayla Anson's account last Friday probably wasn't the first time, and Kayla Anson probably isn't the only one whoever it was took money from."

Four

I

For Margaret Anson, the only real blessing was that it was Monday. On Monday, people had to be where you expected them to be. The long weekend had been an agony beyond anything she could have imagined. It had been a little like being in jail, with the press people in the road day and night and nowhere to go that she could have gotten to. This morning it had occurred to her that she could have gone away completely. She could have gotten on the train and gone to the city and put up at a hotel, or even left the country. She had her passport in a leather passport holder in the bottom of her bag. She supposed, if she'd done it, that she would have been followed. Maybe she would be followed everywhere now. Maybe it would only last as long as it took to put someone in jail for these two murders, assuming they ever put anyone in jail for them at all. She was still angry beyond belief that Zara Anne Moss had been in her garage. Surely there was somewhere else the girl could have gone, somebody else she had wanted to see. Surely there was some place the girl might have fit. All that batik cotton and jangly cheap gold jewelry, like an actress playing a Gypsy in a cut-rate movie. All that simpering innocence.

Derek Chase would have come out to the house for this conversation, but Margaret had been unable to stand the idea of spending the entire day in the house. The Swamp Tree Country Club wasn't really much better, but at least it had a decent menu and private rooms for members who needed to conduct confidential business. Besides, there was a factotum at the door and various guards around the place. It was for members only. The press would not be allowed to bother her here.

She had called ahead and reserved conference room

four. It was the small one, the one almost nobody ever wanted, and she had known before she asked for it that she was most likely to get it. She brushed by the doorman and Thomas Mortimer in the hall. They were murmuring solicitations in her direction, but she didn't want to hear them. She didn't feel that she needed condolences of any kind. Kayla was dead and that was the end of it. She saw Ruth Grandmere and Sally Martindale working busily over papers in one of the offices. She had heard terrible, satisfying things about Sally Martindale—that her husband had left her, that she had so little money that she was sometimes unable to heat the house. Shirtsleeves to shirtsleeves in three generations. That was what people had said when she was growing up, pointing to the new money that was pouring in in the aftermath of the war. Things were faster now, and less forgiving. People were going from shirtsleeves to shirtsleeves in a single lifetime.

She got to conference room four and opened the door. Derek was already there, seated at the table with his attaché case open and a small set of papers lying spread out in front of him. He was not a young man, although he was younger than she was—in his late forties, she would have guessed. He was thinning at the top, the way so many men do. His grandfather had been with her father at the Hill School.

Margaret went into the room and closed the door behind her. Derek looked up and stood when he saw her. She shook hands with him and then sat down herself.

"Margaret," he said. "Please believe me. I was so sorry to hear about Kayla, to hear about this young woman—"

"We could get past this part," Margaret said. "I don't need your sympathies about Kayla. And the young woman has nothing to do with me."

Derek had the good sense not to look surprised. By now he knew her very well. He sat down and moved his papers around on the desk.

"I should think that at the very least you would be worried about the young woman," he said. "Having two dead bodies in your garage in three days is not likely to look entirely innocent to the police."

"I'm sure it won't. It doesn't matter."

"Doesn't it?"

"Well, Derek, I didn't kill her. I had nothing to do with whoever it was did kill her. That should be enough to keep me out of trouble, don't you think?"

"Maybe and maybe not."

"I think it's going to turn out to be one of those serial killer people. Somebody roaming all around killing young women of a certain type. Although I will say that I don't know what type Kayla and this one might have had in common. Really, she was—I don't even know how to describe it. Ridiculous, I supposed."

"Zara Anne Moss was ridiculous."

"Oh, yes. That was her name. That was ridiculous by itself. Zara instead of Sarah. My mother always stressed the importance of giving children solid, traditional names. They don't date. But of course I couldn't do anything with Robert. Robert wanted a daughter named Kayla, and Robert got a daughter named Kayla. Robert tended to get whatever he wanted."

"And you didn't mind," Derek said, "finding the body in the garage? Finding a dead person?"

"Of course I minded. I'm just not being overemotional about it. Why should I be?"

"No reason at all." Derek looked down at this papers again. "So, you want me to go over your position vis-à-vis the estate?"

"I want you to tell me something about it, yes. They've already been out here, you know. Kayla's trust lawyers. The ones Robert picked. They came to the house and searched her room. I nearly threw them out."

"Why didn't you?"

"Because I didn't really know what my position was. I think that now that Kayla's dead I own the house. I know that I have a life interest in it, but I don't know if there are conditions under which that interest could be terminated.

And they'd love to get me out of there, the whole lot of them. They didn't even like Kayla living with me."

"You didn't like Kayla living with you," Derek said. "I was always rather surprised that she agreed to it. Now that she was eighteen, I mean. She had control of a good deal of money. Why didn't she just leave?"

"Leave and get her own house and sign up for an ordinary public school and finish her senior year that way?"

"Something like that, yes."

"She thought of it," Margaret said. "We talked about it. Or rather, she talked about it to me, and to Annabel Crawford and Peter Greer."

"And?"

"I take it they didn't think well of it, or they talked her out of it. Annabel isn't really interested in graduating from some public high school. She likes being the world's ultimate debutante. And Peter—" Margaret made a gesture in the air.

"I thought Peter was out of the picture."

"I thought so, too. I know Kayla was sour on him. He called and she didn't return his calls, or mostly she didn't. But she saw him last week. They had dinner together out in Southbury. She got home very late."

"Maybe they were gearing it back up again."

"He wanted to marry her," Margaret said. "I know all about that. He's really the worst kind of social climber. But Kayla wouldn't have married him. She—was—enormously annoying about all kinds of things, but she wasn't quite that stupid. I've often wondered what happened at that dinner out in Southbury. I've wondered if she dropped him flat."

"Yes," Derek said. "Well. If you want to look at the structure of the estate—"

The structure of the estate, Margaret Anson thought, and then she sighed a little.

They were all so self-protective, these people. None of them could look life in the eye and accept it for what it was. None of them could accept *themselves* for what they were. But she could. In that way, she was much better than Kayla had ever been, or Robert, either. She was much better than Mr. Gregor Armenian Demarkian, who had come into her house and thought he was tricking her into talking to him. Margaret never talked to anyone she didn't want to talk to, and she never said a single thing she didn't want to say. She wondered what Derek would think if she told him what had really gone on in her mind when she first saw Zara Anne Moss lying dead on the floor of her garage, with her eyes bugged out like the eyes of a carnival doll.

Instead, she got down to business.

"I don't want to talk about the structure of the estate," she told him. "I want to talk about whether or not I'm going to come into some money."

2

It took everything Sally Martindale had not to ask to leave the office early—everything she had and everything she was likely to have for days to come. Ruth Grandmere was going methodically through every account file, one by one, file after file, even though she wasn't finding anything. She couldn't find anything. The files were in perfect order. The only way Ruth would know which ones had been doctored would be to talk to the people they belonged to, and even then she might not know. Some of these women were extremely bad about money. They didn't know how much they had or how much they'd spent or when they'd taken out cash and when they hadn't. Sally wished she had been more careful to take money out only when the account holder was actually at the club. She'd been careful to take it in the same amounts the account holder took himself. She'd been careful in a million other ways. Not careful enough, but careful. Ruth Grandmere was not going to find anything wrong in these accounts today.

Even so, by one o'clock, when it was time for her to leave, Sally was as limp as overboiled vegetables. She had been sweating so much that the back of her dress was soaked through and her hair looked as if it had been in a shower of filthy water. If Ruth had asked her to stay on longer, she would have found an excuse to go. She couldn't have stood the tension for another minute. As it turned out, Ruth herself was fed up and wanted lunch. She left the office first. Which was what gave Sally her chance.

She needed more than two hundred dollars now. She needed at least a thousand. Fifteen hundred would be better. If she went out to Ledyard with pocket change, she would never have a hope of doing what she needed to do. She started plugging numbers into the computer, and this time she wasn't careful at all. She had no idea who was or wasn't in the club at the moment. She didn't even care. She only cared that she not deplete any account to the point where it might cause a member to be charged off, or take so much from any one place that the taking would be obvious. In the end, she had to access twelve different accounts. She'd put herself in a whole new kind of danger. If anybody ever lined up this day's activities in one place, they would see immediately what was wrong. They'd see the rash of charges all made within the same two minutes and know that she, and only she, could be responsible for them. Her muscles seemed to be quivering under her skin. She thought she was going to be sick.

When she was finished, she had to look at the notepad next to her on the desk to see how much she'd taken. She had lost count somewhere in the process. Then she tore the page out of the notebook and tore it into little shreds. Then, just to be safe, she went down the hall to the ladies' room and flushed them down the toilet. When she got back to the office, it was still empty. She felt a shot of adrenaline up her spine—if Ruth had come back from lunch, this would all have been useless. She would have doctored the accounts and gotten nothing out of it at all. Instead, she had timed it perfectly.

She went to the cash drawer and took out twenty-five hundred dollars in twenties and fifties. There were hundreds in the drawer, too, but she didn't want to touch those. They made her feel funny. The club usually had ten thousand dollars in cash on hand on any ordinary day. They never went through that much, but they always had it, just in case.

She tried to put the money in her wallet and found it wouldn't fit. She stuffed it into the little inside zipper pocket instead. It still bulged. If she had known she was going to do this, she would have brought a bigger bag.

Nobody who saw her would think the bulge in her bag was twenty-five hundred dollars of the club's own money. She knew that. They would think she was carrying tennis balls, or that she had her period. She put her bag over her shoulder and looked out over the office. Everything seemed to be all right. Everything seemed to be where it was supposed to be. It was so damned hard to concentrate.

She left the office and went down the short hall to the lobby. She said good-bye to the doorman and walked out the front door. She walked out across the parking lot to her car and climbed in behind the wheel. She was finding it almost impossible to breathe.

She got the car started and moving down the long drive to the road. She made herself think about the steering wheel and the gas pedal and the brake. She made herself think, hard, about Ledyard and the slots. That was what she was going to do today, the slots. No blackjack. No roulette. Just slots. She was going to take quarter after quarter, token after token, and hit those machines for the rest of the afternoon, for as long as it took to get the jackpot bell to ring and the money to come pouring down the chute at her, the money that she would then be able to bring back to the club and use to make everything right.

That was what she needed to do. She needed to make everything right. She needed to get her luck going for once. She had terrible luck. She had always had terrible luck. Her life had been ruined by the way her luck was always getting in her way.

Somewhere out on the highway, she began to calm down—but by then she was halfway across the state, and she couldn't remember most of the driving she had done. She was also doing eighty miles an hour.

She made herself slow down—all she needed now was to have some state trooper pull her over and ask to go through her bag—and then she realized that there was only one way she was going to be able to get through the rest of this day, until her strategy paid off and she had money again, until she had gotten herself out of this trouble.

She forced one part of her mind to concentrate on the road, and she let the rest of it drift. She put herself squarely into the future, with the coins falling into her lap, and then with the meeting there would be in the casino's office. She made herself see the man from the IRS and the check that would be made out in her name. She made herself see herself taking that check to her own personal bank and putting it in as a deposit. In Connecticut, the law required banks to make the funds from a local check available on the next business day. She made herself see herself in the morning, transferring the money she needed to transfer from her own account to the club's account, and fixing all the records for as far back as they needed to be fixed.

There was only one problem with that. She couldn't remember how much money she had taken, or from whom, or when. She hadn't written it down, and she had done it so often by now that she didn't know if she would ever be able to track it all down.

3

Eve Wachinsky woke up from her fever on Monday afternoon. She had actually woken up a couple of times before then, but she'd still been hot and confused. She'd only been sure that she was in a hospital room, in a hospital bed, and that people kept telling her she was going to be all right. She didn't think she really was all right. All her muscles ached. Her eyes felt ready to fall out of her head.

Now she turned over in bed and saw a young woman

sitting in a chair near the broad plate glass window, reading an oversized paperback book. *In Praise of Folly*, it was called, by Desiderius Erasmus. Eve had never heard of a writer named Desiderius Erasmus. She hadn't heard of many writers at all, although she knew who Stephen King was, because she had seen him once on *The Tonight Show*.

She tried to sit up and found it too hard to do. She was too weak. And she was starving. She tried again and let out a little moan. The young woman at the window put her book down and looked up.

"Oh, my goodness," she said. "You're awake. I'd better call the nurse."

"Accident?" Eve asked.

The young woman had come up to the bed and begun to ring the buzzer there. She shook her head at Eve's question and said, "No accident at all. Spinal meningitis. Very nasty. I was worried about you for a while there yesterday. Do you remember who I am?"

"No."

"I'm Grace Feinmann. I live across the hall from you in Watertown. You came out into the hall, and you were really feeling awful—"

"Yes," Eve said. She did remember. It was fuzzy, but she could remember. Lying on the carpet in the hall. Feeling that it wasn't possible to stand up. Feeling that she had to get to the hospital and that she would never be able to drive. And then this young woman had come and taken her to a car.

"Eve," Eve said.

"Oh, I know," Grace said. "Your name is Eve Wachinsky. We had to go through your wallet to find your information. So that we could check you into the hospital. I hope you don't mind."

"No," Eve said. "Hungry. I'm—hungry."

A nurse came to the door and looked in. "Oh, wonderful," she said. "You're awake. I'll call Dr. Carpenter right away."

"She says she's hungry," Grace Feinmann said.

"I can get her some chicken broth. That's on the chart. For more than that, we'll have to talk to the doctor. I'll be right back."

"I hope chicken broth is okay," Grace said.

Chicken broth was fine. What Eve really wanted was to sit up. She tried again, but fell back almost as soon as she got up. She shook her head.

"I—want to—sit—up," she said.

"Oh, I can do that," Grace told her. She fumbled around at the edge of the bed, and Eve heard machinery under he whirr. The top half of the bed slid upward. It wasn't exactly like sitting up, but at least it wasn't lying flat on her back, either.

"There," Grace said. "I hope that helps."

"Yes," Eve told her. "Thank you."

"We really have been terribly worried. Nobody knew exactly what was going to happen to you. It was very frightening. The doctor said you must have been having symptoms for at least twenty-four hours. Meningitis doesn't hit like this without a day or so of feverishness and achiness that comes before. But I told him, people just don't go to the doctor for things like that. Not unless they have just tons of health insurance, and I couldn't find any health insurance for you at all. I hope you don't mind that we went through all this stuff. We didn't mean to invade your privacy. We were just trying to do what was best—"

"It's all right," Eve said.

A tall nurse's aide came into the room, carrying a tray with two Styrofoam cups full of chicken broth on it. The cups had white plastic lids on them. The nurse's aide put the tray down on a rolling table and pulled the rolling table over to the bed.

"You can have ice water if you want. To go with the broth. Mrs. Corcoran said it would be all right."

"Yes, please," Eve said.

The nurse's aide disappeared and appeared again a few seconds later with a plastic pitcher and a small glass. She put them down on the rolling table next to the broth and disappeared.

"Here, I'll pour some water for you," Grace said. "This seems like a really strange hospital to me. It's almost as if it were empty. The hospitals I'm used to always seemed crammed full of people."

Eve managed to drink some water. Her mouth felt instantaneously better. She hadn't realized how dry it was. She reached for one of the Styrofoam cups of broth and tried to get the lid off. She cup was warm to the touch. The lid wouldn't budge.

"I'll get that," Grace said, and did. Then she handed Eve the opened cup of broth and stepped back. "You're going to be weak as hell for a week, Dr. Carpenter said. Oh, I'm sorry about the language. I mean, I'll be more careful if you want me to be. I keep forgetting that not everybody talks like a bunch of graduate students."

The broth tasted wonderful. It felt wonderful, too. Eve could practically feel her mind clearing and the fuzziness draining away. She tried sitting forward again and found that this time it was not impossible. It wasn't easy, but at least it wasn't impossible. She took another long sip of broth and then a deep breath. It only hurt a little.

"I've caused you a lot of trouble," she said finally.

"No, no," Grace told her. "It wasn't any trouble. And to tell you the truth, sitting here with you in the afternoons has been a big help to me. I mean, I have all this reading to do, and when I'm home I get distracted by the television or the CD player or something else and I don't get it done. Or the phone rings. There's always something. But when I've been here I've been able to concentrate, you see. So it's really worked out."

"Oh," Eve said.

Grace had left her book on the chair she had been sitting in. Eve looked at it again, but it was no more comprehensible than it had been. She tried to put together some kind of idea of Grace's life, and couldn't do it. None of the people Eve knew read many books, and the books they read had titles like *Love's Tempestuous Flower* or *Blood Vengeance*. Grace had said something about being a student, but Eve didn't think that could be right. Grace looked too old to be a student.

Eve took another long sip of broth. She was glad she had a second cup of it. The first one was going fast. And she was hungrier by the minute.

"So," Grace said, "I talked to Darla Barden. You'll have your job when you get out of here. She seems like a very nice woman. Oh, and I got the key from the super and went in and tidied up your apartment a little. Not that it was a mess or anything, but I was looking for your insurance card and there were a few dishes in the sink and I did them. Oh, and I kept you all the stories about the murder."

"Murder?"

"Two murders," Grace said. "First the murder of Kayla Anson, which is really the big noise, and then yesterday there was somebody else. The woman who lived with Faye Dallmer. You know Faye Dallmer, she writes those books about organic gardening and whatever. So this woman was murdered, the second one, and they found her in the same place they found Kayla Anson, in the Anson garage, you know, and now there's a famous detective here from Philadelphia looking into it all. At any rate, I thought it would be a distraction, if you know what I mean. Everybody in town is talking about it and practically nothing else."

Kayla Anson was dead? And also Faye Dallmer's friend, what's-her-name, Zara Anne Somebody. Eve rubbed the side of her face and tried to think.

In the world in which Eve Wachinsky had grown up, people like Kayla Anson and Zara Anne Somebody did not get murdered. Gang girls got murdered, and old ladies who lived in bad neighborhoods in Waterbury and had to walk to the bank and the grocery store. Women like Eve herself got murdered, too, if they were married and their husbands got liquored up. Eve had once gotten a black eye from a boyfriend who had snorted three lines of cocaine after drinking half a bottle of vodka and then decided that he didn't like the smirk on her face. That was the boyfriend before the last one. Part of her was really happy that she hadn't had more boyfriends than she had had.

She took another long gulp of chicken broth and finished the cup. She reached for the other cup and got the lid off this time without difficulty. Grace beamed at her as if she had done something very clever.

"So," Grace said, "let me fill you in. Let me tell you all about the murder and all the rest of it. Really, it's the most interesting thing that's happened around here in the last century."

Five

I

It was Stacey Spratz's idea that they should do something about lunch that was "convenient." It took Gregor Demarkian a while to realize that Stacey wanted to go out for fast food—wanted it, in fact, as ardently as Bennis Hannaford ever wanted Godiva chocolates, or Tibor wanted an evening at La Vie Bohème, where they made perfect flaming orange chicken. There was a Burger King on Main Street in Watertown, and a McDonald's on Straits Turnpike near the Middlebury town line. If you wanted something more esoteric—Taco Bell, say, or Arby's—you had to go into Waterbury, or out to the new mall. Stacey Spratz did not want anything esoteric. He wanted a Big Mac Extra Value Meal with a Barq's root beer. He was willing to settle for a Whopper if Gregor had strong preferences in the direction of Burger King. Gregor didn't think he had eaten in a fast-food restaurant of any kind since he'd been reassigned off kidnap detail, and that was—what? Thirty years ago? McDonald's had only just been starting up then. They'd sold hamburgers for fifteen cents.

"Go to McDonald's," Gregor said, thinking that one place would be as awful as another as far as the food was concerned. "But stop at the inn first. I want to run up to my room and check on some things."

"It's not exactly on the way," Stacey Spratz said.

"Make a detour. I want to check my messages. And I want to check on Bennis. I've left her flat for the past two days."

"The real problem up in the Hills is that there isn't anything, you know what I mean?" Stacey Spratz said. "There's trees and scenery and lots of old New England, but you have to drive for an hour before you can get a decent hamburger. Or do any shopping that isn't going to cost you like you were John D. Rockefeller. Do you think the Rockefellers have as much money as Bill Gates?"

"I doubt it," Gregor said. Sometimes he thought Stacey must have one of those learning disorders—attention deficit disorder, one of those things—because it seemed like the only explanation for why he jumped from subject to subject the way he did.

Stacey pulled into the parking lot of the inn. Gregor tidied his stack of notes into a pile and put them up behind the sun visor on the passenger side of the car.

"You can come in if you like," Gregor told him.

"I'll wait in the car," Stacey told him. "If you don't mind. I mean, I don't want you to feel hurried or anything like that. But you did say you wouldn't be long. So I thought—"

"I won't be long," Gregor promised. "You can wait in the car."

He got out into the crisp cold air as quickly as he could, if only to forestall the need to listen to Stacey going through yet another stream-of-consciousness philosophy. He walked across the parking lot to the inn's front entrance. He thought it had to be the height of the lunch hour. The parking lot was full of vehicles, when it was usually at least a third empty. Women were coming and going in groups of three and four. The working women wore shirtwaist dresses and little heels. The wives wore shorts and tennis shoes and white socks. It was as if everybody was in uniform.

Gregor stopped at the front desk and found that no messages had been left for him. Then he went upstairs and walked down the long hall to his and Bennis's room. The hall was dark as always, but dark in the way that the halls in the homes of very rich people are dark—dark because of its length and height, not because of was cramped or without ventilation. It was incredible, the way he worried at the whole concept of rich and poor now that he was here. In spite of the fact that nobody ever talked about it—that nobody even mentioned the odd extremes of wealth and poverty that seemed to be as much a part of the landscape of this place as maple trees and swiftly flowing streams—it was on his mind all the time.

He opened the door to his own room and stepped in. He called out Bennis's name and got no response. It occurred to him that he should have checked for her car in the parking lot. It was an unusual car. He usually had a hard time missing it.

He went into the small bathroom and washed his face. He went to the bedroom and found his good hairbrush. He was feeling ragged and filthy. That was what came of riding around in cars all day. He was feeling reluctant to go back to Stacey Spratz, and the car, and the prospect of McDonald's. He was going to have to get over that.

The phone rang while he was in the bedroom. He went to the small table at the side of the bed and picked it up.

"Bennis?" he said.

"No," a familiar voice said. "Donna. I'm glad I got you. Where's Bennis?"

"Out driving around, I'd guess. How are you?"

"If Bennis is out driving around, does that mean you're stuck in the hotel?"

"It's an inn, and I'm not stuck. I'm being driven around by a police officer. Who's expecting me downstairs at any moment. Are you all right? Is something wrong?"

"Not exactly. I'm glad I got you. I talked to Bennis earlier."

"And?"

"And I thought of something. With Peter, you know."

"Peter."

"Peter Desarian. You know Peter. Peter is Tommy's father."

"Yes, yes," Gregor said. "It's just that there's a Peter involved in this mess up here. He was Kayla Anson's boyfriend."

"Well, Peter Desarian would love to be the boyfriend of some woman with two hundred million dollars. He'd probably even marry her. At the moment, however, he's trying to stop Russ from adopting Tommy, and that means that I've got to do something."

"I remember," Gregor said. He sat down on the edge of the bed. What was it that Donna had said?

"Anyway, I talked to Bennis about this," Donna said, "and she said that if you even heard about it you'd have a fit, but I thought I'd ask. It couldn't hurt to ask. And I want to know *why* you'd have a fit."

"Why I'd have a fit about what?"

"I was thinking that the best thing to do would be to charge Peter with child abuse. The next time he comes to see Tommy, which is practically never, but now with all this stuff going on in court he wants to come up and take Tommy out for the day. And you can just guess how Tommy feels about that. This is not good just to begin with. And I thought that after Peter brought Tommy back I could say—"

"Don't even think about it."

"That's what Bennis said. But why not?" Donna demanded. "It's not like I'd be doing any real injustice to Peter Desarian, is it? He'd deserve the trouble he got into. He deserves more than that right this minute."

"Do you think you could get Tommy to lie?" Gregor asked. "Do you think you could get him to lie consistently enough so that nobody would ever find out that he'd lied?"

"I don't know what you mean."

"I mean child abuse charges have to be substantiated. If you made a charge against Peter, the court would be required to bring in psychologists, pediatricians, whole rafts of people to see if you'd made it all up. And they'd be assuming that you *had* made it all up."

"Why?"

"Because you aren't the first person who's ever thought of this. In the past ten years or so there have been a raft of these cases, and judges are fairly fed up. Fed up enough so that the first thing that would happen is that the judge wouldn't believe you. And the next thing that would happen—assuming Tommy couldn't keep himself from telling the truth, which is probably the case—is that the court would reject your bid to terminate Peter's parental rights."

"They're going to do that anyway. You said that yourself."

"Yes, I did," Gregor said. "And it's probably true. But that's all they'll do with things as they are now. If they think you're engaged in some kind of vendetta—that you've become emotionally unstable and are unable to provide Tommy with a positive image of his father—they might end up handing custody over to Peter."

There was a long silence on the other end of the wire.

"Peter wouldn't take it," Donna said finally. Her voice was very unsteady.

Gregor sighed. "Peter wouldn't take it, but that harridan mother of his might. Do you really want to jeopardize Tommy's future this way? Is it really necessary?"

"I want Russ to be able to adopt Tommy."

"I know you do."

"I want Tommy to have a father, Gregor. A real honest-to-goodness father."

"He's already got a father, in Russ, even without the adoption. The adoption is a legal construct, that's all. It would be better if it went through. Life wouldn't end if it didn't go through. Your marriage wouldn't end. Tommy's relationship with Russ wouldn't end. There's no need for a scorched earth policy to deal with Peter Desarian at this time."

There was another long pause on the phone. Gregor wondered where Donna was—in the living room of the apartment above his own, in the living room of the new townhouse down the block, sitting on the steps of Lida Arkmanian's townhouse with a cell phone in her hand. He wondered if Donna was trying to keep this secret, or if she'd decided that there was no hope of that in any case.

"I think a scorched earth policy is the only way to deal with Peter Desarian," Donna said. "If that had been my policy from the beginning, I would have ended up in far less trouble."

"You would have ended up without Tommy. On this one, Tibor's right. Don't regret what gave you the best thing you have."

"Well, Gregor, let me tell you. Don't blame me if I wish the whole thing had happened by artificial insemination. How long are you and Bennis going to be out in Connecticut?"

"I don't know."

"Well, the papers are full of you up here. You wouldn't believe it. Do you know who did it yet?"

"No."

"Too bad. I used to think you always knew, right from the start. You just looked over the suspects and you could tell. Tell Bennis to call me when she comes in."

"I'll leave her a note."

"There really does have to be something I can do about Peter Desarian, Gregor. There really does. I'm not going to just sit back and let him get away with this."

"Don't do anything without the advice of your attorney," Gregor said.

"Very funny. But I mean it. I'm sick of being a football. I'm sick of that idiot just tearing my life up every time he gets bored. And I don't believe for a second that he cares one way or the other if Russ adopts Tommy. He's just trying to spoil things. It's what he *does*."

"Don't do anything stupid," Gregor said again.

"I do stupid things every day. I don't seem to be able to help myself. I won't charge Peter with child abuse."

"Good."

"I won't even have a fit when he comes to spend his day with Tommy."

"Also good."

"But that doesn't mean I'm going to like it. I've got to get out of here, Gregor. I've got to help Lida Arkmanian make pastry. If you come back fast enough, you may get a chance at some pretty good food. Father Tibor has decided that the street ought to hold an Armenian festival."

"What?" Gregor said.

"I've got to *go*," Donna said.

The phone went to dial tone in his ear. Gregor held it back and looked at it. An Armenian festival? What kind of an Armenian festival? And when? In some ways, he hated to be away from Cavanaugh Street. As soon as he got out of touch, people in the neighborhood started *doing* things.

He put the receiver back in its cradle and stood up. He would leave a note for Bennis and then he would go back down to Stacey Spratz. He just really wished that he could remember what Donna had said that had caught him up so short.

There was another advantage to being back on Cavanaugh Street. His mind worked better there. He didn't forget things he should remember.

He went to the little desk in the corner of the room and started looking through it for notepaper.

                                    2

The most difficult thing about any case of murder, Gregor had always thought, is getting used to the fact that everybody is going to lie to you. And he did mean *everybody*. Even people who could not possibly be suspects in the case, who had iron-clad alibis, who had been in labor at the time the murder happened or who were too close to blind to be able to fire a fatal shot—even those people lied, and lied often, when presented with the police in search of an explanation for why a dead body had ended up dead. The truth of it was, of course, that people simply lied all the time. Even he lied. Nobody wanted to present themselves to the world in the full reality of what they were in the privacy of their own minds. Nobody was the person he wanted himself to be, or even the person he thought he ought to be. Nobody was without some corner of his life that embarrassed or shamed him.

The problem with the way people lied in murder investigations, though, was that they lied about specifics. They said they were places they hadn't actually been, or weren't in places they had been. They fudged times. They invented emotional attachments to the deceased that had never existed, or put indifference in the place of what had been a hot and angry connection. Some of them were like Margaret Anson, clear enough about the reality that had been but not exhaustive. You got one part of the story and nothing else.

At the McDonald's on Straits Turnpike, Stacey Spratz insisted on getting out to eat.

"I don't like to eat in the car," he told Gregor. "It's too much like—I don't know. Some movie about some loser who couldn't get a wife, I guess."

Gregor didn't like eating in cars, either. It reminded him of kidnapping detail. Everything about driving always reminded him of kidnapping detail. He was sure that kidnapping detail had been the most miserable experience of his life, although not the most painful. The most painful had been watching his Elizabeth die.

He got out of the police cruiser and followed Stacey Spratz into the McDonald's. It was a big, airy space with a sunroom built onto the end and furniture made of blond wood. There had been a fair number of cars in the parking lot, but the restaurant was almost empty. There were no lines at the registers at all.

"I always get a Big Mac," Stacey said helpfully. "But some people prefer a double Quarter Pounder with cheese."

Gregor didn't want a double Quarter Pounder with cheese. He wanted a bowl of *yaprak sarma,* followed by a plate of something sweet, like those farina-and-honey cakes Lida was always making lately that he didn't know the name of. He wished he hadn't left Cavanaugh Street in such a hurry this time. When Lida and Hannah Krekorian knew he was leaving and going to be away for any length of time, they sometimes packed him big picnic baskets full of Armenian food.

He ordered a crispy chicken sandwich and large everything. It startled him a little to find that instead of being given a Coke, he was given a cup and sent to fill it up on his own.

"It's because you get free refills," the young woman at the counter explained helpfully.

If Gregor had known he could refill his drink at will, he would have gotten a smaller one. He took his tray to the soda machine and pushed the button for ice. Something that sounded like a volcano opening up in front of his face started spewing little nuggets of cold into the air.

"I'll get that," Stacey said, coming up behind him.

Gregor let him get it, too. He was not cut out for this sort of thing. He liked restaurants with waiters, even the kind of waiters who insisted on telling you their first names.

Stacey threw little packets of ketchup and a small mound of napkins on Gregor's tray. He got a cup lid and a straw for the Coke. Then he picked up the tray and headed for the sunroom in the back.

"This way," he said. "I got us a table in the warm."

The table was a large square. The chairs were just the kind Gregor liked, sturdy instead of ornamental. He sat down and looked at his food with uncertainty. Even when he and Bennis were traveling in the car, and going a long way, they brought their own lunch instead of stopping at fast-food places. The only people he knew who spent time in McDonald's with any regularity were Donna and Russ, and they did it so that Tommy could get the toy in the Happy Meal.

"So," Stacey said, as Gregor said down. "Have you got it figured out yet? Do you know who killed Kayla Anson?"

"No."

"Didn't you think that thing at the Swamp Tree was weird? I keep running scenarios through my mind. Somebody killed her and then went out to the country club and cleaned out her account. Somebody had already cleaned out her account and she found out about it and that's why they killed her. Somebody—"

"It was the blonde woman," Gregor said, trying out his sandwich, which was, in fact, not actively bad, although it had too much mayonnaise on it. "Sally Martindale."

Stacey looked startled. "What was Sally Martindale?"

"The person who took the money. She's the—what? The bursar? Something like that?"

"Well, yeah, I know, but—"

"No buts," Gregor said. "I'll guarantee it. My guess is that she's been stealing from quite a few accounts over an extended period of time. The question is if she's been careful or not. If she's been careful, they won't catch her, no matter how hard she tries. If she hasn't been, they will. That is, assuming that she manages to stop taking money now that she knows they're looking out for it."

"But of course she'd stop," Stacey said. "I mean, if she's really the one. Why wouldn't she stop? She an educated woman. We're not dealing with one of these west mountainers, you know, or the idiots down in Waterbury. Sally Martindale has an MBA."

"She's also a compulsive gambler."

"What?"

"Trust me. I know the signs. I know them backward and forward. Is she married?"

"She used to be. To Frank Martindale, this hotshot arbitrage lawyer. Except I've never known what arbitrage is, exactly. Just that he got paid a ton of money for it. But they got divorced a year or so ago—ah."

"Exactly."

"Jesus," Stacey said. "Did she kill Kayla Anson, too? To hide the fact that she'd taken the money?"

"I don't think so," Gregor said. "I wouldn't rule it out at this stage, but I don't think it's very likely. She doesn't have the nerve. It took nerve, killing Kayla Anson. And then killing Zara Anne Moss. In the garage like that."

"Do you think Kayla Anson was killed in the garage?"

"No." Gregor drummed his fingers on the table. It was a good table for drumming. It sent up a satisfying hollow-wood sound, even though the wood was probably not hollow. Gregor pulled the pile of napkins off his tray and his pen out of the inside pocket of his jacket. The trick to writing on napkins was to write on them folded, not spread out. If you spread the napkin out, it tore with every movement of the pen.

"Look," he said. "Kayla Anson had to have been killed sometime between the time that Zara Anne Moss saw the BMW driving down the Litchfield Road, followed by the Jeep, and the time you saw the same BMW speeding through Morris."

"Why?"

"Because it doesn't make any sense to think that Kayla Anson herself would have been speeding. If she'd been willing to speed, why wouldn't she have been doing it when Zara Anne Moss saw her? What did Zara Anne say? The Jeep was following so closely behind that it was almost bumping into the BMW's bumper. But Kayla Anson did not speed up, or at least didn't speed up significantly. Which indicates to me, at any rate, that she didn't like putting the pedal to the floor."

"Ah," Stacey said. "I see what you mean. But that's still conjecture."

"Yes, it is. But you've also got the body, which from everything I've heard about it had been dead at least some time before Bennis Hannaford found it. And you've got the garage, which showed no sign of anything in the way of evidence that a murder had been committed there. I read those reports you gave me. There was absolutely nothing."

"Maybe there wouldn't have been anything, if the murder had taken place in the car."

"In that case, the murderer must have been Margaret Anson. She's the only one who could have committed it in the car and in the garage and not have had to worry about leaving evidence of herself someplace on the property. And she's my favorite suspect, at the moment. The most likely person, so to speak. But even if it *is* Margaret Anson . . ."

"Yes?"

Gregor's drumming became a pounding. "There should be footprints."

"What?"

"There should be footprints. Or something. The Jeep had to have been ditched first. Or ditched and then come back for. I wish I had a map."

"I can get you maps—"

"Not that kind of map," Gregor said. "I keep telling you, I want to draw a map that shows where everything is. How far it would be to walk. Because whoever killed Kayla Anson had to do a fair amount of walking on the night of the crime. He had to ditch the Jeep completely or ditch it and then come back for it. He had to get home. You ride around on these roads out here and you feel that everything is a million miles apart. The whole scenario seems impossible."

"Things aren't millions of miles apart," Stacey said. "But you keep saying 'he.' Are you so sure it isn't Margaret Anson?"

"No, I'm not. I was just speaking the way we were taught to speak before political correctness. And Margaret Anson would have the easiest time of it here—ditch the Jeep, bring the body back in the car, park it in the garage, and walk across the drive to her own living room. Much the simplest possible sequence of events."

"But you don't believe it," Stacey said.

"I believe that I need to make that map," Gregor said. "Let's go somewhere and do it. There has to be somebody around here who would understand the kind of thing I mean and has some decent information about distances. And after that, we can talk to Peter Greer."

"Why Peter Greer?"

"I'll explain to you about Peter Greer later. Let's go."

Stacey Spratz looked down at the table and blinked.

"But Mr. Demarkian," he said. "You haven't finished your fries."

Six

I

The last thing Annabel Crawford wanted to do, this afternoon or at any other time, was to drive out to Margaret Anson's house. To *Kayla's* house, she kept telling herself, as if, if she said it often enough, she could stop thinking of that place as having nothing to do with Kayla at all. It was just a place for Kayla to die in, that's what Annabel thought. All that worried nattering on the television news was just so much nonsense. Of course Kayla had died there, in the garage, with the bats roosting in the rafters over her head. She had died there just the way that woman from Faye Dallmer's place had died there. It was a miracle that the bats hadn't had at both of them—or maybe they had. That was the problem with knowing so little firsthand, with not being able to see for yourself. It was impossible to get the whole thing straight in her mind. Maybe the bats had roosted in Zara Anne Moss's hair. Maybe they had pecked against the window of the car where Kayla's body was, desperate to get in.

Annabel had spent all afternoon at the club—again. Since Kayla had died, she seemed to hate the idea of being home. Jennifer was at home, treating this whole thing like one more soap opera, except that Jennifer didn't watch soap operas. Soap operas were not considered a good thing by the run-of-the-mill Litchfield County lady. They were too low-rent, for one thing. They were the kind of thing that housewives in small Cape Cod houses with jobs at the local Kmart watched and thought they were getting a glimpse into the life of upper-middle-class suburban ease. The *clothes* were all wrong. That's what Jennifer and her friends always said, when they talked about the women in those Cape Cod houses, the women who contributed ten dollars in cash to the latest Cancer Society fund drive. Annabel sometimes wondered what it was like, living the way those people lived, going to public schools, doing your own lawn, having a bedroom that was barely as big as her walk-in closet back home. She couldn't imagine it. She had always lived like this. She always wanted to. She didn't believe Mallory Martindale when she said that that other way was real life, and that this was all a fantasy that they were indulging in only because they could. Mallory Martindale said that she was going to go to nursing school and then get a job in a hospital somewhere. She was going to have one of those Cape Cod houses of her own, if she could ever afford to buy a house.

"I'm not going to kill myself to try to keep *this* up," she'd said, and then she had pocketed Annabel's money, the money for the dress.

Annabel didn't know if she was happy to have the dress or not. She only knew that Mallory was happy to have sold it to her. She thought that what Mallory was doing was insane.

What she was thinking of doing was insane, too, but that was a more complicated thing. Deciding that you'd rather be rich than poor should have been a no-brainer. Annabel paused in the hall outside Ruth Grandmere's office and looked around. The administrative hall at the club was always mostly deserted. It was as if none of the members wanted to be seen in the vicinity of the actual work that had to be done to keep the club running. Annabel knocked on Ruth Grandmere's door and looked inside. The office was empty, but there was what seemed to be a propped-up white card at the end of her desk. Annabel went in and read it.

Mortimer, it said. *I'm in Sally Martindale's office.*

Annabel backed out into the hall. That was odd. She had seen Ruth walking around a little while ago, and she had simply assumed that something had happened to change the schedule. Ruth was never on duty at the same time as Thomas Mortimer.

Sally Martindale had the bursar's office. Something had

happened to her marriage, and now she had to work at the club. Annabel couldn't imagine that any more than she could imagine Mallory in nursing school. She went down the hall and found that the bursar's door was open. She stuck her head inside and saw that Ruth Grandmere was alone. She felt instantaneously better. She had to talk to someone. The situation was getting critical. She couldn't have talked to Sally Martindale to save her life.

Ruth Grandmere was sitting at Sally Martindale's desk, bent toward a computer screen, with a frown on her face. Annabel knocked tentatively on the open door. Then, when Ruth didn't budge, she knocked again.

This time, Ruth heard. She turned away from whatever was engaging her attention, but for a moment it was as if she couldn't recognize the person in the doorway. It made Annabel feel very strange, as if she had ceased to exist. Then Ruth seemed to snap to attention, and her gaze cleared, and she smiled.

"Annabel, hello. I'm sorry. I'm afraid I'm a little distracted."

"That's all right," Annabel said.

"I wish I understood more about computers than I do," Ruth Grandmere said. "And more about money. It seems odd to me, to get to my age and understand so little about money. Can I ask you a question?"

"Of course."

"Do you often take money out of your account here? In cash, is what I'm talking about. Do you take money out frequently?"

"I don't take it at all. I just charge stuff."

"But what about when you've run short of cash?"

"I don't think I ever have. Not out of here. And in town you can use the ATM."

"Yes," Ruth said. "Yes, you can." She looked back at the console, tapped a few keys, and waited. Then she shook her head again and sighed. "You didn't take one hundred twenty-five dollars out of your account last August twenty-second?"

"On August twenty-second, I was in Martha's Vineyard. We're always on the Vineyard in August. We go to stay with my grandparents."

"Do you? I didn't realize it was all of August. Good God, but this is a mess, isn't it? I don't know what we're going to do about it.".

"Do about what?"

Ruth Grandmere seemed to come to again. This time, she looked sheepish.

"Don't mind me," she said. "I'm just rambling on. It isn't very important, really. We've just got a lot of computer mess-up in the records, and they'll all have to be straightened out. Was there something you wanted that I could help you with?"

Annabel shifted from one foot to another. The idea of Ruth Grandmere working on Sally Martindale's computer was intriguing. Where was Sally Martindale? How messed up could the records get, that Ruth would come in when she was supposed to be off-duty just to get them straightened out?

Annabel looked at the floor, and then at the ceiling.

"The thing is," she said. "It's about Kayla."

"Kayla?"

"I was going to ask for your advice," Annabel said. "I mean, you know what my mother is like. She can't keep her head about anything, really. And so I didn't want to ask her. But I thought you might have an idea."

"If there's something important going on in your life," Ruth Grandmere said, "you should talk to your parents, no matter how hard it is. I know what it's like around here, Annabel. I know that it's sometimes very hard for young people to go to their parents with a problem when their parents have spent years, spent years—"

"Pretending that their children don't exist?" Annabel said. "Yes, I know about that, too. But that wasn't the kind of thing I meant."

"What kind of thing did you mean?"

"It's just that—if you had some information, about

Kayla, that might be of some use to somebody, would you tell them?"

"What kind of information could you have about Kayla?"

Annabel really wanted to sit down. Now that she had started this, it didn't seem like such a good idea.

"It's just—something I came across. Something Kayla told me. And I keep thinking that Margaret Anson ought to know."

Ruth Grandmere was no longer paying any attention to the computer console at all. She was turned around on her swivel chair, giving Annabel her full attention.

"If there's something you know about Kayla Anson that has to do with her murder, you shouldn't tell Margaret. You should tell the police. Or that detective, that Mr. Demarkian."

"It's not that kind of thing. At least, I don't think it is."

"What kind of thing is it?"

"It's hard to explain. But Margaret is the one who ought to know. Because Margaret is the—what do you call it? The heir. Isn't she?"

"I don't know," Ruth Grandmere said.

"I don't see that the information has anything to do with her murder. I mean, it was months and months ago that we talked about it. But it was supposed to be—private, I guess. Nobody was supposed to know. So I thought that maybe Kayla hadn't made a record of it, and Margaret Anson wouldn't know."

Annabel had been half-staring at the ceiling again while she said all this. When she turned her attention again to Ruth Grandmere, she saw that the older woman had become almost comically agitated. She was half-rising out of her seat. Her eyes had become very wide. Annabel stepped back, startled.

"Listen to me," Ruth Grandmere said. "Make sense, for once in your life. Two people are already dead. Do you understand me?"

"Yes, I know, but the thing is—"

"The thing is nothing," Ruth insisted. "Two people are dead, and they were both found in Margaret Anson's garage. Both of them. If you don't know what people around here have been saying about that, you haven't been listening."

"I do know," Annabel said. "But—"

"No buts. I'm not going to say that I think that Margaret Anson murdered her own daughter in her own garage, because I suppose you should treat people as innocent until proven guilty. But you must know as well as I do that Margaret is capable of it. If you've got some information, no matter how trivial you think it is, you should take it to the police."

"Yes," Annabel said. "Yes, I know."

Ruth reached out and touched her shoulder. "I want you to promise me that you won't go hauling off to Margaret's house and laying this thing all out for her. You'll talk to the police instead."

"The police really aren't going to be interested."

"That's fine. After the police say they aren't interested, then you can go to Margaret Anson. But not before. For your own safety. Okay?"

"Okay," Annabel said.

Ruth Grandmere relaxed back into her chair. "That's all right then. As long as you're going to be sensible."

Annabel made polite little noises, but Ruth didn't hear them. She was back at the computer console again, concentrating as hard as if she were taking an exam. Annabel backed quietly out of the office and into the hall.

Of course she knew the sensible thing to do was to tell the police anything that might be relevant—or even anything vaguely odd, in case it might be relevant. And what she knew was definitely odd. The problem was, it really didn't concern anybody but Margaret Anson, which meant that it was Margaret Anson who ought to be told. She ought to be told soon, too, because the longer it went before something was done about it, the harder it would be to actually do anything.

Assuming, of course, that there was anything to be done. Assuming that Kayla hadn't taken care of it herself months ago. She had said that she was going to take care of it.

Annabel let herself out of the administrative hall and into the main body of the club. Then, on an impulse, she walked out of the club's front doors and into the parking lot. Even if Margaret had killed Kayla, it had nothing to do with her. This wasn't the kind of information you murdered somebody for. This was the kind that made you end up giving them a reward.

Annabel got into her car and started it up. Her jacket was still in the club. She'd have to come back for it later.

What she needed to do now was to drive out to Margaret's house and lay it all out on the table. She didn't have to worry about Margaret Anson getting violent, because she was sure that Margaret would never do anything conspicuous in front of all those reporters parked in front of her house. *There* was a trait that all the Litchfield County ladies shared. They all hated publicity.

Of course, Zara Anne Moss had been killed in Margaret's garage and at a time when Annabel supposed that there must have been reporters in the road, but for some reason that fact didn't seem to change the equation in any way that mattered.

2

Martin and Henry Chandling were waiting on their front porch when Stacey Spratz drove up with Gregor Demarkian, and Martin thought immediately that he'd never in his life seen a less foreign-looking man than this one with the big shoulders and the much-too-heavy coat. It made him a little peeved. He had been expecting something a little more definite, someone like Peter Lorre, maybe, or like Yakov Smirnoff. He had most certainly been expecting an accent, which only seemed natural for a man with a name like Gregor Demarkian. If Gregor Demarkian was a real American instead of an Armenian, why hadn't he changed that name? Any normal person would have become Gregory Marks by now.

The state police cars were a little larger than the ones the towns in the hills used for their local police department. Gregor Demarkian didn't have to unfold himself too thoroughly from the front passenger seat. Still, he was a large man, much larger than the ones Martin was used to. Martin guessed that he was at least six three, and he didn't have to guess about the gut. It was pitiful, the way some men went to seed.

"Doesn't look like much, does he?" Henry asked, as they watched the two men walk toward them. Neither of them moved. Neither of them would have moved even if they'd been offered money. There was a standard to maintain.

"Martin? Henry?" Stacey Spratz said. "This is Gregor Demarkian."

"We see that," Henry said.

"We were just up at the Litchfield County Museum," Gregor Demarkian said.

"He brought that thing down here himself, that's what we think," Henry said. "That Jake what's-his-name. He brought it down here just to make a fuss so that his museum would get in the newspapers. Then somebody came along and murdered that rich girl, and that took care of that."

"We want to go up the hill and see where the Jeep tipped over," Stacey Spratz said.

Martin tipped his chair back a little farther. He had to be careful, because he'd tipped himself over backward once or twice already this year. Now he thought, uncomfortably, that the rumors they'd been hearing were true. The Jeep was involved in the death of Kayla Anson, somehow. Whoever had brought it here had been dumping it after he'd used it to—what? Martin wasn't very clear on that. He thought Kayla Anson had been killed in a different vehicle altogether, possibly in her own car. He only knew that the Jeep had to fit in one way or another.

He let all four feet of his chair hit the floor and heard Henry do the same.

"Come on up," Henry was saying as he got to his feet. "It's right up the path. It isn't far at all."

"It seemed far on the night," Martin said. "In the dark."

"We thought it was kids," Henry said. "We're always getting kids. Kids like to muck around in graveyards."

"They like to overturn the gravestones," Martin said helpfully.

In the full light of day, it wasn't a long walk up to the cemetery at all. It didn't seem treacherous, either. The path was well-packed and broad enough not to be claustrophobic. When you could see it, there was nothing to stumble over.

They got to the top of the hill. Martin and Henry stood back to let Stacey Spratz and Gregor Demarkian go before them. There was really not very much to see. The Jeep had been a heavy vehicle, so there was still some impression in the dirt, but not much. The grass had sprung back into place.

"If we'd have known it was going to have something to do with the murder," Martin said, "we'd have been more careful. We just thought it was kids."

"This was at what time?" Gregor Demarkian asked. "Do you remember?"

"Sure we remember," Henry said. "It was just after midnight. That was part of the point. They always wait to midnight to get going. They think it's funny."

Gregor Demarkian was circling the few indentations in the ground that were left as evidence of what had happened to the Jeep. Martin thought he looked like a dog trying to get comfortable enough to go to sleep. He stopped and looked back in the direction of Martin and Henry's house. Then he did another circle of the area and looked down the hill.

"What's down there?" he asked.

"Capernaum Road," Henry said. "Town-maintained dirt. Except I think it's Watertown, not Morris."

"It is Watertown," Martin said.

"All these towns up here sort of wrap around each other," Stacey Spratz said to Gregor Demarkian.

Gregor Demarkian was looking at the ground again.

"Does anybody have any idea of how the Jeep actually got here? Did it drive up from the house?"

"It couldn't have," Henry said. "We would have heard it. We were sitting right there in our front room."

"How about down from the Litchfield County Museum?"

"It couldn't have gotten through," Martin said. "There's a path to that but it's a footpath. It's not wide enough for a Jeep."

"Trees," Henry said solemnly.

"All right," Gregor Demarkian said. "That seems to leave two possibilities. Either in from the road out front, or up from down there. There was no indication?"

"It's all rocks," Stacey Spratz said apologetically. "There's nothing to leave tire tracks in. Everybody likes gravel drives."

They all looked down at the hill that led to Capernaum Road. That was rocks, too, but bigger ones than what would be on a gravel drive. Martin thought this was really pitiful. On television, when the police conducted investigations, they used state-of-the-art equipment and mobile crime labs. They were able to find microscopic cloth fibers on blades of grass.

"I don't know what you're going to find up here, just looking around," Martin said. "They took the Jeep away the next morning. That was Saturday. And then we tidied up some. That's what we're paid to do. Keep the cemetery tidy."

"The cemetery is not in use any longer?" Gregor Demarkian asked.

"Well, of course it's in use," Martin said. "We've got dead people up here. Dozens of them."

"He means in use by people today," Henry said. "They don't bury anybody new up here, that's what he wants to know. They haven't buried anybody new up here for a long time."

"How long a time?" Gregor Demarkian asked.

"Maybe a hundred and fifty years," Henry said.

"There are still Fairchilds out there someplace," Martin said. "They've got a right to be buried here if they want to be. 'Cept none of them ever seem to want to be."

"Do they visit their dead?" Gregor Demarkian asked.

"Of course they don't." Henry said. "Do you visit the graves of people in your family died around Civil War? Nobody visits graves that old."

"Mr. Demarkian's graves would probably be in Europe somewhere," Martin said.

Gregor Demarkian made another circle of the area. Then he straightened up. "All right," he said. "That's the most I can do here. The Jeep was really banged up?"

"It was damned near totaled," Henry said.

"You can go down to Faye Dallmer's place and see it," Stacey Spratz said.

"What I want to know is whether it was more banged up than it should have been just from driving up to this part of the cemetery. Even if, say, it came from down there."

"It looked like it had been in a head-on collision," Henry said.

Gregor looked from one to the other of them and nodded. "All right," he said again. "That's what I needed to know. I thank you both for taking the time and the trouble to help us out."

"It was no problem at all," Martin said.

"It put a little interest in the day, if you want to know the truth," Henry said. "Not a lot happens up here. You get bored."

"I don't get bored," Martin said.

They walked down the hill toward the house and Stacey Spratz's state police car. What Martin had said was perfectly true. He didn't get bored—listless, sometimes, but not bored. But then, he didn't think of the Jeep and the murder of Kayla Anson as putting a little interest into the day. He didn't know how he thought of them.

They got to the state police car. Gregor Demarkian got into the front passenger seat. Stacey Spratz opened the driver's side door and leaned on it for a moment.

"We'll probably have to come back," he said. "We'll give you a call."

"Fine," Henry said.

Martin went back up on the porch. It was definitely colder than it had been. He should have worn his barn jacket instead of just this thick flannel shirt. He wondered what would happen to him when he died. He couldn't be buried in the Fairchild Family Cemetery. If he died before Henry, maybe Henry would have him cremated. If he died after, there would be nobody to do for him at all.

Henry came back up on the porch.

"You ever think about dying?" Martin asked him.

"No," Henry said.

"You want to tell me why you told that Demarkian man we were sitting in the front room when the Jeep crashed, when you know as well as I that you were out in back and I was on the porch?"

Seven

I

Later, Gregor Demarkian would wonder if he had gone about it wrong—if there was something he should have done that he didn't do, if there was something he did do that he should have left undone. At the time, he hardly thought of himself as making a decision. There was so much going on in the case, so much that he didn't understand. He was captive to Stacey Spratz and his state police car, too. Gregor didn't think he had ever been in a place where what he needed to see so was spread out, or separated by so much dead space. He supposed Donna Moradanyan Donahue would not be happy about his calling good forest land and open meadows "dead." In spite of the fact that she was staying on Cavanaugh Street, she declared great affection for nature and the outdoors. Gregor had never understood it, himself. He was an urban animal, born and raised in the middle of Philadelphia, forever afterward more comfortable with asphalt than mulch. He also tended to assume the existence of public transportation, which was not a safe assumption. Out here, he could die of exposure waiting for a bus.

"I have an appointment for us with Greer at his house," Stacey Spratz said. "You won't believe this place. Cedar modern, post and beam, millions of windows. Hangs off the side of a hill, you think it's just going to collapse one day in the rain. But it's been up there for five years."

"Only five years? I thought Greer had been in business for longer than that."

"I don't know how long he's been in business, I only know when he built the house. I do remember when the business went big, though. It was about two-and-a-half years ago. All of a sudden, there were ads everywhere. He must have spent a mint."

"Or the company did."

"I never get how that works. My brother-in-law, he's got a body shop business out in Manchester. If the company spends money, he spends money. It's all his money one way or another, you know? But some of these guys, the company gets big enough and it's not all their money anymore."

Gregor tried to think of a way to explain the principle of legal incorporation to Stacey Spratz, and failed at the attempt. He had known officers like Spratz often in his years in the FBI, especially after the founding of the behavior sciences unit, where liaisons with local forces were a matter of almost daily routine. Stacey Spratz would spend his career in a uniform. He would be honest and efficient. He might even be promoted to sergeant. Beyond that, he would not be able to go, no matter how often he pushed all the right buttons, crossed all the right Ts, dotted all the right Is. He lacked both imagination and sophistication. Out here, most of the time, that didn't matter. In a major city, like Hartford or Bridgeport, it would be fatal. That was the trouble with the state police. It covered a lot of territory. Any serious promotion would require Stacey Spratz to go into places he was not familiar with and deal with people who were far more cynical, and unrelenting, than any people he had so far known.

They had gone for miles without seeing any other indications of civilization than speed limit signs—didn't they name the roads out here? Gregor wondered. Didn't they feel the need to post the route numbers?—when they came to a clearing on the side of the road. The clearing had a sign out in front of it that said LINDA'S PARTY STORE, and beyond the sign a low clapboard building that looked like it might once have been a house. It also looked about ready to fall down. Gregor didn't think it could have been painted in a year.

"Pull in here," Gregor told Stacey. "I want to make a phone call."

"Phone call?"

"There are two pay phones right over there."

The pay phones were standing side by side on black metal posts just outside Linda's Party Store's front door. Gregor had no idea why Southern New England Telephone had thought it worth their while to install two of them. Gregor wondered if Linda managed to make any money. Maybe the local people thought it was worth their while to drive all the way out here for liquor. Maybe they weren't really "all the way out here" at all, but had traveled another one of their pretzel routes and ended up almost back to where they had started.

Stacey pulled into the parking lot next to the phone. Gregor got out of the car and rummaged around in the pockets of his trousers for change. Linda's Party Store had made a halfhearted attempt to decorate for Halloween. There was a jack-o'-lantern next to the front door. There was an orange banner on the side of the building with a picture of a black cat on it. Gregor was suddenly homesick for Cavanaugh Street and Donna Moradanyan's lunatic decorating, even though he knew that she hadn't done it this time. He didn't know what he was going to do when she moved and started decorating a different building. Maybe he and old George Tekemanian would be able to convince her to come back and decorate theirs, as well.

He found a pile of change in one pocket and put it out on the little stainless-steel ledge above the hanging phone book. He reminded himself that if he could remember his calling card number, he wouldn't need change for the phone so often. He reminded himself as well that if he could only remember to bring his calling card along in his wallet, he wouldn't need to remember the number and he wouldn't need the change at the same time. He was just so paranoid about carrying around cards. He'd seen too many people get their lives shredded because they'd lost control of their plastic.

He punched a bunch of coins into the machine and dialed the inn. It was only after he'd done it that he realized he was making a local call. It was really impossible to find anything at all around here, or to know where anything was. When the woman at the inn picked up, he asked for his own room. Then he listened to the phone ring for a while and wondered what had happened to Bennis Hannaford.

She must have been in the bathroom, or asleep, he decided, a second later, when the phone was picked up. She certainly sounded tired. He tried to lean against the side of the booth and found he couldn't do it. It was one of those new booths that weren't booths at all, but little freestanding cubicles, practically out in the air and in public.

"Bennis?" He said.

"Oh," Bennis said. "It's you. I was wondering what you're doing."

"We're on our way to interview Kayla Anson's boyfriend. Except that he's not a boy. If you know what I mean."

"Peter Greer. Who owns Goldenrod."

"Right."

"I've been lying down."

"I thought you might have been. That's rather why I called. I was getting a little worried about your health."

There was a little pause on the other end of the line. Gregor thought that Bennis must be dragging on a cigarette. He thought that even though he hadn't heard her light up, and he should have, if she had been asleep when he called.

"My health is fine," she said finally. "I'm just a little tired. Maybe I'm just a little depressed. This hasn't been a lot of fun."

"No, I can see where it wouldn't be."

"Are you going to be long?"

"I don't know," Gregor said. "I expect it depends on how things go with Peter Greer. And then what else Stacey has for me. I'm trying to convince him to draw me a map."

"Probably a good idea."

"Definitely a good idea, but it isn't going over very well. I think he doesn't understand how confused I get. It can be very frustrating."

"I think I have to lie down again," Bennis said. "I really am tired beyond belief. I'm sorry, Gregor."

"Just as long as you aren't angry with me," Gregor said. "I don't know why, but I keep getting this feeling—"

"I'm not angry with you. Believe me. I'm not angry with you in the least. I'm just—tired. And distracted. Okay?"

"Yes," Gregor said.

"I'm going to get a little more sleep."

"All right. I'm going to let Stacey Spratz drive me around. You can get in touch with me if you want to, you know. All you have to do is call the state police dispatcher and tell him who you are. I put you down as one of the people they're supposed to notify me immediately if you call."

"Who else did you put down?"

"Old George Tekemanian and Tibor."

"Not Donna?"

"I'd never get off the phone."

"I'm going to get off and close my eyes."

"Right," Gregor said. And then, because the situation seemed to call for something more, "I missed you. When you were out here and I wasn't. Did you know that?"

"Yes. I missed you, too. Go work."

Gregor put the phone back and stepped away from the booth. He wished he had some other name for it besides booth. It wasn't a booth. He didn't know what it was.

He went back to the car and got into the passenger seat. The engine was still running. Stacey had Big D 103 FM on the radio and was singing along to the Beach Boys doing "Sloop John B."

"Everything okay?" he asked, when Gregor got back into the car.

"Fine," Gregor said.

Everything was fine, too. Gregor was sure of it. He thought the nagging doubt at the back of his brain was just a residual nattering from his obsessiveness about love earlier in the week. He could be obsessive about just about anything if he let himself.

"It's not all that far from Peter Greer's," Stacey told him. "It's just a little bit farther up in the hills."

2

Peter Greer's house was in New Preston, and "a little bit farther up in the hills" was a good way to describe it, although Gregor might have dispensed with the "little." The hills were relentless. Gregor had no idea what people did out here when it started to snow—and they had to do something, because there suddenly seemed to be a lot more of them than there had been. It wasn't that the area was built-up. There was nothing at all like a subdivision, for instance, or a city block. There were, however, a lot of houses, both close to the road and farther back, placed every which way on lots that all seemed to be protected by low stone walls. Every once in a while, there was a wall with a driveway entrance but nothing else to be seen. The house beyond was protected by shrubbery or a thick tangle of trees or sheer distance, so that it couldn't be seen from the road. Peter Greer's was one of these houses. At first, all Gregor could see was a square stone pillar with the number 267 attached to it on a burnished bronze plaque, and an over-sized blue mailbox.

"If I lived out here, I'd live close to the road," Stacey said. "I mean, think of the days when you don't want to go out, but you have to get into your car just to get to your mailbox. Either that, or trek through the snow and the rain just to find out that all you've got is another mailing from Publisher's Clearinghouse."

Peter Greer's driveway was narrow and rutted. Stacey Spratz's patrol car bumped along, threatening to blow a tire every few feet.

"Gravel drives cost a mint to keep up," he said. "And people run out of money and they stop doing it, and this is what you get instead."

"Not good," Gregor said.

"Well, the idiot has probably got an ATV. That could explain it, too."

ATV. All-Terrain Vehicle. It took a while for Gregor to translate it, and by the time he did they were in the rounded open space in front of the garage. The car sitting there, giving off waves of heat, was a Ford Taurus sedan. It was a new sedan, but as Gregor went around the back of it he could see that it was a rental, from Enterprise, one of the cheapest outfits around. Even so, if it had been his car, Gregor would have wanted to give it a better driveway.

Stacey Spratz called in their location and the phone number where they could be reached until further notice. Gregor got out of the car and looked at the house. It was a remarkable piece of architecture, and "hanging off the side of a hill" wasn't a bad way to put it, either. The thing must have been bolted into the rock. It went down a sheer cliff above a small stream, and the stream was *very* far down.

"This thing would give me nightmares," Gregor said.

"Me, too," Stacey said.

The front door was opened and a tall, thin, intensely well-dressed man stepped out. Gregor was interested to note that he could tell that Peter Greer was "intensely well-dressed" even though the clothes he was wearing were nominally casual—jeans, button-down shirt, sweater. The shirt was a good broadcloth, though, and the sweater was cashmere. Even the jeans looked expensive.

"Mr. Demarkian?" Peter Greer said.

"I'm Gregor Demarkian," Gregor said.

"Mr. Greer and I have met," Stacey Spratz said.

Peter Greer stepped back and motioned Gregor and Stacey into the house. The inside turned out to be just as spectacular as the outside had been. Just inside the door was a foyer. The ceiling of it rose two-and-a-half stories above their heads. Beyond the foyer was a living room, which also had a ceiling two-and-a-half stories tall. It also had a solid wall of windows looking out on the sheer drop and the stream below.

"This is a remarkable house," Gregor Demarkian said.

"Yes, isn't it? Lindal Cedar Homes. That's the company that made the kit that it was built from. Custom designed, by the way. I saw an example of their work up in Salisbury and I had to have one."

"It must have cost a lot of money."

"I think it makes sense to spend money on where you live, don't you? After all, you're going to spend most of your time there."

Most people spent a significant part of their time at their offices, but Gregor didn't mention it. He assumed Peter Greer worked hard enough. Starting a successful business and turning it into a player in the national market was not a hobby. He allowed himself to be led into the living room and offered a chair. The chairs, and the sofa, were all navy blue leather.

Peter Greer went to the bar built into the side of one wall and poured himself a Perrier and lime. He gestured to Stacey and Gregor, offering, but they both declined.

"So," he said. "You've come to talk about Kayla. And to get my alibi."

"Something like that," Gregor agreed. "Do you have an alibi?"

"I don't know. I can't figure out what time I'd need to have an alibi for. The news reports have been very confusing."

"Why don't you just tell me what you did on the night Kayla Anson died?"

"I worked late. I do that a lot. We have a new ad campaign ready to launch. I was checking out the print ads. We're doing some television, too—once L. L. Bean started doing television, the rest of us had to, but if you ask me, it's a pain in the ass. But I wasn't ready to look at the television stuff anyway. I just looked at the print."

"Were you with someone while you worked?"

"I was all by myself," Peter Greer said. "Chessy Barre would usually have been with me. She's my personal assistant. But she'd been out all day. She had some kind of food poisoning."

"And this was from when to when?"

"I don't know what you mean by from when to when. I got to work at eight-thirty on Friday morning. I usually do get to work at eight-thirty in the morning."

"And you stayed at work?" Gregor asked. "All day? Without leaving?"

"Oh, no. I left at five or a little after and ran up to Subway in Watertown to get something to eat. I usually pack something from here. I hate fast food. But I hadn't intended to work late that night, so I was stuck."

"And your office is where?"

"On the Litchfield Road, in Watertown near the Morris line."

"And there were people who saw you at work when you left at—five?"

"Or a little after, yes. There were probably a dozen people who saw me then. We go from nine-thirty to five-thirty instead of nine to five."

"How about when you got back? Did anybody see you then?"

"Not a soul," Peter Green said. "By the time I got back it was after quitting time, and they were all gone. I hear there are places in this world where people work late with joy in their hearts, but Goldenrod is not one of them."

"Yes," Gregor said. The FBI hadn't been one of them, either, for most of the people who worked there. "So you got back at—?"

"About six-fifteen."

"About six-fifteen. And you stayed until when?"

"I don't remember. Eleven, eleven-thirty. Something like that."

"And then you came home?"

"Yes."

"Straight home?"

"Yes. There's nothing much open at that hour unless you want to go into Waterbury. And I didn't."

"Was anybody here when you got home?"

"No," Peter said. He finished his Perrier and went back for more. "There was a message on the answering machine, though. A message from Kayla. I didn't think anything of it at the time."

"Did you keep it?" Stacey Spratz asked.

Peter Greer shook his head. "It wasn't a message to keep. It was mostly just hello and how are you and can we talk sometime. That kind of thing. It rather surprised me, really."

"Why?" Gregor asked.

"Because we'd pretty much broken up," Peter said. "I mean the whole thing was rather insane all the way along, wasn't it? She was much too young for me. I don't mean I was cradle robbing when we started seeing each other. She was eighteen, and she wasn't an unsophisticated girl. But there were—gaps. Gaps in understanding. I should have realized that it wouldn't work out."

"What kind of gaps in understanding?" Gregor asked.

Peter Greer shrugged. "Gaps in understanding about work. I founded a company, and I run it. That takes a lot of time, and sometimes it means I have to take financial risks that leave me rather short of money. Kayla wasn't used to not being the center of attention and she wasn't used to not being able to do things because there simply wasn't any cash. I don't know. Maybe it was class as much as age. Do you see what I mean?"

"I see what you mean," Gregor said. "Are you short of cash?"

"Right now? No. About three or four months after Kayla and I started dating, though, I took the company through an expansion period. It was either expand or die."

"And you expanded."

"Thank God," Peter Greer said.

Gregor went to the wall of windows and looked out. He wished immediately that he hadn't. He didn't usually have a fear of heights, but this view gave him one. He retreated.

"So," he said. "Tell me about Kayla Anson. And about

you. Where you met her. What she was like."

"We met at the Swamp Tree Country Club," Peter said, "which is where everybody meets everybody out here. Or at least, where everybody like us meets everybody else like us. There was a dinner dance. The club has them about once a month. Kayla was there with Margaret. Oh, and with her friend. Kayla's friend, Annabel Crawford."

"And what was Kayla Anson like?"

Peter Greer shrugged again. "I think the tendency is to think of girls like Kayla as extraordinary—people do it with Chelsea Clinton, as well. Girls in the spotlight, so to speak, who get a lot of publicity, who have to live public lives. We like to think of them as unusual people with unusual strengths."

"And Kayla Anson wasn't that?"

"Kayla was Kayla, that was all. She was an East Coast debutante. More intelligent than most, more grown-up than some, fairly steady emotionally and philosophically. And of course she was attractive, although she wasn't really beautiful. That's the other tendency we all have, with girls like Kayla. Even when they're plain as toast, we like to describe them as beautiful."

"I think it's remarkable that you started a relationship—I presume a sexual relationship—with a woman you were able to look at so . . . judiciously."

"Well," Peter Greer said, "maybe I wasn't so judicious in the beginning."

"What about Kayla Anson? Was she judicious about you?"

"I think she was just—bored. Bored out here. Bored with going to parties. Bored and looking for somebody or something to distract her. And I was that somebody."

"What ended it?"

"Kayla ended it," Peter Greer said. "One night about two months ago, right out of the blue. Although I can't really say I was all that surprised, once I thought it over. We were both just sort of marking time."

There was a faint trilling sound. For the first few moments, Gregor didn't recognize it as the ringing of a phone. Peter Greer did, and strode over to the end table near the couch to pick up. He said, "Peter Greer here" instead of "hello," and then he listened.

Finally he looked up and held the phone out in Stacey Spratz's direction. Stacey was near the window wall, looking green.

"It's for you," he said. "It's your dispatcher. She says it's urgent."

Stacey Spratz came forward and took the phone. Gregor thought he was being very careful not to look at either one of them, but that might have been nothing. That might have been Stacey still embarrassed at how badly he was taking the view. Stacey listened for a while and then grunted. He said, "Yes, yes, I understand" and "we're leaving as soon as I hang up." Then he handed the phone back to Peter Greer and looked at Gregor.

"Jesus Christ," he said. "There's another body in Margaret Anson's garage."

PART THREE

One

I

To call what was going on in the road outside Margaret Anson's house a circus would be to make it sound more dignified than what it was. What was going on in the road outside Margaret Anson's house was a form of lunacy. Gregor Demarkian had never seen anything like it, not even in the days after the Monica Lewinsky case started to go nuclear—and that, at least, had involved a president of the United States. It was hard to tell what it was people thought they were doing here. Vans that had been politely in the road only a few hours ago were now parked up on the grass. Reporters who had stayed where they belonged on the public pavement were now creeping up the long gravel drive, only to be turned back by one or another of the state police sentries who had been posted to deal with just such a problem. There were police everywhere, more police than Gregor had seen in one place since coming to Connecticut. Some of them were state police and some of them belonged to the Washington Police Department. Their cars were everywhere, parked on the sides of the drive, crammed into the roundabout in front of the barn. Their uniforms were the one consistent feature of the landscape.

Stacey Spratz pulled carefully into the drive, waving at the sentry there to make sure he understood that they were official and therefore allowed to pass—but instead of passing he found himself stopped, and the car beginning to rock.

"What the *hell*," he said.

Gregor could see what was happening. There were two people nearly plastered to the window at his side. There were people everywhere.

"We're being rocked," he said. "From the back."

Stacey Spratz looked into the rearview mirror. Gregor

turned around in his seat. There were two men back there, leaning against the left side of the car and pushing. Every time they surged forward, the car swayed and shuddered.

"Jesus Christ," Stacey said. "They're going to turn us over."

Gregor didn't think it was impossible. The rocking had picked up momentum. Stacey didn't dare rev the engine, for fear he would end up killing someone—and in the long run that would ruin him, even if the death were accidental, even if it were entirely justified. The car was now sometimes lifting off the ground on the left side. It wasn't lifting very far off, not yet, but it would get farther. Gregor tightened his seat belt.

"I'm going to make a break for it," Stacey said.

"No." Gregor leaned across the front seat and hit Stacey's horn, as long and as loud as he could. He didn't know what make of car this was—he didn't know what make of car any car was, unless somebody told him—but he knew in no time at all that this one had a very loud horn.

"You're breaking my eardrums," Stacey said.

The two men who were rocking the car had not been deterred by the noise. They were still rocking. Gregor looked up the drive and saw what he had hoped to see. Four tall state policemen were heading in their direction, coming at a run. It took them a couple of seconds to assess what was going on. Then they ran at the two men rocking the car as if those men had been boxing dummies.

"Get ready to get out of here as soon as they peel them off," Gregor said.

"I'm watching," Stacey said.

The two men gave one last heave. It was as if they were willing to risk anything to get the car turned over. It didn't work. The car went up dangerously on one side, but it came down again. Seconds later, Gregor saw the crowd of state policemen pull the two men off and away.

"Go," he told Stacey Spratz.

Stacey didn't need the advice. He hit the gas, hard. The car jerked forward as if it had been launched. Ahead of them, the next sentry stood back to let them pass. They shot up the drive in the direction of all the police cruisers. They came to a stop just in time.

"Jesus," Stacey said.

Gregor opened his door and swung his feet out. He was surprised to find that he was shaking. He wasn't sure why. These were reporters he was dealing with. They wouldn't have torn his arms off. He looked back down the drive and saw that both of the men who had been rocking the car where now in handcuffs, and surrounded by a large part of the crowd. Absent any other kind of a story, their story would do.

"Mr. Demarkian?" Stacey Spratz said.

He was standing in the drive next to Mark Cashman, who looked as ashen as Gregor had ever seen a man look in his life.

"She's in the barn," Mark Cashman said. "Just like Zara Anne Moss. She's been dead—I don't know. For a while."

"Maybe we ought to go in and look around," Stacey said.

"Tom Royce is in there," Mark Cashman said. "Along with a million other people. Except it's different from the last time. I don't know what I mean."

"I do," Gregor Demarkian said.

"I was thinking maybe I wasn't cut out for this," Mark Cashman said. "I didn't sign on for—I don't know what. You can go fifty years in a town like this and never see a single murder."

"Could we get down to practicalities here?" Gregor asked. "Could you tell me who was murdered?"

"Oh, Jesus," Stacey Spratz said. "I didn't even think about that. I just came hauling out here and I thought— Christ."

"It was Margaret Anson," Mark Cashman said. "Is Margaret Anson. I don't know how to put it."

"All right," Gregor said. "How did the police find out she was dead?"

"We got a call. From Annabel Crawford. She's—her

parents have a place in New Preston. She's sort of famous around here for having more fake IDs than an international terrorist. We've all picked her up at one time or another. But—"

"But?" Gregor prodded.

"Well, there's no harm in her," Mark Cashman said. "She doesn't drive drunk, and she never drinks more than about two beers, so she usually manages to keep the guy she's with from getting behind the wheel and killing somebody else. She's always with some guy. I mean, she would be. Wait till you see her."

"She's one of those debutantes," Stacey Spratz said.

"She's still here?" Gregor asked.

Mark Cashman nodded in the direction of the house. "She's in the living room. She's a mess, really. And I don't blame her."

"I'm going to go talk to Mr. Royce," Gregor said. "Unless either of you mind?"

Neither of them minded. Mark Cashman seemed as if he would never mind much of anything again, and Stacey Spratz was obviously reluctant to go anywhere near the barn. To Gregor, police work had always had some connection with violent death. In the last ten years of his career, it had had no other connections at all. It seemed strange to think that there were men who wore police uniforms who had never seen violent death at all—and didn't even want to.

Gregor left Mark and Stacey standing where they were and walked over to the barn. The state policeman on duty on the door nodded to him politely and let him pass. Gregor walked into the dark building and saw the body on the floor. It was right inside the bay, as if Margaret Anson had been on her way out into the drive when she'd been caught from behind. Because Gregor was fairly sure she had been caught from behind. He could see Kayla Anson being tricked by a murderer who came at her from the front, and certainly Zara Anne Moss, but Margaret Anson would have known better than to turn her back on anyone.

Tom Royce was bagging things. Gregor had never understood much about that part of police work. He went to stand in the circle around the body. This time, the white athletic shoelace was clearly visible. It was dug into the soft skin of Margaret Anson's neck, like a cookie cutter half-pressed into dough. Margaret Anson had not been an attractive woman in life. She was even less of one in death.

Gregor cleared his throat. Tom Royce looked up and then stood up, visibly stretching.

"It's you," he said. "I thought you'd be along."

"And?"

Tom shrugged. "And what? My guess is that it's the same person, with the same method, but you'll have to wait for the lab analysis and the autopsy. But it blows my favorite theory all to hell."

"What was your favorite theory?"

"That this was a serial killer we were dealing with. Somebody who liked to off young women. Young women with long brown hair, specifically. That's the way serial killers work, isn't it?"

"There are elements to these crimes that don't fit the pattern," Gregor said. "The use of the garage, for one thing. Unless you meant that you thought Margaret Anson was the serial killer in question."

"No. No, I didn't. We had one, you know. A serial killer. Up in Hartford last year. Killing prostitutes. Why do you think so many of them kill prostitutes?"

"Prostitutes are available," Gregor said. "They're supposed to go to dark places alone with strangers."

"I guess. She hasn't been dead all that long, by the way. Not as long as Zara Anne Moss had been. The girl who found her said she was still twitching."

"The girl was twitching, or the body was?"

"The body was."

"That could have been an illusion," Gregor said. "Somebody who wasn't used to seeing dead bodies. Somebody who wasn't really thinking straight."

"Absolutely," Tom Royce said. "But you know what it's

like. We have to listen to everybody. We have to know what everybody is saying."

"I'm surprised you listened at all. I didn't think it was customary for deputy medical examiners to sit in on interrogations. Or even casual inquiries."

"I eavesdropped. Everybody eavesdropped. You couldn't help but eavesdrop. She was hysterical."

"This was Annabel Crawford?"

"Right. I felt sorry for her. I still feel sorry for her. I wish—"

"What?"

Tom Royce shrugged. "Nothing that makes any sense, I guess. That none of this had happened. That I was back in Hartford checking out the latest drug hit. That's where you expect dead bodies. Not in places like this."

This was nonsensical, but Gregor didn't say so. People said a lot of nonsensical things in murder investigations. Besides, he knew, in a way, what Tom Royce meant.

"I think I'm going to go talk to this Annabel Crawford," he said. "Unless you've got something else I need to know. Something unusual for once."

"No, not a thing. Well, except for the door, and I don't think that's really unusual."

"What door?"

Tom Royce pointed across the barn, to the far corner at the back. "That door. I think she must have left it open all the time. At least, it's been open all three times we've been here. Although why, I'll never know."

"Why not?"

"Well, there's nothing out there, that's all. You run right into a wall of trees. The only thing I can think of is, when the door was put in there was yard back there and then it got grown over. If that makes sense to you."

"It makes sense to me. Just a minute."

Gregor crossed the barn and stood in front of the door. It was still open—the forensics people would be careful not to change anything they didn't have to change in the barn, just in case—and he could see that Tom Royce had been exactly right. There was literally a wall of trees out there, although there was probably a way through them if you worked at it. Gregor could see no signs that anybody had worked at it.

He went back to the bay where the body was. Tom Royce was down on his haunches again, putting something into a plastic bag with tweezers.

"I'm going to go see about Annabel Crawford," Gregor said.

"Good luck," Tom Royce said.

Gregor almost pointed out that their luck was already bad. If it hadn't been, Margaret Anson would be more than a body lying on the floor of her own garage.

2

The back hall of Margaret Anson's house was just as dark as Gregor had remembered it, and the ceilings in the rooms were just as low. It struck him again how odd it was, that someone with Margaret Anson's money would have wanted to live cramped up like this. A sense of history was all very well and good, but this was taking it much too far. Even the colonial settlers would have jumped at the chance to live in a redwood modern, after having to live for any amount of time in something like this.

Mark Cashman led him through the house, although this time he didn't need leading. As they walked, Gregor could hear the muffled sounds of crying. Mark Cashman could hear them, too. He nodded in the direction of the living room and said. "She's been like that since we showed up. At least. In fact, she's a little better now. For a while there, she was completely hysterical."

"How old is she?"

"Eighteen."

"Eighteen and brought up in a nice family in a nice world. I don't think hysterical is out of line under the circumstances."

"I don't, either. But it has meant that she hasn't been easy to deal with."

They got to the living room and Mark Cashman stepped back to let Gregor enter first. Gregor went through the door and found a small blonde woman sitting on the long main couch, one fist pressed to her lips and her eyes red. Even with the mess her face was in, though, it was easy to see that she was a very pretty young woman, all porcelain skin and big china blue eyes. She had on the flowered skirt and crewneck cotton sweater that Gregor had come to think of as a Litchfield County uniform.

She looked up when he came in. As soon as she saw him, she straightened up and put her hands in her hair. Her hair was a mess. The attention she gave to it didn't help.

"Oh," she said. "Oh, it's Mr. Demarkian, isn't it? I saw your picture in the newspaper. And on television. A couple of nights ago. Maybe yesterday."

It would almost have to have been yesterday. Gregor sat down in the high-backed wing chair to the side of the couch and leaned in her direction.

"Would you mind answering a few questions for me?" he asked. "It wouldn't be like answering regular police questions. It wouldn't be on the record for anybody but me."

"I didn't even mind answering police questions," Annabel said. "Although I suppose I shouldn't have. I should have called my father and gotten him to get me a lawyer. But it wouldn't have worked, you know, because he's never at home. My father. My father is never at home. And my mother is hopeless."

"Yes," Gregor said. "Can you tell me what you were doing here? Were you a friend of the family? Did you come out to visit Margaret?"

"What? Oh, not exactly. I mean, I did come out to visit Margaret, yes, but not to just visit. And I was Kayla's friend, her best friend, I guess. We were in boarding school together." Annabel flushed. "We got expelled together, too. And I guess it was my fault."

"So you came out to pay your condolences to Margaret Anson."

"No," Annabel said. "No, I didn't. She wouldn't have wanted to hear them. She wouldn't have let me into the house."

"Then why did you come out?"

"I did call before I came. I wasn't going to. I was at the club, you see, and the whole thing was bothering me. So I got in the car and started out here, but then I changed my mind and I drove around a little. And then I stopped at Popeye's in Morris and used the phone and called Margaret. And she told me to come right out."

"Very good. This was when?"

"Right before I came out."

"I meant what time," Gregor said. "Can you remember the time?"

"Oh, no. No, I can't. I never wear a watch, you see. I don't—I don't like what they look like. But it was right before I came out. I went right back to my car from the phone and then I drove straight here. It couldn't have taken five minutes."

"We might be able to work it out," Mark Cashman said. "If she called the police more or less as soon as she got here—"

"We'll think about that in a moment," Gregor said. "I want to do this in order. You talked to Margaret Anson and she agreed to let you come out. But you say she wouldn't have been amenable to a condolence visit."

"It wasn't a condolence visit. It wasn't anything like that. It was about money."

"Money?"

"Kayla's money," Annabel Crawford said. "I knew that as soon as she knew it was about Kayla's money, she would let me come. It was all she cared about, really. Money. She said she cared about family and tradition and all the rest of it, but it wasn't true. She only really ever cared about money."

"And there was something you knew about Kayla Anson's money that Margaret Anson didn't know."

"I don't know if she didn't know it," Annabel said, sounding anguished. "That was the point. I didn't know if anybody knew it but me. And I thought I had to tell. You know. I just thought I had to."

"You thought you had to tell what?"

"It was about six months ago, I think. And Kayla and I were down at the Danbury Fair Mall. I don't know. We were bored. You know how that is. And we were sitting at a table in the food court, and she was going through her bag looking for something. She had this big tote bag she carried around a lot. And she spilled a bunch of stuff all over the floor. So I bent over to help her pick it up. And there it was. I couldn't miss it."

"There what was?"

"A receipt for a certified check. For one hundred and thirty-five thousand dollars."

Gregor sat back in the wing chair. "That's a lot of money. Do you know who the check was written out to?"

"It was written out to herself. To Kayla Anson."

"To herself?"

"I think she wanted it in cash." Annabel looked confused. "I know this doesn't make any sense. It didn't make any sense to me at the time. But it's what she said. She said she needed the money to help a friend and she needed it in cash. Oh, and that it was only a loan. But I didn't understand why she had to have it like that, you know, instead of writing out a regular check."

"And this was when?"

"I'd guess about six months ago. At the very end of spring or the start of summer. We were sort of at loose ends."

"In May."

"Maybe more like June."

"Did she ever mention this money to you again?"

"No," Annabel said. "But I mentioned it to her. Just about four weeks ago. I asked her if her friend she'd loaned the money to had ever paid her back."

"And what did she say?"

"She said that it didn't have anything to do with her anymore. And I asked her what that meant, but she wouldn't tell me. She just kept saying that she didn't need to talk about it because it wasn't her problem any longer. And that was that."

"That was that."

"I just wanted Margaret to know," Annabel said. "Because it was such an awful lot of money. And I kept thinking there was something strange about the whole thing. And I didn't just sort of want to let it drop. Do you know what I mean?"

"Yes, as a matter of fact, I do."

Annabel Crawford took a deep breath. "So I came out here to talk to Margaret," she said. "Except when I got here Margaret was dead. I pulled my car into the drive and I got out and I looked through the garage doors just by accident, you know, and there she was."

"There was no policeman guarding the drive?"

"When I came in? No."

"What about reporters?"

"There was one van down at the bottom of the road, but that was it. I don't think whoever was in there was paying much attention to me."

"And after you found the body, you did what?"

"I came in the house and called the police."

"Right away?"

"Yes. Yes. I didn't want to be here alone with—with that."

"The door to the house was unlocked?"

Annabel Crawford looked momentarily confused. "Well, yes, it was," she said. "Shouldn't it have been? I mean, I don't know anybody out here who locks their doors. Especially not in the middle of the day. Why would they bother?"

"One more thing," Gregor said. "Did you tell anybody, anybody at all, that you were coming out here? Did you tell anybody why?"

"Not a single person," Annabel said. "I didn't even see anybody to tell."

"Fine," Gregor Demarkian said.

He got out of his chair and motioned Mark Cashman to follow him. When he got to the hall, he motioned back in the direction of the living room and said, "You'd better find that young woman a doctor. She's in shock, and if she goes long enough without having it treated, it's going to matter."

Two

I

The first thing Eve Wachinsky noticed when she entered Grace Feinmann's apartment was the piano—except that it wasn't a piano, exactly. It was hard to tell what it was. Grace had taken her keys and run across the hall to get some things for her to wear while she was recuperating on the sofa bed. Eve went over to the "piano" and ran her hand across the top of it. It had two keyboards, one on top of the other. That was one strange thing. It was painted so elaborately, it looked like one of those movie animations of an LSD trip. Its legs were longer and thinner than the legs on a regular piano, too, so that it looked less like a musical instrument than like a piece of furniture. Eve wondered if Grace played it. Grace played a lot of classical music. Eve had heard it coming through the walls. She had always assumed it was coming from CDs and audio cassettes.

Grace came back through the door, carrying Eve's green polyester pajamas and her red terrycloth bathrobe.

"Here," she said, putting them down on the arm of the couch. "You'll feel much better once you've had a real shower. You can never shower for real in a hospital room. I'll get across the hall and clean up tomorrow. I'd do it today, but I'm just exhausted. I've got a performance in two weeks. I've been practicing until I drop."

Eve ran her hand over the "piano" again. "Is this what you perform on? It's not like any piano I've ever seen before."

"That's because it's not a piano. It's a Peter Redstone harpsichord. And that's what I perform on, yes. That and the virginals. Except that I started out on the piano. Everybody does."

"I'm sorry," Eve said. "I'm very ignorant, really. I never, you know, went to school much."

"Well, I wouldn't worry about it if I were you. Not everybody has heard of the harpsichord even if they did go to school a lot. And practically nobody has heard of the virginals. That's my project at the moment. I'm trying to buy a mother-and-child virginals."

"It sounds like something you'd hear about in church."

"It's an instrument like the harpsichord, actually. It's smaller, though. And with the mother and child, you have the main instrument that you sit at and then there's what looks like a drawer in the side, and when you pull it out it's another virginal. That you can play. If you see what I mean."

"I see why they call it mother and child."

"It's what's keeping me broke at the moment. Buying the virginals, I mean. I really wanted to do it right this time, so I'm having the Hubbard people make them for me, and then I'm having Sheridan Germann decorate it for me, and by the time it's all done it's going to cost nearly thirty thousand dollars. That's why I'm living here. I teach at Fairfield University in the music department, and they pay really well, for a music department. But not well enough to afford something like that without very low expenses and a second job."

Thirty thousand dollars. Eve had never made all of thirty thousand dollars in a year. She took her hand off the harpsichord. It hadn't occurred to her that it might be expensive. Now it seemed as if it could be worth a fortune. She moved away from it toward the couch. There was a picture on the end table in a frame, showing Grace in what looked like a leotard under a long black skirt, with a harpsichord on one side and a large man on the other. The photograph was signed *All my best, Igor Kipnis.*

"That's me at the Connecticut Early Music Festival," Grace said. "Last year. I played a selection of songs written by Henry the Eighth. And that's Igor Kipnis, who is one of the two greatest harpsichordists now working. He kept trying to get me to go back to performing full-time."

"Why don't you perform full-time?" Eve asked.

"Because no matter how hard I practice, I'm never going to play like Igor Kipnis. Or Gustav Leonhardt. Or any of those people. I'm just not a world-class player. I'm good enough to teach. Why don't you sit down and I'll make you a cup of coffee. Or tea. Or even hot chocolate. I can always drink hot chocolate."

"Oh, yes," Eve said. "Tea, I guess. I really wish you wouldn't go to any trouble."

"It's no trouble. Why don't you turn on the TV and check around. I'll bet at least one of the stations has more on that murder we were talking about. Except it's two murders now."

Grace hurried off into the back of the apartment. Eve found the television remote on the table and pushed the power button. A picture popped up on the small screen, wavered for a moment, and then settled. The set seemed to have been left at News Channel 8. Eve sat down on the couch and hunched forward to watch.

It took a moment or two to figure out what was going on. Eve hated news bulletins. She found them far too confusing. During The Monica Lewinsky Mess, as Darla had called it, Eve had taken to playing movies on the television at work. It was the only way she could make sure that whatever she was watching would not be interrupted by "late-breaking news." Eve hated late-breaking news even more than she hated news bulletins.

Grace came back into the living room, saw what was on television, and stopped.

"What's this?" she asked. Then she hunched forward and listened.

"There's been another murder," Eve said, because this was something she had managed to figure out. Another murder, of someone named Margaret Anson, in her own garage. Wasn't Margaret Anson Kayla Anson's mother?

Grace was looking a little green. "This is terrible," she said. "This is really terrible."

Ann Nyberg was manning the anchor desk for what looked like a long special report. Every once in a while, a map would flash on the screen, but Eve couldn't make head or tail of it. She had never been very good at reading maps.

"We must stress," Ann Nyberg said, "that there are a lot of unanswered questions in this case. Police still do not know who was driving the 1996 Jeep Wrangler that was seen following Kayla Anson's car on the night of her murder, or how the Jeep became badly damaged, or who dumped it in the Fairchild Family Cemetery in Morris. Police also do not know—"

"Don't you love Ann Nyberg?" Grace said. "I always watch her when she's on. She's my favorite one."

"The Capernaum Road," Eve said.

"What?"

Eve bit down on the knuckle of her right index finger. It was so hard for her to think. It had always been so hard for her to think. She would never have been able to put together the kind of life Grace had, with different jobs and different friends and projects that stretched years into the future. She had a hard time dealing with the crossword puzzles in the *Waterbury Republican*, and those were crossword puzzles for dummies, not hard ones like some people did.

"Kayla Anson was murdered on Friday night. Didn't you say that?" Eve said.

"That's right."

"And this thing with the Jeep. That happened on Friday night, too? That the Jeep got messed up and was found in the Fairchild Family Cemetery?"

"I think so. But I've kept all the news stories. We could look at them and find out for sure. Why?"

"Somebody would have told, don't you think? I mean, it was an official report. It came through the town of Watertown. It would have been written down somewhere and somebody would have seen it."

Out in the kitchen, the kettle began to blow. Grace

looked over her shoulder in that direction with more than a little impatience.

"I'll get that in a minute," she said. "Tell me what you're talking about. What was an official report?"

"It would have been written down," Eve said again. "They would have seen it. They've probably thought about it already, and decided it doesn't mean anything. I'm probably just being stupid."

"I've got to go get the kettle. But I don't think you should just decide that you're stupid. If you think you know something, you should tell somebody. You should tell the police."

"It's just that it's so close. To the cemetery. And something must have knocked it over. They don't fall over by themselves. And it would do a lot of damage, too. Usually it would just knock the whole thing over."

"Oh, for God's sake," Grace said.

The kettle was whistling and whistling. It hurt Eve's ears to listen to it. She still couldn't make up her mind. She hated to look stupid in front of people, and this was just the kind of thing that would make her look stupid for years. Everyone in town would know. She would hear about it every time she went to Adams for the groceries or to Brooks for her hydrogen peroxide and witch hazel.

The kettle stopped whistling. Grace had gone to get it. Now she came back to the living room, holding it in her hand.

"I don't think you should just decide you're stupid," she said. "I think if you think you know something, you should go tell someone. If you don't want to tell the police, go tell that detective they brought in. That Gregor Demarkian. But tell somebody. There are three people dead in less than a week. There's some sort of homicidal maniac on the loose. Anybody at all could be next. Even you."

Even me, Eve said to herself inside her head, but the thought did not compute, it did not make an impression. What did was the idea of this man, this Gregor Demarkian, who was not from town and did not know her, and who might be persuaded to listen to what she had to say but not tell anybody else she had said it. Unless she was right, of course, and then he could tell anybody he wanted. Then she wouldn't look stupid, but smart.

Grace disappeared into the kitchen again and came back holding a big mug of tea. She put it down on the coffee table in front of Eve and then went away to get sugar and milk. When she came back again, Eve had made up her mind.

"This Gregor Demarkian is staying some place in Washington, isn't he? At the Mayflower Inn or somewhere? Could we go there?"

2

Zara Anne Moss's mother was a Litchfield County lady, the kind that Faye Dallmer could recognize on sight and twenty yards away. She had on a long flowered skirt and a black cotton crewneck sweater and espadrilles, and the espadrilles were the kind that came directly from Spain and frayed at the end of every summer. These were fraying now. Their fraying was a sign of status. Faye had once spent an entire year figuring out the various indicators of status in the Northwest Hills. That was in the days when she had still been married, and when she had thought that she might put the knowledge to the conventional use of social climbing. It seemed odd to her now that she had ever cared at all for social climbing.

Dorothy Moss did not look as if she had ever spent a day in her life worrying about social climbing, mostly because she probably didn't have to. She had the thin, high-cheekboned face of the kind of woman who had gone to a Seven Sisters college and majored in the History of Art. She did not look anything at all like her daughter.

"I have heard of you, of course," she said, "long before Zara Anne came out here to stay. And after I knew she was here, I went out and bought a couple of your books, just to see. You write very well."

"Thank you," Faye said.

"And I was relieved, if you want to know the truth. That she was out here, I mean. Not that you write well. She had been—around—quite a bit. There had been—incidents."

"Ah," Faye said.

"Drugs, mostly, I suppose," Dorothy Moss said. "There were always drugs, in high school, in college. Marijuana, most of the time. But sometimes mescaline. Which seems to be something like LSD."

"It's a plant," Faye said. "It causes hallucinations. Some people take it instead of the chemical drugs because they think it's more natural."

"Well, Zara Anne was always very committed to doing the natural. Natural food. Natural fibers. I didn't realize there were natural drugs. And of course she was always committed to the supernatural, too. Are you a practitioner of Wicca?"

"No," Faye said.

"You've written about it."

"It goes with the territory. A lot of people who are interested in what I do are interested in Wicca. Sometimes I write about it."

"I think Zara Anne was a practicing witch."

"She tried to be."

Dorothy Moss's mouth twisted into something that was not a smile. She was sitting in the middle of Faye's couch, with a mug of Faye's herbal tea on the coffee table in front of her. She looked out of place, and Faye had no idea why she was here.

"That's the thing, isn't it?" Dorothy said. "She tried to be. Nobody can really be a witch. There are no witches. But Zara Anne tried to be. And I thought it was safer for her here, with you, than it would be if she'd stayed drifting around the way she had been. You seemed—stable, somehow. As if you knew what you were doing. And reading what you wrote, I didn't think you did drugs."

"I don't."

"I would never have guessed that Zara Anne would know Margaret Anson. Or that she'd even consent to going to her house and talking to her. I wish I understood why it was she went out there. I wish I understood anything about her, really. We were very close when she was small. Then she became an adolescent, and everything changed. I talked to a psychologist about it. He told me to just relax and wait, that when she got older she'd change her mind. But she never did. In the end, we couldn't get together at all without fighting."

"I never got along with my mother, either," Faye said.

Dorothy Moss shook her head. "I suppose you're wondering what I'm doing here. I'm wondering a little myself. I think I just wanted to see where she'd been living, what her life had been like, in the last few months before she died. We found her once, maybe three or four months after she left college, living on the street in Boston. Just sitting there on the pavement with a cup to collect charity in."

"I don't understand," Faye said. "Had there been an argument? Was there a reason why she couldn't go home?"

"No reason at all. We would have been glad to have her. She'd gone to Boston to set up as a—as a fortune teller, I suppose you'd say. She wanted to read Tarot cards and do horoscopes. And she had some money with her when she left, money enough to get started, I would have thought. She cleaned out her entire savings account. Then she gave it all away to somebody, to some man. 'Loaned' it to him, is how she put it. But he disappeared, of course. Most people would have expected him to. She didn't have much of a sense of self-preservation."

"Maybe that explains how she got out to Margaret Anson's house. Maybe she got a call, or somebody stopped in, and she just—trusted the person."

"Yes, maybe so. I suppose that's as good an explanation as any. But really, I just wanted to see, you know. I wanted to see what this place was like. I wanted to see how she was living. You've made it very lovely here."

"Thank you."

"It's good to know she wasn't cold, or living in filth, or hungry. You start out with so many more elaborate hopes for a child. That she'll grow up to have a brilliant career. That she'll marry well and produce half a dozen happy children. With Zara Anne I had to give all that up early. She was very bright—she would never have been admitted to Trinity if she had not been very bright—but she was never really stable."

"Yes," Faye said. This, at least, she could verify as true. Zara Anne had not been stable. Not at any time while she had been living in this house.

Dorothy Moss stood up. Like most Litchfield County ladies, she was a little too thin. The bones in her neck stood out like cords.

"Well," she said. "I'll leave you now. I've seen what I came to see. I want to thank you so much for letting me come. And for talking to me. I find that I haven't assimilated it yet. That she's gone. She was in and out of our lives so much, it still seems to me that she must be coming back."

"Yes," Faye said again.

"Of course, some of that is due to my own weaknesses. I've let her father do all the arrangements, you see. I haven't taken any part in them. I haven't been able to. Do you have any children?"

"No," Faye said.

"Then I don't suppose you'd understand. I wouldn't worry about it if I were you. Some things it's a blessing not to understand."

Dorothy's black leather Coach bag was on the floor. She bent over, picked it up, and put it on her shoulder.

"Well," she said. "Thank you again. And thank you for the tea. Now I must be going."

"Oh," Faye said—but she didn't really have time to say anything.

Dorothy Moss was fast. She was out of the living room and at the front door in no time at all. Faye trailed after her, not sure if she wanted to catch up and make all the customary condoling noises or not. By the time she reached the door, Dorothy was out in the drive and at her car. Faye stopped in the doorway and waved back when Dorothy waved to her.

She wasn't going to make condoling noises after all. She wasn't going to say a thing that made sense, any more than she had said a thing that made sense in all the hour that Dorothy Moss had been in her house. She wasn't even going to be able to think anything that made sense.

She saw Dorothy's car pull out onto the Litchfield Road and head in the direction of Watertown. She retreated into her foyer and shut the door firmly on her sight of the day.

Eventually, she was going to have to open the roadside stand again. She was going to have to go on with her life. She was going to have to go through the motions. Already there had been one or two incidents, when people who had driven all the way out from New York City found that they couldn't do the shopping they'd come to do after all.

Really, Faye thought, it wasn't that she was bereft at the lost of Zara Anne Moss. She hadn't even liked Zara Anne much in the end. It was the circumstances that were making her crazy, and that she couldn't shake off.

It hadn't even occurred to her that violent death was different than other kinds of death, and now she was drowning in a sea of confusion.

She didn't think she'd get straightened out again until she found herself in need of money. The practical, as she had told her husband once, would always trump the metaphysical.

3

Bennis Hannaford hadn't brought a lot of clothes with her to the Northwest Hills. She never brought a lot of clothes with her when she traveled. A veteran of book tours, she knew that clothes were more a problem than an asset. They made it difficult for you to get away quickly. This time, she had only to pack two skirts, two silk blouses, and a dress. Her laundry was already in a plastic bag at the bottom of her suitcase. She could wear her jeans and her turtleneck and her sweater for the drive home.

Assuming, of course, that she was able to drive home. She didn't see how she could avoid trying. The car was here, and there wasn't anything in the way of public transportation. Her cough, though, had become a steady hacking convulsion. At least once or twice every half hour it bent her over double. She was finding it impossible to breathe.

She was also bringing up more blood. That was what had decided for her. She had brought up two big wads of it, on two separate occasions, since this morning. Something had also happened to her smoking. She had been a two-pack-a-day chain smoker for decades, but she had always felt in control of her addiction. She had always been able to put the cigarettes aside for a few hours if she needed to, to ride in an airplane or sit through a movie. Now she couldn't put the cigarettes aside at all. She wanted to smoke all the time. If she didn't have a cigarette lit and to hand, she was positively frantic. It didn't make any sense. It was also scaring her to death.

"Listen," she'd told Tibor on the phone, when she'd called to tell him she was coming home. "Call Dr. Gerald Harrison and tell him it's me and it's an emergency. I'd do it myself but I'm in a hurry and I don't have my book with me. Tell him it's a big emergency. I'm not even going to come to Cavanaugh Street. I'm going to drive right to his office. I'm going to get there at about seven o'clock."

"Seven o'clock at night? But, Bennis, the doctor will not be in his office at seven o'clock at night."

"He will be if you call him and tell him I need him to be there. Tell him it's an emergency, Tibor. Tell him it's a big one. Do it now."

"Bennis—"

"I've got to get on the road," Bennis said.

Usually, Bennis was infinitely patient with Tibor. Tibor

had been jailed in the old Soviet Union. Tibor was the best priest Holy Trinity Armenian Christian Church had ever had. Tibor was her friend.

But right now, there was nothing and nobody more important than her moving, driving, going, getting where she had to be. Where a doctor could check this out. Where she could find that she was afraid for nothing, and that she wasn't going to die. There it was, right there, at the back of her mind. She was afraid she was going to die.

At the last minute, because she had to tell him something, she wrote Gregor a note and taped it to the mirror in the bathroom, where he would be sure to see it as soon as he washed his hands.

Had to go back to Philadelphia. Love you, Bennis.

She didn't think she wanted to write down any more. She didn't think she wanted to explain.

If she wrote it down—if she put it into words—it would turn out to be true.

Three

In the media atmosphere that now existed, it was going to be almost impossible to get anything done. Gregor had known that, vaguely and subconsciously, when Stacey's police cruiser had been rocked on Margaret Anson's drive. He knew it sharply and without question when it came time for them to leave, and he saw that they would still have to face the reporters massed into a knot in the road. Standing on Margaret Anson's front steps, Gregor thought the route to 109 was completely impassable. A couple of the vans had been parked sideways across the road, blocking it to all through traffic. Reporters on foot were everywhere. The state police guards that had been stationed at the end of the drive were proving to be completely inadequate. The words *feeding frenzy* didn't begin to describe what was going on.

"They're mad at us," Stacey Spratz said, sounding puzzled.

"We're not telling them anything," Gregor said. "Never mind that we don't have anything much to tell them."

"We don't have anything."

Gregor shook his head. "It's the skeleton. That's the key. The skeleton had to have been put there for a reason."

"You're sure? It could just have been kids. Really. That museum thing is left unlocked all the time. And the kids always know where stuff is."

"If it hadn't been for the Jeep, I'd agree with you. But the Jeep was there, and the skeleton was there. We have to assume that the point was to divert our attention from something, but what?"

"It didn't divert our attention from the Jeep," Stacey Spratz said. "We went over it with a microscope."

"And?"

"And, the report was in that stuff I gave you. Some paint

flecks here and there. That's all. The paint flecks didn't belong to the BMW."

"Well," Gregor said, "they wouldn't. The BMW wasn't hit by anything, as far as I know."

"Not as far as we could tell."

"So that takes care of that. But if it wasn't the Jeep, it had to be something. The murderer wouldn't take the risk of dragging that skeleton through the brush just for kicks, even if it is only ten or fifteen yards. Ten or fifteen yards and up to the right of the house. What's to the left of the house?"

"To the left and to the back, the cemetery. We went that way."

"Right. We'd better get out of here, then. There has to be something, but I don't know what it is. And I desperately need some coffee."

Gregor also desperately needed some food—for some reason, the McDonald's hadn't really managed to stay with him; it seemed odd, considering the fact that everything had been fried—but he didn't want to suggest it and find that Stacey knew yet another fast-food place he was dying to visit. Taco Bell. Kentucky Fried. Gregor missed Cavanaugh Street more than ever. At least on Cavanaugh Street he could get something decent to eat.

Stacey Spratz was more worried about the logistics of the situation.

"Maybe I can get them to form a wedge that would get us out. If they don't do that, I don't know how we're going to *get* out. Have you ever seen anything like this?"

As a matter of fact, Gregor had seen things like this, on a number of occasions, but before they had always involved serial killers who had targeted young children, or high political figures. He didn't know what was going on in Washington, Connecticut, except, perhaps, boredom. Why the national media were behaving the way they were, he couldn't have said. Someday he was going to have to sit down and think through the entire idea of celebrity. Why some people had it. Why other people paid attention to it.

Why so many people thought it was important. Sometimes he thought he was looking at an addiction, or a mania.

"Let's do what we have to do," he told Stacey Spratz. "But let's do it fast."

2

In the end, Mark Cashman came with them, too.

"It counts as work," he said. "And I'm officially off-duty. And I need to talk to somebody."

Gregor and Stacey didn't complain. Instead, with Mark at their side, they headed for Waterbury, where the Barnes & Noble had a Starbucks.

"It's far enough away so that we won't be tripping over reporters," Mark said, "and I can get a café mocha."

There was a danger that they would have to trip over reporters anyway. At least two tried to follow them, pulling out behind them on 109 and sticking close enough so that one of them bumped the back of Stacey's cruiser at least twice. On a major highway, they could have picked up speed and tried to outrun them. On the back roads of the Northwest Hills, it was impossible. What Stacey did was dodge. Down one side street and up another, onto dirt roads, around the bends of hills that seemed to rise and fall without sense or reason. It took nearly half an hour, but they lost both the cars that were following them.

"And now that they're lost, they'll really be lost," Stacey said. "You can drive around all day up here and never see anything but more trees, if you don't know where you're going."

"Well, I don't want them so lost they can't go home," Mark Cashman said. "The last thing I want is a bunch of New York reporters wandering around for the winter, with me supposed to be taking care of them."

"I think the CNN reporters are from Atlanta," Stacey said.

Gregor ignored them both, and headed straight for the

doors of Barnes & Noble as soon as Stacey parked the car. Inside, he went to the fenced-off area where Starbucks had its tables and pushed two small square ones together. Then he sat down on a rickety chair and got out his notebook. He was usually very organized about his work. It made him half-crazy to be in a situation like this one, where it seemed impossible to organize anything at all.

Stacey went to the counter to buy coffee. Mark went to the desk and bought all the local papers.

"Here we are," he said, throwing them down on the table so that they covered Gregor's notebook. "They're old news now, of course, but they're all paying attention to us. To you, Mr. Demarkian, I guess. The *Torrington Register-Citizen* doesn't like you."

"The *Waterbury Republican* loves you," Stacey said, putting the coffees down. "Does this sort of thing happen to you all the time? 'The Touching Story of Gregor Demarkian's No-Longer Unrequited Love.' I mean, I know it's at the bottom and everything, but it's the front page."

"They'll have one of those features in the *LCT* next thing you know it," Mark Cashman said. "Big picture of Gregor here. Big picture of Miss Hannaford. Big story about how fascinating his life is that he gets to look into all these murders."

Gregor pulled his notebook out from underneath the papers. "Can we get down to business? Because the problem is, gentlemen, that although by now it ought to be perfectly clear who did it, I don't think there's any way to prove it. Not any way at all. Which does lead us to a certain amount of difficulty."

Stacey and Mark looked at each other.

"I don't know about anybody else," Mark said carefully. "But it isn't obvious to me. It isn't in the least bit obvious to me. So maybe you just ought to tell us—"

"No," Gregor said. "Pay attention for a while. Think. Kayla Anson died because of the money—"

"How can you know that?" Stacey demanded. "How can you possibly—"

Gregor held up his hand. "Think," he said again. "Anything that ever happened to Kayla Anson happened about money. It almost had to. She inherited, what, a couple of hundred million dollars? Almost a billion dollars? Like it or not, for someone like that, the bottom line is always going to be about money. But in this case, Kayla Anson did something that rich girls are taught never to do. She loaned money to a friend. She loaned a great deal of money to a friend. A hundred and thirty thousand dollars."

"She might have loaned it to a friend," Mark Cashman said slowly, "but she might not have. The cashier's check was in her name. She might have been paying a blackmailer."

"A single payment of one hundred thirty thousand dollars? Have you ever known a blackmailer to ask for only one payment?"

"There may have been more payments," Stacey said. "We don't know until we check. Maybe she'd been paying blackmail for years."

"She couldn't have been paying it for years," Gregor said. "She only recently turned eighteen. Before that, she wouldn't have had access to very much, except for her allowance. But by all means check. I think you'll find there was only the one check. The really significant thing here is that she had the check made out to herself, rather than to the person she was giving it to."

"I don't get that," Stacey said. "Does that mean she had to get the money in cash and hand over bills?"

"No. She could have endorsed the check on the back and handed it over. It's done all the time when people buy cars."

"Then what difference would it make?" Mark asked.

"The bank would have a formal record—and Kayla would have a receipt she would need to hand over for her tax record—of the actual person to whom the check was made out. But when the check was cashed with the endorsement, the bank would simply file it away. There would be no way for Kayla's lawyers, for instance, or her mother, to find out anything about the check except that she had it made out to herself. They couldn't know just by looking who she had given the money *to*."

"You mean she didn't want anybody to know who was getting the cash," Stacey said. "But why not? It was her money."

"Maybe the person getting the cash didn't want anyone to know," Mark said.

"Very good," Gregor said. "And there might have been some of that. But I think that the real reason was that she didn't want to face ridicule, or censure, from her advisors or from Margaret. The person she gave the money to was not exactly a good credit risk. Among other things."

"So this was six months ago," Mark said. "What happened next? Was the money supposed to be paid back?"

"I think Kayla Anson decided she wanted to get the money back, yes," Gregor said. "That she wanted it more or less immediately. I also think—do you remember what Annabel Crawford said? She asked Kayla about the money and all Kayla would say was that it wasn't her problem anymore. If it wasn't her problem, then it must have been somebody else's. My guess is that she was intending to turn over collection efforts to her lawyers."

"Intending to?" Mark asked. "You mean you don't think she actually did?"

"If she had, there would have been no point in killing her," Gregor said. "Never mind in killing two other people. And it's more than that. The original murder—the murder of Kayla Anson—was incredibly elaborate. I don't care what you read in Agatha Christie. Murderers in real life do not tie themselves into pretzels creating complications just for the hell of it. Murderers do what they have to do. Which means everything that's happened so far has been necessary."

"The Jeep," Stacey said. "Why was the Jeep necessary? Why not just use his or her own car and get to Kayla that way?"

"Because the car would be recognizable. Far too recognizable."

"Why follow her at all?" Mark asked. "Why not just arrange a meeting out at wherever and go from there?"

"Well," Gregor said, "possibly because Kayla would not have agreed to a meeting wherever. What's more likely, though, is that our murderer didn't want Kayla casually telling someone else that the meeting was going to occur, or worse, just bringing along a friend, like Annabel. The idea was to leave no trace."

"For somebody who wanted to leave no trace, this murderer sure created a lot of fuss," Mark said. "Skeletons. Overturned Jeeps. Whatever."

"I know," Gregor said. "Obviously, there's something about the Jeep, or about the area around the cemetery, that made the diversion of the skeleton necessary. I just don't know what yet. Maybe we ought to go back there again later this afternoon."

"Tomorrow morning," Stacey said. "It's going to be dark now anytime. It gets dark early here in the fall."

"But wait a minute," Mark said. "What about Zara Anne Moss? Why all that fuss? I still don't believe she saw who was driving that Jeep. She couldn't have. All she would have seen is a dark rectangle and a blur of white for the body. That's it."

"Absolutely," Gregor said. "What Zara Anne Moss saw was obviously the murderer on foot."

"What?" Stacey said.

Gregor sighed. "On foot," he repeated. "Think about it. The murderer used Faye Dallmer's Jeep. In order to do that he or she had to get Faye Dallmer's Jeep. Nobody connected with this case lives in walking distance of Faye Dallmer's place—"

"No," Stacey said. "Nobody does."

"—although it is in walking distance of the Fairchild Family Cemetery, if you go across a field. Whoever it was had to drive out there to the Litchfield Road, walk to the Dallmer place, steal the Jeep, and then wait, on a side road along the way, for Kayla to come along in that BMW of hers. But in order to do all that he or she first had to walk, and the walk made the murderer vulnerable. If Zara Anne Moss hadn't been stupid, if she hadn't been so much in need of calling attention to herself, we'd have our evidence, our murderer would be in custody, and two people would still be alive."

"Where was the third car?" Mark asked slowly.

"I don't know," Gregor said.

"How did the murderer get Zara Anne Moss out to Margaret Anson's house?" Stacey asked.

"The murderer asked her to go and the murderer came by to pick her up. Maybe it was a question of having Zara Anne walk down the Litchfield Road a ways to a meeting place. You might want to check that out. Somebody may have seen them. But don't think that Zara Anne wouldn't have gone. She was so desperate to be important. Isn't that what everybody says about her? She wanted it so much. All the murderer had to do was to make her feel important. She would have gone anywhere."

"Even though she had good reason to believe that this person had killed somebody and she had evidence that could send him or her to jail." Mark Cashman shook his head.

"I doubt if that occurred to her," Gregor said. "She was very naive, really, in a lot of ways. She was also somewhat detached from reality—again, given what everybody says."

"Everybody says right," Stacey said. "She was spacey as hell. Talking all the time about having visions and being able to see into the heart of evil and auras coming from the Jeep. None of us took her seriously."

"The murderer did," Gregor said. "The murderer probably also realized that he or she had been spotted. The murder of Zara Anne Moss would have been easy, as long as there's a back way into that barn, which I think there is. There's a door, remember?"

"It opens onto a lot of vegetation," Mark Cashman said. "That wouldn't have been easy."

"It wouldn't have been hard, either," Gregor said. "I've been meaning to ask you or Stacey to send somebody out there to look around. I don't think anybody will find anything, except maybe the grass being tamped down in a couple of places, but I'll bet you anything that you can get to another road that way, someplace to park a car—"

"There is another road," Mark Cashman said. "Jewelry Lane. It's dirt and there's nothing on it close to One-oh-nine, but it's there."

"A perfect place to park a car," Gregor pointed out, "if you're trying to get into that barn without being seen by the reporters in the street. Of course, with Margaret Anson the murderer wouldn't have had to go to that much trouble. He would only have had to come the back way himself. And Margaret was no Zara Anne Moss. She would have known that our murderer was probably dangerous."

"And she would have turned her back on this person anyway?" Stacey asked.

"Well, she did," Gregor said. "Arrogance, maybe. Or possibly the mistaken impression that murder is hard to commit. It would be for most people, of course. It isn't for some people. Anyway, that's the way I think it all lays out. It's too bad I can't prove any of it."

"You don't have to prove it all," Mark Cashman said. "You don't really have to prove any of it in the sense of any of the particulars. We just need to find something that will connect this person to Kayla Anson and to Kayla Anson's death. That could be—anything."

"I know," Gregor said.

"If you told us who it was, we might be able to do it," Stacey said. "Once you have an idea of who the perpetrator is, it's a lot easier—"

"I know," Gregor said again. He thought for a moment and pulled his notebook closer to him. Then he ripped out a blank page and wrote down a name.

"Do me a couple of favors," he said, pushing the page into the middle of the table. "Check this person's bank accounts. And check the car ownership records. Find out if this person owns an unusual and easily recognizable car."

Stacey Spratz picked up the paper and stared at it. "Jesus Christ," he said.

Mark Cashman sighed. "I already know about the car. It's a Ferrari Testarosa. Four hundred thousand dollars' worth of vehicle and bright red. And I didn't even *think* of it."

Gregor Demarkian took a long drink of his café mocha, thinking at once that it was too sweet for coffee and that he would really like to go somewhere and lie down.

3

Gregor also wanted to go someplace and talk to Bennis, and so he had Stacey drive him out to the inn. It wasn't the most convenient of arrangements—Stacey was going to have to come out and pick him up again in a couple of hours—but Gregor was beyond caring about convenience. He couldn't remember being this tired since he got back from North Carolina, and yet this case was far less awful than that one had been. At least here, he was dealing with adults, instead of an infant. At least here, he knew what was going on.

He picked up his keys at the desk and went upstairs. He let himself into the suite and looked around. He could tell as soon as he stepped into the little living room that something was different, but he couldn't tell what. He went into the bedroom and paused. Then he went into the bathroom and saw the note.

Had to go back to Philadelphia. Love you, Bennis.

Gregor pulled it off the bathroom mirror and stared at it. Then he went back into the bedroom and looked into the closet. It was empty of all of Bennis's clothes. Bennis's one small suitcase was gone from the bench at the end of the bed. Bennis's mess was gone from the single bedroom chair. That was why the suite had seemed different. Bennis's clutter was missing. The place was neat.

Gregor sat down on the edge of the bed and tried to think. The worst-case scenario was that he had done something terribly wrong and didn't even know it. Bennis was angry with him. Bennis was furious with him. Bennis was never going to speak to him again. The second worst-case scenario was that something had happened to someone on Cavanaugh Street, and Bennis had gone back to help out. Maybe they had been trying to get him all day, and he had been unreachable because he had been in police cruisers and country clubs. Maybe something had happened to Tibor. Maybe something had happened to old George Tekemanian, who was well into his eighties now and no longer in good health.

Gregor picked up the phone and dialed Tibor's number. The phone rang and rang. Tibor might be out, but he also might be deep in a book. Gregor had once sat in his living room and watched him not hear the phone ringing for twelve full rings, because he was reading his way through *The Stranger Beside Me* by Ann Rule.

Gregor let the phone ring twelve times, and then fourteen, and then twenty. He asked himself if he was being sensible here—even if Tibor was there, if he were that involved in a book he would never hear the phone anyway—when the phone was finally picked up.

"Yes?" Tibor said.

Gregor relaxed immediately. It had gotten to the point where Armenian accents always made him relax completely.

"Tibor," he said.

"Ah," Tibor said. "Krekor. It is you. It is good that you have called."

"Is Bennis there with you?"

"No, Krekor. I don't even think she could be in Philadelphia yet. It hasn't been that long. And she wouldn't be here. She is going to her doctor's."

"Which doctor?"

Tibor appeared to think about this for a moment. "Not the lady doctor. The other one."

"Gerald Harrison."

"Yes, that one."

"Why?"

"I don't know, Krekor. But she had me call him for her. To tell him she was coming. And she said to tell him it was an emergency."

Gregor took a deep breath. "How could it have been an emergency?" he asked reasonably. "She drove down to Philadelphia, didn't she? She took her car."

"Yes, Krekor, she is driving."

"Then she must be well enough to drive. What kind of an emergency could there be that would make it necessary to see her doctor—when? When do you figure she'll get to Philadelphia?"

"Around seven o'clock, Krekor. Yes, I know. It's crazy. I can't make it out. But that was what she wanted. I am surprised she didn't tell you."

"I was out."

"You were investigating a murder, Krekor, yes. I understand that. But I think you'd better come home as soon as you can. Because Bennis does not panic for no reason. So I think it possible that this is serious."

Gregor ran his hands through his hair. Serious. Yes, he could see that it might be serious. There was always the chance that a health problem could be serious. Even a little health problem that you didn't think much about at all.

Suddenly, he couldn't stop thinking about Bennis's cough.

Four

I

Somebody—Mallory, probably—had put a jack-o'-lantern on the top of the steps that led to the front door, and lit a candle in it. Sally Martindale parked the car halfway up the drive and sat looking at the light. There were lights on in the house, too, in the keeping room and beyond. The car was making that rattling noise that said it was almost out of gas. Sally Martindale was out of money. She thought she should have kept some of it to get home on, considering how much she had started with, but in the end she hadn't been able to stop trying. That was what mattered, trying. She had always believed that. It just seemed, sometimes, as if trying didn't work for her. She tried and tried, and everything came apart.

This was the way the house looked best, in the almost dark, with the lights on. You couldn't see anything at all of the fact that she hadn't had enough money to keep it up in the last year or two. The paint peeling on the northern side didn't show up in the dark. Neither did the sag in the railing on the little porch that led to the side door. Even the windows might as well have been washed. When she and Frank had still been together, she had had people in to take care of what needed to be taken care of: Ray's Remodeling to repair sags and rebuilt porches; Proe's Lawn Service to do the grass and the shrubbery and the gutters; Martin and Sheedy to paint inside as well as out. Now she didn't even have the lawn service. Mallory had gone to Sears and bought a lawn mower. She shaved the grass short once a week when she had a little time away from her classes.

I'm going to go to jail, Sally thought, and then she rubbed the palms of her hands over her face, over and over again, as if she were trying to rub out a makeup stain. Her head hurt. Her body felt drained of blood. She had cried off and on on the drive home—cried bitterly and without shame, since no one was able to hear her—but now she was just tired, and beyond caring. What she couldn't get out of her mind was herself at Mallory's age, standing at the mailbox of her parents' plain asphalt driveway, opening the letter that told her she had been accepted at Smith. She could see the houses that surrounded her, ordinary little Cape Cod houses with plastic awnings over the windows and plastic flower boxes attached beneath them. She could hear Didi McConneky and Linda Giametti laughing in that high-pitched way they had when they were talking about boys. She was, she had thought then, on a long and exciting journey out—out of a life in little houses like these, out of too many pregnancies too early, out of following soap operas instead of the exhibition season at the Metropolitan Museum of Art. She had had a vision of herself, grown up and on her own, and in the end it had been a vision about money. Later, at the end of her second year at Smith, she had gone to Linda Giametti's wedding, and that had been about money, too—money spent on a wedding dress and a reception that was as much as some people used for the down payment on a house, money charged to credit cards and taken out in loans, money thrown away on a spectacle that lasted only a few hours on a single day. She had felt as if she had a secret that no one else could share. She knew what really mattered, and how to make sure that her life would have some meaning. She knew how to get away from all this.

Now she got out of the car and looked around. It was cold, this late in October. Tomorrow was Halloween. If Linda Giametti could see this house, she would not know that there was something about it that was better than her own. She would like the size, but she would think that its age spoke against it. She wouldn't be able to understand why Sally hadn't opted for vinyl siding. Maybe the truth was that you could never get out. You always ended where you started, even if it seemed you didn't.

Mallory was in the kitchen. Sally could see her moving around in there. She looked at the sag in the porch rail near the kitchen door and the jack-o'-lantern near the front one and opted for the sag. Everything in her life sagged these days. What difference did it make?

The kitchen door actually let her into the pantry. Sally put her pocketbook on the floor and called out, "Mallory?"

"In here."

Sally picked her pocketbook up again. She didn't know what she was doing. She wasn't thinking straight. She went into the kitchen and saw Mallory with her back to her, working at the big black eight-burner restaurant stove.

"Well," she said.

"Ruth Grandmere called," Mallory said, without turning around. "She said it was important. In fact, she said it was urgent."

Sally pulled out one of the chairs at the kitchen table and sat down. It was an Eldred Wheeler chair and an Eldred Wheeler trestle table. The set had cost something like fifteen thousand dollars, new.

Mallory turned around and faced her. "I think you've been caught," she said.

"Maybe," Sally said carefully. "Maybe not. As of this morning, they knew somebody had been taking the money. They didn't know it was me."

"From Kayla Anson's account."

"Oh, from all the accounts, or a lot of them. I never took from men. They pay too much attention. I never took from women lawyers, either. The housewives were the best. Most of the time, they didn't have the faintest idea what was going on."

"Do you know how much?"

"Before today?"

"You took some money today?" Mallory looked startled. "After you already knew they knew that something was wrong?"

"I was going to fix it," Sally said. "I thought that if I

could only do it right, if I could go out to Ledyard and really make a stand—"

"Oh, for God's sake."

"If I could do it right, I could fix it. So I took—I don't know. Some money. Fifteen hundred, maybe. Or twenty-five hundred. I can't remember."

"How can you not remember?"

"Because I can't."

"Jesus."

Sally started to rub her face again. Mallory was pacing back and forth. This was all so complicated. Mallory just didn't understand it.

"It was because it wasn't fair," Sally said finally. "They just—those people—the Ansons and the Crawfords and the Ridenours—those people just are, if you know what I mean. They don't have to do anything. They just are. But people like me have to work at it. And luck isn't evenly distributed."

"I think," Mallory said, "that you're having a nervous breakdown."

"If life were fair, I would have won today. I would have come home with a whole pile of money and I would have been able to put the money back, and there would still be enough left over, you know, to get us by. Because I really don't know what to do, Mallory. I really don't. We barely had enough to get through last winter, and now it's worse. I'm behind on everything. People call here all the time, the credit card companies, those people, they call all the time. You don't know what it's like. And I don't know what to do. And now this. I suppose they'll put me in jail."

"I don't think so," Mallory said. "Not as long as you pay the money back."

"I can't pay the money back. It must be ten thousand dollars by now, counting today. Maybe even more."

"You can sell the house," Mallory said. "That will pay back the country club, and it will pay off the credit card bills, and it will leave you enough for another house—"

"A *smaller* house," Sally said, feeling suddenly savage.

"A more *sensible* house. Just like your father wanted us to have. While he moved into a duplex penthouse on the Upper East Side and bought a place on the Vineyard for his sweetie pie."

"Listen," Mallory said. "This is not about my father. This is a crisis."

"He caused the crisis."

"Maybe he did. But you don't want to go to jail. And I don't want you to go. And there's no reason why you should. We can sell the house. We can get something smaller. We can make do. I can go to nursing school—"

"Your father will pay for—"

"I don't want him to pay for, except nursing school if he's willing. It makes perfect sense. It's a good field. If you specialize in surgery or crisis pediatrics you can make a pile of money. I can turn it into something else later. It's a start, Mother."

"It's the kind of thing the girls I grew up with did, if they were considered bright. Nursing and teaching. The two main professions for lower-middle-class women."

"You care too much about class."

"The world cares too much about class," Sally said. "What do you think would happen to us, if we did what you want us to do? Do you think we would still have any friends? People would mean well, of course, but it wouldn't last long. They'd get sick of our poverty and drift off. We'd be—alone out here."

"We're going to be just as alone out here if you go to jail for embezzlement," Mallory said. "You're not making any sense."

"I kept thinking I could do it," Sally said. "I went out there and I played the slots for hours. Hours and hours. I worked so hard. When I was growing up, it was a kind of truism. If you worked hard you got what you wanted. But it didn't happen this time."

"I don't think working the slots is what they meant by working, Mother."

"No," Sally said. "I suppose it wasn't."

Mallory went back to the stove. She was cooking dinner. That was good. Sally could use something to eat. She hadn't eaten for hours and hours. She hadn't wanted to waste the money, in Ledyard, on food.

When she was growing up, the purpose of her life had been clear: to get out, to get free, to escape. If she was going to end up right back where she started, then what had been the point of it all? Had she really had to come to Connecticut to see her daughter train as a nurse, or to live out her life in a little ranch house with a patio out back? Had she really come all this way just to be the person she could have been if she'd stayed at home? Life was a tunnel, that was what she thought. Life was a black hole that sucked you in and kept you captive.

Mallory came to the table, bearing a small plate of fried chicken.

"You'd better call Mrs. Grandmere back," she said. "It's not going to do you any good to postpone all this until tomorrow."

2

Ever since Jennifer Crawford had come out to Margaret Anson's house to pick up Annabel in the Volvo station wagon that served as the family "country" car, she had been nattering—and all the time she had been nattering, Annabel had been trying not to listen. Now that they were at home, the nattering had gotten even worse. Jennifer fussed, that was the problem. Jennifer always fussed. At the moment, she was fussing about the state of Annabel's sweater, which she thought of as completely inadequate.

"In my day, sweaters were made of wool," she kept saying. "I don't know who got this idea to make them from cotton. At least wool sweaters kept you warm."

Annabel was warm enough. She was almost hot. Toward the end of the time she had spent at Margaret Anson's house, a woman who had identified herself as a doctor had come along and made her drink two stiff shots of Johnny Walker Black. Annabel had had to swallow them in two swift single gulps, like guys doing divebombers in a bar.

"It's what they seem to have around this place," the doctor had said cheerfully. "At my house, all we have is beer."

Truthfully, Annabel couldn't quite understand why she wasn't drunk. She thought she ought to be flying. Instead, she was just a little hot, and desperately tired. She just didn't want to sleep. Every time she allowed her eyes to close, she saw Margaret Anson's face, in death, with the eyes bugged out and the neck at that uncomfortable tilt. She put out her hand again to touch the body and felt that it was already cold. What she couldn't get out of her mind was the really important question. She wanted to know if Kayla had felt like that, too, when she was dead.

"I've been thinking," Jennifer said now. "Maybe we ought to go back into the city for the rest of the fall. You're coming out in the city as well as here. There's no reason why we shouldn't be in Manhattan."

"I'm all right," Annabel said.

"Well, yes, sweetie, I know you are. It's not that I don't think you're all right. It's me, really, I guess. I'm sure this has upset you enormously. It's upset me. And I suppose I don't really want to be around it while it's going on."

"Maybe they wouldn't let me leave," Annabel said. "Maybe I'm a suspect."

"Oh, surely not, sweetie. You couldn't be a suspect. What an absurd idea. Nobody would think that for a minute."

"That Mr. Demarkian thought it."

"What?"

"Mr. Demarkian. The detective. He thinks I'm a suspect. I talked to him today. I don't see how you can blame him. I was Kayla's friend. I was right there where Margaret Anson was—was—" Annabel took a deep breath. "Dead," she finished.

"I don't see what your being Kayla's friend has to do

with it. And as for Margaret Anson, well, let's face it. If that Mr. Demarkian is making a list of people who hated her enough to kill her, it would look like the Manhattan phone directory."

"I want a cup of tea," Annabel said.

What Annabel really wanted was a cup of tea with another shot of that Johnny Walker Black in it, but she wasn't going to ask for it. For all her fake IDs and raids on bars for St. Pauli Girl Light, she really neither liked nor approved of alcohol. She didn't really like the way people got when they drank, and she especially didn't like the way so many of the people she knew seemed to be unable to go a day without drinking. Even people her own age. There had been girls at boarding school who had kept flasks in their underwear, so that they'd be able to take nips off them every once in a while during the day. Annabel knew everything there was to know about buying liquor in secret in small towns near fancy schools, about getting the liquor back into the dorm without being seen, about drinking without getting caught at drinking. It came with the territory.

Jennifer came bustling over with a cup of tea. Annabel hadn't even heard the kettle whistle.

"Listen," Jennifer said. "Even if they do have to think of you as a suspect, because police procedure is police procedure, you know. I understand how it is. Even if they have to do that, you could still come in and spend the fall in the city with me. You could go shopping. You could go to the theater. There would be something for you to do there. Unlike here. Where you're stuck. So to speak."

"I wanted to call Tommy about the car," Annabel said.

"The car?"

"The night Kayla died. I was out with Tommy Haggerty. He got drunk as a skunk and I left him in the bar and drove his car back here so that I could get home. It was parked in our driveway all that morning, Mother, for God's sake. It was fire engine red."

"Well," Jennifer said, "as long as you don't drive with

anybody who's drunk. That's all I ask. Just stay sober yourself or have a designated driver."

"Yes, I know. But the thing is, I don't drive all that well in any case, and I clipped a mailbox. So the paint got scraped on the front near the headlights on the passenger's side. And I've been wondering if I should offer to pay for the repairs, you know, or if the fact that he made a mess of himself and forced me to find my own way home should be enough in the way of payment. And I still don't know what to do. But I've got to do it."

"Now?"

"No," Annabel said, feeling confused again. "No, I guess not. I don't know. I was just thinking about it."

"I think you're in shock," Jennifer said firmly. "You should put something serious in that tea. Enough honey to make it thick, that would work. Let me get you some honey."

"I don't like honey."

"I know you like to watch your weight, Annabel, but this is no time for it, trust me. This is a time to take care of yourself. I wish I had some chocolate in the house."

"What were you like, when you were my age?" Annabel asked. "Were you like you are now? Were you different?"

Jennifer stopped in the doorway. It was a dramatic pause, but it was in character. The rest of the Litchfield County ladies would pause like this, too. We look a lot alike, Annabel thought, and then wondered why she'd thought it. Most of the time she believed that she looked nothing like her mother at all.

"What an odd question," Jennifer said. "Of course I must have been different. I was much younger then. Let me get you that honey."

When people died, their faces froze in place. They stared into the future and saw nothing. You could see it in their eyes. Someday, her own eyes would stare into the future like that, and it would all be over.

Annabel Crawford had a terrible, gnawing feeling that she ought to do something about this, now, that she ought to change herself in some way so that this wouldn't happen. If she wasn't careful, she would turn into her mother. If she wasn't even more careful than that, she would end up dead. The need to act was so intense and so immediate, she nearly leapt to her feet and ran around the room. Then she thought that that was not what was wanted of her, that there was something else out there that was up to her and needed to be done.

She just couldn't think of what it was she was supposed to do.

3

When Bennis Hannaford got to Gerald Harrison's office, the light was on in the two front windows, and there was a note for her on the door.

Ring twice so I'll know it's you. G.

Bennis rang twice, and then the coughing started again. She wrapped her arms around her chest and doubled over. By now, she had been coughing so often and so violently for so long, her lungs hurt whenever she started in again. Out on the Pennsylvania Turnpike coming into Philadelphia, she had once again thrown up blood. She was going to do it again, right here. She hacked and hacked, hacked and hacked. Just as she brought up a big splatter of red, Gerald opened his door.

"Jesus Christ," he said, looking at the mess on the floor. "How long has this been going on?"

"The cough or the blood?"

"The blood."

"Since yesterday."

"What about the cough?"

"For a couple of weeks."

"Come on in," Gerald said. "In about two minutes, I'm going to make you go to the hospital, but for the moment I want to check you out."

Bennis straightened up and stretched. It hurt to stretch.

It hurt to breathe. It hurt to have the hall light glowing over her head.

"He's going to say he told me so, you know that," she said. "They're all going to say they told me so."

"They ought to. You should have given up cigarettes ten years ago. You should never have started."

"You think this is caused by cigarettes?"

"Yes, Bennis," Gerald said patiently. "Whatever this is, it was probably caused by cigarettes."

Bennis walked past him into the office. The reception room was carpeted in deep pile and decorated with huge plants—trees, really—in equally huge planters. The walls were covered with photographs of patients successfully treated. Nobody ever kept photographs of the ones who died. She wondered if Gerald would take her own photograph down off the wall if she died, and then she told herself to stop it. She was being morbid. She was being nuts.

In the back hall, Sheryl Lynne, one of the nurses, was fussing around in an examining room. She smiled politely at Bennis—Bennis was sure she just *loved* having to stay late, just so some Main Line postdebutante could have an examination after hours—and pointed the way into the room they were going to use. Bennis felt the cough welling up in her chest and tried to hold it back, if only to avoid the pain. It didn't work. She began to hack and hack again. She brought up more blood.

"Oh, my God," Sheryl Lynne said.

"Go sit down," Gerald said, coming up behind them both.

Bennis put a hand against the wall. She was so cold, she couldn't stop herself from shaking. The whole world seemed to be made of ice. The coughing had stopped but she didn't feel any better. She felt worse. She felt worse and worse all the time.

"Go sit *down*," Gerald commanded her, giving a little push to her back.

Bennis scurried into the examining room. The examining

table was too high up. She sat down on the little wooden chair instead.

"What is it?" she heard Sheryl Lynne ask.

Gerald Harrison sighed. "Pneumonia, for one thing. What else is the matter in there, I can't tell at the moment. You'd better call me an ambulance."

"No," Bennis said. "I've got—I've got my car."

"Tell the hospital I'm going to want an immediate admission. I'm going to need an IV and I'm going to need a ton of antibiotics. There's no way she came down with this yesterday. She must have been walking around with it for days. Get the ambulance, Sheryl Lynne. Do it now."

"My car," Bennis said.

"Shut up," Gerald said. "What it is you have against consulting a doctor when you get sick, I'll never know. It's like you've got a vested interest in creating emergencies."

Not quite, Bennis thought, as she drifted into oblivion—but then she did drift into oblivion. The world was dark and endless, and the only person in it besides herself was Gregor Demarkian.

By the time the ambulance showed up, Bennis was thinking of nothing at all.

Five

I

What Gregor Demarkian really wanted to do was to find some form of public transportation and go right back to Philadelphia, and to Bennis, as soon as possible. What he had to do was to find some way to give the Connecticut State Police hope that they might be able to arrest a person who had already committed three murders in four days, and who seemed to have no interest whatsoever in stopping. That, Gregor knew, was a misperception. This murderer was not a lunatic—a "homicidal maniac" as some people liked to call them. Gregor had known a few homicidal maniacs in his time, and taken an interest in a few he had not been professionally involved with. The truth was, none of them had seemed very much like maniacs to him. Some of them had been the kind of person one expected to find accused of serial murder—drifters, loners, badly dressed, badly smelling, with a history of lost jobs and erratic behavior. Some of them had been far more ordinary men. There was Ted Bundy, who could have had a life if he'd managed to keep his sexual impulses on track, or if he'd even wanted to. There was Frederick West, in England, just a few years ago, who had had a life, and a wife and a job and a house, and used all of them to murder young girls who happened to be waiting for a bus at the stop on the street just outside his front door.

Serial murderers were odd people, in ways which were not all that obvious. Gregor had spent ten years of his life trying to understand them, and he still went over the problem in his mind from time to time, and kept up on the research. By now he was convinced that there were probably at least two kinds, which he privately labeled the smart ones and the stupid ones. In reality, it was probably a difference between the ones who were otherwise sane and the ones who were full-blown schizophrenics. In every case he had ever known, though, the bottom line had been about sex. The eroticization of death. The sexuality of violence. The confusion of orgasm and anger. If nothing else about the murders here in Connecticut proved that they were not committed by a serial killer, there was the fact that they had nothing to do with sex.

Crazy people kill for sex. Sane people kill for money.

As a motto, that was terrible. It wasn't even true. At four o'clock in the morning, when he couldn't get hold of anybody on Cavanaugh Street and those people he could get hold of didn't know what was happening to Bennis, when he wanted to sleep so badly he could scream and yet he couldn't make himself do it, when it seemed as if all the radio played was the Beach Boys singing "Fun, Fun, Fun"—it would have to do. Eventually, he gave up and watched television, which consisted of bad movies on one channel and ads for Jeff Fox doing the weather on another. The channel with Jeff Fox was the one Bennis liked to watch. It started its morning news at five. Gregor left it there. Eventually, he fell asleep sitting up in a chair, thinking about the British police with their wrecking crew, going into Frederick West's house and taking down the walls, digging up the cement foundation in the basement, finding bodies everywhere.

Asleep, he dreamed about Bennis, alone and in trouble, somewhere he couldn't get to her.

2

In the morning, when Stacey Spratz had picked him up and deposited him in the big conference room at the back of the Washington Police Department's building, Gregor was not only depressed, but just as depressed as everybody else. The table in the middle of the room was now even more full of papers than it had been the first time Gregor had ever seen it. Reports were everywhere, succinct and legalistic at the same time, describing time of death, cause of death, accompanying circumstances. Gregor could have recited the evidence by rote. He thought Stacey Spratz, Mark Cashman, and Tom Royce could, too. None of it mattered unless they could get this case into a courtroom, and at the moment they couldn't have done that if they'd done nothing else but try.

"This is why I never wanted to be part of a big-city police department," Mark Cashman said. "This and getting shot. But there must be a lot of this in a city, cases you can't close even though you know how to solve them, cases you can't prove. It would drive me nuts."

"You'd think there would be something," Tom Royce agreed. "I mean, how many times can someone commit murder and not leave a piece of solid evidence around? Just one piece."

"Did anyone go out to Margaret Anson's house and try the back door to that garage?" Gregor asked them.

"I did," Mark Cashman said. "There was no go. You could tell that somebody had tramped around back there, but once you get past the bush at the very top of the hill, right next to the garage, there's a path. It could have been anybody."

"Doing anything," Stacey Spratz said.

"You'd think there would be something," Tom Royce said again. "A coat sleeve caught on a branch and torn. A footprint preserved in the mud."

"What about the bank accounts," Gregor said. "Have those been checked out yet? After all, a deposit of over a hundred thousand dollars is at least a start—"

"We're getting there," Stacey Spratz said. "We had to get some kind of court order. We ought to have that information some time later today."

They all looked at each other. The bank accounts would at least be something, assuming they showed what they ought to show. There was a large urn of coffee in the middle of the table. Gregor stood up and got himself some. He'd drunk so much coffee by now that he felt like an electrical outlet. He was wired to the hilt. When this was over and the adrenaline went down, he was going to fall over like a tree.

They had just begun to go over it all again—the paths, the bank accounts, the distance from the Litchfield Museum to the Fairfield Family Cemetery—when there was a knock on the conference room door and a young woman stuck her head in.

"I know you said you didn't want to be disturbed," she said, "but there's a woman outside who says she has to see Mr. Demarkian. I mean, there are two women together, but it's just the one who has to see Mr. Demarkian. She says it's important. She says it's about a telephone pole."

"What?" Mark Cashman asked.

"Send her in," Stacey Spratz said.

"Maybe we should try not to intimidate her," Gregor said.

He could have been talking to the air. The young woman had disappeared. A few seconds later, she appeared again, this time with two other women in tow. One of them was middle-aged and distinctly pudgy and tired-looking. The other was young, thin, and somewhat New York-ish, complete with the sort of wiry shock of hair people used to call a Jewish Afro. The pudgy one looked around the room and started to panic.

"Now," Gregor said, getting out of his seat and going over to her. He knew without question that the pudgy one was the one who wanted to talk to him. The young one had been brought along for moral support, or for courage. Gregor took the pudgy one's arm and guided her to a seat. "Now," he said again, "if you'll just sit down, Mrs—"

"It's Eve Wachinsky," Mark Cashman said. "She's from Watertown. She was a couple of years ahead of me in high school."

"Oh," Eve Wachinsky said. "Maybe I shouldn't do this—"

"She's worried that you're all going to laugh at her," the young woman with the Afro said. "But I've listened to what she has to say, and I think she ought to tell you. She really should. So if it's not important, just blame it on me."

"Who are you?" Gregor asked.

"My name is Grace Feinmann. I'm her neighbor across the hall. We both live in the same building out by Depot Square in Watertown. And you've got to be careful, because she just got out of the hospital yesterday. She had meningitis."

"If I hadn't been sick, I would have said something sooner," Eve said. "It's just that I was—it's just that I was—"

"On Friday night when Kayla Anson was murdered, she worked the night shift at Darla Barden's answering service," Grace said. "She got back home about six in the morning and just collapsed in the hall. Because she was sick. So you see, she didn't even hear about the murder and then she was in the hospital—"

"I had a fever," Eve said. "It was a big fever and I couldn't think. And now I have medical bills, you know, thousands and thousands of dollars in medical bills and I don't know how I'm going to pay them—"

"You're going to apply for patient assistance," Grace said. "I'm going to help you fill out the forms. You've got to tell him what happened at Darla's."

"Oh," Eve said. "Yes. I know. Only, the thing is, they must have made a record of it. At the time, you know. And you must have seen the record. So you must know all about it. So you must not think it's important. But Grace said maybe you don't know at all, maybe something slipped up."

"What is it we might not know about?" Gregor asked patiently.

"The telephone pole," Eve said.

"The telephone pole," Gregor repeated.

Eve nodded. It wasn't just that she was scared, Gregor realized. It was that she was still weak from sickness. She shouldn't be out in the open like this. She ought to be home in bed.

"On Friday night, there was a telephone pole," she said. "It went down on Capernaum Road. I'm not sure about the time, but I think it might have been between eleven and twelve. That I got the call, I mean, not that the pole went down."

"Capernaum Road," Gregor said. "Why is the name so familiar?"

"You're probably thinking of the Bible."

"No he's not," Stacey said. "Capernaum Road is the dirt road at the back end of the Fairfield Family Cemetery."

It was going to be a while before the adrenaline drained completely. Gregor could feel it. This was something far more dramatic than a second wind.

"How far is it from the cemetery?" he asked.

"About as far as the Litchfield Museum is in the other direction," Stacey Spratz said.

"Right." Gregor turned back to Eve Wachinsky. "A telephone pole went down. How did you hear about it?"

"Darla does the emergency calls for the town," Eve said. "And Rita Venotti called me and told me to call Craig and get a crew out there to, you know, fix things up or get SNET to fix them, because there are all kinds of wires on those poles or else the poles are close to the electrical wires or something. I don't know how it works. But anyway, there had to be someone to take care of it. But it should be written down somewhere. That the crew was sent out. And that something happened. Especially since it was so odd."

"What was odd about it?" Gregor asked.

"Well, it was like Craig told me later," Eve said. "When he called in, you know. And he was really very upset, because when he got out there it was a real mess and he'd had to spend hours, and it looked like it was going to be some kind of vandalism. They all hate vandalism. Nobody wants to be out of bed and running around in the woods somewhere at two o'clock in the morning just because some kid got stupid. And with power lines involved, you've always got the problem that somebody could get killed."

"Yes," Gregor said patiently.

"Anyway," Eve said. "The thing is, Craig said later that when they got the SNET guys out there, they—the SNET guys—they said that it looked to them as if somebody had taken a vehicle and just rammed the pole over and over again. That somebody was trying to knock it over. And Craig said to me that it really didn't make any sense. To knock the pole over you'd have to do a lot of damage to your car. Even if you had a truck, it would end up a mess. And nobody would do that on purpose, you know? Unless you were trying to mess up the vehicle. Which really didn't make a lot of sense."

"The Jeep," Mark Cashman said.

"Exactly," Gregor said.

"You see," Grace Feinmann said. "I told her over and over again that it wasn't stupid, but she wouldn't listen to me."

"But it is stupid," Eve said suddenly. "I mean, it must have been a big deal. They were out there all night, the crews were, getting it fixed. They might have been out there even the next morning. You know how long things like that take to fix. The news must have been just everywhere. If it was important, why didn't they—"

"The news on Saturday was all about Kayla Anson being murdered," Grace Feinmann said firmly. "If Saddam Hussein had landed in Washington and offered to join the United States Marine Corps as a regular recruit, it wouldn't have made a dent."

This, Gregor Demarkian thought, might possibly be true—but it was probably going to turn out to be mostly his fault. They would look at the records and the records would be there, clear and obvious on the page. The problem would come down to the fact that he did not know where things were up here. He hadn't been able to put two and two together.

Now he downed the rest of his coffee and started to shove papers into his big yellow folder.

"You were not stupid to come here," he told Eve Wachinsky. "In fact, you performed a very valuable service.

Sometimes, the answer is staring you in the face but you don't know it's there. It takes somebody with a different perspective to point it out to you."

"Oh," Eve said, blushing. "Oh, dear. Well. I mean. Thank you."

"I *told* you so," Grace Feinmann said.

"I take it you want to go out to Capernaum Road."

"As soon as you can get me there," Gregor said. "And I want Miss Feinmann here to take Mrs. Wachinsky back to her apartment and put her to bed. Immediately. She's in no shape to be out. Are the rest of you gentlemen going to come with us?"

"I'm just so glad I didn't do anything stupid," Eve Wachinsky said. "I don't know why it is, but I seem to spend all my time doing things that are stupid."

Gregor Demarkian knew how that felt, but at the moment he didn't have time to think about it.

3

Out on the Capernaum Road, it was as if nothing had ever happened. No telephone pole had ever come down. No live wires had ever lay stretched across the road. As soon as Stacey Spratz's car pulled over to the shoulder—if you could call the start of wild-growing grass a shoulder—Gregor got out and looked around. There wasn't much to it. The road was only a few hundred feet long. On one end was Route 109. On the other was Route 63. The dirt was well-tamped and packed solid, probably because a lot of people used this road as a shortcut between the two routes. It would be faster than going all the way out to the intersection.

There were five telephone poles along the road, all on the side away from the hill that led to the Fairchild Family Cemetery. Gregor walked from one to the other of them, carefully inspecting each of them at their bases. They *all* looked as if they had been smashed into and knocked over, that was the problem. He came back to the police car and looked up the hill.

"That hill is rocky like that, all the way up?" he asked Stacey Spratz.

"All the way up," Stacey agreed.

"Meaning the Jeep could have been driven straight up and into the Fairchild Family Cemetery without leaving a trace."

"After it had been smashed into a telephone pole hard enough to knock the pole over?"

"Why not? It still runs. It was returned to Faye Dallmer banged up but still going. That's what the report said."

Another car pulled into the road and up onto the grass. Mark Cashman got out and walked over to them.

"I talked to SNET. It was the second one in from Sixty-three. And it fell toward Sixty-three, too."

"That way." Gregor pointed away from the part of the hill that led up to the cemetery.

"Right," Mark Cashman said.

"I had it backward, you see, that was the problem," Gregor said. "I thought that the murderer must have hit Kayla Anson's BMW with the Jeep. The murderer was following Kayla close enough to bump her, according to Zara Anne Moss. I thought that what must have happened was that something from the BMW got onto the Jeep, and then it needed to be disguised. But if you think about it, that doesn't make much sense. The Jeep was being driven very oddly some of the time. People would have seen it. People might have remembered it and commented on it. In fact, people did see it and comment on it. And so what? The Jeep didn't belong to the murderer anyway. The murderer could leave any evidence on it at all, and it just wouldn't have mattered."

"Then why smash up the Jeep?" Stacey asked. "Why knock over a telephone pole."

"Because the Jeep smashed into something else," Gregor said. "It smashed into the murderer's own car."

"The Ferrari," Mark said.

"The problem," Gregor said, "was that the Jeep, which lots of people could have seen and remembered, and would know was following Kayla Anson's BMW, the Jeep now had trace evidence of the murderer's own car. There's an efficient area of police work for you—we can get all kinds of things off a car that's hit something. So the idea was, I think, to have it hit something else and far more violently. To layer evidence on top of evidence. To give the impression that we had found the source of the crash, on the assumption that we wouldn't go looking for another one."

"There's still a chance that something is left on that Jeep," Mark Cashman said. "We can get it from Faye for a couple of days and check it out."

"You do that," Gregor said. "What about the Ferrari? Can we get to that?"

"I don't see why not," Stacey said. "It can't have disappeared."

"It's likely to be someplace not immediately available," Gregor said. "At somebody else's house. Or in the garage. If the Jeep smashed into it, there may have been some damage."

"Well, there's only one place in this part of the hills that fixes Ferarris," Stacey said. "That ought to be easy enough."

"Did the telephone company people take pictures?" Gregor asked.

Mark Cashman turned on his heel and went back to his car. Gregor looked around the Capernaum Road one more time. There really wasn't anything much to it, and yet there had to be more than he could see. The need to walk, and the need for secrecy, required it.

"Stacey?" he said. "Is there any road branching off this road? Not the routes on either end. A road."

"Go on up to about the fourth pole," Stacey said. "You'll see it going into the woods on the left. On the pole side, I mean. It isn't really a road anymore. The town doesn't maintain it. There used to be a house up there back about fifty years ago, but there's nothing now. Why?"

Gregor walked up to the fourth pole. He had been there before, and he hadn't noticed it, but it was there—a road in the process of self-destruction. The weeds were high in the center of it. There were rocks everywhere. Still, the edges of what had once been a traveled pathway were clearly visible, if you took the time to look.

"What's wrong?" Stacey asked, coming up behind him.

"You need to get some people up there," Gregor said. "That's where Kayla Anson died. Up that thing. That's where the BMW and the Jeep and the Ferrari were parked. Nobody would ever have known they were there."

"Taking a four-hundred-thousand-dollar Ferrari up that thing is asking for trouble."

"Under the circumstances, I think that was a minor consideration. But you can see what happened. The murder venue had to be out of the way. So did the places where the switches were made. Capernaum Road itself wouldn't do. It was too well-traveled. People probably use it for a shortcut—"

"All the time."

"—and that means the chance of getting caught at any moment. So you come up here instead, and it's quiet and out of the way, and nobody will see you. But you have to keep your lights low or off. If you don't, somebody might see *them*. So you come barreling back up here after you dump the body, you need to move the Jeep for some reason, and instead you smash into your own car. If that hadn't happened, I think the Jeep would still be on this road."

"This whole thing sounds nuts," Stacey Spratz said.

"Not nuts. Just careful. And very elaborate. Some people like to be elaborate."

"Some people should be locked up for more reasons than one."

"Get some people out and at work," Gregor said. "Find out about people passing on One-oh-nine that night. Not this part of it, the other side of Four Corners, on the way to Margaret Anson's house. That has to be—what? Ten or fifteen miles. It was a long walk."

"*Walk?*"

"Didn't it bother you at all, about the times? The Jeep is following Kayla Anson's car at six o'clock at night or so. All the rest of these things don't start happening until nearly midnight."

"This is worse than nuts," Stacey Spratz said.

But, Gregor thought, it wasn't nuts at all. He wished it were nuts. Nuts was easier to deal with than premeditated.

4

Half an hour later, sitting in the parking lot of the Adams Super Food Store in Watertown while Stacey ran in to buy a six-pack of Coke, Gregor Demarkian finally gave in to exhaustion. He could feel it start almost as soon as Stacey left the car. He turned up the radio and found that Big D 103 FM out of Hartford was once again playing "Fun, Fun, Fun." He thought of Bennis Hannaford and her little tangerine orange two-seater Mercedes convertible. Then the music changed to the Beach Boys doing "Sloop John B" and he thought about Cavanaugh Street, where everything was empty and sad because Donna Moradanyan hadn't been able to concentrate on decorating for Halloween. In fact, it *was* Halloween. The days had been going by with such formless insanity, Gregor hadn't realized it.

Like most people who have spent a significant part of their lives in law enforcement of one kind or another, Gregor Demarkian didn't like Halloween. That was the holiday when people felt justified in causing pain, and fear, and death. The streets were full of people who thought they had made pacts with the devil.

Gregor put his head back on the seat, and closed his eyes, and dropped into unconsciousness.

Six

I

It was one of those days that felt like rain even though it wasn't raining. The air was wet as well as cold. So many leaves had fallen from the trees that there was a rustling along the ground in even the slightest wind. Martin Chandling kept putting his hands up to touch the top of his head, to see if raindrops had fallen there. Then, when his hair seemed dry but all too thin, when the slick curve of baldness underneath was all too evident, he put his hand down again and tried to get some work done. He had a lot of work to do. It was going to be Halloween tonight. Maybe it was Halloween even now. Out there somewhere there were teenaged boys, hot-rodding up and down the back roads. They had six-packs of Coors in the back of their trucks and their radios turned up loud. They had girls who had convinced themselves to love them, and later, when it got dark enough and they got tired of scaring lonely women driving home by themselves in the dark, they would take the girls out onto the dirt lanes where there were no lights. Martin had taken girls out onto the dirt lanes himself when he was seventeen. He could still feel the cold on his back as they squirmed underneath him. He could still remember not caring if he froze to death.

Right now, he had to clean out the gutters. They were clogged full of leaves, and if it did rain in the next couple of days, the clog would bring the gutters down. He tried to remember what it had been like, to make love to a woman, even when he was married, but all that stuff was pretty hazy now. He remembered high school better than that, when he and Henry had walked through the halls with their books and their high-topped sneakers, and the girls they both secretly wanted—the blonde ones with the Villager skirt-and-sweater sets, the ones who looked like magazine models and who were going away to Connecticut College or Smith—wouldn't even talk to them. Cecily Harkness, that was the name of the one Martin had liked best. She had gone to Vassar and then married a man from Goshen who had gone to Yale. He sometimes saw her in the Danbury Fair Mall, going in and out of Lord & Taylor looking like an advertisement for a country club. Except that country clubs didn't have advertisements. Had he realized, even then, that life didn't usually work out for people like him?

He got out the stepladder and popped it open next to the big casement window block that looked into the kitchen. He climbed up a few steps and saw that the leaves were all bunched down at one end, the other end, and he would have to move his whole operation to the far side of the house. He got down off the stepladder and wiped the palms of his hands against his jeans.

"Damn," he said. But even he thought he sounded as if he didn't mean it.

Henry came around the side of the house. Henry had been looking fidgety all morning, but Martin had put that down to the fact that Demarkian and those people had been out here again. Although they'd left the two of them mostly alone this time, Martin had to admit. They'd been out there pacing around on the roads. Martin had thought that Demarkian was going to break his ankle.

"So," Henry said, looking up as Martin climbed the stepladder again. "I thought maybe we should talk."

"Talk about what?" Martin asked. The clog was too tight to be shook loose by a hard stream of water. That was too bad, because blasting the sucker with the hose was definitely the easiest way to take care of a problem like this. Martin was going to need a stick, or the handle of the rake.

"This is a mess up here," he told Henry. "We've got to do something about it."

"I said maybe we should talk," Henry said again. "I've been thinking."

"About what?" There was a stick right there on the ground that looked like it might do. Martin got off the ladder and picked it up. It was bent, but thickly round. He broke a little piece off the end of it to make it a more manageable size and started up the ladder again.

"I don't see why what we have to talk about can't wait till supper," he said.

"Martin, for God's sake."

Henry put his arm out and on Martin's arm. Martin looked down on it like it was a large dragonfly that had come out of nowhere and chosen him to roost.

"What the hell," he said.

"Listen," Henry said. "It's about this place. The cemetery. It's about us being here in the cemetery. Or about me being here in the cemetery."

"What about it?"

"Well," Henry said, "the thing is, I don't want to do it anymore. Do you see that? I mean, we've been doing it for years. And I'm sick of it."

The ladder seemed suddenly very high, much too high to climb. Martin put the stick on the ground and tried to think.

"But you can't just stop doing it," he said finally. "They'd kick us out of the house. It isn't our house. It belongs to the Fairfield Foundation."

"I meant I was sick of the house, too."

Martin rubbed his palms against his jeans again. There seemed to be nothing else to do. "I don't get it," he said finally. "Where would we go? What would we do?"

"We don't necessarily have to do anything," Henry said. "You could stay here if you wanted to. I could go on my own."

"I couldn't handle this place by myself."

"You could hire a helper. Get one of those boys who's always driving us so crazy. One of them would probably be more than happy to have a part-time job."

"You don't want me along with you," Martin said. "Wherever you're going, you don't want me to be there, too."

Henry sighed. "It's not that I don't want you to be there,

too. I just want you to do what you want to do. That's all. I just want to stop going along to go along. I'm an old man. I want to do something fun before it's too late."

"Fun," Martin said.

Then he turned around and lifted the ladder off the ground. He snapped it closed and put it under his arm. These were familiar things he was doing, the things he did every day. This was the life he knew. Henry was crazy to be talking about fun.

"I'm going to go put this away in the barn," he said, keeping his back to his brother. "You go do what you want."

"Listen," Henry said. "We can get Social Security in a few years. Do you realize that?"

"So what?"

"So it's enough to live on, some places. And we wouldn't have to stop working. We could flip burgers or something. There would be jobs."

"Where?" Martin demanded. "In Waterbury? Why would I want to flip burgers in Waterbury?"

"Not in Waterbury. In Florida. We could go to Florida. I've got some money put by. We could buy a trailer, one of those things, or a little ranch house. They don't cost much in Florida. Maybe sixty or seventy thousand dollars in some places."

"Nobody can buy a house for sixty or seventy thousand dollars," Martin said. "You can't buy a garage for that."

"Up here you can't. Down in Florida you can. I've been checking. Down in Palm Harbor, that's a place. And it's getting cold, can't you feel it? It's going to be cold as hell all winter."

"It's always cold as hell all winter."

"So you like that?" Henry asked. "Why? Why should we both be miserable for months at a time? Why shouldn't we go to Florida?"

Martin put the ladder down on the ground, on its side. The leaves were thick around his ankles. Somebody would have to come out here and rake. The raking would take all day, and when it was done it would have to be done again. Then the snow would begin to fall, and somebody would have to shovel out the driveway and the walk. Him. He would have to shovel out the driveway and the walk, unless Henry did it, and Henry couldn't do it if he was in Florida.

"We've never been to Florida," Martin said finally, as if that ought to answer everything.

Instead, Henry was hopping around from one foot to another, grinning like he'd just finished a bottle of whiskey.

"That's the point," he said. "We've never been there, and it's warm, and we can go to Disney World."

Disney World.

For the first time in his life, Martin Chandling thought he was getting a migraine.

2

By late on the afternoon of Halloween, everybody at the Swamp Tree Country Club knew what had happened with Sally Martindale. Everybody knew what the deal was going to be, too, because members had been eavesdropping outside old Mortimer's door all afternoon. Mortimer was not being particularly quiet in there—in fact, most of the time he was shouting. It was Ruth Grandmere who was keeping her head and being practical about things. If it hadn't been for Ruth, Mortimer would probably have had the police come right to the club and cart Sally Martindale off to jail.

"It was gambling," Marian Ridenour confided to Peter Greer as she pulled out a chair to sit down at his table. "Can you believe that? She was taking all this money and going out to Ledyard to play the slots. Hundreds of thousands of dollars of it."

"It wasn't hundreds of thousands of dollars," Jennifer Crawford said, pulling another chair over to the little table. "It was only about ten thousand, and mostly she wasn't gambling with it. Apparently, she's been living out there in that huge house for months without enough money to pay the bills. She'd had her heat shut off last winter."

"Oh, I'd heard that," Marian said. "Somebody said—I don't remember who—that she'd had to apply for heating assistance from the state. And yet Mallory was here, the whole time, trying to be a debutante."

"Oh," Jennifer said, "Mallory isn't going to be a debutante anymore. She's going to go to nursing school. Which is much more sensible, really, if you think about it. It never does any good to be unrealistic about your circumstances."

Peter Greer had intended to be alone, but at the moment he found this particular conversation soothing. It was so— Swamp Tree Country Club; so—Litchfield County. It occurred to him that there were dozens of women in this small square part of the state who were perfectly sane, who did not think gossip and status were the bedrocks of life, and some of them were even rich. None of them belonged to the Swamp Tree. And yet this was what he wanted. This was what he had always wanted. He wondered what that said about himself.

"What do you think about it?" Marian asked him. "Are you just shocked beyond words?"

"Not really," Peter said. "I suppose it was hard to keep up after Frank left."

"Oh that," Jennifer said. "Well, of course, nothing on earth could excuse Frank's behavior. But you have to wonder. You really do. You have to wonder if he had cause."

"Why?" Peter asked.

"Well, because of this," Jennifer said. "I mean, she couldn't have been very stable, could she? And Frank had to live with her. He'd have known something was wrong long before we would. Maybe he saw it happening. This breakdown, or whatever it is she's having."

Peter cocked his head. "Her husband left her for another woman and stiffed her on the settlement so that she got practically no cash when she'd been used to living well, and you don't think that's enough of a reason for her to have a breakdown?"

"Well," Marian said, "you've got to remember. She used

to have a job. She worked for Deloitte. And they fired her."

"She came up for partnership and didn't make it," Peter said. "Most people who come up for partnership don't make it."

"Still," Marian said. "You've got to wonder if they saw something, too. Now that we know, you see, it all begins to make sense. The odd things she did. Her peculiar behavior. And her behavior really has been peculiar."

"She'd come to dinner at your house and then she wouldn't invite you back," Jennifer said. "Ever."

"She didn't have enough money to entertain," Peter said.

Jennifer brushed this away. "It wouldn't have had to be anything elaborate. I never do anything elaborate myself. It's a waste of time. But anybody can afford a nice little buffet with drinks on the side. Really. She wouldn't have had to go to any trouble."

"Champagne cocktails hardly cost anything at all," Marian said.

Peter stood up. The waiter would be by in a moment, but he didn't want to sit still just this once. A champagne cocktail at the club cost four dollars. Even if you assumed the price was inflated, that was still not nothing at all.

He got to the bar and asked for another Perrier and lime. It was much too early to be drinking actual alcohol, but some of the women were doing it. They drank tall, fancy drinks with plenty of soda in them and thought of it as not really drinking. He got his Perrier and lime and looked back at them. Marian was wearing tennis shoes and white ankle socks. Jennifer was wearing a print skirt and a cotton sweater. They all got their clothes at the same places. They all looked alike. He loved that about them, that they were so much of a type, that they didn't bother much with individuality.

"Individuality," Peter's first debutante girlfriend had told him, "is very middle-class."

The doors to the bar were propped open with solid walnut doorstops. Peter looked up as Deborah Candleman came running through them, looking breathless.

"They're coming out," she said to nobody in particular and everybody at once. "They're coming right down the hall."

Peter didn't think a single person in the bar sat still. Marian and Jennifer were on their feet so fast, he didn't even catch them moving. The crowd surged at the doors and then out of them. The hall in question was in the back, and there was a back door there, and they didn't want to miss anything. Peter followed them very slowly, not sure what he wanted to do.

There was a window in the hall outside the bar. Standing at it, it was possible to see the other door, the one Sally Martindale would be coming out of, and the parking lot beyond it. Peter stood at the back of the crowd and looked out on the leaves. The other door opened then and Sally came out with Ruth Grandmere's arms wrapped around her shoulders. Sally was staring at the ground and hugging herself tight. She was taking steps so small, it was as if she were walking on bound feet.

"Oh, look," somebody said. "Doesn't she look upset?"

"Well, she ought to look upset," somebody else said. "Stealing all that money. She ought to look more than upset."

"She won't go to jail for it, though," the first somebody said. "They never do in cases like this. She'll just get to pay it back."

"If she has it."

"They'll work out a payment plan."

"They don't want embarrassing stories about the club in the newspapers."

"She didn't belong here anyway. Anybody could tell that. She was just a nobody from the Midwest somewhere and then she married money."

Peter took a long pull on his Perrier and lime. Out in the parking lot, Sally Martindale was trying to get into her car. All her muscles seemed to be stiff. She was having trouble folding herself into a sitting position. Her face was white. Even at this distance, he could tell that her eyes were red.

"Oh, look at the crocodile tears," one of the women said. "Isn't that just like her, the deceitful little cheat."

Peter went back to the bar, and found his table, and sat down.

He was suddenly feeling violently sick to his stomach.

3

Bennis Hannaford had not meant to turn it into a neighborhood meeting, or an Armenian American convention, or whatever it had become. She had only wanted to have Father Tibor with her if she had to have a biopsy, and that was why she had called him and asked him to come. Now he was here, but so was Donna Moradanyan Donahue and Lida Arkmanian and Hannah Krekorian and even Sheila Kashinian, who had been driving the nurses at the nurses' station totally berserk for nearly half an hour. Sheila Kashinian wanted to redecorate the ward, in primary colors, to make it more cheerful for the patients.

"It really wouldn't *take* anything at *all* to get it *done*," she kept saying, in that Philadelphia-accented grating caw of hers, loudly enough so that they could probably hear her down in surgery.

The good thing was, the doctor would only allow two people at a time in Bennis's room with her. That meant that Tibor and Donna were right here at her bedside, but the rest of them were down the hall. They would all want to come down and talk to her eventually, but Bennis thought she would deal with that when the time came. If she could deal with anything. She was washed out and weak. She was so exhausted, she sometimes dropped off in the middle of conversations she was having herself.

"I still say," Donna was saying, "that we ought to call Gregor and tell him what's going on. He's not going to be at all happy to show up here and find Bennis in a hospital bed when he didn't even know she was sick."

"He knows she is sick," Tibor said, in his very careful, thickly accented English. "I have told him that she has gone to see the doctor. I have told him that she has had an emergency and that he should come home. What else should I have told him?"

"You should have told him the doctors think she might have cancer," Donna said.

Bennis turned over in bed. She wanted a cigarette. That was the truth. She wanted a cigarette so badly, she was almost ready to cry. More than that, she wanted to be able to breathe.

"Oh, God," Donna said. "We've got her upset. Bennis? Bennis, listen, I didn't mean to upset you, I really didn't. I just meant that Gregor really needs to know what the situation is. It's not fair to him—"

"Nobody knows what the situation is," Bennis said, forcing herself to sit up. "They found a spot on my lung. They don't even know what it is yet."

"Yes," Donna said. "Yes, I know."

"Jesus Christ," Bennis said. "You don't have to be so damned optimistic about it."

"I am optimistic about it," Tibor said. "I have talked to God. That is my job. But I am not optimistic about you when this is over, because I do not think you will quit smoking."

Bennis lay back down again. Quit smoking, quit smoking, quit smoking. How long had she been smoking? She couldn't remember. Since she left high school, she thought. She'd started sometime in college. She rolled over on her side and curled into a fetal position. She needed more covers. She needed more blankets. She was so cold. She should have thought to get Tibor to bring something for her from home. If he was going to bring Donna with him anyway, Donna could have gone into Bennis's apartment and found everything that was needed.

"Look," Donna said now. "We've caused a relapse."

"We would not cause a relapse if you would not lecture

her about cancer," Tibor said. "It does nobody any good at this point to jump to conclusions."

Bennis turned over on her back again. Then she sat up again. It made her feel dizzy.

"Listen," she said. "I want the two of you to get out of here. And then I want to see Lida."

"Of course," Donna said quickly. "We're making you exhausted. We'll send Lida and Hannah in and—"

"No. Just Lida. I'll talk to Hannah later. Maybe. If I'm up to it."

"Hannah is going to be very upset about it," Donna said dubiously. "Are you sure you want to, well, you know—"

"I need to talk to Lida," Bennis insisted.

Tibor and Donna looked at each other. Bennis wished they weren't behaving so much as if they were granting her her last wish. Then they each leaned over the bed in turn and kissed her on the forehead.

"Just a moment," Tibor promised. "We will send Mrs. Arkmanian down to talk to you."

Bennis took the time just after they left to rearrange the pillows so that she could sit up better. Then she remembered something she had forgotten about hospital beds and went looking for a button. She found it on a sort of remote-control thing that wasn't really remote, since it was hooked into a wire. She couldn't think what to call it. She pushed the button and the top half of the bed began moving upward.

Lida came in just as Bennis found a bed position she liked. Lida Kazanjian Arkmanian had been the prettiest girl in Gregor Demarkian's grammar school class, and she was still a remarkable-looking woman, with high cheekbones and good hair. She also had a truly remarkable three-quarter-length chinchilla coat.

"I wish I had that," Bennis said, as soon as Lida came in. "I'd use it as a blanket."

Lida shrugged off the coat and spread it out over Bennis on the bed. "This should be better than what they give you here. And later this afternoon, maybe I'll bring you some real blankets and some food. Will they let me bring you food?"

"Absolutely. I can eat anything. I'm supposed to eat anything. It was just last night and this morning you know, when they were leading up to the biopsy."

"Yes," Lida said.

Bennis hunkered down under the chinchilla coat. "Look," she said, "I don't mean to pry or anything, but are you still in contact with my brother Chris?"

Lida cleared her throat. "Yes. Yes, as a matter of fact, I am. Not quite in the same sort of contact I once was, if you understand—I don't know, Bennis, but I think I'm getting old—but we still talk at least once a week."

"Good. Because Chris and I hardly talk at all, and I lost his new address after he moved last spring, and now I want to get in touch with him. Do you think you could get in touch with him for me? Do you think you could tell him I want to talk to him?"

"Of course I can, Bennis. I can do that tonight. Do you want him to fly out here? Do you want him to be with you?"

"No, that's not necessary, really. I just want to talk to him. I can't tell Gregor everything, after all. Sometimes I try, and he just doesn't get it."

"None of them get it, Bennis. At your age, you ought to know that. Some of them are very sweet, of course, but none of them get it."

"No, I guess they don't. But I want to talk to Chris anyway. Okay?"

"Of course."

"Now, do you think you could do me a bigger favor and tell the assembled horde out there that I'm not up to seeing any more visitors? Just tell Hannah I fell asleep or something, will you? I'll make it up to her later."

"She'll be very upset."

"I know she will. But I just—can't, if you know what I mean. I just can't."

"It will be all right, Bennis. We'll work something out. And maybe you should sleep."

"I will sleep. They'll come in here in about half an hour and fill me full of Demerol. I won't be able to help but sleep."

"That wasn't what I meant."

"I know."

"I will be going now," Lida said. "Do you want to keep the coat?"

"Somebody would steal it."

"Yes."

Lida picked up the coat and put it around her shoulders. Then she leaned over and kissed Bennis on the forehead, too. Bennis couldn't remember a time in her adulthood when so many people had kissed her on the forehead.

As soon as Lida was out of the room, Bennis put the bed back down flat and turned over on her side.

If it really was cancer, she had no idea of what she was going to do.

Seven

I

They impounded the car.

That, and picking up Faye Dallmer's Jeep, was all they could think of to do. The financial records would be on their way as soon as all the authorizations were in and the bankers felt protected from any possible future lawsuits. Gregor Demarkian did not think there was much chance that what he believed would be there would not be there. After all, nobody takes a hundred and thirty thousand dollars in cash and just leaves it lying around the house. Something has to be done with money of that kind. Someplace has to be found to put it. Even in the event of the nearly unthinkable—that the check had been cashed and the cash put into a safety deposit box, say—there would be some record of the check *being* cashed. No bank would ever have handed over the money without it.

The question was—was it going to be enough? That was the difficulty with well-heeled, well-educated perpetrators. If they kept their heads, they could get away with almost anything. Evidence was such a tricky thing. "Beyond a reasonable doubt" was even trickier. And then there was the obvious, well known to every law enforcement officer and every district attorney: juries hated to convict personable, successful, well-mannered white people. Gregor had seen it a hundred times, in cases he had been personally involved in and in cases he had only followed in the newspapers. Rapes so egregious they left the victims scarred for life. Assaults so violent the victim required decades of plastic surgery before he would be whole again. Even murders, done carefully, so that the evidence was obvious only to those people who had to deal with evidence all the time. Sometimes, Gregor thought that juries these days were made up of people who had watched entirely too many episodes of *The Fugitive*.

In the long late afternoon, sitting in the conference room at the Washington Police Department, Gregor watched what evidence they had piling up. There was, he knew, also the status differential. In general, juries tended to find the lives of men more important than the lives of women—where they might convict a woman of murdering a man, the same evidence would be deemed insufficient to convict a man of murdering a woman. This was also the case for blacks and whites, and for rich people and poor people. It was as if crime were being judged on a discount scale, or maybe as if the days of aristocracy had never ended. On the other hand, it didn't really do to be too rich, or too young, or too arrogant. Juries were not made up of members of the Swamp Tree Country Club. The question in this case was how a jury would gauge the life of Kayla Anson. Zara Anne Moss would be too kooky. Margaret Anson would be too old and too easily portrayed as a bitch. It was Kayla Anson whose death a jury might be willing to avenge, and then mostly because they would see her as assailed on every side, a victim of forces that saw her less as a person than as a fountain of money. Poor little rich girl. Cinderella in a golden tower. Gregor didn't understand why people couldn't see things clearly, and understand that murder was always wrong, even if the person who had been murdered was better off dead.

It was about quarter to five when he decided that he couldn't wait any longer. He had already tried to call Cavanaugh Street four times, and on the two occasions when he'd found somebody to talk to, their answers had been vague and unsatisfactory. He was worried as hell, and the more he tried to concentrate on the case, the more worried he got. Bennis had gone to the doctor's. That was last night sometime. After she'd gone to the doctor's, though, he had no idea what had happened to her. She hadn't gone home. He'd called her apartment more times than he could count. He'd called his own apartment half a dozen times, in case she'd decided to use it instead. She liked some of the games she had given him for his computer, that she did not have for her own. He'd called Donna Moradanyan Donahue, too, but that had elicited nothing but the information that she still didn't know what to do about Tommy's natural father. He had called Father Tibor Kasparian, but Tibor just kept lapsing into Armenian and Latin. He knew without a doubt that they were all keeping something from him. He didn't for a moment like the ideas he'd had for what it might be.

"The problem," Mark Cashman said, when Gregor had made his suggestion, "is that we're not really clear on location. It's going into Friday night—"

"I know," Gregor said. "Try that country club. The Swamp Tree. That seems like a good bet for Friday night. Under the circumstances."

"Right," Stacey Spratz says.

"And if I'm right, make sure you do something to hold the situation steady. Enlist the aid of the club manager, what's his name, Mortimer—"

"It's the weekend. It would be the assistant club manager, Ruth Grandmere," Mark Cashman said.

"Even better. But we've got to do something."

Stacey and Mark looked at each other. They thought they ought to do something, too, but Gregor knew that this was not the sort of thing they thought they ought to be doing. They wanted to go into someplace or the other with their guns drawn and a SWAT team at their backs, although Gregor doubted there was a SWAT team in all of the Northwest Hills. In Waterbury, maybe, although Waterbury didn't look like it would be able to afford one. Why was he thinking about SWAT teams?

All the explanations he could imagine for Bennis's sudden disappearance were bad. She had had an accident and was lying in the hospital somewhere—although Tibor and Donna had both been adamant that there had been no accident. She had decided that the relationship wasn't working out and had gone off somewhere to think. She had met up with an old lover and not been able to resist a nostalgic fling. On second thought, that last one didn't make much sense. Bennis was never on good terms with the lovers she left, and she was always the one who left. Bennis's forte for the last four or five years, before they'd started this up together, had been a form of emotional hit-and-run.

Mark Cashman came back and gave him the thumbs-up. "At the country club," he said. "You want us to drive you out there?"

"You want us to wire you?" Stacey asked helpfully. "Then we'd be able to hear everything the two of you said and maybe—"

"Get the case thrown out of court over illegal evidence," Mark Cashman finished.

Gregor got up. The conference table was littered with Styrofoam coffee cups and the wrappers from dozens of packages of junk food. Hostess cupcakes. Twinkies. Doritos chips. Potato chips. Slim Jims. Gregor had actually eaten a Slim Jim. It had been as tough and unyielding as one of the plastic dog chew toys Sheila Kashinian kept for her Pekingese. He was going to have to get back to Cavanaugh Street just to make sure he didn't starve to death.

He dug his notes out from underneath the debris, and headed out to the car with Stacey and Mark.

2

The Swamp Tree Country Club looked much better at night than it did in the day. It looked bigger, for one thing, because the lights that came from inside it seemed to stretch in two endless lines from the brightly lit entry in the center. They all stopped in the foyer and got permission to go on through. It wasn't difficult, because this time they were expected. Gregor half expected Ruth Grandmere to come out to greet them, as Mortimer had, but she stayed out of sight. The foyer was decorated in silver and white, as if for a wedding, but no wedding seemed to be going on or to have gone on. Gregor found the explanation on the events board,

an elaborate affair of wood cut into slots and square
wooden blocks with letters on them that had to be threaded
through. It was the kind of thing nobody would ever own
unless he had an employee who was available to go to the
trouble. HARVEST MASKS DANCE, the events board said.
DINNER, 8 P.M. DANCE 10 P.M. Debutantes.

Stacey and Mark were both nervous. Stacey was more
nervous than Mark.

"Is there a bar?" Gregor asked them.

Stacey pointed solemnly down the hall to their right,
where a discreet little sign jutted out saying CLUB ROOM.
Gregor headed for it, not bothering to check if Stacey and
Mark were following. He didn't want them in on this conversation anyway, and they knew it. They'd even honor it.
It was part of the consideration you got for being a consultant.

Gregor went into the club room and looked around. At
first, he thought he might have been mistaken. There were
dozens of people at the tables and the bar, but none of them
seemed to be Peter Greer. Then he saw him, sitting off by
himself at a corner table for two. He most certainly was
trying to fend off intruders, because he'd picked the one
spot in the room where it would be virtually impossible for
anyone to join him. Gregor threaded his way through the
other tables, past women still in sports clothes, past other
women still dressed for the evening. All the men, except
Peter Greer, seemed to be in suits.

"Do you mind?" Gregor asked, when he got to Peter's
table.

Peter looked up and shook his head no. "Not at all. I
was just sitting here being morose. Have you heard about
our crime at the country club?"

"No."

"Sally Martindale, the club bursar. And a member here,
which isn't all that usual. But it was complicated. She was
caught embezzling funds from the member accounts."

"Ah. Actually, I had heard something about it. I didn't
realize that that was what you were talking about."

"You didn't come here to discuss Sally Martindale."

A waiter appeared out of nowhere. Gregor asked for a plain Coca-Cola. Peter asked for a Glenfidditch on the rocks. It wasn't what he'd had before. Whatever that was in the glass the waiter was taking away, it had been clear and bubbly.

"So," Peter said after the waiter had left. "You were going to say."

"Kayla Anson," Gregor said.

"Oh, absolutely. Kayla Anson and Zara Anne Moss and Margaret. Margaret was a bitch, did you know that?"

"I had gotten that impression, yes."

"Everyone got that impression. The woman was truly a piece of work. Even Kayla hated her, and God only knows she hated Kayla. She hated Kayla the way the Republicans hate Bill Clinton. Or worse."

"Margaret Anson would have been the easy one. She was right there. You wouldn't have had to get her out there. My guess is that she called you, almost as soon as Annabel Crawford called her. Because unlike Annabel, she would have known who got the money."

"Margaret," Peter Greer said carefully, "always had a very suspicious mind."

"Zara Anne Moss was harder. You had to get her out to the Anson place. I think at that point, you were still trying to throw suspicion on Margaret. That was a large part of the idea from the beginning. So you called her up and you made an appointment and you said—what? That Margaret wanted to see her? That you did? That there were spirits in the garage out at the Anson place that wouldn't be quiet until they'd been healed by a witch. She could have told somebody where she was going."

"Did she?"

"No."

"It wouldn't have fit her," Peter Greer said. "She loved to be mysterious, did you know that? She loved to make everything an enigma."

"I'm sure," Gregor said. "She also saw you bumping the

Jeep into the back of Kayla Anson's car, but she wasn't really smart enough to put two and two together and figure out who you were. She might have eventually, though. So you decided not to wait."

"I'm not very good at waiting."

The waiter was there with their drinks. Peter picked his up off the tray without giving the waiter a chance to hand it to him, tilted his head back, and swallowed half of it. Then he looked up at the waiter and said, "Why don't you get me another one right away?"

The waiter left. Gregor said, "When you killed Zara Anne Moss, you went around to the back of the house to avoid the reporters. You came up through the woods from One-oh-nine and in through the back door of the garage. You went out that way, too."

"Did I?"

"But the most elaborate of the three was the murder of Kayla Anson, because it had to be so carefully planned. So carefully planned that you wouldn't be forced to do another one. You never wanted to do more than one."

Peter finished the rest of his scotch. The waiter came back with his second. This time, Peter put the glass down in front of him and didn't touch it.

"You knew Kayla Anson was coming back from Waterbury and you knew approximately when. You knew which way she would come, because she didn't like driving on the highway at night and if she wasn't going to do that there really was only one way. You drove your own car out to Capernaum Road and then off onto the little dirt access road and parked. Then you walked to Faye Dallmer's and stole the Jeep. It wasn't far to walk. It was less than a quarter of a mile."

"Things are very close around here," Peter said.

"Yes, they are. Much closer than I'd realized, when I started. The roads make it confusing. But you weren't limited to the roads. So you stole the Jeep, and you parked it off to the side someplace, and you waited for Kayla Anson to come through. And when she did, you pulled out onto the road and followed her, as closely as possible, until you got to Capernaum Road. At that point, you forced her off to the side and onto Capernaum Road. Then you forced her off to the side again on the dirt access road. It wouldn't have been hard. You only needed to do some ordinary crowding and to not care if the Jeep got hurt. And she wouldn't have had anyplace to go but where you wanted her to go."

"And?"

"And," Gregor said, "you got out of the Jeep and she got out of the BMW, and then you hit her over the head and shoved her into the passenger seat of her own car. And then you strangled her. Because she wanted the money repaid. And when she wasn't getting satisfaction from you, she'd decided to tell her lawyers about it and let them handle the collection. I take it you're more or less flat broke."

"Everybody who runs a small business is more or less flat broke."

"You didn't want anybody to know you'd borrowed the money. You never wanted anybody to know that. Because you like all this. You like people like these to be your friends. And you couldn't borrow money from your teenaged, over-rich girlfriend without giving yourself the kind of reputation the people here would not forgive. They would have winked at sex, or even at drugs and drinking. But they have no mercy on people they think are out to take their money."

"It's like walking over the Grand Canyon on a tightrope," Peter said. And then he smiled, and shook his head, and drank his scotch.

"You strangled Kayla Anson in the front passenger seat of her own car. Then you got into the driver's seat of that car and drove out to Margaret Anson's place. You left the car in the garage. If Margaret heard it, she'd just think Kayla was coming home. After you dumped the body there, you got out of the car and left by the garage's back door. You went through the little woods there to One-oh-nine. And then you walked back to the Litchfield Road."

"That's a long walk," Peter said. "Have you any idea how long a walk?"

"Sure. It's just about ten miles even. I checked. But that explains the times, you see. Because a number of other things happened that night, but they didn't happen until nearly midnight. They couldn't happen. You were walking back, and taking your time about it, too. There was no reason to be in a hurry. Nobody ever goes onto that access road, and if they did, what would they find? Your car and the Jeep. As far as you knew, nobody could connect the Jeep to Kayla Anson anyway."

"I must have been cold."

"In more ways than one. When you got back to Capernaum and the access road, I think you had to move the Jeep in order to get your own car out. On that part, I'm not completely sure. But whatever the reason, you got into the Jeep and started to move it and miscalculated in the dark, because you were trying to do all this without lights. You didn't want anybody coming by on Capernaum to see you on that road. And while you were moving the Jeep, you smashed into your own car and caused a lot of damage. A fire engine red Ferrari Testarosa. That's why you're driving a rental car at the moment. I noticed it when we came to your house to talk. We have the Testarosa, by the way. We impounded it this morning."

"Marvelous."

"You needed to do something to erase the traces of the Testarosa from the Jeep. You did the only thing that might have a hope in hell of accomplishing that. You staged another collision. You drove the Jeep down to Capernaum and rammed it into a telephone pole, several times. You knocked the pole over. Then you took the Jeep up the hill into the Fairchild Family Cemetery. But you still didn't think you were safe."

"Obviously."

"So you went around back and up to the hill, trying to see if there was anything you could find that would help take our attention away from Capernaum, to move it in the other direction. Just in case. What you found was the Litch-field Museum, complete with a brand-new skeleton exhibit and doors left unlocked and security system left turned off. So you took what was on hand—the skeleton—and went and put it down on the Chandling brothers' front porch. And it worked. Everybody worried about the skeleton. Everybody concentrated on how that and the Jeep were connected. It didn't occur to anybody, then, that they weren't connected, at least not in any straightforward sense. It didn't occur to anybody, then, that the skeleton wasn't the point."

"It occurred to you."

"That's what I'm called in to do," Gregor said. "That's my job. Anyway, you left the Jeep in the Fairchild Family Cemetery, turned over on its side for good measure. You went back to the access road and got back into the Testarosa. Fortunately, it still ran. So you just went home. The next morning, you took the car into the shop and got yourself a rental. And the rest, as they say, is history."

Peter Greer stirred his scotch, very carefully. It occurred to Gregor that he really did not like the look of unblended scotch. It was clear, and it looked thick, like anisette. Gregor really did not like anisette. Peter Greer took a long drink and put his glass back on the table.

"The thing is," he said, "it isn't history. That's the point. It's a nice story, but you haven't any proof of it. Not really."

"You must have deposited the money," Gregor said. "There's that. And there's the car, and the Jeep, which should yield some interesting results, once they've been tested."

"I suppose so. But you know, I'm not a fool. I know you can't use most of this as evidence. You can't even use anything I say here as evidence. You haven't given me my Miranda warnings, and you're employed by the police."

"Do you want me to give you your Miranda warnings?"

"No."

"Did you kill Kayla Anson?"

"Oh, yes," Peter said. "And Zara Anne Moss and Margaret, too. But I'll deny it if it ever gets to court, and you know I will. I should have killed Margaret first. She was something worse than a bitch. She liked to destroy things just for the sake of destroying them. She wanted to destroy me."

"She may manage it, in the end."

"Maybe. But not without a fight. Never without a fight. I've fought all my life, to have money, to have status, to be *here*. I'm not Sally Martindale. I won't confess and make it easy for everyone. I won't indulge in one of the cheaper forms of repentance."

"Connecticut has the death penalty these days. Repentance might not come cheap."

"I'll take my chances. You would, too, if you were in my shoes. Anybody would."

"Possibly."

Peter finished the rest of his scotch and stood up. "I've got to go down to the locker room and have a shower and change," he said. "I'm an escort at that party tonight. When I was in high school, the debutantes wouldn't even talk to me. Now they line up to see who I'll deign to escort to the country club ball. I've planned it all very carefully. I don't intend to give it up."

"And if you get arrested?"

"I'll cross that bridge when I get to it. Good evening, Mr. Demarkian. I hope you have a nice trip back to Philadelphia, whenever it is you intend to go."

Peter had not been gone from the table for a full second before Mark and Stacey rushed up. They were too frustrated-looking to have been able to hear any part of that last conversation, or they had only heard Gregor's own part of it, which of course would be of no use to them at all. It was what Peter had said that they needed to hear. All Gregor could do was tell them, knowing that they would know, just as he did, that the information was useless.

"Well?" Mark Cashman demanded.

"Well," Gregor said. "It's time we found me a way to get back to Philadelphia."

3

In the end, they drove him all the way down to Bridgeport to catch the train. It was all they could do. Gregor thought about hiring a limousine, but he couldn't find a limousine company willing to take him all the way to Pennsylvania. Mark Cashman checked into commuter flights, but there was nothing leaving Hartford until eight o'clock the next morning, and Gregor didn't want to wait that long. He also didn't want to ride in a little commuter plane, but he didn't say anything about that. It made less than no sense to tell everybody on earth just how much he was afraid of flying.

Stacey couldn't go, since resident troopers were required to be available at all times, through radio connections if in no other way. Mark had only to wait half an hour until he was officially off-duty. In the meantime, Stacey drove Gregor back to the inn and gave him a chance to pack.

"I'm going to be sorry to see you go," he said, while Gregor piled shirts into his suitcase in a jumble. "You were the first really interesting person I'd had to talk to in months."

Interesting, Gregor thought. And then he let it pass. He let everything pass. Now that he was sure about Peter Greer, he had nothing on earth to think about but how worried he was about Bennis.

EPILOGUE

I

For more than a day, Bennis Hannaford had been afraid of what would happen when she had to see Gregor Demarkian again. There was so much he had every right to be angry with her about: the fact that she'd gone so long without telling him how seriously ill she felt; the fact that she'd left Litchfield County without giving him a chance to ask her for explanations of any kind. It didn't help that she still felt so enormously awful, or that she couldn't seem to sleep without dreaming of the biopsy. She thought that it would be a much better idea to put people who had those things under general anesthetics instead of local ones, so that they wouldn't have to see so much of what was going on. Actually, she had been given something general. She thought it might have been sodium pentathol. She thought she might have been in a kind of twilight sleep, so that she knew what was going on without really knowing. Maybe what she remembered wasn't a memory at all, but just a re-creation, built out of her fear. The needle coming down to the center of one side of her chest. The doctor bending over her with a mask on his face that showed only those eyes. She had imagined, at the time, that he would know what the tumor was made of as soon as the stuff rose up in the hypodermic. That was why his eyes looked as blank as mirrors, like one of the evil robots in an *Outer Limits* episode.

It would be *The X-Files* now, Bennis told herself, turning over onto her side so that she could look out the two plate glass windows that made up much of the outer wall. All she could see was the dead flatness of Philadelphia in the latening autumn. The sides of the buildings looked as if they had been sprayed with chalk. The roofs looked as if they had been eaten away by bugs. Cavanaugh Street never looked ugly like this, not in the worst of weather. If she sat up a little and looked off to the side, she would be able to see a cemetery.

Why was it that hospital rooms so often looked out over cemeteries?

She was turning onto her back again and trying to sit up when she heard Gregor in the hall. He had a deep voice that carried, blocking out anything else that might be going on around him. She could tell he was coming close by the way the sound was getting louder as he moved.

"Three twenty-one?" she heard him say—and then nothing. The nurses' voices were much too quiet.

Bennis turned over on her back and pressed the control button. The back of the bed behind her slid upward, and she slid upward with it. She still felt too weak to sit up on her own, but she was still doing better than she had been the night before. She got hold of the side rail and pulled herself upright that way.

She was just stretching forward a little to unkink her back when the door to her room opened and Gregor walked in. For some reason, it startled her that he looked just the way she remembered him. He was big. He was going to seed a little, especially around the middle. He was wearing a suit. Bennis thought that she herself probably looked like hell, but she had no intention of looking into a mirror and finding out for sure.

"Well," she said.

Gregor came all the way into the room and shut the door behind him. "I was here last night. Did you know that? You were asleep."

"The nurse left me a note."

"I was here for a couple of hours, with Tibor. Then he made me go home."

"It was probably a good idea."

Gregor went over to the windows and looked out. "I talked to Gerald Harrison last night. He's supposed to come in and talk to you this morning."

"Did you?" Bennis said.

It was funny, but she seemed to have become weightless.

She thought that if she looked down at herself, she would find that her body had disappeared. She was nothing but a disembodied spirit, hovering in the room. Except that she was violently, undeniably sick to her stomach. If she had known where the barf pan was, she would have thrown up in it. She thought she might end up having to throw up on the floor.

"I don't know if I want to talk to Gerald Harrison," she said.

"You want to talk to Gerald Harrison. The biopsy report is back."

Bennis tried to take a deep breath. It didn't work. There was no air in the room. Gregor had his back to her.

"So?" she said. "What is it? Are you having a good time with this? Why won't you just talk to me?"

Gregor turned around. "I'm trying very hard to find a way to say what I want to say."

"To say what? Am I going to die?"

"Only if I kill you. Which is a distinct possibility at the moment."

There *was* air in the room. There *was*. Bennis couldn't remember ever having needed so much air. She let herself fall onto the raised back of the bed and collapse. And then, for no reason at all, she was crying.

"I'm sorry," she said. "I don't know what's wrong with me."

"Pneumonia of apparently long standing, for one thing. Malnutrition. Exhaustion. I think Gerald has a list."

"But the tumor wasn't malignant."

"It wasn't even a tumor." Gregor came and sat at the edge of the bed. "As far as Gerald can figure out, what you've got is some slight scarring. He thinks you've been walking around with the pneumonia for maybe over a month. Smoking all the time. Never getting enough sleep. Not eating. And otherwise doing yourself damage."

"Oh," Bennis said. "Oh, God."

"Yes, well. He wants you to stay in the hospital for at least a week. He says if your insurance won't cover it, your bank account will. I think it's a good idea. Tibor says he'll board up the door to your apartment so that you can't come home."

"I'd be happier at home." Bennis sat forward again. For some reason, it was easier than it had been.

"You'd go to work in three hours," Gregor said. "And you still need more tests. Messing yourself up with pneumonia may not be as bad as lung cancer, but it can still kill you if you aren't careful. Besides, here in the hospital, they won't let you smoke."

"I've noticed that."

"I thought you had."

"Maybe we can compromise on something a little less than a week," Bennis said. "Forget the cigarettes for a moment. I'd be better off where I could get some decent food. Maybe somebody would be willing to take me in. Maybe Lida would let me sleep on her couch."

Gregor looked up at the big plate glass windows. He still had something on his mind. Bennis squirmed on the bed. There was really no way for her to get comfortable. She wanted to be sitting in her big leather armchair at home. She wanted to be—alone.

Well, no. She didn't want to be alone. She just didn't want to hear whatever it was Gregor had to say.

"Listen," he said finally. "Do you know what cancer is?"

"What?"

"Do you know what cancer is?" he asked again. "Elizabeth died of cancer. Elizabeth my wife. You do remember that I once had a wife."

"Of course I remember. That wasn't fair, Gregor."

"I'm not trying to be fair. I'm trying to make a point. Elizabeth died of cancer. It was ovarian cancer, in her case. But cancer is cancer, in some respects. It took her five years. Five years is a long time."

"I know."

"I don't think you do. I don't think you can begin to realize what it is to watch somebody die and take five years to do it. To watch the progressive deteriorization of everything you've ever loved. To watch the pain, the continual and unbearable pain, that no amount of drugs can relieve. To make it through the emergencies, the ambulance rides, the ICU admissions, the feeding tubes, the IVs and blood transfusions. I think that part of my life was like a tunnel, a tunnel of defeat that I thought was never going to end. And yet, you know, I am who I am. I couldn't stop fighting for her. I couldn't stop hoping for her. I think she was ready to die a long time before I was ready to let her go. People always say that they watch pain like that and compassion makes them want to see the end come soon. Well, it didn't for me. I couldn't believe that I could fight that hard for something and not win in the end."

"Gregor—"

"Stop. Listen to me. Let me say what I've got to say."

"All right."

He was still looking out the window. She wished he would turn and look at her. She thought that if he did, he would be struck speechless.

"I am who I am," he said finally. "If that biopsy had come back and the news had been bad, if you had been diagnosed with lung cancer, I would have done for you what I did for Elizabeth. I would have fought for you, for years if it had been necessary, for any extra time we could manage to have together. I would have fought doctors and hospitals and drug companies. I would have organized your life so that no part of it fell through the cracks, so that no emergency happened to you while I was out of the way and unable to cope. I wouldn't have been able to help myself. I know we don't say it to each other, not seriously. When we use the words we joke around. We're so sophisticated, it's practically a terminal condition. But I love you, Bennis. I think I have for years. And it's not a joke."

"I love you, too, Gregor. And I have for years. And it was never a joke."

Now he turned to look at her. "Good," he said. "Because I'm here to hand you an ultimatum. And I mean it. If you had been diagnosed with cancer, I would have fought for you, but you weren't. Right now, except for that scarring, your lungs seem to be perfectly clear. Which is lucky for you, and lucky for me. And that puts the future on an entirely different footing. Do you hear me?"

"Of course I hear you. I think I hear you. You're just scaring the hell out of me."

"That's good, too," Gregor said. "Because I want you to get this through your head. As of this very moment, right now, not a second later, you have quit smoking. Cold turkey and forever. You will never smoke another cigarette as long as you live. Because if you do, I'll walk. I'll pack my things and go to Europe and stay there. I'll leave no forwarding address. I'll disappear so thoroughly that you'll never be able to find me, and I'll stay gone until I have you out of my system, no matter how long it takes."

"Jesus Christ," Bennis said.

"Well, Tibor would say that wasn't a bad name to call on. I say do whatever it takes, but get it done. I saw one woman I loved die of cancer and I don't want to do it again."

"What if I quit and I get cancer anyway? It happens to people. What if it happened to me?"

"Then I'd find a way to live with it. As long as you'd quit. But you have to quit."

She was crying again. She could feel the tears rolling down the sides of her face. She wanted to make it stop and she just couldn't do it.

"This is crazy," she said. "This is just crazy."

Gregor stood up and came closer to the head of the bed. He leaned over and kissed her gently, on the lips, but so sexlessly that it might have been the kiss of a child.

"I'm going to go back to Cavanaugh Street. I'll be here again this evening, with food, if I can talk Lida into it. I can't believe I won't be able to. You get some rest."

"I want a cigarette so badly, I'd kill for it," Bennis said. "Do you realize that?"

"I don't care what you want, Bennis. Only what you do. At least in this case. Get some rest."

He kissed her again, on the forehead this time. Then he left the room and closed the door behind him. Bennis hit the control button on the bed and laid herself out flat, with her eyes shut.

She couldn't just quit smoking, just like that, with no preparations and no program. She had to ease off gradually. She had to give herself a start date and then smoke like crazy up till then. She had to—what?

For the very first time in her life since the day she had first picked up a cigarette, it occurred to Bennis Hannaford that she was not in control of her smoking, and that she could not stop anytime she wanted to.

2

Half an hour later, Gregor Demarkian got out of a cab on Bridgefort Street and walked the block and a half to the intersection with Cavanaugh. It was a bright, cold, energetic first of November, and all around him were the signs that Halloween was only barely over. The row houses on Bridgefort Street had pumpkins on their front steps and crepe paper black cats in their windows. One or two of the car windshields had been soaped. A couple of the ground floor windows had been soaped, too. He knew that when he got to Cavanaugh Street, nothing would have been soaped. People didn't do that kind of thing there.

He turned the corner and looked down the long three blocks to the awning of the Ararat Restaurant, where he should have had breakfast this morning. He hadn't been able to, because he'd been too agitated about his coming talk with Bennis, he hadn't been able to stand the idea of sitting still. Down a block there was a little cluster of people in front of one of the houses. If he wasn't mistaken, they were in front of the house where his own apartment and Bennis Hannaford's were. He looked at the scattering of Halloween decorations that would stay up for another few days, the pop-up black cats and the banners with stylized witches on them. Then he started down the block, wondering if Father Tibor was at home or doing something at the church. He thought that he had meant everything he had said to Bennis, but that if in the end he had to leave her, it would kill him.

He had gone about half a block when he realized what he was looking at. Donna Moradanyan was standing most of the way up a tall ladder she had placed on the side of their building, tacking something underneath the sill of what looked like one of his own windows. Old George Tekemanian, her son Tommy, and Father Tibor were all standing on the ground, watching her. Donna was decorating. Donna was *decorating*.

Gregor walked the rest of the way to his building and the people standing in front of it and looked up. Donna seemed to be stringing long lengths of chocolate brown crepe paper across the front of the building. Farther up, she had strung a little roundish area in beige.

"Now what?" Gregor asked the bunch of them.

"We're going to be a turkey," Tommy Moradanyan said happily. "The whole building."

"Donna said it was too late for Halloween," old George Tekemanian said, "so she would decorate for Thanksgiving."

"She has enough crepe paper to wrap the whole street," Father Tibor said. "Krekor, seriously. You would not believe it."

Gregor would believe it. Donna had once wrapped their building up in crepe paper to make it look like a heart for Valentine's Day. She had once wrapped the entire front of the church to look like a Christmas tree. Tibor hadn't been able to decide if that was a form of heresy or not—it was a pagan symbol, but it was on the outside of the church; the church allowed icons but not graven images, and this was halfway between the two—but in the end he had let it stay, mostly because it was going to be so much work to take it down and Donna wouldn't do it herself until after Epiphany. Still—

Gregor went to the foot of the ladder and looked up. "Donna?" he called. "What's going on?"

"I'm decorating for Thanksgiving."

"I can see that. I thought you said you had too much on your mind to decorate for anything."

"Yes. Well. That changed. My mind is now perfectly clear."

"Donna?"

"Did you hear that Russ is going to be my dad?" Tommy Moradanyan said. "And I'm going to have a new name. I'm going to be Tommy Donahue instead of Tommy Moradanyan. But that's not until later, when we go to see a judge. I don't understand that part. But I can call Russ Dad now. It's allowed."

"Right," Gregor said.

"I don't understand, either, Krekor," Tibor said. "All of a sudden, this morning, we have this, and she is decorating for to make a turkey. I have been worried that she has done something—inadvisable."

"What about you?" Gregor asked old George.

Old George shook his head. "You know what it's like, Krekor. I'm an old man. Nobody tells me anything. They give me silver-plated peach pitters with digital control panels." He waved the gadget in the air. Then he waved the peach.

"Donahue is Russ's name," Tommy said cheerfully. "We're all going to be named Donahue after we see the judge, even me. It shows that we're a family."

Gregor looked up the ladder again. "Donna?"

Donna seemed to pause and then make up her mind about something. She shoved the rest of the crepe paper she was carrying onto his own window ledge and came on down to the ground.

"It's settled," she said, as soon as she hit solid earth. "Is that okay with you? Peter has agreed to voluntarily relinquish his parental rights. He went into his lawyers' office this morning and signed a letter of intent. They faxed me a copy."

"Why?" Gregor asked.

"Why did they fax me a copy?"

"Why did he agree?"

Donna folded her arms across her chest. "I turned him in to the Deadbeat Dad program."

Gregor's mouth dropped open. "For God's sake," he said. "You didn't want—"

"It doesn't matter what I wanted," Donna said triumphantly. "He had a court order to pay child support and he didn't do it. I never went to court and said he didn't have to. The court never said he didn't have to. He's three years behind and he owes me better than fifty thousand dollars. So I turned him in. And they showed up at where he works yesterday, and they took him out in handcuffs. Right in the middle of the day. What do you think about that?"

Gregor started to laugh. "I think it was a stroke of genius," he said.

Donna had been ready to argue again. Now she stared at him instead. "Oh," she said. "Well, Russ was kind of upset. Because our position was always that we didn't even want Peter's money, you know, and that Peter had no hand in raising or supporting Tommy so that—you really don't think it was the wrong thing to do?"

"No. No. It was wonderful. I just wish I'd been there to see it."

Donna looked sheepish. "I wish I'd been there to see it, too, but they won't let you go along. I asked. Was that bad of me?"

"Probably."

"I don't care."

"I don't blame you."

"Well, anyway, it worked out. You know. And now Tommy and Russ and I can, you know, get everything to normal. And that kind of thing."

"Right," Gregor said.

"I'd better get back to work." Donna turned away and went back up the ladder. When she was halfway up, she turned and looked down on them all. "I promised the Melejians that I'd decorate the Ararat to look like a cornucopia with a bunch of fruit falling out. I'll be over there later this afternoon if you want to come look."

"I'm going over there in less than a minute," Gregor called back.

Tommy was hopping around from one foot to another, stopping every once in a while to try out old George Tekemanian's new gadget. Peach pits littered the front steps of the house. Pitted peaches and unpitted ones were piled up on a plate that had been left on the sidewalk—a blue-and-white plate that belong to Lida Arkmanian's best Royal Doulton set.

Gregor grabbed Father Tibor by the arm and starting leading him down the street in the direction of the Ararat. He was starving, and it was suddenly a very good day, in spite of the situation with Bennis. Maybe the truth was that he had very suddenly decided that everything would be all right, that Bennis would find a way to quit smoking for good, that his life was not going to fall apart. Maybe it was just that he was home, in the only home he had ever really had, in adulthood or out of it.

"Listen," he told Father Tibor as they walked together down the street. "Let me tell you what I've figured out about love."

Turn the page for an excerpt from
Jane Haddam's next book

TRUE BELIEVERS

Available in hardcover from
St. Martin's Minotaur

It was still full dark when Marty Kelly left home, so dark that there were haloes around all the street lights, as if the lights had metamorphosed into miniature blue moons. For a while, it seemed odd to him that he should be standing out here in the night like this. He'd done enough of this kind of thing in his life, in spite of the fact that he was only twenty-six, but all the other times he'd been anything but stone cold sober.

"Alcoholics," Bernadette had told him, the first time he'd brought her to this place. "Alcoholics and druggies. This place is full of them."

At the moment, this place was full of nothing. Marty could see with perfect clarity down the long alley between the trailers, and there wasn't so much as a light on in one of the living room windows. Even Marty's own mother seemed to be asleep. Marty shifted from one leg to the other, put his hands in his pockets, tried to think. If Bernadette found out that Geena's trailer was dark, she'd want him to go down and check. It was Friday night. Geena worked on Friday nights, if she was able—and for some reason she still got work, almost as much of it as she'd gotten when Marty was small and her face had looked less like a piece of onionskin that had been crumpled into a ball and thrown into a wastepaper basket. In those days, the men had come in the afternoons as well as at night, and when they did, Geena would shove Marty into the back bedroom and fix the door so he couldn't get out. If the man was fast, it didn't matter. If he wasn't, Marty would find himself sitting on the bedroom floor for hours, hungry, bored, ready to explode. When he had to relieve himself, he would get an empty beer bottle out from under the bed and go in that, praying like crazy that he didn't have to relieve himself in the other way. When the fights started, he would wedge himself into the small closet and shut the door, hoping like hell that nobody would find out he was there. Every once in a while, the fights got bad enough to make somebody notice. Something would crash through the living room window. Something would spill out into the alley where other people could see. Then the police would come and he would have to hide even more carefully. He would have to practically stop breathing. If the police found him, they would call the child protection people, and that was the very worst thing of all.

"She might be sick," Bernadette would say, if she were standing out here next to him. "One of those men who visit her might have done something to her. You can't just leave her alone. You have to go see."

Marty turned back to look at the truck. Bernadette was sitting upright in the passenger seat, her seatbelt already on, her eyes closed. Her sense of duty was one of the things he loved most about her, mostly because he'd never met anybody else who had it. Bernadette believed that wives cleaned house and got dinner for their husbands. Their trailer was always spotless, and if she had to work late and couldn't be there when he got back from the station, she left a covered dish in the refrigerator with instructions for him to heat it in the microwave. Bernadette believed that good people went to church on Sunday, and that they did more for their church than sit at Mass looking holy. She volunteered for two different missions, and helped out at the Episcopalian church across the street when they had need of it. She hadn't even seemed to mind that most of the people at the church across the street were gay. Bernadette was holy, but she wasn't one of those people who had her nose stuck in the air.

Marty had learned to nurse a single beer all Saturday night so that he'd be in shape when the alarm went off at six on Sunday morning. Sometimes, he stopped cold in the middle of installing a carburetor or changing the oil on some car that hadn't had it changed in the last six years and felt a kind of shock. He was still living where he had always lived, but he might as well have been living on a different planet. He didn't know anybody else whose trailer looked like his, or who had a savings account, either. It was incredible what happened when you kept your drinking to a six-pack a week and didn't do drugs at all. In the beginning, he had only gone along because he was in love, and because he couldn't believe that Bernadette loved him back. In the end, he had had to admit that she was right about everything.

"*Used* to have a savings account," he said now. He was looking at his mother's dark living room window again. It was the first of February and very cold. In any other year, there would have been snow. He turned back to look at Bernadette. She hadn't moved.

"Listen," Bernadette had told him, when they were first going out. "It's not luck. It's not that you have to get lucky. It's that you have to have a plan. If you have a plan you can do anything. Don't you see?"

One of the things Bernadette had done was to make him stop playing the lottery. She had made him take the money he would have spent on lottery tickets and put it in a jar behind the kitchen sink. At the end of a month, she had dumped it all out on the kitchen table and shown him how much there was—and there was nearly three hundred dollars, enough for the utilities two months running, enough for a payment on the truck. Marty thought he would remember it all the rest of his life, the way she had been that night, her red hair caught back in a barrette, her great blue eyes looking bluer than usual in her pale freckled face. She had been so beautiful, she had made him hurt.

"You have to have a plan," she had told him again. "You have to think things through."

He'd never been too good at that: thinking things through. He wasn't good at it now. He had a sudden vision of the first time she had fallen down in front of him, bucking and shaking, her eyes rolling back in her head—but the vision went black in no time at all. He knew what he had done, the first time she had gotten sick and every time thereafter, but he couldn't remember himself doing it.

He forced himself to look at Geena's window, yet again. He forced himself to walk down the alley to Geena's front door. The inner door was open, in spite of the cold, but at least the storm windows were in in the outer door. He'd put them in himself, in November, because Bernadette had reminded him to. The windows were all clean, too, because Bernadette had cleaned them, the way she went down to Geena's when Geena was sleeping off a drunk to do the dishes or vacuum the floors or get the laundry to the Laundromat so that Geena wouldn't smell.

"She's your mother," Bernadette had said, running her fingers along the edge of a sewing needle she had been trying to thread for the last half hour. "You have to honor your mother, even if she hasn't been a very good one."

Sometimes, Marty wondered what it was God thought He was doing. He was supposed to have some very important plan—and there had been times when Marty had claimed to understand it—but the truth was that everything seemed to be a mess. Nothing made sense. Nothing ever went right for more than a minute at a time.

Marty went into Geena's trailer and turned on the light. He could hear Geena snoring in the back. He could see the small plastic statue of the Virgin Bernadette had put up on the wall next to the front door, as if that alone would be enough to make Geena want to change. Bernadette had statues of the Virgin everywhere, and rosaries, too. She had a Miraculous Medal with a blue glass background that she wore around her neck, always, no matter what. Even in these last few months, when they had not been going to St. Anselm's at all, Bernadette had not stopped wearing that medal.

Sometimes, when Geena fell asleep drunk, she fell asleep naked. Marty didn't know how old she was, but he thought she might be going through menopause. She got hot at night, and even hotter when she was plastered, and then she took off her clothes and left them on the floor. He held his own breath and listened to hers. It was even and untroubled. It didn't sound as if she were sucking in her own vomit. If she were lying naked, he should cover her—but he didn't want to see her that way. It made him sick to his stomach, and angry in a way he couldn't explain.

He listened for a moment more, and then went back outside, closing the inner door behind him, because that would at least let Geena's trailer warm up. The moon over his head was full and clear. The air around him was very sharp. His hands were cold enough to feel stiff. He walked back to the truck and got in behind the wheel, moving carefully so that he did not startle Bernadette. He found himself wishing that her eyes were open, so that he could look into them, so deeply that he could see the bottom of her soul.

Instead, he got the truck started and the heater turned on, and then headed out down the dirt track toward the town road. It was going to be a long drive into Philadelphia, and there would be traffic even at four o'clock in the morning. If they got there too late, Mass would be starting, and they wouldn't be able to do what they needed to do. He should have listened to Bernadette in everything, without exception, even in those times when he had been so frightened he hadn't been able to listen at all.

He had just turned onto the two-lane blacktop when Bernadette shifted in her seat and seemed to shudder. He leaned over and put his right hand over hers, to comfort her in sleep.

It was only when he felt the marble coldness of her skin that he remembered, for the first time in an hour, that Bernadette was dead.

A COLD DAY IN PARADISE

STEVE HAMILTON

Other than the bullet lodged less than a centimeter from his heart, former Detroit police officer Alex McKnight thought he had put the nightmare of his partner's death and his own near-fatal injury behind him. After all, Maximilian Rose, convicted of the crimes, has been locked in the state pen for years. But in the small town of Paradise, Michigan, where McKnight has traded his badge for a cozy cabin in the woods, a murderer with Rose's unmistakable trademarks appears to be back to his killing ways. And it seems as if it will be a frozen day in hell before McKnight can unravel the cold truth from a deadly deception in a town that's anything but Paradise.

CDP 12/99

Winner of the Edgar Award for Best First Novel, author Eliot Pattison masterfully scales the heights of the genre with this gripping thriller that follows the tradition of *Gorky Park* and *Smilla's Sense of Snow*.

THE SKULL MANTRA

Edgar Award Winner
ELIOT PATTISON

When the grisly remains of a corpse are discovered, the case is handed to veteran police inspector Shan Tao Yun, a prisoner deported to Tibet for offending Beijing. Granted a temporary release, Shan is soon pulled into the Tibetan people's desperate fight for its sacred mountains and the Chinese regime's blood-soaked policies when a Buddhist priest, whom Shan knows is innocent, is arrested. Now, the time is running out for Shan to find the real killer ... An astonishing, emotionally charged story that will change the way you think about Tibet—and freedom—forever.

"Superb...breathlessly suspenseful."—*Kirkus Reviews* (starred review)

"A top-notch thriller!"—*Publishers Weekly* (starred review)

"Pattison provides truly remarkable transport...a riveting story."
—*Booklist* (starred review)

"A stark and compelling saga...As in Tony Hillerman's Navajo mysteries, Pattison's characters venerate traditional beliefs, and mystical insight as a tool for finding murderers."—*Library Journal*

"A thriller of laudable aspirations and achievements."—*Chicago Tribune*

"One of the hottest debut novels of the season."—*Minneapolis Star-Tribune*

AVAILABLE WHEREVER BOOKS ARE SOLD
FROM ST. MARTIN'S PAPERBACKS

SM 10/00

Don't miss these spellbinding Inspector
John Rebus novels from acclaimed,
award-winning author

IAN RANKIN

"This is crime fiction at its best."
—*Washington Post Book World*

"A brilliant series....The work of a master."
—*San Francisco Chronicle*

KNOTS AND CROSSES
Rebus's city is being terrorized by a baffling series of murders, and
he isn't just a cop trying to catch a killer—he's the man who holds
all the pieces of the puzzle...

TOOTH AND NAIL
Sent to London to help catch a vicious serial killer, Rebus must piece
together a portrait of a depraved psychopath bent on painting the
town red—with blood...

MORTAL CAUSES
A young man's tortured body is found in a medieval cellar far
beneath the Edinburgh streets, and to find a killer, Rebus must travel from the city's most violent neighborhood to Belfast, Northern
Ireland—and make it back alive...

HIDE AND SEEK
In an Edinburgh housing development, a junkie lies dead of an over-
dose, his body surrounded by signs of Satanic worship. Rebus knows
it was no accident. Now, to prove it, he's got to scour the city and
find the perfect hiding place of a killer...

Rankin 3/00